ON THE SIDE OF THE ANGELS, SHE FACED A DEVIL'S DILEMMA . . .

Alissa's heart sang in her breast. He would allow her to remain safe at Hawkstone! "Mr. Braxton, how can I thank you?" she said in a rush, a smile lighting her eyes.

"Don't thank me," Jared said curtly. "Not until you've heard my terms."

Alissa sobered. "What are the terms?"

Jared viewed her for a long moment. "We are to be married."

"Married!" she cried, springing from her chair. "You must be . . . daft!"

Jared's temper flared. "Agreed, I am daft!" he shouted, his eyes hard as moss-covered stone, "but the terms do not change. It's the sheriff or me. Now *choose*, woman!"

Masque of Enchantment

Charlene Cross

POCKET BOOKS

New York   London   Toronto   Sydney   Tokyo   Singapore

An *Original* Publication of POCKET BOOKS

POCKET BOOKS, a division of Simon & Schuster Inc.
1230 Avenue of the Americas, New York, NY 10020

ISBN: 0-671-67699-7

First Pocket Books printing February 1990

10 9 8 7 6 5 4 3 2 1

POCKET and colophon are registered trademarks of
Simon & Schuster Inc.

Printed in the U.S.A.

To my husband Ron:

Without you, all would be dark and silent. Thankfully, though, my life is aglow with the sweet strains of laughter. No one else could ever bring me such joy. I love you.

Masque
of
Enchantment

*There's a divinity
that shapes our ends . . .*
—William Shakespeare

CHAPTER

One

England
April, 1840

A thick mist rose from the black waters of the Thames to slowly snake through the narrow maze of cobblestone and brick, enfolding all of London in its heavy embrace. Gaslights stood as lone sentinels along the deserted streets. Dim flames flickering in midair, they resembled a legion of lost spirits, lighting a pathway straight into hell. The entire city, now lifeless as a corpse, fell silent, entombed by the deepening fog.

Quickened footfalls broke the silent void as Alissa Ashford raced along the sidewalk, urgency driving her onward. *Home, home,* the word cadenced through her mind; a searing pain ripped through her side. An uneven rise in her path snagged her toe; a startled cry escaped her lips as her groping fingers snared the damp stone wall beside her, stopping her fall.

Thankful that the dense haze concealed her, Alissa leaned back against the cold, hard barrier, drawing a deep, fortifying breath to soothe her burning lungs, while quavering fingers massaged her tender side. She knew she should be on her way, but her feet refused to move. Her legs shook, then the trembling slowly crept upward. A violent shiver racked her entire body, as though a ghost had brushed her soul— the ghost of Charles Rhodes?

1

The frightening thought reestablished her need for haste, and Alissa pulled her black velvet cloak more securely around her, forcing her legs into action. She had to return to Mrs. Binnington's and retrieve her possessions, for it was imperative she flee London before someone discovered what she had done.

A distorted rumble suddenly filtered through the murky haze, surging then subsiding, like the ebb and flow of an ocean's tide. Alissa stopped and listened. Again, it loomed upward, only to be devoured by the dense fog. She peered through the mists, but the sound had no form. Uncertain of its origins, she pressed herself into the shadows.

Once more, it reverberated, rolling like distant thunder, growing louder, closer; it was accompanied by a ghoulish creak. Palpable fear rose to choke her as she imagined some supernatural entity stalking the deserted streets, searching for her. The ghost of Charles Rhodes! she thought again. And again, she shivered.

Muted hoofbeats broke through the precipice of her fear; iron scraped stone, and Alissa immediately realized it was a conveyance. With a quick scamper, she sought refuge in a narrow doorway and flattened herself into the corner. Then, as the clop, clop, clop of horses' hooves drew closer, she pulled back, her breath held tightly in her lungs.

As the vehicle came alongside her, her acute eyes searched the fog, and she wondered if it was a coach. Or it might be a prison wagon, she thought frantically, dispatched from Bow Street on its way to Mrs. Binnington's with a contingent of constables enlisted to escort her to Newgate, where she'd await trial for the murder of Charles Rhodes.

She shuddered as she imagined herself cast into the prison, left there to rot. Undoubtedly, all of London would decry her heinous crime—a crime she had good reason to commit. Yet, she knew her claim of self-defense would do little to persuade the throng of her innocence. No one would believe the word of an actress—an actress who had not yet gained the affection of the masses—that the viscount had tried to force himself on her. True, she bore the marks of his savage assault. Yet she was certain his father, the Earl of Creighton, would deny her accusations and testify she'd led poor Charles on, asserting that she'd bashed his son's skull after young Rhodes had spurned her.

Nausea overtook her as she remembered the drunken sot's hands groping below the neckline of her gown, biting painfully into her tender flesh; bitter bile surged to her throat as she relived the feeling of his wet, thick lips slobbering across her own. Still able to taste the leavings of his whiskey-laden breath, stale with cigar smoke, Alissa felt certain she'd vomit. Her nerves close to shattering, a scream rose within her. Willfully, she stifled it and erased the disgusting vision of her attacker from her mind.

Deathly silence met her ears, and as Alissa cautiously peeked from the edge of the doorway, she noticed the vehicle had stopped several yards beyond her hideaway. Fearing she had indeed let loose a bloodcurdling scream, she pressed herself into her corner, her ears finely tuned to every sound.

"Mr. Stanley," a deep baritone voice called through an open coach window, "where in blazes are we?"

"Don't know, gov'nor," the driver answered. "Cain't see a bloody thing in this here fog."

"Pull ahead to the signpost."

"Don't know what good it'll do. Ye know I cain't read."

"Just do it, Mr. Stanley," came the terse reply.

The coach lurched forward; a vivid curse escaped its interior. Several yards ahead, it stopped equally as fast, and another expletive colored the air.

Finding her courage, Alissa braved another peek from her niche. The coach door swung open, and a man of tall stature alighted from the vehicle, brushing at his evening clothes as he stepped down. "Henceforth, Mr. Stanley," he said with an edge to his voice, "you'd best keep those horses under control, or I'll demote you to stable boy and hire myself a more capable driver."

"Sorry, gov'nor. The reins slipped out'a me hand."

"Most likely, it's you who's slipped. Keep a tight cap on that bottle in your pocket, sir. I might find it a handicap, since Her Majesty is so young," he said, sarcastically, "but I'd hope to reach our destination sometime during Victoria's reign!"

Alissa watched as he strode to the signpost, where his eyes searched the lettering. Then, without warning, he spun in her direction. In that same instant, the fog lifted from around him, and the glow from the gaslight caught his features in bright relief. A dark scowl crossed his handsome, angular face as his gaze riveted itself to the doorway where she hid. Afraid she'd somehow drawn his attention, she dared not move.

A black cat suddenly bounded from the doorway just beyond and scurried past her hideaway. Seeing it, the tall man relaxed. His deep laughter rumbled across the void, and in a whirl of cape, he strode back to the coach, his booted feet striking the cobblestones with a smart click. "Shouldn't be too much farther, Mr. Stanley," he said, swinging inside the coach. "Just keep to the street we're presently on." The door closed with a thump.

"Hie-yup!" the coachman shouted, and the large bays clopped off at a steady pace.

When the coach lanterns shrank into small specks in the undulating mists, Alissa fled her sanctuary and on light feet flew to the safety of Mrs. Binnington's. Entering through the back door to escape detection should anyone still be in the front parlor, she turned the key behind her and breathed a sigh of relief. As her hood fell from her head, she brushed a loose strand of mahogany hair from her cheek; then the ties on her cloak came free while she rushed around the oak table, heading for the back stairs. Just as she reached their shadows, the connecting door to the hall swung wide; Alissa halted in her tracks.

"Alissa, dear, you gave me a start!" Mrs. Binnington's age-spotted hand covered the jump of her heart. Then she smiled. "I didn't hear you come in." She headed toward the wash cupboard to place a soiled bundle of linen in the wicker basket. "I have some sad tidings to share," she lamented from inside the closet. "Poor Miss Pembroke passed on earlier this evening. The undertaker just left. I need to contact her new employer, but I suppose it can wait until he arrives. 'Tis sad, indeed, but the poor woman was so weak. Such a frail thing." She gathered some fresh bedding and retreated from the small room. "A shame she didn't

4

have any relatives to be at her side, but, praise the Lord, she went peacefully when her time came."

Mrs. Binnington shut the door and turned to find Alissa clutching the back of a chair. All the blood had drained from the girl's face. Then she noticed Alissa still wore her stage makeup. Her huge eyes looked like two shards of blue glass, staring from a white mask; slashes of rouge, redder than the devil's suit itself, streaked her high cheekbones. Her trembling lips bore no color at all, and to Eudora Binnington, they seemed more pale than the late Miss Pembroke's.

"Alissa, what's wrong?" Eudora dropped the linens and rushed to her side. Fearful the girl might faint, she quickly helped her into the chair and patted the insides of Alissa's wrists. "What is it, dear?"

Staring at her landlady's gently lined face, yet not seeing her, Alissa remained mute. Death, she thought, it seemed to follow her everywhere. At the theater. At Mrs. Binnington's. Her own mother's, not six months before. Did it stalk her now in the form of a hangman's noose?

The press of a cool cloth against her brow snapped her from her trance. She blinked and tried to smile, but it ended in a weak twitch of her lips. "Thank you," she whispered as she took the cloth from Eudora. "I just felt a bit lightheaded. I'm quite fine now."

"Here, take a sip of brandy, dear," Eudora offered after she'd retrieved the bottle from the oak hutch, pouring two fingers' worth into a glass. "It will put some life back into you."

Alissa obeyed and grimaced as the fiery liquid scorched its way to her stomach. Almost immediately, a soothing warmth spread through her veins, thawing the icy chill from her bones. She sipped the amber liquid again.

Carefully studying the girl, Eudora knew that something horrible must have happened to her. It had nothing to do with Agatha Pembroke's death, either, for Alissa barely knew the woman. As she scanned Alissa's petite form, Eudora noticed that, besides her makeup, she still wore her Grecian costume. The gossamer bodice, peeking through the edges of her cloak, was torn; purple streaked the top of her youthful breast. On closer inspection, Eudora discovered it was a bruise.

Determined to have the truth, she sat facing Alissa. "Tell me what's happened," she said softly, nodding toward the torn gown. "I know you're in some sort of trouble, and I won't let you carry this burden alone. Your mother would never have forgiven me if I didn't do everything in my power to help you." Her warm hands covered Alissa's cold, tightly gripped fingers, resting atop the table. Then Eudora's hazel eyes beseeched as she coaxed, "Please tell me, child."

Alissa fought the tears glazing her blue eyes and looked at Mrs. Binnington. Tall and statuesque, her dark hair streaked with silver, Eudora was very precious to Alissa. The woman was all she had, the only person she could rely on.

"Alissa," Eudora coaxed again. "Tell me."

"I bashed Charles Rhodes's skull in," Alissa stated and braced herself, awaiting Eudora's reproving gasp. It never came.

"The fiend deserved no less," Eudora replied without emotion, squeezing Alissa's hand. "The Young Turk has bothered you long enough. You should have done it sooner."

Alissa's voice was throaty, yet even, as she looked directly into the elder woman's eyes. "He's dead."

Eudora never batted an eye, she simply nodded. But, though she seemed calm on the outside, her mind raced as she tried to think of a way to protect Alissa, for she was well aware of the Earl of Creighton's reputation in seeking revenge, even when he'd not actually been wronged. The man was a tyrant; Alissa would never stand a chance against him. Certainly the sweet child had suffered enough distress since her mother's death. Suddenly an idea sprang into Eudora's head, and she rose from her seat. "Come, we must get you out of London before the earl learns of his son's death. I believe I have a way to do it."

With a curious look on her face, Alissa followed her landlady up the steps. They passed rapidly down the hallway to the front of the house and stopped at Mrs. Binnington's quarters.

"Go inside, dear," Eudora instructed, "and take off your costume. Cleanse your face, too. Use the creams on my dressing table." She gently patted Alissa's arm. "Lock the door after you. I'll be back in a moment."

Stepping into the rose and cream-colored room, Alissa secured the door behind her. As always, she stood in amazement. Her landlady's quarters looked like a shrine: one wall decorated with painted woodcuts, tint-stenciled posters, playbills, and other memorabilia from her past life on the stage. Alissa wished she had time to peruse the collection again, but she knew time was the one thing she could least afford to spare.

She dropped her black velvet cloak over a chair's back, then removed her costume and threw it onto the wool carpet. Feeling chilled in her undergarments, she donned Eudora's heavy velvet robe, then sat at the dressing table, where she gazed into the mirror and gasped at her reflection. She looked a total fright!

Her wealth of heavy, mahogany hair fell, tangled. Her once perfectly applied makeup was smeared, her eyes and cheeks now grotesquely streaked. Beneath the paint, her complexion was pale, wan. Horrified, Alissa compared her appearance to that of an aged streetwalker more than twice her own nineteen years.

Uncapping a jar, she quickly creamed her face, wiping the ugly mask away, then went to the basin and, using a clean facecloth and lavender-scented soap, scrubbed her skin until it glowed. Next, she removed the remaining pins from her long hair and, returning to the vanity, combed her fingers through it, freeing the tangles. As she did so she wondered what she would have done without her beloved landlady's help.

Once an acclaimed actress, Eudora had been a friend of Alissa's mother, who'd also been an actress. While Rachel Ashford had remained on the stage, even after Alissa's birth, Eudora had given up the profession when she married. The union had produced no children, and when George Binnington had passed on suddenly a year back, leaving some debts, Eudora opened her home to boarders.

She catered mostly to stage professionals, for her brick and stone house was ideally located not overly far from Covent Garden and the Drury Lane Theatre. Alissa also suspected Eudora enjoyed the company of her peers. Perhaps it was because the woman longed for the days of her lost youth plus the excitement that seemed to radiate from those in the theater. Indeed, everyone here spoke Eudora's language. But, whatever her reason for opening her home, Alissa felt it was a godsend. For after her mother's death from a lung ailment, six months past, she found the small house they'd leased was far too expensive for her meager salary alone, so she'd moved to Mrs. Binnington's. Since then, the older woman had become surrogate mother to Alissa, the daughter Eudora had never had.

A light rap sounded on the door, and Alissa gathered up the extra length of robe, before scurrying across the room to allow Mrs. Binnington entry.

"Close and lock it," Eudora said after she came through, overloaded with clothing and several pieces of luggage.

The black case Alissa recognized as her own, but the others, the two larger of the three, were a mystery. "These aren't mine," she said as she looked at Eudora, her once smooth brow now furrowed in confusion. "Why have you brought them?"

"They're Miss Pembroke's," Eudora explained, then cut off Alissa's rising protest. "The woman no longer has a use for them—*you* do."

"What are you saying?"

"It's part of my plan to get you safely out of London." Eudora removed the gray traveling dress from across her shoulder where she'd carried it. "Put this on. Hurry, he'll be here any moment."

Alissa's eyes widened. "Who?"

"Miss Pembroke's new employer . . . a Mr. Braxton, I believe."

"Employer?"

"Yes, employer. She was retained as a governess for the man's daughter. Here"—Eudora took a packet of ribbon-tied letters from her skirt pocket—"I believe these were his correspondence with Miss Pembroke. Read them while I get you ready."

"Ready?" Alissa still did not comprehend Eudora's meaning. "What are you going on about?"

"You, my dear, are about to play the most challenging role of your career, and it depends upon you alone whether or not it's a success. The lines will be of your own making, but they'd better be a close match to the late Agatha Pembroke's. With any luck, this Mr. Braxton hasn't met her in person. If we get through the first act, you'll soon be on your way to Scotland."

"Scotland!"

"Yes, Scotland. Away from the Earl of Creighton. Now hurry and slip into the dress. We haven't much time. Your new employer sent word around earlier he'd be here about half past nine. It's well after that now."

Still stunned, Alissa felt uneasy as she stepped into the dead woman's clothing, and once it was buttoned, she discovered the bodice was far too tight. It pressed uncomfortably against her full breasts, making her bruised flesh even more sensitive. The sleeves were too long, capping to the middle of her slender hands, and the skirt was a bit too short, but it would have to do, for Alissa's dresses were much too stylish for a governess to wear. Through instinct alone, Alissa knew the rather austere woman had somehow defined her true self to her new employer, if not in person, then through her correspondence with the man. Frills definitely weren't part of Agatha Pembroke's character.

"The bodice will never do," Eudora said, then directed Alissa to the dressing table. "Lift your arm. Just as I thought. There are a couple of darts I can let out. The creases will show, but if you're careful, no one will notice." She took her late husband's straight razor to the threads, cautious not to cut the material. "There."

The task completed, Alissa breathed easier. The bodice still strained a bit, but nothing like before. Then, while Eudora brushed at the remaining tangles in Alissa's hair, she scanned the letters.

The words that met her eyes were written in a bold, strong hand, and immediately, Alissa noticed the wealth of praises heaped upon Agatha's head by one Jared Braxton. By the tone of his letters, it was obvious he'd been the one to seek her out, not the other way around. She'd come highly recommended by her former employers, who were obviously numerous. Yet, apparently, Mr. Braxton had checked all her references, a good two dozen, which meant he was a thorough man. Or, perhaps it meant he lacked trust in humanity.

As Alissa read the one-sided communications further, she discovered Agatha Pembroke was much more than a simple governess. The woman specialized in teaching children who suffered a physical or emotional handicap. Once her charge was improved, however, Miss Pembroke always moved on to the next position, the next child who needed her expertise, which explained her frequent job changes.

Alissa lowered the letter. Closing her eyes, she said a small prayer for the woman. Never had she suspected the frail, unassuming Miss Pembroke, with whom she'd spoken only briefly, could have possessed such a determined will. She'd given her all to her "children." Agatha Pembroke was a saint, literally.

Again Alissa began absorbing the words to discover Agatha was accepting the position as governess for six-year-old Megan Braxton. Finally, she found she could no longer continue. "I don't think I can do it," Alissa whispered as the letter lowered to her lap. She looked at Eudora's reflection in the mirror. "Mr. Braxton's daughter has been mute these past two years, ever since her mother's death. Eudora, he's expecting a miracle worker. I can't purposely deceive him."

"The poor child," Eudora said sympathetically. "But, dear, what makes you think you couldn't perform the duties of a governess? If Agatha could, God rest her soul, surely you can."

"I think not." Alissa quickly explained the contents of the letters. "Miss Pembroke was a very special woman with a very special talent. I simply can't deceive the man. It wouldn't be right."

The brush stopped its movement along Alissa's lustrous hair. "If you don't go with him to Scotland, you'll surely be enjoying your next meal at Newgate." Eudora's words were short, to the point. "You won't harm the child any, and Miss Pembroke is no longer able to help her. More than likely, no one can . . . not anymore." Her stern gaze penetrated Alissa's through the mirror. "You have to go, deception or not!"

Then she dropped a bath cloth around Alissa's shoulders and dumped two handfuls of talc onto her waist-length hair.

Alissa coughed, then sneezed. "What are you doing?"

"I'm dulling the sheen of your hair."

Eudora worked the powder to the roots, then brushed the residual free. Forgoing the usual center part of the times, she pulled the long tresses straight back and knotted the heavy mass into a tight bun at Alissa's nape, covering it with a chenille net.

Next, she retrieved a small leather case from the bureau and instructed Alissa to face her. Then she spread a light cream over the girl's soft skin before applying a special mixture of moist powders, stroking upward to the roots of Alissa's hair and down the length of her ivory neck. Using a rabbit's foot and a sponge, she blended the makeup, darkening the hollows of Alissa's cheeks and the delicate skin beneath her eyes with a deeper shade of powder, until she was satisfied with the results.

"Now, close your eyes." She brushed the fine hairs of the rabbit's foot across the blue-veined lids, dabbing at the tips of Alissa's long, dark lashes in the process. Finally, she straightened a hairpin, held it over the lamp's flame, and allowed it to cool. With its blackened tip, she emphasized the fine lines near Alissa's eyes, making it appear she had crow's-feet. Blotting more powder near Alissa's eyes, Eudora said, "There. Look at yourself and tell me what you see."

Alissa turned and stared into the mirror. "I look almost a dozen years older."

"Good. Miss Pembroke was thirty, if she was a day. What else do you see?"

"A very frail woman who has been recently ill."

"Excellent. Mr. Braxton's earlier message said he hoped she was well enough to travel. I assume Miss Pembroke informed him of her chill. I posted several letters to Scotland over the past few weeks, but nothing since she took her terrible turn. The poor woman lived here only a month. Odd how very fragile life is. Why, Mr. Binnington—" She cleared her throat. "Well, now, I believe you're ready. Take this case with you," she said as she replaced the powder mixtures, rabbit's foot, and sponge inside. "Use them every day, but be careful in bright sunlight, though I sincerely doubt the northern climes have much. There's enough here to last quite a while. I'll send another batch on to you when you need it."

Eudora scribbled down Mr. Braxton's address on a scrap of paper, then quickly moved to Agatha Pembroke's luggage. Opening each bag, she searched for an empty space within and packed the makeup case away. Then, using the cover of her skirt, she secretly slipped a sealed note from her pocket. Her hand dipped into the suitcase, whereupon Eudora hastily tucked the note beneath the folds of a worn nightdress. She straightened, her gaze centering itself on the young actress.

Alissa was too busy viewing herself to notice her friend's movements. "You're an expert at makeup, Eudora. I can't believe this is me!"

"Oh, go on with you," Eudora said, moving to Alissa's side. "You should know an actress never forgets how to apply her makeup. I've just learned a few new tricks playing with it over the years." She smiled and winked, then grew serious again. "Now, here's a small tin with some powder for quick touch-ups. Carry it in your purse." She removed a copy of Rede's *The Road to the Stage* from her vanity drawer. The manual was considered an actor's bible for makeup. "Take this, too. I've jotted down my improvements on Rede's methods in the margins. And here are some special creams I've concocted. They'll keep your skin from rashing out."

She took the lot to Agatha's case and slipped them inside. "Let's see, now," she said, her mind rapidly running through a checklist as her forefinger tapped her top lip. "I packed half your undergarments, a couple of nightgowns, and several dresses. Your mother's jewelry, too. The rest I'll leave in your room should the constable ask to check it. That way, with your clothing here, he'll think you're still in London and you'll be back for your things. It may delay him. At least, he'll probably confine his search to the immediate area. By the time he discovers otherwise, you'll be safely in Scotland. I'll claim you owe me board money and insist on keeping your possessions as payment. They'll be here . . . uh . . . when you return." Eudora wisely caught the word *if* before she said it. "Quickly now, slip into these shoes. The ones you have on are totally out of character."

Alissa looked at her feet, noting her soft kid slippers. Again, she felt uncomfortable, for, in actuality, she'd be walking in a dead woman's shoes. An omen? she wondered, slipping on the serviceable high-topped boots, buttoning them.

"There, is this more like our Miss Pembroke?" she asked as she straightened and stood. Then she noticed Eudora folding her velvet cloak and the torn costume. Before she could voice her protest, Mrs. Binnington stuffed them into the valise, along with her kid slippers. "Can't you throw that horrid thing away?" She took a step, intending to remove the costume herself, but her feet slid inside the shoes, and she almost fell onto her nose.

Fortunately, Eudora caught her. "Steady, dear. You don't want to tumble down the stairs into Mr. Braxton's arms when he arrives, do you?"

"Certainly not," Alissa said with a demure sniff, trying to make light of her situation for the moment. "Miss Pembroke would never do such an unladylike thing."

"Then you'd better do a few struts, back and forth, before he comes. When you're settled in Scotland, see if there's a shoemaker handy and have him fashion you a new pair in a smaller size."

"I'll do that." As Alissa took several practice steps, her feet felt like they were swimming in a sea of thick leather. A few more steps, however, and she was certain she'd mastered her walk, but with the next one, she tripped again, then laughed. "I think crawling would be far safer."

"You'll overcome this minor problem. You've no choice."

"The costume, I—"

"You'll have to take it with you. If they find it, they'll know you were here," Eudora explained, apologetically, closing the cases. "I would burn it, but I'm afraid to chance it. It will take too long, and time is something we don't have." Then she asked, "Young Rhodes . . . is it possible he's been found?"

Alissa had almost forgotten him—almost. She sank onto the satin bed cover. "I don't know. I—I—"

Eudora came to Alissa's side and sat next to her, placing a comforting arm around her slim shoulders. "Are you able to speak of it?"

Tears gathered along the cups of Alissa's lower lids as she looked at Eudora. "It was ghastly. He . . . he was hiding in my dressing room. I tried to fight him off b-but he . . . he was far too strong." She shuddered violently as she remembered how his hands had clutched at her, touched her where no man ever had. "I—I managed to escape him for a moment, but he blocked the door. I ran behind the dressing screen, and he came after me. The pressing iron was still in its stand from when I used it earlier. I grabbed it and swung with all my might. He sank like a rock. There was a horrible gash at his temple, blood poured everywhere. I was so frightened, I just grabbed my cloak and ran."

"Did anyone see you?"

"Yes, Madame Vestris. She was checking on the players, hurrying them on- and offstage as she usually does. I must have looked a fright, for she asked if I was ill. I told her yes. I was completely surprised when she said I should leave immediately. She even said she'd hire a coach to take me home. Then she disappeared to find another actress for my part. I didn't wait. I ran all the way here."

Eudora was glad to hear Rhodes was behind the screen in Alissa's private dressing room—the first one the poor child had ever had, too, granted for her very first lead in one of Shakespeare's comedies, *A Midsummer Night's Dream.* If anyone came in, they wouldn't notice him immediately. And she was equally surprised to hear of Madame Vestris's sudden change of character. The woman usually brooked no excuses; she'd little use for an actor who claimed he or she was ill.

"I suppose she didn't want you fainting onstage," Eudora said. "Madame has always been a hard taskmaster, even more so since she and young Charles Mathews have taken over management at Covent Garden. But enough of her." She waved away their discussion of Lucia Elizabeth Vestris Mathews—Madame Vestris, as she still wished to be called —and her husband, Charles. "Did anyone on the street see you?"

Alissa thought of the man in the coach, then shook her head. "No, no one saw me."

"Good."

They both started as they heard a loud knock on the front entry.

Eudora glanced at the small timepiece on the night table by her bed. It was a quarter past ten. "Stay here until I call you," she instructed. "No matter who's at the door, remember, you're Agatha Pembroke."

"I'll remember. But what of the others? They'll know I'm not Agatha."

"Fortunately for us, our other tenants are out for the evening. They don't know of Miss Pembroke's demise."

"I'm so frightened. Not only for myself, but for you, too. What if they find out you've helped me?"

"My dear, you were far too young to see the great Eudora Wembly on stage, but if you had, there would be no question about my safety. This old mare can still outact any of the young fillies prancing the boards today."

Alissa breathed a sigh of relief, realizing Eudora's words rang true, then she hugged her. "Thank you for everything. It breaks my heart to leave you. I'll write when I get to Scotland."

"You had better. I'd never forgive you if you didn't. Keep in touch as often as possible." The knock sounded again, louder. Eudora released the young woman from her arms, then rose and went to the door. "Did Mr. Braxton mention whether or not he's met our Miss Pembroke?"

"No."

"Well, we'll soon discover if he has."

Eudora was out the door, and Alissa found she was unable to wait. Quickly she slipped on a pair of Agatha's worn gloves and the woman's oversize bonnet, tying the frayed ribbons under her chin, then draped Agatha's coarse wool cloak over her shoulders.

Poor Miss Pembroke, Alissa thought. She certainly had no eye for fashion. But, at the moment, *that* was the least of Alissa's worries. As she took one last glance in the mirror, she noticed the letters. Fetching them, she stuffed the lot into Agatha's shabby purse and left the room. On light feet—as light as her new shoes would allow—she hurried to the head of the stairs.

Suddenly she stopped and stared in disbelief.

"Ah, Miss Pembroke," the deep baritone voice called up to her. "I'm delighted to see you are well." Then the tall man turned to his driver. "Mr. Stanley, come help with Miss Pembroke's bags."

CHAPTER

Two

Alissa gazed down at the towering man as he moved gracefully to the bottom of the stairs. Dressed in black evening attire and draped by a black cape lined with red satin, he cut an excellent figure as his clothes molded themselves across his broad shoulders and narrow waist. His handsome face radiated a healthy hue, and she imagined he spent much time out of doors, unlike the pale gentlemen of the theater with whom she was acquainted.

He doffed his top hat, and bowed his head—thick with dark, rich hair—in formal greeting. "Miss Pembroke." His deep-toned voice resonated up the stairwell. He straightened, and a smile cut across his magnetic features. "Jared Braxton, at your service."

Alissa felt an odd twitter, similar to the soft brush of a butterfly's wing. It was the same feeling she suffered moments before she went onstage. The man's a devil, she thought as she viewed his self-confident mien. Dismissing his possible kinship to Lucifer, she composed herself and descended the stairs, puzzling over how the man in the coach and Agatha's Mr. Braxton could be one and the same. But, more importantly, she wondered if he'd already met the late Miss Pembroke. From where he viewed her at the bottom of the stairs, he might have mistaken her for Agatha. But as she drew closer, he might realize she was an imposter.

Alissa braced herself for their face-to-face encounter. But as she reached the third to the last step, she slid in Agatha's shoes, losing her balance. Keen reflexes allowed Jared to catch her arm before she completely upended herself, and he assisted her until she reached solid footing.

"Thank you." Alissa's whispered words floated upward to the man who stood head and shoulders above her. Suddenly she realized the curtain had risen—Act I, Scene i—and could only pray it would not fall before this farce of a melodrama had been played out! Pulling free of his firm grip, she explained, "I suppose I'm not yet as steady on my feet as I had thought."

"It's understandable. Your illness has naturally weakened you." Jared had noticed her quick escape from his supporting hand. Perhaps she was embarrassed, he thought, for she had almost tumbled at his feet. Not wanting to distress her further, he stepped back a few paces. "I apologize for my late arrival," he continued, his deep, mellow tone vibrating through her, "but my man became confused in the fog. We took several wrong turns before we finally found the correct street. Unfortunately, I'm no longer as familiar with London as I once was."

"Apology accepted, Mr. Braxton, but you are not to be held accountable for this dismal night," she said in Agatha's proper tone as she desperately tried to rid herself of his compelling charm. He possessed an extraordinary power to attract the opposite sex, she knew. *Beware!* her inner voice warned. *He's a devil—a devil!* "London is notorious for its sudden blinding mists," she continued priggishly. "It's a common occurrence."

She's certainly a prim little baggage, Jared decided while he perused her. Plain as a brown paper wrapping, too. Then he wondered if his precious Megan would take to this woman. She seemed too staid and standoffish to establish an easy rapport with any child, let alone his own.

Perhaps, he concluded, she felt uncomfortable in the presence of a man—he in particular. Having saved her from certain disaster, he'd felt her stiffen under his touch. But he couldn't very well have let her fall flat on her face! Whatever had caused her prudish behavior, it was no concern of his.

Her exceptional talents had come highly recommended, and he was anxious to return to Scotland so she could put her expertise to work. Above all else, Megan needed her help.

"The fog is one thing I've not forgotten about," he offered, again smiling. When he viewed her more carefully in the dim light, he noted the dark circles under her eyes and the gaunt hollows in her cheeks. Although he was eager to be on his way, he thought better of it. "Miss Pembroke," he ventured, "considering the late hour and your weakened condition, perhaps we should wait until morning before we—"

"No!"

Alissa and Eudora had cried the word in unison, then they both fell silent. Obviously the solicitous Mr. Braxton had been taken aback by their distressed outburst. Hoping to rectify the situation, Alissa drew from all her training on the stage. Straightening her shoulders, she looked directly into Jared Braxton's eyes—long-lashed green eyes that could melt a woman's heart. Or freeze it just as quickly. "What Mrs. Binnington and I meant was she has already let my room. The new tenant has moved in, so I no longer have a place to stay. Besides, the sooner we leave for Scotland, the sooner I can begin working with . . . uh, Megan," she quickly supplied, having almost forgotten the child's name. "My time is precious." Alissa's tone grew pompous, too much so, even for her own ears. Yet she forged onward in the same vein without thought of possible repercussions. "I simply cannot abide delays. Other children do need my help. So let us not tarry, sir."

One dark brow arched as Jared stared at the haughty woman. He hoped she wasn't threatening him, for demanding females set him on edge, and his tolerance toward this one was slipping fast!

Already in ill humor, precipitated partly by the fog, but mostly by his disappointment at losing out on an introduction to a very intriguing young lady, earlier in the evening, Jared felt like exiting without a backward glance. But a vision of his daughter passed before his eyes, and he decided he must remain civil, no matter how much he detested the thought of doing so. For Megan, he would do anything.

Then something caught his attention. Although the woman appeared to be on death's doorstep, her eyes were a clear, sparkling cobalt-blue. Indeed, they had far too much life in them for someone who had recently been so ill. His curiosity aroused, he stepped closer, hoping to examine the insolent woman more thoroughly.

His steady gaze upon her, Alissa's immediate reaction was to retreat, but she stood her ground, offering up a thousand praises that the lighting was somewhat inferior. That, plus the jutting brim of the poke bonnet, kept her face shadowed. Yet, she felt her composure waver. The man made her nervous. He was far too forceful, too imposing for her liking, and something in his manner told her that he viewed the opposite sex with disdain. But perhaps it had nothing to do with women. Maybe he had hit upon her attempted deception!

With her gaze never vacillating from his, she made a final push. "Well, Mr. Braxton, do we leave? Or shall I consult my list for another name—one who will be more appreciative of my time and expertise."

Jared's eyes narrowed. Ultimatums boded ill with him, as well, and despite his earlier decision to endure her irksome manner, he found he could no longer keep up the pretense. "By all means, Miss Pembroke," he stated in clipped tones. "We shall be on our way." He turned to the wide-eyed man in the doorway. "Mr. Stanley, fetch Miss Pembroke's luggage." With that, he strode through the entry, the heels of his black boots echoing his anger as he disappeared into the night to cool his rising temper.

Alissa's questioning gaze sought Eudora's. With a reassuring nod, the older woman turned to the short, wiry man still hovering on the doorstep and smiled. "Mr. Stanley, please follow me."

"Yes, mum," he said, head bobbing, hat in his hand. But when he reached Alissa's side, he stopped and ducked his head again. "Don't pay him no mind, miss. He's in a foul mood tonight, me gettin' lost and all." He looked at his well-worn hat as he twirled it nervously in his calloused hands. "Uh, if ye don't mind me sayin' so, Mr. Braxton's a bit touchy with the ladies. Has been ever since—" He

20

cleared his throat, and Alissa realized Mr. Stanley felt uneasy about his shared confidences. "His daughter, Megan, she's his whole life, now. She needs yer help, so if ye could find it in yer heart to overlook his fits of temper, I'm sure, uh . . . that is . . ."

"I understand, Mr. Stanley," Alissa reassured him as she lightly touched his forearm. "Believe me, his daughter is my first and foremost concern."

And indeed she was, as Alissa doubted the wisdom of continuing her charade. Megan Braxton deserved far better than Alissa, posing as Agatha Pembroke, could ever give. In the end, the child might suffer a devastating blow to her emotional health if Alissa's duplicity was found out, which seemed inevitable.

Eudora watched Alissa's thoughts gallop full speed across her face, thoughts that could lead her straight to the gallows. "Mr. Stanley, Miss Pembroke's bags are in my room," she said. "If you don't mind retrieving them yourself, I have no objections."

His craggy face split into a crooked, long-toothed grin. "That'll be fine, mum. Be most happy to fetch 'em."

"Upstairs, and first door on the left. You'll find three cases there and a small trunk in the hallway." Then Eudora waited until Mr. Stanley was out of earshot. "The play will let out at eleven and someone will surely find the viscount's body, if they haven't already," she whispered. "There's not much time. At best, a half hour. You've no choice but to go." Alissa started to protest, but Eudora cut her off. "At least use Mr. Braxton's coach to get safely out of London. Once you've reached Scotland, if you decide not to portray Miss Pembroke any longer, so be it! You can escape the man well before you ever meet the child. Please, Alissa," she implored. "Use your head. You must leave. *Immediately.*"

Alissa sighed. "Eudora, I . . . oh, all right. I'll do what you ask. But I don't like it."

"You don't have to like it. When you find the opportunity to flee Mr. Braxton's company, do so as quickly and with as much thought as possible. Whatever you do," she added, "don't leave a trace of yourself. I detect the man has little patience with dishonesty, especially in a woman. And take care not to provoke him. I suspect he's only willing to tolerate the impression you've made as Agatha for his daughter's sake, and hers alone. Heaven only knows what he'll do should he discover you're not the woman he believes he hired."

"I'll be careful. I fear I overacted my part, but the man makes me exceptionally nervous."

"Agatha certainly was prim and proper, but she had far less spirit than you've displayed. My suggestion is to keep Alissa's temperament under control, then you'll have mastered your part as Miss Pembroke."

"I'll try," Alissa said, but feared it would be a futile attempt. Then she wondered why the man couldn't have been a dull, unassuming individual equal to the late Miss Pembroke. She'd have no problem playing her role, then. As it was, though, she would have to watch her every step. In more ways than one, she thought, gazing down at her oversize shoes.

With a grunt, Mr. Stanley reappeared at the top of the stairs, and both women glanced at him. Knowing she had but a few seconds more, Eudora affectionately squeezed Alissa's hands. A hug might have drawn suspicion. "God keep you safe, dearest, and write me as soon as you can." Then she turned. "Ah, Mr. Stanley," she called cheerfully. "You found them without any trouble, I see."

"Yes, mum," he answered as he juggled the cases: two gripped in a small, but meaty right hand; the third tucked under his arm; while the trunk, secured in his left hand, bumped down the steps beside him. "Uh, mum," he said when he reached the bottom, a somewhat awed expression on his face. "If ye don't mind me askin' . . . uh, was ye an actress?"

Alissa stiffened and quickly looked to Eudora.

"I saw 'em posters and stuff. Ye was quite a looker, ye was . . . I mean, ye still are, mum, but . . . uh . . ."

"That's quite all right, Mr. Stanley." Eudora smiled as relief washed over her. "Thank you for the compliment, but as you have guessed, that was years ago."

"Yes, mum, but yer still a fine-lookin' woman."

"Mr. Stanley!" Jared Braxton sharply addressed his man

from the shadows beyond the opened door; Alissa jumped. "If you are through chatting," he said, sarcasm lacing each word as he entered the foyer, "we'll be on our way."

"Aye, gov'nor, I was just leavin'." He lifted the heavy trunk again, and headed for the door. "Sure has a frightful case of the mulligrubs, he does!" the man grumbled loud enough for his master to hear.

Jared's dark scowl followed Mr. Stanley's hasty escape. If he didn't owe the disrespectful cuss his life—the man had fished him from the waters near the docks in Glasgow after he'd been set upon by thugs, twelve years past—he'd boot the old salt straight into the Thames! Then he turned a corrosive eye on Alissa. "Miss Pembroke, if you would, please?"

She gazed at his proffered arm, wondering how long he had been on the doorstep, then became fearful that he had overheard Eudora's words. No, she quickly decided, for if he had, he would have instructed Mr. Stanley to dump her bags, and the two would have departed. But not before he'd delivered a caustic, well-deserved rebuke at her person.

Holding her head high, Alissa moved to his side. "Thank you, Mr. Braxton." Her voice rang strong and steady. Yet, oddly enough, she discovered she clutched her purse in front of her. It was a worthless shield, indeed. "I appreciate your consideration, but I can manage on my own." His arm slowly fell away, and she turned her gaze to Eudora. "And thank you, Mrs. Binnington, for all you've done. My stay here was most pleasant." Although her words were formal, the deep affection she held for her friend shone in her eyes. Suddenly she felt the sting of tears, and before they fell, she quickly swept down the steps, leaving Jared Braxton behind.

Jared watched as Mr. Stanley assisted the odd, little woman into the coach. Estimating her age close to his own thirty-two years, he decided she was a plain, impertinent female who held little attraction for his gender. Yet, there was something about her graceful carriage that contradicted his opinion. And her *eyes*. Unable to fathom what it was, he felt certain a dark secret lay behind those clear, blue irises. Knowing his frame of mind slanted distrustfully toward all women, however, he quelled his suspicions. "Mrs. Binnington." He nodded his good-bye, then he, too, descended to the coach.

Eudora watched as he swung into its interior, then the conveyance rolled away into the misty night. She kept her vigil until it turned the corner, then closed the door and fell back against it. "God help her," she whispered, "should he ever discover the truth."

As the lumbering coach rolled and swayed along the dark streets, Alissa sat in the corner of the dimly lit vehicle, gazing out the window. In turn, Jared Braxton sat opposite her, perusing his daughter's new governess. She felt his steady gaze, yet he said not a word. The silence prevailed until finally her taut nerves could no longer withstand the lengthening void.

"How far do you think we shall travel tonight?" she asked, her gaze turning from the street.

"As long as Mr. Stanley can keep atop his seat. I've made arrangements with several coaching inns for fresh horses along the way. If possible, we'll travel the night. I assume that meets with your criteria for speed and efficiency? I certainly wouldn't want to cause you any unnecessary delays, Miss Pembroke." Then he fell silent, his eyes never leaving her.

Alissa held his gaze for a moment and looked out the window again. She refused to answer his snide comment, for she sensed he was purposely trying to bait her! Heed Eudora's counsel, she reminded herself. Control your temper and all will go well. But no matter how hard she tried to convince herself of it, his continuous stare began to fray the edges of her sanity. She almost blurted the truth, when the sudden pitch of the coach caused her to swallow her confession. With a violent jolt, the coach stopped, and she flew forward, her face smashing into Jared Braxton's broad chest.

His quick hands caught her before she flopped to the floor between them. Gently he settled her back onto the seat. Long fingers gripped her upper arms, pressing against the sides of her full breasts, while his eyes remained intent upon her face. A peculiar scent invaded his nostrils, and he identified it as lavender and . . . *brandy?* No, Jared decided. Most likely, it was some type of medication, prescribed for her condition. "Are you all right?" he asked, concerned.

"Quite," she answered stiffly, worming her way from his grasp. Uncomfortably close, his face only inches from hers, an odd chill shivered through her body. Then, realizing her bonnet was askew, she quickly pushed it forward to shadow her face. Nervously she brushed at her clothing, hoping to distract his searching gaze.

In that instant, a rise of angry voices drew Jared's attention, and he stepped over her feet and out the door, leaving it slightly ajar. Alissa breathed an audible sigh of relief. With a curious ear, she listened to Mr. Stanley's tirade from atop his perch.

"Ye bloody fool, cain't ye see I had the right o' way?" And, with an expert's flair, he added a colorful phrase, causing Alissa to blush.

"Mr. Stanley!" Jared intervened sternly. "Calm yourself! I'm certain these good men have urgent business."

Wondering what could be causing the commotion, Alissa poked her head outside. Instantly she withdrew it. Her heart racing wildly, she started to tremble. Quickly she debated whether she should flee or if she should stay in the coach. Her decision made, she huddled deeper into her corner and pulled her cloak more securely around her. For what seemed an eternity, she waited and prayed.

"Back it up, Mr. Stanley." Jared's call finally filtered to her ears, and with a thump, the coach wheel rolled from the sidewalk. A few seconds later, he settled into his seat again.

"What was that all about?" Alissa asked cautiously.

"Mr. Stanley and a prison van decided to occupy the same width of street at the same precise moment. Fortunately, he was able to avoid a disaster."

Certain the van was on its way to Eudora's, she was thankful they'd left when they had.

"Was there any mention of their mission?"

"They were in a hurry. They didn't have time to make polite conversation."

"Oh," Alissa commented, relieved to hear it.

"Do murders intrigue you, Miss Pembroke?"

25

Her gaze snapped to his face. But nothing in his close scrutiny indicated he suspected anything. "Murders?"

His green eyes remained steady on her face. "Yes, murders."

"Did they mention such?"

"No, but I presume by their haste, they weren't merely after a pickpocket." Jared continued to watch the tight-lipped woman across from him. "Well, do they?"

"Do they what?"

"Murders . . . do they interest you?"

"How utterly ridiculous you should ask such a thing," she answered primly and watched as a rather strange grin split his chiseled lips. Despite herself, she could not help but stare. As an actress, she was no stranger to kisses, she simply did not offer them freely. But as she gazed at Jared's handsome mouth, intuition again told her, if he were to use those pliable lips on a woman's, they could be either persuasive and tender, or hard and demanding, whichever he chose. She shook the thought from her head. "You have a dark and disgusting mind. Murders, indeed!"

"My apologies, Miss Pembroke," he said as he settled back. "I dispute your comment about my mind. But of course, that is a matter of opinion. I asked because I was just curious as to why you were so interested in the constable's . . . uh, 'mission,' as you put it."

"I, too, was just curious."

No longer able to hold his amused gaze, she lowered her eyes. Then she saw it. Powder smudged his black cloak, and she knew precisely what it was! When she'd rammed, headlong, into his hard chest, her cheek had grazed its solid wall and part of her makeup had remained behind. She raised her hand to cover the exposed area on her face. With several subtle strokes, she tried to blend the missing patch over. A quick glance at her glove, however, told her she was botching the repair job by wiping more off.

Jared saw the gentle caresses and remembered how she'd crashed into him. "Have you bruised yourself?" He leaned forward and reached for her hand. "Here, let me have a look."

"No!" Her strident voice echoed around the coach before

it settled into deathly silence. Suddenly she realized how sharply she'd spoken.

His hand still in midair, Jared had not moved; his eyes were like hard, moss-covered stones. From the moment she'd practically fallen into his arms, while descending the staircase at Mrs. Binnington's, he'd noticed a definite show of wariness toward him, almost to the point of hostility. Why, he couldn't fathom, but he was going to get to the bottom of it, now!

"Do I frighten you, Miss Pembroke?" His brow curved upward over one narrowed eye as his hand finally dropped to his hard, muscular thigh with a noticeable slap. "For if I do, let me assure you, you've conjured up all sorts of wild feminine fantasies in that *odd* little mind of yours which have nothing to do with reality! My only interest in your person is to keep you safe and well until you have helped my daughter. When you've accomplished that, I'll be most happy to pack you and your belongings onto the first coach headed toward the next name on your list. Is that understood?"

Wide-eyed, Alissa studied his face. He seemed to dare her to say no. "Y-yes, quite."

"Good. Now let's try to make this trip as amicable as possible. We have a long way to travel. Hopefully, we can come to some sort of truce to make its passing more pleasant. Agreed?"

"Agreed," she answered quietly, sufficiently cowed. Then she quickly tried to explain away her bad manners. "I apologize for my outburst, Mr. Braxton. I fear, however, I'm extremely tired, which, unfortunately, has made me quite edgy. If I could impose on you to dim the lamp, perhaps I could get some rest. I'm certain my mood will improve with sleep." Her words ended, the coach hit a bump; her forearm collided with her tender breast. Pain pulsated through the bruised tissue, and her hand automatically dropped from her face to soothe and protect the area.

Not missing her wince, Jared noticed how her hand covered her chest. Immediately, he wished he'd shown a bit more decorum, instead of lashing out at her in a temper. "Your heart?" he asked solicitously.

27

Not understanding his meaning, Alissa blinked, then frowned. "What?"

"Your heart." He nodded to her hand. "Is it paining you?"

Her hand climbed to her cheek. "W-why do you ask?"

Aggravated, Jared wondered if the woman had gone daft. Realizing she still probably harbored visions of him pouncing upon her and forcefully having his way with her, he almost chuckled aloud. The only emotion Agatha Pembroke stirred inside him was anger. Taking care he did not look anywhere near the vicinity of her bosom again, he cleared his throat. "I am merely concerned, Miss Pembroke. If you'll remember, in your letter, you said your childhood illness left you with a weakened heart. If you are feeling ill, I'll have Mr. Stanley dispatch us to a physician, at once."

"No. Please, don't bother. The pain comes and goes. I—I try not to think about it." Her tongue suddenly tasted bitter. Deceit did not come easily to her, yet the deceptions were mounting, lie upon lie, until she feared her towering falsehoods would tumble down around her. But, in truth, she did have pain, and if he mistook it, it was no fault of hers. *Liar,* she berated herself silently, but she said aloud, "Thank you for your concern, Mr. Braxton. Please, don't make too much of all this. As I said, I'm just overly tired." And she was.

"Then you must rest." He leaned forward and removed an oversize lap robe from the custom storage box beneath the seat. "Here, this will keep you warm." Before she could protest, he spread the cover across her legs, his movements detached and efficient.

"Thank you." Alissa's voice trembled when she finally spoke, her gaze moving unsteadily over his face. He was far too handsome, she thought, and far too commanding. In all aspects of his life, she knew, Jared Braxton was a self-assured man, including with the ladies. But she suspected his relationships, if he had any, were merely for pleasure, playful dalliances that left no lasting emotions. Yet, despite her knowledge, he left her feeling breathless.

Suddenly she wondered about his late wife. There was no

mention in his letters to Agatha of what had caused her death, simply that his daughter, Megan, had been mute since it happened. But Alissa felt certain there had been some terrible tragedy surrounding the poor woman's demise, especially for it to have affected the child so.

She wanted to ask, but she was far too weary, the unsettling effects of her own traumatic experience having finally taken their toll. "The lamp, please, Mr. Braxton," she whispered, stretching the robe up over her shoulders. "I simply must rest."

"Certainly." He reached up and lowered the wick; the flame slowly smothered into darkness.

"Thank you." Alissa breathed the words across the void, then settled deeper into her corner. Moments later, her protective hand slowly fell from her face, and soon, the steady roll of the coach lulled her into a restless sleep.

As they made their way from London out High Holborn to Cow Lane, up St. John's to Islington Road, Jared sat quietly, gazing at Alissa's shadowy form. Strange, he thought. First, it was her eyes, now her voice. He hadn't noticed it before, but in the darkness, its melodious quality had caught his ear. He was certain he'd heard its song somewhere before.

Impossible, he thought, while stifling a yawn. Then he began seeking a more comfortable spot to settle in. But, after several minutes of thrashing about in his seat, he found the annoying Agatha Pembroke wouldn't leave his mind. So, despite his desire to do otherwise, he finally gave in and allowed his thoughts free rein.

Odd little wren, he decided as he viewed her obscure figure through the shadows again. With her drab coloring and flighty disposition, she indeed reminded him of the small gray bird; as did her voice, which could be sweet as a wren's song or as harsh as its chastising prattle. Likewise, he conceded, she probably equated him with a treacherous bird of prey, a hungry hawk silently swooping down upon its quarry, its talons poised and ready for the kill. For it was obvious she had disliked and distrusted him from the start. Puzzled, he wondered if it was only he who provoked such a guarded response. Or did all his gender? Pondering the thought, he decided her uneasiness most likely stemmed from an unhappy episode with a man.

Miss Pembroke having an affair! Not likely! The woman was far too dull to spark even the smallest flame of desire in any man. She certainly left him cold. Yet, even though the vapid Miss Pembroke held no interest for him, personally, it was quite possible that another man had been attracted to her—once. But why was he giving this woman a second thought? True, outwardly she was colorless, yet he sensed something unseen within her, an inner mystique that tempted him to tear through her plain wrappings and discover if there were, indeed, a glowing radiance hidden deep inside.

With the sudden realization of how utterly ridiculous his thoughts were, he snorted aloud. Alissa stirred and moaned softly; the cover fell from her shoulders. Jared reached across the space and draped it back over her. She moved again, and he quickly jerked his hand away and held his breath, strangely fearing her wrath should she discover him fussing about her. With another soft sound, she slipped back into a fitful slumber, and he relaxed when her even breaths met his ears.

He frowned into the darkness and decided he must be insane! Surely, his abnormal thoughts and his peculiar need to be attentive were the direct result of his being without the sweet pleasures of a woman for . . . how long? Well, it wasn't so long he couldn't remember. But just the same, it was long enough. Certain *that* was the reason behind his ridiculous reverie, he settled back, and with a somewhat sour glance at the sleeping woman across from him, he rested his head against the coach wall.

Then, needing to be entertained by more pleasing thoughts, his contemplations turned to a different woman, one whose appeal truly did whet his masculine appetite. As he remembered the excitement he'd experienced when he'd first seen her earlier this evening, he wondered why she had disappeared, never to return. He searched his memory for her name, but it eluded him, and he patted his breast pocket, seeking the folded paper placed there for safekeeping. It was gone. And so was her identity, lost forever. Yet his visual recollection of her remained strong. Soft and enchanting, her grace and beauty filled his head as he pictured her bathed in limelight, strolling through a forest's glade in a magical fairy kingdom. With a lazy smile on his face, Jared joined his sweet vision, his *Hermia,* and drifted into a pleasurable, yet troubled sleep.

CHAPTER

Three

Dappled beams of golden light shone through the small window, the night's dreary mists having lifted into a glorious morn. Huddled into her corner, Alissa absorbed the sun's rejuvenating rays, and like a flower, she turned her face more fully toward its energizing warmth. Sighing contentedly, she snuggled deeper under the woolen robe and listened to the steady vibrations: the trotting cadence of shod hoofbeats, the creak of the coach springs, the rumbling roll of the wheels. Momentarily, she was lulled into a false sense of security. Then, with a start, she abruptly came awake. Blinking several times, she pushed her bonnet forward; a quick glance confirmed her first waking thought. Jared Braxton was staring at her.

"Good morning, Miss Pembroke," he said in a cheery, singsong manner. His straight teeth flashed in the sunlight, their stark white brilliance a direct contrast to his sun-bronzed skin. "I trust you slept well."

Her wary eyes met his, noting his cocky grin. "Exceptionally," she answered, her voice husky with sleep. Suddenly his idle scrutiny made her extremely uncomfortable. His *too* sweet smile instantly unnerved her, and she feared he'd discovered the truth about her while she'd slept. Like a playful, yet cunning cat about to pounce on a trapped mouse, was he waiting to do the same? "And you, Mr.

Braxton?" she asked politely, as she began folding the lap robe, while bracing herself against the possibility of a lethal blow. "I trust you also rested well?"

"Extremely," Jared replied. His curious gaze followed her every move. Nothing has changed, he told himself. She's as fidgety now as she was last night. "I'll take that." He reached for the robe and made accidental contact with her hand. Instantly, she recoiled as if he'd stung her; the covering dropped to the floor between them. He quickly retrieved it, then shoved the rumpled thing into the storage box beneath the seat. "Would you feel more comfortable, Miss Pembroke, if I were to draw a line down the middle of the coach?" he asked sarcastically, then continued, not giving her a chance to speak. "Or perhaps we could fashion a barrier of sorts. Aha! The lap robe. We could tack it to the walls. That way, you could have your side, and I, mine. What do you say? Shall we improvise?"

Alissa realized he was baiting her again. "Don't put yourself out for my sake," she answered with an airy wave of her gloved hand. "There is plenty of space for the two of us. However, if you would like privacy, do as you wish."

His smile had long since faded, and for a lengthy moment, Jared eyed her. Then, with purpose, he said, "My wish, Miss Pembroke, is you would keep inside your skin and stop leaping from it every time I accidentally touch you. I thought it was understood I have no desire, in the strictest sense, to cast myself upon your person, yet you continue to react as though I do."

"I simply don't like being touched—by anyone."

In her eyes, Jared saw a flicker of . . . what? Revulsion? And it seemed to be coated in hatred. He was sure something dreadful had happened to her in the past. Without thought, he asked, "Was it a man who caused this unreasonable fear?"

"That is none of your business, Mr. Braxton," Alissa retorted stiffly. She turned her face away and stared through the window. She'd tried to cast out the horrid memory of Charles Rhodes's attack and had almost succeeded, until Jared Braxton reminded her of it. Tears gathered in her eyes, and she fought to keep them from spilling over.

So, Jared thought, carefully surveying her. He'd been

right. Dear God! his mind exclaimed. Surely she'd not been . . . raped! He truly hoped for her sake—any woman's sake—that was not the case. But it would explain her behavior, her feeling of being repulsed by his nearness, his touch.

Immediately regretting his callous query, for the memories he'd brought forth with it were obviously more than she could bear, he breathed a heavy sigh. "Miss Pembroke, you are right. It *is* none of my business. Yet, if I may be so bold, I ask you do not condemn all mankind for what one of my gender has done."

Alissa faced him and noticed his eyes showed sympathy. Pity, too? Apparently he had deduced the truth, but she suspected his final conclusion to be far more violent and degrading than what had actually transpired between Rhodes and herself.

Should she condemn all mankind for what one had done? As she viewed him, she suddenly realized she'd not been portraying Agatha Pembroke at all these last few moments —nor the night before. Indeed, her reactions to Jared Braxton's touch, no matter how slight, had been her own. Oddly, though, the sensations he evoked were in no way related to the disgusting, nauseating feelings Charles Rhodes had managed to summon within her. Truly, they were as different as night and day! Yet Alissa feared Jared Braxton just the same. He moved slightly, and her eyes met his, and she wondered if he expected an answer.

Having observed the conflicting flurry of emotions as they skipped across her pale face, he said, "Your pardon, Miss Pembroke, but I—"

"I will consider your statement, Mr. Braxton," she said, quietly. "For now, I would prefer a change of subject."

"As you wish," he stated, his tone considerate. Then, as she remained under his careful regard, he silently began to reassess the wisdom of hiring her.

Blast it all! If it were not for Megan, he'd order Mr. Stanley to turn the coach around and take the woman back to London, posthaste. Realistically, he couldn't tolerate the idea of tiptoeing around his own home, afraid of saying or doing something that might set the nervous Agatha Pembroke into a twitter. Certainly, he had sympathy for her obvious distress, whatever its cause. His own past was filled with hellish hosts of its own. A burning vision of Celeste suddenly appeared before his mind's eye. The image pierced his brain, his soul. With force, he ejected the unwanted memory, barricading his thoughts against a second unwelcome infiltration.

When he had finally recovered, Celeste's ghost safely locked away, he decided, before they had traveled another furlong, he would question Megan's new governess further. "Miss Pembroke," he began, "about our arrangement concerning your employment—"

"Yes, Mr. Braxton," Alissa cut in, rambling on in haste. "I've been anxious to discuss your daughter."

"Yes, but—"

"Please tell me about her." Alissa had deliberately sliced off his words, for she desperately needed to discuss something, anything, so long as it would turn aside her wayward thoughts.

"First, Miss Pembroke, I must ask, do you feel you are capable, uh"—he paused to select the right word—"*health-wise*, to assume this position?"

Alissa answered as Agatha. "My health, true, is not as good as most, but who is more important? Megan or me?"

Jared settled back and viewed her with a discerning eye, for he knew she was trying to turn the tables on him. "I need not answer. You already know she is my entire life. And that is precisely why I need to be certain you are capable of handling this position."

Was she? Alissa wondered. No, but what choice did she have? "What have you told her about Ag . . . uh, me?" she stuttered, almost slipping.

"I did as you requested. But I'd like an explanation for your reasoning."

Alissa panicked. What, precisely, had Agatha told him in her letters? Quickly she searched Jared's closed face for a clue, but she found none and decided it was time she confessed. "Mr. Braxton," she began tentatively, trying to hold his gaze. "I feel I must tell you . . . I, uh . . ."

"Miss Pembroke, I assure you I am not a stickler for formalities," Jared stated, assuming she was having difficulty choosing her words to answer his question. "If you don't want to be called governess, nurse, nanny, or any and all of the above, that's fine with me. I was just wondering why. As you requested, I've already told Megan you are a friend who's coming for an extended stay. She also understands you'll eventually part our company."

"Excellent," Alissa said on a breathless sigh. Unknowingly, Jared had helped her discover the unique approach Agatha had used over the years in dealing with her many charges. Then, wisely or unwisely, she held her confession. Instead she decided to answer his earlier query and chose her words carefully. "The term 'governess' implies authority, Mr. Braxton, which, in turn, causes a child to erect a protective barrier. Any natural openness two equals might normally share would be destroyed. True, I am her elder, but after I've gained her trust, she'll consider me her friend, not her keeper." Then Alissa found herself very interested in Megan, and last night's questions sprang to the tip of her tongue. "Will you please tell me more about her . . . and your wife's death?"

Jared's gaze remained steady on her face. "Perhaps it would be best if you ask the questions, and I shall try to answer them."

Alissa noticed his clear green eyes were suddenly shuttered; his demeanor cautious. Perhaps his memories were still too painful to openly discuss his wife's passing, especially with a stranger. Heartlessly, though, she had managed to resurrect them from the dark tombs of his mind, where he'd buried them. Belatedly Alissa realized none of it was really any of her business. "I feel I have trodden into an area where I shouldn't have," she said, her regret displayed in her soft tone. "Please forgive me."

"If you are to help my daughter, you must know of her past, correct?" His unwavering gaze questioned her as well, and Alissa nodded. "Then, Miss Pembroke, I will supply the details."

"She's been mute since your wife's death?" Alissa questioned, remembering the statement from his letter to Agatha, and watched as Jared turned his head briefly to look out the window. When his gaze again met hers, it had hardened, considerably.

"Yes." The word came out on a low, steely note. "Megan

suffered a severe emotional trauma when she was four years old. There was a fire; Celeste, her mother, perished in it. Fortunately, Megan and I escaped, but she's been unable or unwilling to speak ever since. It's been two years. I've taken her to physicians, one after another, and they all say there is no physical abnormality. That's why I sought you out."

With the recent loss of her own mother, Alissa could easily respond to his daughter's hurt—the pain, the feeling of betrayal. Tears suddenly gathered as she thought of Rachel Ashford, but she quickly brushed her mother's memory aside, for she was certain to flood the coach if she continued to think of her. Then, unheedful of her action, Alissa stretched her hand across the small space and touched Jared's as it rested along his muscular thigh. "Your wife's death was very tragic. I'm certain the loss has been great," she said sympathetically. "For Megan, and for you."

Jared bestowed a lingering glance on her hand; Alissa immediately withdrew it. "For Megan, yes," he said, "and that's precisely why I must know if you are capable of handling this position. If not, I will have Mr. Stanley turn us around, and we shall head back to London."

Jared Braxton's words were expressed without emotion, and Alissa was taken aback. *For Megan, yes.* But what of himself? What had transpired to make him seem so bereft of feeling for his late wife? Decidedly, it was indeed strange for a man to show not an ounce of remorse over the loss of a loved one, especially his mate. Unknowingly, she expressed her confusion aloud, "Why?"

"Because," he said, again misinterpreting her meaning, "Megan isn't a very trusting child, especially of women. If—and I emphasize the word *if,* Miss Pembroke—by some chance you're able to establish a rapport with her, I want to be certain you'll be capable of carrying through on all you've promised for her. If not, it's best we turn back now. I'll not allow any further destruction of her emotions."

Like a heavy stone cast through the smooth surface of the water, self-condemnation rippled outward through Alissa's mind, until her guilt-ridden conscience filled itself with ever-widening circles of remorse. She knew she could not fulfill any of his expectations, especially when he seemed to have placed his last ray of hope on Agatha Pembroke. Her shame mounted, brick upon brick, until she felt she would suffocate. Having known it was wrong from the start, she now truly realized Megan Braxton's mental health was far more important than her own needs. And, again, despite the possible ramifications, Alissa attempted to state the truth.

"Mr. Braxton, I must explain something. I—I hope you will be understanding when I've finished." She tried to hold his gaze, but she found it impossible and shifted her concentration to her tightly gripped hands. "I—I—"

"Yes, Miss Pembroke," Jared broke in. "What is it?" The woman seemed to have gone even more pale than before. How, he was at a loss to say! "You what?"

"I—I . . ." She hesitated again, then looked at him. Suddenly she feared his wrath, for she suspected it could be more destructive than a raging tempest.

Becoming frustrated with her inability to verbalize her thoughts, Jared edged forward in his seat, tempted to pull the words from her throat. "Miss Pembroke, *please!* Be out with it!"

"I, uh . . . I," she stuttered again, for Jared was starting to glare. Then, like a frightened rabbit under the watchful eye of a wily fox, all her courage fled. "I have to use the convenience!" she blurted nonsensically.

Jared threw back his head, and his deep laughter rang through the confines of the coach. "Your wish is my command," he said, when his laughter finally subsided into a chuckle. Leaning toward the door, he rose slightly and opened it, then shouted up to his coachman. "Pull into the next inn, Mr. Stanley."

"Aye. Be about five minutes to the Bell in Stilton."

"Good." He glanced back at Alissa, noting the tight expression on her face. "Hurry, please. Miss Pembroke is in dire need."

"Aye, gov'nor," Mr. Stanley called, snapping his whip; the steady pace of the bays increased to a full gallop.

With the sudden surge, Jared lost his balance. As he cursed Mr. Stanley's parentage, his arm thrust forward, his hand hitting the seat near Alissa's head, stopping his descent to her lap. Then, he shoved himself back into his own seat. "My apologies," he stated. "Obviously, Mr. Stanley is most sympathetic to your plight."

Under her makeup, Alissa turned red to the roots of her hair, embarrassed by her ridiculous outburst. Jared's laughter continued to ring inside her head, as did his vivid expletive, and she found she still suffered the effects of their near collision. The combined force of his handsome face, having been so close to hers; of his clean, masculine scent, laced with a hint of spicy cologne, its headiness still surrounding her; and of his exquisitely carved mouth, which she'd glimpsed fleetingly, prompting her to wonder again about its masterful embrace, made her feel somewhat giddy. Confused by her teeming emotions, she instantly wondered what she'd gotten herself into!

Jared viewed her odd coloring with dismay. It was, to his estimation, the strangest hue of yellowish-pink he'd ever seen on a human. He could only equate it with the decaying salmon that washed up on the banks of the River Ettrick near his home, not far from Selkirk.

Fearing she was becoming ill, he tried to soothe her. "We'll be at the inn in a moment. I'll arrange for a private room for your needs. After you've rested and eaten, we'll be on our way, either to my home or back to London, whichever you choose." Alissa started to speak, but he waved her off. "You can give me your answer after you've rested. However, Miss Pembroke, should you decide to continue on, be very certain you are capable of fulfilling your promise." The coach slowed, and Jared glanced out the window. "Ah, we're here."

Alissa's gaze followed his, noting the hustle and bustle along the busy section of the Great North Road. Two inns, the Angel and the Bell, sat opposite each other, staring stonily across the twenty-yard span separating them, for their competition was fierce. Coaches entered and exited both inns at a pace that was hard to believe. Jared Braxton's own coach stood in line, waiting to enter through the gates into the courtyard of the Bell. In the midst of all the hubbub, flocks of gray geese waddled along the middle of the thoroughfare, scurrying from under horses' hooves and coach wheels as they were herded south to the London market. Oxen, as well, traveled in the same direction on newly shod hooves, the iron shoes preventing injury or wear along the way.

Alissa hadn't expected all this frenzied activity. Instantly she feared she'd be recognized by one of the numerous travelers taking repast at the inn. Then she decided it was unlikely. Yet, she'd feel a great deal more secure if there were fewer people milling about.

As the coach slowly made its way through the stone archway into the courtyard, Alissa looked at Jared. "How far have we come?"

"Seventy-five miles."

Her eyes widened. "On one team of horses?"

Jared chuckled. "Hardly, Miss Pembroke. We stopped several times during the night for a fresh pair. You slept soundly through the entire event."

"Oh," Alissa commented and glanced out the window.

Soundly? Jared questioned silently. Not quite! She'd stirred several times while in the throes of a bad dream. What had she muttered? *Run, run, he's after you. No! Roads. . . .* Jared had missed the rest, her babble nothing more than incoherent little sketches. But later, she'd moaned, then shouted, *His blood!* or *God's blood!* Whichever it was, he couldn't recall. How she'd managed not to awaken herself, he had no idea, for he'd practically jumped from his seat when she'd yelled the words. Then he wondered if last night's tactless queries had possibly stirred the specters of her past into action, causing her nightmares. His brow furrowed, and again, he doubted the wisdom of continuing on their northward journey.

The coach finally pulled to the entry, and Jared stepped from its interior. Preoccupied with her thoughts, Alissa slid to the edge of her seat. With any luck, she'd be able to escape him here in Stilton and book herself on a stage, heading north, or west. Anyplace, so long as it was away from Jared Braxton and her pursuers. If she were careful, she could find her way from the Bell over to the Angel and board the next public coach and be safely on her way. But first, she needed to fetch her hidden savings from her case. Unfortunately, there wasn't even a farthing in Agatha's purse.

Jared offered his hand. "Miss Pembroke."

Alissa placed her small hand in his, noting its gentle strength. Then in a rustle of skirt, she alighted with grace.

"I see we are making progress."

Confused, she gazed at his handsome face. "Progress?"

"Yes." He nodded toward their joined hands.

Realizing his meaning, Alissa slowly slipped from his grip. "I suppose we are, Mr. Braxton."

"Good." He withdrew a step, deciding not to press her too quickly. "Fears can be overcome, if one only tries."

"I'm certain they can," she said as she glanced around the bustling, sun-fused courtyard. While she pushed her bonnet forward, she searched for a feasible escape route.

Jared noted how she always fussed with her bonnet, apparently trying to hide her face, and suspected her plainness made her feel self-conscious. Yet, he remembered, while viewing her this morning, he'd noticed she had good bone structure, plus a classically straight nose, and nicely shaped lips, the lower slightly fuller than the upper. If it weren't for her deathly ill color, she might be quite pleasant to look upon. Or at least passable, he conceded. "Shall I have Mr. Stanley fetch a bag from the boot?" he asked, dismissing his wild meanderings.

"Yes, please. The small black one."

"Certainly." He strode several feet from her side, then looked up at his tired coachman. "Mr. Stanley, please bring Miss Pembroke's small black case when you come."

"Aye. I will, soon as I tend to the horses."

"You'd best tend to yourself, Mr. Stanley. A hot meal shall await you when you're through."

"Right, gov'nor," he said with a tip of his hat, then guided the coach to the livery area.

"After you, Miss Pembroke."

Jared swept his arm before him, and Alissa headed toward the door. But before she could enter, a small, rotund man came scurrying up from behind them. Without so much as an "excuse me," he nudged Alissa aside, and heaved himself through the opening, leaving her wide-eyed and mouth agape. Such rudeness was uncalled for, she thought, glaring at the man's back. Apparently, Jared thought the same.

"Hold, sir!" He grabbed the man's collar and yanked him back through the entry. "A lady was before you. You'll wait your turn."

The smaller man pivoted, ready to take issue. But when he saw the size of his towering opponent, he thought better of it. "Begs yer pardon, ma'am," he said with a gulp, "but I have urgent business with the Justice o' the Peace. He's here breakfasting with his regulars," he added, referring to the local constables. "There's been a bit of trouble in London, and word's out to check all coaches headin' north." Normally, he would never have shared the information, but the look in the tall stranger's eyes had loosened his tongue. "Excuse me, but I must be goin'." He bobbed his head and started to make his way back through the door, but Jared's words stopped him.

"We've just come from London. Is there a great emergency?"

Suddenly Alissa felt nauseated, weak. Keeping her head bowed, she listened to the man's every word.

"Nothin' serious. Just some viscount gettin' his head split in two by an actress at Covent Garden. They're lookin' for her. Cain't say I'd like bein' in her shoes when they find her."

Jared turned curious eyes on the man. "Covent Garden, you say?"

"Sure 'nough. Been there, has ye?"

"Several times."

He reserved the knowledge that the last time was only yesterday. Then he wondered if the young actress—his *Hermia*—and the woman the harried man had mentioned were one and the same. He had dreamed of her last night—held her in his arms and felt his masculine needs stir. Then just as his lips were about to meet her yielding mouth, his gaze traveling over her vague features, his vision of her became distorted, then changed. The face of Agatha Pembroke had appeared in her place! Needless to say, he'd jerked himself awake. As he thought on it, Jared shuddered anew, wondering how such a lovely fantasy could turn into such a distasteful bugbear.

Clearing the distressing episode from his head, Jared said, "Please go ahead." He waved the man through. "Your mission is obviously most urgent."

To Alissa's relief, the small man puffed himself up and waddled through the door. With an odd rolling gait, he sped out of sight. Fortunately, she had escaped detection *this* time. But for how long? Especially with the Justice and his regulars in the building! Then she felt Jared's hand on her arm, urging her forward. But her feet refused to move; they seemed rooted in the stone step. Finally, she gazed up at him. "I fear I really must find a place to rest." Anyplace! she thought in desperation. So long as it was away from the many curious eyes at the inn.

Viewing her, Jared was amazed at the ghastly colors the peculiar woman could turn. Before it was yellowish pink, now it was paste gray, an exact match to the stone wall behind her. Without hesitation, he hustled her through the doorway, practically carrying her to the counter, pushing several patrons aside who were in his path. "I need a room, immediately," he said to the clerk without preamble.

"You'll wait yer turn," the young man answered, echoing Jared's words spoken outside the door.

"I need a room, my good man," he repeated with controlled force, his voice low, threatening. *"Now!"*

Indignation written on his face, the clerk raised his narrowed gaze, ready to refuse. However, he took one look at Jared's hard green eyes and glanced at Alissa. "God A'mighty! She ain't dyin', is she?"

"Not if you get her a place where she can rest, undisturbed—*immediately.*"

"Yes, sir." The clerk called a young servant girl to the counter and handed her a key. "Take this here lady upstairs . . . be quick about it."

"Thank you," Alissa whispered. As she turned to follow the young woman, she heard the clerk's aside to Jared.

"She ain't catching, is she?"

"No, young man. She has a frail heart."

"Should I fetch a croaker?"

"If she needs a physician, I'll let you know."

Pretending to be extremely weak, Alissa followed slowly up to the second level. Once inside the room, the young woman curtsied and hastily started to flee. "Wait!" Alissa called. The girl slowly turned to face her; Alissa noticed she kept her hand on the latch. "Could you please tell me if there's a public stage due at the Angel soon?"

"Can't say. I don't work at the Angel, mum. This here's the Bell."

"I know it is!" Alissa practically snapped the words, time

being of the essence. The girl edged herself closer to the door, her back now against the latch. Obviously, she was frightened, and Alissa realized why. "Please, don't be afraid. I assure you I have no disease, nor am I contagious." The girl still seemed cautious, but at least she'd stopped her anxious movements. "How many stages pass this way?" Alissa questioned, hoping to get *some* information from her.

"Oh, lots, mum. But I don't know the times, especially at the Angel."

"Do any head west from here?"

"None I know of, mum," she said, shrugging. "London'd be your best place to catch one, I'd say. 'Course, you could go north to Leeds. I have an uncle there, and I took one once to visit him. I suppose you could catch one going west from there."

Frowning, Alissa thought of her options. London was definitely out of the question. Yet she had hoped she could travel a different road than Jared, but the Great North seemed to be the way of both their paths.

Both women jumped as a sudden rap sounded on the door. The latch turned, and without waiting for Alissa's call, Jared strode through, carrying her black case. The servant girl quickly scurried out, almost beneath Jared's feet. He frowned at her abrupt departure, then closed the door. "It's difficult to get good help these days," he commented as he walked toward the bed where he set the bag. "I've ordered up a tray for you. I took the liberty of sending a lad over to the Angel for some of Miss Worthington's famous Stilton cheese. I hope you enjoy it."

"I'm certain I will."

"Is there anything else you need?"

Alissa shook her head. "Rest, that's all. I thank you for your concern."

Jared hesitated, momentarily, then he retraced his steps to the door. "I'll have someone come stay with you."

"No! I mean, I'd rather you wouldn't. Everyone here seems a bit nervous. I think they're afraid I might carry the plague. Besides, I know my own needs better than anyone. Truly, Mr. Braxton, there's no cause for alarm."

"Are you certain?" he asked, but she didn't answer. She just stared. "Miss Pembroke, please understand, if you feel the need for a physician, tell me. You won't be putting anyone out by doing so." Jared took a step toward her, and Alissa immediately backed away. Suddenly he realized he'd shut himself in the room with her. There had been no intent on his part, yet she possibly thought otherwise. "Should you decide you've changed your mind, please let me know." With that, he left the room.

As soon as the door closed, Alissa rushed across the room, her feet sliding inside Agatha's shoes. Turning the key, she threw the bolt. Then she fairly flew to the window. Fortunately, she'd been given a room opposite the entrance to the Angel. She yanked aside the lace curtain and viewed the traffic along the Great North for several furlongs in each direction. For once, luck was with her. Within moments, a large stagecoach, pulled by four strong bays, came rambling through the stretch, heading north, stopping at the Angel. The lettering on the side, the words rising one over the other, read: Edinburgh–London.

The curtain dropped; Alissa ran to the bed and opened her case. She knew she had little time. Public coaches never tarried. Within minutes, it would be gone, and with it, her hopes of escape.

Lace-trimmed chemises, petticoats, pantalettes, a corset or two, plus her dresses flew through the air, landing all over the quilt-covered bed as she searched for the white stocking containing her savings. Finally, reaching the bottom of the case, she turned it upside down, giving it a violent shake. Nothing! Again, she searched the scattered pieces, turning each garment inside out, feeling each stocking from toe to top. Why, she didn't know, for the particular stocking she wanted would be quite visible to the naked eye, its small, rounded bulge stuffing the toe.

Distraught, Alissa rubbed her fingers across her forehead, hoping to stimulate her thoughts. Where could it be? she wondered, her hand bumping the bonnet's brim. In a fit of temper, she yanked the ribbons free and tossed the obnoxious thing across the room. Then her eye caught the remnants of her makeup left on her glove, and she realized she'd managed to wipe more off.

Why? Why? *Why?* she wanted to scream, aloud; but somehow she managed to hold it inside. Oh, how she wished she could scrub herself from head to foot, discard the horrid clothing and the oversize shoes and just be herself once more. But the disguise was all she had to get her safely out of England.

The stage! She rushed back to the window, praying it was still there. Indeed it was, but Alissa stiffened when she saw the activity around it. The rotund little man who'd brushed her aside, earlier, stood next to another, more dignified-looking gentleman, whom Alissa believed to be the Justice of the Peace; two other men helped the women passengers, one at a time, alight from the coach's interior. The Justice tipped his hat, then questioned each woman as she stepped down. When the last woman appeared at the door, the fat little man pointed an accusing finger, shaking it with vigor, while a cry erupted from his pudgy mouth.

With a force Alissa deemed unnecessary, the two regulars practically dragged the poor woman from the coach. Then, suddenly, another man literally leapt into the picture, bounding from the passenger seat atop the stage. Rage filled his features as he shoved the constables aside, then he placed a protective arm around the shaking woman's shoulders. The two men instantly backed off.

"Keep your filthy hands from my wife!" the man shouted, his angry voice filtering through the windowpane into Alissa's ears. "I shall have your heads if you touch her again!"

The man seemed so enraged Alissa expected to see him slap his glove across the face of each man involved, challenging all to a duel, commencing immediately. Should he do so, there was no doubt in her mind that, whether he fought each one individually or the foursome together, he would be the victor.

Then Alissa noticed the traffic on the Great North had stopped; spectators surrounded the coach, more than mildly interested in the outcome of the foray. Suffering from embarrassment, the woman apparently wanted to make peace, for she placed her gloved hand on her husband's chest and whispered something to him. The man nodded, then withdrew his arm from her shoulders, bumping her bonnet. Alissa gasped as she watched it fall from the woman's head, a head filled with a wealth of mahogany hair.

Suddenly she realized why they'd singled out this particular woman. She'd been mistaken for Alissa Ashford, actress and murderess!

Defeated, Alissa moved to the bed and sank to the down-filled mattress. Even if she had found her money, she'd never have escaped Stilton, not when they were searching the coaches, not even in her disguise. Still, there remained the possibility she could offer a bribe—her mother's jewels—to a farmer or to a private coachman. But it seemed unlikely. Word was already out, and Alissa suspected everyone would be extra cautious until the murderess had been captured.

With a sigh of resignation, knowing she'd have to continue north with Jared Braxton, she began retrieving her clothing. Perhaps Eudora had packed the stocking in Agatha's luggage. Then she remembered Eudora's words: "I packed *half* of your undergarments . . ." Half certainly was not all, and Alissa realized her money was still in London, hidden in the back of her bureau drawer along with some worn stockings that Eudora probably ignored in her haste to get Alissa safely out of London. Unfortunately, Alissa had forgotten to ask.

Resigned to her fate, she realized that not only would she have to continue with Jared, but she'd also have to rely on him for support. And she'd have to become Agatha Pembroke to get it.

Alissa clutched a petticoat to her breast. Bowing her head, she closed her eyes; her head moved in a negative gesture. If she had an ounce of courage, she'd stop her ridiculous charade, fleeing one country, then most likely another, and march herself down the stairs, straight to the Justice of the Peace. As she seriously thought about it, the courts versus Jared Braxton, she knew her best chance would be with the former. Undoubtedly, a hangman's noose would be far kinder than the punishment Jared Braxton would surely mete out, should he discover her deception.

Footsteps sounded outside her door, then she heard the whiny voice of the servant girl; Jared Braxton's deep voice countered, "She's not a threat to you, so hold your tongue." Then a knock sounded on the door.

Alissa didn't answer. Her makeup was smeared, her

bonnet was in the corner, her clothing was still scattered across the bed, and only a few feet away stood her executioner! If he were to discover her like this, he'd know she'd been pretending all along!

The knock sounded again, louder, harder, and in a flurry of activity, Alissa stuffed her clothing into the case, snapping it shut. As she rushed to the mirror, Jared's rap sounded again, but she still ignored it. Plucking the tin of makeup from her purse, she did a quick repair job, which took only seconds, then she hurried across the room and snatched the bonnet from the floor. She squashed the thing onto her head as Jared fairly pounded the solid door asunder.

He jiggled the latch. "Miss Pembroke, open up!"

Taking a deep breath, Alissa spun toward the panel. Hurriedly, she started toward the door, slid inside her shoes, and lost her balance. Her arms flailed as she tried to correct herself. But she overcompensated and fell backward, landing on her seat with an unladylike plop.

Outside, Jared heard the thud; he glanced at the girl holding the food-laden tray. "Do you have a key?"

"No, sir," the wide-eyed girl answered. "They're all downstairs on a ring."

Jared quickly ran his hand along the sturdy wood, then set his shoulder to it. Solid, through and through, he concluded. He looked at the girl, then back to the door. "Oh, hell!" He growled the words just before his booted heel hit the latch. The splintered panel crashed against the wall, and Jared burst across the threshold to stop short.

"Why, Mr. Braxton, you startled me!" Alissa exclaimed from where she primly sat on the edge of the bed, a small book held in one hand, the other over her wildly beating heart. "One would think a simple knock would have sufficed!"

Jared eyed her suspiciously. "One would think so, Miss Pembroke," he said, and the grating quality of his voice scraped along Alissa's nerves. "Since I nearly beat the door in two, I'd like to know what in blazes you were doing in here!"

"Doing?" Alissa asked innocently.

"Yes, doing!"

"Why, I was reading."

"Reading!" he exploded, his hand raking through his thick, dark hair.

To Alissa, it looked as though he were about to pull it from its roots. "Yes," she said as she waved the copy of Shakespeare's *Sonnets* in the air, silently thanking the dear departed Agatha for having it in her purse. "It relaxes me."

"My dear Miss Pembroke, *relaxes* is hardly the proper word. You'd have to be stone-dead not to have heard me!"

If he only knew, she thought, but said aloud, "I apologize, Mr. Braxton, but when I become absorbed in Shakespeare, a cannon could discharge beside me and I'd never know it."

Jared's eyes narrowed. What trick was she trying to pull? When he was on the other side of the door, it had sounded as though she'd been chasing herself around the room. But now she sat, all neat and tidy, just like he'd left her, her ridiculous-looking bonnet still crowning her head. Did she ever take the blasted thing off? Then he noticed her face was that godawful salmon color again. As he viewed her, he couldn't decide which suited her best, paste gray or yellowish pink.

"Uh, sir," the girl said behind him. "Do you mind if I bring in this tray?"

"Here, I'll take it." He hefted the heavy thing from her hands. "Please inform the innkeeper of the damages and have him include it on my bill. We'll be leaving shortly."

"Yes, sir." She dipped a curtsy while perusing the tall, handsome man with feminine interest. Then she peered around Jared. " 'Bout the coach, mum—"

"Oh, yes, thank you," Alissa cut in as she sprang from the bed, "but I won't be needing the information."

The servant girl shrugged and, with one last look at Jared, left the room.

"Coach?" he questioned, his dark brow rising.

"Yes, uh, I inquired about a coach back to, uh, London," she answered, turning her back to him, knowing she was adding another lie to her list. But she also knew there would be yet another and another.

He eyed her skeptically. "Why?"

"I felt, if we were to part company, here and now, there was no need for you to travel all the way back to London. I'd simply have taken a public coach."

"Then you've made your decision?"

Alissa turned to face him. "I have."

"And?"

"I've decided to go on to Scotland."

"As you wish." He set the tray on the side table. "Eat hearty, it's a long way to Selkirk. We'll be leaving within the half hour." He strode to the door, where he turned and looked her squarely in the eye. "I hope, for your sake, you've made the right choice." Then, with a curt nod, he left.

Not only had she heard the warning, but Alissa had read it in his green eyes. As she stared at the lopsided door, which stood slightly ajar, she whispered, "I hope I've made the right choice, too, Mr. Braxton. Believe me, I do."

CHAPTER

Four

Scotland

As the coach swayed up the long drive, Alissa gazed in awe at the enormous house, stretching upward, three stories, into the overcast sky. Low-hung clouds swept the peaks of its slate-tiled roof; thick, hanging mists curtained its gray stone facade, creating an eerie appearance.

A sudden chill shivered along her spine. She wondered if they had somehow taken a wrong turn. Her brow furrowed, hoping against hope they had. Then she noticed two wings jutting forward from the core of the house. Charred stones framed the windows on the eastern-most wing, resembling the blackened eyes of a plague-riddled corpse. No longer able to deny it, she finally admitted the ugly mars were the remnants of a fire. Indeed, *this* was Mr. Braxton's home.

With a loud snort, Mr. Stanley stirred in his seat. As he smacked his lips, his head lolled lazily against the interior wall of the coach, where it rested. Opening a bleary eye to see Miss Pembroke across from him, he suddenly realized where he was and jerked upright. His hand stroked over his balding pate, smoothing the few hairs that resided there. "Sorry, miss," he said in a hoarse whisper, "I must'a dozed fer a minute."

Alissa bit her lower lip, trying to contain her laughter. His snores had vibrated steadily for a good two hours, if not longer. "That's quite all right, Mr. Stanley. You deserve a long rest. In but a few moments, I'm certain your bed will offer great comfort."

His head twisted, and he glanced through the coach window. "We're at Hawkstone." He sounded somewhat amazed. "Guess I dozed a bit longer than I'd thought."

"Hawkstone, you say," Alissa mused aloud, gazing again at the huge mansion. "Mr. Stanley," she began, turning her attention to him, "how is it Mr. Braxton can afford such an enormous place?"

The coachman fidgeted in his seat; his fingers scratched the back of his neck, his gaze shying away from hers. "Cain't say, miss. His lo . . . uh"—he coughed, fitfully, and cleared his throat—"Mr. Braxton don't exactly share his finances with me."

While he busily straightened his rumpled clothing, the same ruse she'd used whenever she wanted to distract Jared's attention from the issue at hand, Alissa viewed him distrustfully. Nonsense! The past few days had been harrowing, to say the least, making her suspicious of everyone and everything. "It's an impressive home," she stated simply, not wanting to distress the man further.

The coach swayed slightly as the horses accelerated their pace, gaining speed for the final uphill stretch to the house, and she wondered how the master of Hawkstone was faring from his long stint in the bleak elements.

When they'd left Stilton, over a day ago, a surprised Alissa had watched Jared, still attired in evening clothes, climb to Mr. Stanley's spot atop the coach. At the time, she'd thought him extremely considerate, for his man, eyes spiderwebbed in red, could not go another furlong without sleep. Now, as she thought on it, she wondered if he'd changed places simply to avoid her. It mattered not, she concluded. In actuality, she'd been equally relieved to escape his presence, as much as he'd been hers. Possibly more so!

Over the passing miles, the two men had shifted positions every four hours. Mr. Stanley had slept soundly during his breaks, and when Jared entered the coach, Alissa had pretended to do the same. They'd stopped for hot meals, a periodic change of horses, and once for several hours' rest, Jared changing into more appropriate garb. Then they were off again to travel throughout the long night.

Alissa's nerves suddenly quavered. Their journey at its end, she thought of Megan Braxton. Beyond those dismal stone walls resided her charge, and her guilt soared anew. It's wrong, her conscience admonished harshly. Knowing it was too late, she closed her eyes and offered a silent prayer of penitence.

The coach pulled to a stop at the huge stone entry; the carved doors swung wide. A rather austere-looking woman stepped from the house, head held high. Her brown hair peeked from beneath a white cap; her back stood rod-straight. Dressed in somber gray to match the gloomy weather, she waited on the doorstep, her face totally devoid of expression.

"That's Leona Dugan," Mr. Stanley stated with a sniff, supplying the answer to Alissa's unspoken question. "She's the housekeeper here at Hawkstone."

"Why, Mr. Stanley, you sound as though you're not overly fond of her."

The disgruntled coachman glanced at Alissa. "She's a mite strange, she is."

Curious about his statement, Alissa opened her mouth to inquire on it, but the coach door opened, and Jared offered his hand. "Miss Pembroke."

Her bones stiff and achy, Alissa grimaced as she tried to slide to the edge of her seat. Noticing her distressed look, Jared reached deeper into the coach, took her arm, and gently urged her forward. Then his firm hands spanned her small waist, and with little effort, he hoisted her from the interior, settling her to the solid ground, and held her, giving her his support.

As the blood started to recirculate through her lower extremities, a surge of heat tingled to Alissa's toes; needles pricked painfully under her skin, and her legs wobbled like a newborn colt's. Unnerved by Jared's familiar touch, she was, by the same token, thankful for his steadying hands.

Amazed, Jared discovered that she was sleek and soft beneath the worn material of her gown, not the skin and bone he'd imagined, and his errant fingers moved upward in gentle exploration. Startled, Alissa's head snapped up; the stiff brim of her bonnet striking him square in the jaw.

Immediately, he kicked back his head, fearing she'd strike again.

"I can stand on my own now, thank you," she announced curtly. Yet, her cool tone belied the warm sensations coursing through her body. Confused, she pushed his hands aside. Suddenly her legs gave way, and Jared caught her arm before she landed on the ground in a heap.

"Obviously, you cannot," came his clipped reply. Angered that he'd allowed his male curiosity to play a game of seek and find with this pretentious woman, he scowled at her and took a firm grip on her elbow. With long strides, he escorted her to the stone steps.

Her feet sliding inside Agatha's shoes, Alissa found herself hard-pressed to keep up, especially with her legs still tottering beneath her. Yet, she held her protest, for her eyes were on those of the reed-thin woman standing by the doorway. A disapproving look came from the housekeeper, causing Alissa to shrink inside. Alarmed, she thought the woman might be clairvoyant and had guessed she was an imposter. But she quickly dismissed the idea and squared her shoulders.

Jared easily climbed the steps, Alissa in tow. "Miss Pembroke, may I present my housekeeper, Leona Dugan."

Alissa extended her hand. "How do you do," she stated in a friendly tone, trying to break the woman's glacial reserve, but she received only a curt nod in return, and Alissa's hand drifted slowly to her side.

"Megan has been impatient for your return," Leona said, ignoring the newcomer, her dark brown eyes held rigidly on her employer. "I've sent Mary up for her. She's been in her room since you've left. She's hardly eaten a thing."

Forgetting decorum, Jared released Alissa's arm and strode through the doorway, anxious to see his daughter.

Alissa followed Leona through the massive carved doors into the grand entry to stop short. Her eyes wide with wonder, she stared in disbelief. The dismal facade outside had done little to prepare her for the opulence within.

White marble, with periodic insets of black, formed a diamond pattern beneath her feet. The floor, edged in black, met white marble walls, shooting upward, two stories high.

Alissa's neck craned backward as she gazed in awe at the high ceiling, backdropped in blue. Gilt-winged cherubs danced among sun-rayed clouds, expertly stroked by an artist's hand. A crystal chandelier hung from the ceiling, hundreds of tapered white candles ensconced in its holders, but only a few were lit to chase away the gloom of the day. "Magnificent," she whispered, not realizing she'd spoken the word aloud.

Then her gaze turned to the grand staircase, directly opposite the door. Its blood-red carpet swept up the virgin white marble to a landing, then detoured left and right, then up again, but Alissa's eyes remained on the child dressed in emerald green, resembling a miniature adult. Her dark, wavy hair, secured by a band of green ribbon, trailed down her back. Timidly she stood on the third to the last step. Amazed, Alissa instantly noted how much she favored her father.

"Megan, sweet princess." The throaty words were whispered as Jared angled around an ornately carved table, almost toppling the centuries-old, hand-painted vase gracing its top. "Did you miss me, sweet?" he asked as he swung her high into his arms, holding her close. "I promised I wouldn't be gone long, and I kept that promise, didn't I?"

Not a sound came from between the child's lips as she retained a deathlike grip around her father's neck, a bright sheen of moisture glazing her green eyes. The sight of father and daughter tore at Alissa's heart. For it was evident Megan had feared never seeing her one remaining parent again.

Then she felt the sting of tears behind her own eyes as she thought of Rachel, the only parent she'd ever known. Her hand rose to the hollow between her breasts. Unknowingly, she searched for the precious remembrance, her last link to her mother. But it wasn't there. As Jared released Megan, setting her slippered feet to the floor, Alissa quickly composed herself, her hand dropping from her breast.

"Megan," he said as he urged his daughter toward Alissa, "I want you to meet someone." Megan stayed slightly behind her father, her huge, long-lashed eyes staring up at the stranger. "This is the special friend I told you about.

She'll be staying with us for a while." He turned. "Miss Agatha Pembroke, this is my daughter, Megan."

At her father's direction, Megan offered a slight curtsy, but she kept behind him, her eyes searching Alissa's face. Alissa smiled reassuringly, and said, "Megan, my name is A . . . Agatha, and you may call, uh, you may know me by that name. I've heard so much about you, but your father neglected to say how very pretty you are." Alissa heard Leona's disdainful sniff, but she ignored it and forged onward. "He spoke only of his deep affection for you and of how anxious he was to return home to Scotland and to you." She glanced at Jared, noting his arched brow. "I hope you aren't upset with me because your father was kind enough to fetch me from London. And, of course, during my stay, I do hope we'll become fast friends."

Her words reaped no reaction from the child, only a blank stare. Then Megan tugged at her father's trousers. Jared focused his attention on her, watching as she rubbed her stomach.

"The child's hungry," Leona piped in a rancorous voice. "She's taken little nourishment since your departure. I'll take her to see cook." Leona reached for Megan's small hand, but the girl grasped her father's and pulled. "Obviously, she's afraid to let you out of her sight."

Jared gazed down into his daughter's wide, pleading eyes. "Are you hungry?" Megan nodded. "Then let's see what cook has for us, shall we?" Megan relaxed, again nodding, and Jared turned his attention to Alissa. "Will you join us, Miss Pembroke?"

"If it is acceptable to you, I'd rather find my quarters, so I may bathe and rest a bit."

"Certainly. Mrs. Dugan will see you to your room. I'll have cook send up a tray."

Relieved, Alissa glanced at Megan. The child seemed equally happy that she would not have to share her father's attention with some stranger. Megan might want to be close to her father, but Alissa certainly did not.

"We will talk, later," Jared said, then swept Megan high into his arms and carried her toward the back of the enormous house and the kitchens.

Alissa watched the departing pair, and envy stabbed at

her heart, for she'd never known a father's love. Megan was most fortunate, she thought.

"Follow me." Leona Dugan turned on her heel, lifted her starched skirt, and stiffly proceeded up the grand staircase.

Alissa trailed along at her own pace, gawking at the grandeur surrounding her, but apparently it wasn't fast enough. The housekeeper stopped, her back arrow-straight, hands tightly clasped, and impatiently waited until Alissa caught up. Alissa did not dare fall behind again.

When they reached the second-story landing, the housekeeper marched down the red-carpeted hallway, past several large rooms, one being the formal dining room, which Alissa glanced at briefly. Impressive, she thought, and turned left through a set of carved doors, leading into the west wing.

Near the end of the corridor, Leona stopped and took a set of keys from the holder on her belt. She unlocked the door and turned the solid brass handle. "This is your chamber. I'll have Mary bring up hot water for your bath." With that, the housekeeper retraced her steps, disappearing into an alcove, and descended the hidden stairs.

Alissa stared after her, disturbed by her demeanor, and wondered if it was she who'd caused the woman to act so cold. Then she remembered Mr. Stanley's statement, "She's a mite strange, she is." And Alissa decided the housekeeper's unfriendly reserve was simply part of her personality.

Too weary to really care one way or the other, she dismissed any thought of Leona Dugan and pushed the door wide. A gasp of pleasure escaped her lips as she viewed her room.

Large insets of mint-green silk, bordered on all sides by finely carved cream-colored wood, its raised design gilded, climbed to a white ceiling. Against one wall stood a large bed, draped and canopied in a floral print of green, gold, and blue silk. A small, sky-blue silk-covered settee and two chairs, striped in blue and gold, also of silk, were arranged directly opposite the bed in front of the gold-veined, white marble fireplace. A large off-white carpet, its center threaded with gold, blanketed the better part of the highly polished wood floor. On closer inspection, Alissa discovered the design to be a rose.

A large armoire stood in one corner, a hand-painted

screen in another, and a japanned writing table nestled itself between the tall windows, which were draped in gold brocade. Assorted tables, bureaus, and a dressing table with a mirror completed the furnishings.

Amazed by all this opulence, Alissa viewed the room, again, a frown etching itself into her brow. Never had she hoped to see such a beautiful bedchamber, much less sleep in one. And, again, she wondered about Jared Braxton's wealth.

Yet, amid all this grandeur, Alissa sensed a great sorrow. The feeling seemed to weep from the very walls of this great house. And oddly, Alissa felt a sadness settle around her.

Could her mood be caused by her own hopeless situation, and not by some echoes of the past that might still be reverberating through the yawning corridors of Hawkstone? No, she decided, for she'd somehow felt its melancholy pull the moment she'd walked through the doors. And she wondered what had happened here to cause such a woeful, sinking feeling.

"Miss? Might I come in?"

Alissa turned at the sound of Mr. Stanley's familiar voice and smiled. The smile was for herself, as well as the coachman, as she tried to break free of the gloom encasing her. "Certainly."

His arms filled with her bags, he crossed the threshold and placed the cumbersome luggage at the bed's foot.

"Thank you, Mr. Stanley. You're most kind."

"Yer welcome, miss." Nervously, he toed the carpet. "Uh, I want to thank ye fer comin' all this way to help little Megan. With ye not feelin' well and all"—he shrugged— "well, it's might good of ye."

Alissa discovered she could no longer hold the man's gaze. "I appreciate your kind words, Mr. Stanley," she whispered. "I'll do my best."

A noise at the doorway drew their attention. A young maid, whom Alissa assumed was Mary, struggled into the room, a large bucket of steaming water in each hand. Mr. Stanley quickly took one, then trailed the young woman and disappeared behind the screen in the far corner.

Alissa followed the two and discovered a small alcove set

into the wall. Light streamed through a frosted-paned window onto an ornate brass and copper, claw-foot tub. Elation rioted through her as she watched the clean, clear liquid fall into the huge bath, possibly large enough for two. Heavenly, she thought. She could hardly wait to strip away her clothing and have a long soak. Several more trips by Mary and Mr. Stanley and the bath was filled.

"Can I help ye unpack?" Mary asked.

Anxious to be rid of the two, Alissa said, somewhere between Agatha's proper tone and her own more cordial one, "Thank you, but no . . . Mary, is it?" The maid nodded. "I do appreciate your offer, Mary, but right now I'd like very much to bathe, then rest. Besides, there is very little to unpack. As you can see, I travel lightly."

"As ye wish, mum. I'll bring ye up a tray."

"Just place it outside the door, will you?"

"Sure, mum." Mary eyed the newcomer at Hawkstone. From what she could see behind the ugly bonnet, the woman looked awful peaky. She needs some of cook's special tea, the maid decided. That should put some pink into her cheeks. "Should ye be takin' yer bath, I'll knock to let ye know I'm back."

Despite herself, Alissa suddenly felt tense. She wanted out of Agatha's clothes and into the tub. "That will be fine," she stated more sharply than intended.

"Come, Mary," Mr. Stanley said from where he hovered by the doorway. "Miss Pembroke, here, needs to rest." With a nod, the coachman, along with Mary, took his leave.

Alissa quickly locked the door after them and prayed she was secure inside. The heavy panel seemed strong enough, the lock sturdy. But she remembered the solid door safeguarding her room at the inn and its splintered remnants when she'd left. She viewed the panel again. Since there was no strife between Jared and herself at the moment, she decided not to worry about it. Right now, like a small child, she simply wanted to frolic in her bath.

The hated bonnet torn from her head, the chenille net springing free, Alissa loosened the pins from her hair, then massaged her scalp, her long tresses tumbling around her in wild disarray. Agatha's clothing and shoes clearly marked a path behind the screen as Alissa slipped into the tub, immersing herself up to her neck. *Heaven,* she thought, enjoying the warmth. When the water finally cooled, she scrubbed herself from head to toe, careful of her bruised flesh.

The angry mark was a vivid purple now, with streaks of green and yellow slashing through it. Ignoring it, for it brought back too many upsetting memories, Alissa began washing her hair, then rinsed it with a large pitcher of water left by the tub's side.

She stood, rivers of water running down her sleek thighs, and dried herself vigorously. Wrapping a dry piece of toweling around her pink body, she retrieved her brushes from her case and sat near the hearth and the crackling fire Mr. Stanley had lit to chase the chill from her room.

What to do now? she wondered as she stroked the brush through her drying mane. Again, she thought of confessing, but again, she dismissed it. There had to be some way to extricate herself from this ruse without incurring Jared's wrath. Impossible! Short of disappearing into thin air, she knew she had little chance of escaping him.

A knock sounded on the door, startling her. Believing it to be Mary, Alissa called, "Just leave the tray outside the door, if you will. I'll fetch it later."

"If I had a tray, Miss Pembroke," Jared countered from the hallway with a chuckle, "I'd be delighted to comply with your instructions."

Alissa jumped to her feet; the bath sheet dropped to the floor. Realizing she stood in all her glory, she grabbed the towel, shielding herself. Not knowing what to do or where to hide, she practically wilted into the carpet as the scene at the inn flashed through her mind, repeating itself over and over again. "W-what do you want?" she cried, frantically tucking the bath sheet into place, holding it securely.

"I wanted to know if your room is satisfactory."

"Y-yes . . . very."

"Is there anything you need?"

"No. E-everything's fine."

Jared was fast becoming weary of pressing his ear against the wood to hear her responses. Leaning his shoulder along the door frame, he said, "Miss Pembroke, is it possible for you to open the door, so I might address you face-to-face?"

"No!" The word shrieked through the panel, and Jared drew back. "I-I've just finished my bath," Alissa explained, "and I-I'm in dishabille."

Jared again chuckled as he imagined the prudish woman wrapping herself in every available piece of cloth. He discounted the draperies, for no doubt, she believed she could be seen from the lawns.

"I beg your pardon, Miss Pembroke. I hadn't realized you were indisposed. When you have finished your preparations, I ask that you join me in my study."

"C-certainly," Alissa answered, relaxing.

"On the hour, then?"

"The *hour?*" she gasped, not certain she could transform herself into Agatha so quickly. She glanced at the clock on the mantel. Twenty-five minutes past three. She'd never do it. "I—I really need more time."

Jared frowned. The woman had sounded as though she were readying herself for a ball. "I do have other appointments, Miss Pembroke," he stated, exasperation clearly written in his tone. "I must insist."

Alissa didn't like the sound of his voice. Fearing he'd take it upon himself to assist her into her clothing, she replied, "As you wish. I'll be there on the hour."

"Excellent. I will await your arrival." With that Jared turned on his heel and strode down the hall, his head shaking in weary response. There must be some way to open the lines of communication with this woman, he thought. But for the life of him, he couldn't decide how. *Patience,* he stressed the word in his mind. Unfortunately, that particular trait was one of his weakest.

In her room, Alissa hurriedly rifled through one of Agatha's cases and found a suitable brown dress. A large woolen shawl would serve nicely as a cover-up, since she had no time to perform any alterations on the gown's bodice.

As she fished through another case, finding several petticoats, she discovered some bound journals. Curious as to their content, she opened the cover of one and perused the pages, written in a neat hand.

Alissa breathed a grateful sigh of relief when she discovered the books contained daily entries, denoting each day's progress, or lack of it, on each of Agatha's "children." Meticulously documented, the journals would provide the knowledge needed to help Megan.

"Thank you, Agatha," she whispered. "You've saved my life."

Quickly gathering the journals together, intending to study them later, she noticed a white envelope near her foot. Inside, she found a letter and £20. Unfolding the paper, she read: *Alissa, dearest—This is all I have. I pray it sees you out of danger. God keep you safe.—Eudora.*

If only she'd found the envelope sooner! she thought, agonizing over the unkind twist of fate. Why hadn't Eudora told her about it? But Alissa knew the answer. Her own pride would have made her refuse Eudora's gift, and her friend knew it as well.

Even if she'd known about the money, she realized it would not have solved her dilemma. Her only way of escape from London and Stilton had been through Jared Braxton. Yet, she now possessed the means to carry her to Edinburgh and, perhaps, beyond.

As she mulled the thought of escape over in her mind, she struggled to find an answer. Then, oddly, a picture of Megan Braxton appeared before her. Sad, green eyes stared up at her, and within their depths, Alissa could see the loneliness and the emotional strife that plagued the poor child's soul.

Closing her own eyes, she fought the ache growing within her heart. An urgent need to somehow help the girl suddenly overcame her, and she fought with her conscience, knowing her own survival was paramount to anything or anyone. Then a childlike voice whispered, pleadingly, *"Stay, stay."*

Her eyes flew open, and she glanced around the room to see if someone had entered. She found not a living soul, and an odd chill rushed up her spine. Was she losing her mind?

The journals weighing heavily in one hand, the envelope in the other, Alissa sighed, then tucked the note and money into the cover of the top journal. For now, she would stay.

Placing the daily diaries on a shelf in the armoire, she pushed them well out of sight. Next, her costume and soft kid slippers followed, both wrapped in one of Agatha's old petticoats. Within minutes, she had the cases unpacked, everything stored away, including her own dresses, which she wisely hid behind Agatha's.

What should she do with her mother's jewel case, she wondered, holding it in her hand. The armoire. She'd hide it with the journals and her costume. But, before doing so, she opened the lid and rediscovered the trinkets inside. A sea of memories flooded her mind as she envisioned her mother wearing each piece. Then she touched the small, white satin box, monogrammed in red silk, faded by the years.

She questioned for possibly the millionth time what the *C* stood for, as her fingertip lightly traced its raised, embroidered curve.

Opening the lid, she gazed lovingly at the gold filigreed brooch. Its large cornflower-blue sapphire glistened up at her, smaller diamonds surrounding its breathtaking brilliance. As always, when she gazed at it, she felt her mother's spirit fill her. The remembrance of Rachel's love embraced her, and a serene mood enveloped Alissa.

Yet, there was something more, something beyond Alissa's understanding. The brooch seemed to reach out to her. The sapphire beckoned to her, wanting to share its knowledge of the past, its hidden promises. Now, as always, an overwhelming need encompassed her.

There was a tap at the door, and Alissa snapped the jewel case shut and hid it in the armoire.

"Mum," Mary called, "I've brought the tray."

Alissa relaxed. "Thank you, Mary. Please set it beside the door."

"There's some herb tea here for ye. Cook made it to chase away the stiffness after the long trip. It's best taken hot."

"Tell cook thank you. I appreciate her kindness. And yours too, Mary."

Mary stared at the closed door and placed the tray beside it. "Can I get ye anything else, mum?"

"No. All is well."

Mary turned to leave, but pivoted toward the door again. "Oh, mum, I forgot. The master said ye have ten minutes to keep yer appointment."

Ten minutes! Alissa's mind exclaimed. Thankfully, while she and Mary were carrying on their conversation through the door, she had finished dressing. "Tell your master I'll be there, as promised."

"Yes, mum," Mary replied, then was off to do as bade.

Her gown buttoned, except for a half dozen along the middle of her back, which she found impossible to reach, Alissa quickly smoothed her hair into a tight knot at the base of her neck. Pinning it haphazardly into place, she covered her shining crown with a heavily woven, oversize net. She'd had no time to powder it. Besides, she thought, why was it even necessary? Jared had never seen her without her bonnet, and since the possibility existed he might demand her presence, day or night, she knew she had to devise an adequate, yet simple method to transform herself into Agatha at a moment's notice. She didn't relish the idea of sleeping in her hated disguise. In fact, she refused to do so!

With the tins of Eudora's special powders in hand, Alissa sat at the mirror and darkened the hollows of her cheeks and beneath her eyes, gently blending the areas with her fingertips. Quickly dusting her entire face with the lighter powder, she brushed away the excess. Viewing herself, she discovered she'd managed to effectively capture the persona of Agatha Pembroke. And within only a few short minutes, too!

In the final analysis, she realized her artwork wasn't as elaborate nor as expertly done as Eudora's, but she hoped the disguise was satisfactory. With luck, his first impression of her would stick with him and override any change, should he notice one. It will have to do, she thought as she pulled the hairnet a good inch down over her forehead, then pinched her lips together in a prudish manner. *Excellent!* She could pass as Agatha's twin—almost.

Determined to beat Jared's time limit, which left her only a fraction over five minutes, Alissa gathered the woolen shawl around her shoulders, straightened her back, and with her head held high, marched toward the door. The luxurious softness of the carpet tickled her toes, and she stifled a giggle.

Shoes! She scurried across the room and, without the

benefit of stockings, she stuffed her feet into the leather footwear. There was no time to fasten them.

Then, on a prayer and a steadying breath, Alissa opened the door, shoved the untouched tray inside, and marched down the hallway, hoping Jared would not detect the change in her.

CHAPTER

Five

After wending through the hallways of Hawkstone, losing her way several times, Alissa found herself back in the main corridor, just beyond the grand staircase.

She was at a loss as to where her employer might be, for behind each door she'd encountered, she had found an empty room, with finely appointed furnishings. So far, she'd discovered the formal dining room, the main salon, grandly decorated in gold and white, a music room, a game room, plus several locked doors, but no Jared Braxton.

Another doorway stood before her. Peeking inside, she found it was the library, with deep, rich paneling and an enormous collection of books, expensively bound and obviously well cared for. But, again, no Jared. Confused, Alissa moved on.

Finally, at the end of the hallway, she stopped and perused a pair of red velvet draperies, stretching from floor to ceiling. Curious, she pushed one heavy panel aside to find a set of doors. Her hand reached toward the brass handle. It was locked. Frowning, she gazed upward.

Black stained the white marble framing the doorway, and Alissa realized it was the entry to the destroyed east wing. A chill shivered through her for no apparent reason, and she dropped the drape into place.

"I see you've decided, at last, to keep our appointment,"

Jared crooned, and Alissa whirled, meeting him face-to-face. "And I'd say five minutes late, too," he continued, his brow rising toward his damp hair, a heavy lock of it falling over his wide forehead. *"Tsk, tsk,* Miss Pembroke. Punctuality. My time is precious, and I simply cannot abide delays."

Alissa's eyes narrowed ever so slightly as she realized he'd repeated the very words she'd spouted when they'd stood in the entryway at Eudora's while engaged in their battle of wills. "I beg your forgiveness, Mr. Braxton, but I didn't realize I needed a map to find you. Since you neglected to inform me of the whereabouts of your study, I believe you are equally to blame for my tardiness."

Jared fought the twitch centering on his lips. For some unexplainable reason, he was starting to enjoy their sharp banter. Although her body was weak, her exterior wrappings unappealing, her mind was as sharp as a well-honed blade. She seemed a refreshing change from the beauties he normally gravitated toward, their minds being of little interest to him.

A humorous light entered his eye. "I stand corrected, Miss Pembroke. Henceforth, precise directions shall be given to facilitate your moves within my home." He motioned toward the library. "Shall we?"

Alissa paraded past him, gritting her teeth each step of the way. The arrogant boor! she stormed inwardly. Why, if she were a man, she'd . . . she'd . . . Knowing Jared had the ability to thrash practically any man inside the borders of Scotland, or out, she quickly decided she'd do nothing.

Taking a deep breath, she calmed herself, remembering Eudora's wise counsel regarding her temper. The advice, however, was becoming harder and harder to follow, especially when the man seemed to take delight in provoking her. The pompous fool!—someday, he'd receive his comeuppance. *That* she promised herself.

Jared ambled behind his daughter's governess, noticing her stiff carriage, and could only imagine the curses being heaped upon his head. The formal Miss Pembroke wasn't the pious prude she pretended to be. Of that, he was certain.

Increasing his gait, Jared strode around Alissa, his highly polished black boots ringing against the parquet flooring in the library. Inadvertently, she inhaled his clean scent; her senses piqued. Dressed in tight-fitting buckskin trousers and a white flowing muslin shirt, several buttons left undone to reveal a collection of crisp dark hair, he displayed a casual disregard toward propriety. Feeling a light blush creep up her face, she knew, unequivocally, in his own home, he'd dress, do, and say whatever he wished. And no rule of etiquette would stop him.

"My study is in here." Jared entered the smaller room off the library, and Alissa followed. "Please have a seat." He motioned to the red leather chair across from his solid mahogany desk.

Poised on the chair's edge, her hands clasped tightly in her lap, Alissa watched as Jared folded his long, sinewy frame into a sitting position. His shirt gaped further, exposing more of his muscular chest, and her gaze quickly skittered to the window.

The mists had turned into a steady rain. Urgently wishing she were out in the cold shower, Alissa envisioned herself such, hoping it would extinguish the sudden flame scorching through her body. Unconsciously, her nails bit into her hands as she fidgeted in her seat.

Jared noticed her uneasiness and assumed, as always, she disliked being alone with him. "May I offer you some sherry?" he asked as he started to rise from his chair, hoping the drink would help calm her flightiness.

"Spirits are the devil's henchmen," Alissa retorted sharply and fell silent, wondering why she'd snapped the words. Her only explanation was she'd heard that very phrase from Agatha's lips when an inebriated male boarder at Eudora's had asked the woman to join him in a round.

His hands pressing against his desk, Jared remained somewhere between sitting and standing, a hard eye on the woman opposite him. Finally, with a shove, he gained his full height. "Since you already believe I'm in league with the knave you've mentioned, then you won't object if I partake." Without waiting for her reply, he strode to the cabinet and poured himself a healthy glass of brandy and downed half of it before he returned to his desk.

Wary eyes upon him, Alissa swallowed hard. His glass thudded to the middle of his desk, while he did the same in his chair. Not liking the look in his eye, she was suddenly tempted to reach across the span, grab the glass, and choke down what remained.

"Miss Pembroke, I realize your sensibilities may be somewhat offended by what I do, but you must remember I'm in my own home, and I will not change my habits or my lifestyle for anyone, whether one likes it or not."

He leaned back in his chair, and she found she could not release his stern gaze, no matter how hard she tried. Why hadn't she taken Eudora's money and run when she'd had the chance?

"Also," he continued, his sharp eyes pinning her to her chair, "we unfortunately seem to have a great deal of difficulty in communicating. A conflict of personality, perhaps. But, as you know, there is only one reason why you are here, and only one reason why I allow you here—Megan. I do not seek to become your friend, and I'm certain you feel the same about me. We must find a neutral point, however, a common ground from which to work. If you will remember, I gave you the opportunity to turn back, yet you insisted on coming with me. Since you made that choice, and of your own free will, then I will expect you to fulfill your duties, as promised. And you will not leave here until I'm assured they've been discharged to the best of your ability, and Megan is well on the mend. So, I suggest you find a way to overlook my sins—which I'm certain you believe are many —because, Miss Pembroke, you may be here for a very long time."

Alissa's eyes widened, and she wondered if he intended to keep her prisoner here. My God, what would he do if she failed to make any progress with his daughter whatsoever? She suddenly speculated on whether Hawkstone sheltered a dungeon. Wildly, she envisioned herself stripped to the waist, her wrists chained in irons, breasts pressed to a dank, smelly wall somewhere in the depths of the stone fortress, and Jared standing behind her, shaking free a cat-o'-nine-tails, readying it for her punishment.

"Since it's understood what I expect, do you have a suggestion as to how we can keep from tearing at each other's throats for the duration?"

Alissa heard the words from afar, her mind still whirling

with visions of Jared tormenting her. Unable to speak, she vigorously shook her head no.

"Then may I propose a way for us to see little of each other, but still make the optimum of the time we must be in each other's company."

Alissa nodded, willing to do anything he wanted, so long as she be kept from harm's way and out of his.

"Good." Jared retrieved a scrap of paper from the top of his desk. "To keep your stay here to a minimum, I suggest that you be with Megan as much as possible. Of course, you'll have Sundays off. By choice, you may join us for breakfast at seven; the afternoon meal is also your choice. With my business schedule, I'm not always here for the second meal, so you may wish to dine with Megan on the days I cannot. However, I ask you to join us in the evening at eight. Mrs. Dugan puts Megan down for a nap in the afternoon, usually shortly after her playtime. While she naps, you may do whatever you wish. I expect no less than eight hours per day devoted entirely to my daughter. If you need more, you'll have it. One hour before supper, we shall meet here to discuss Megan's progress, whereupon we'll adjourn to the less formal dining room, downstairs. At your leisure, you may explore the house to acquaint yourself with it. The only places that are forbidden are, naturally, the east wing—Megan is never to go there—and, of course, my own quarters, which are down the hall from yours."

By this time, Alissa had recovered from her ridiculous delusion that Hawkstone hid a prototype left from the reign of Henry VIII. But, as she digested Jared's words that his quarters were off limits, she was flustered anew. Did the man think she pranced in and out of a man's bedroom at will? "Your quarters! Sir, you . . . you—" she sputtered, unable to get the words out.

"Calm yourself, Miss Pembroke. I only mentioned it, should you lose your way as you just did. On occasion, I'm dressed even more casually than this, and I did not wish for you to find me in a state of total undress. Doing so might shock you. Normally, the door is closed, but if Megan comes in, sometimes she forgets to shut it after herself when she leaves. Come no farther than her room, and you'll be safe."

Alissa's gaze narrowed. Certainly the man didn't parade

around naked before his child's eyes! "I'll remember your warning, Mr. Braxton," she said tightly.

Jared read the accusing look she'd bestowed on him. "My child is not a stranger to seeing me shirtless. But I'm not a complete savage, Miss Pembroke, although you undoubtedly believe otherwise."

After a long moment, Alissa tore her gaze from Jared's forceful stare, yet his eyes were still intent on her face. She looked different—less sickly and perhaps a bit younger. Then, exasperated with himself, he shook the thought from his head. Only a short while ago, he'd felt he was beginning to enjoy their duel of words, but now, he was ready to be rid of her. "Does this schedule meet with your approval?" he asked.

Alissa turned her attention to him. "Schedule?"

"Yes, Miss Pembroke. If you'll recall, we were discussing Megan."

"I do recall, Mr. Braxton. And yes, the schedule will do fine."

"Then, supper is at eight."

"If you don't mind, I'd prefer to allow myself some time alone this evening. Likewise, I'm certain you and Megan need private time together."

"As you like, Miss Pembroke." He passed the schedule to her. "I've made some notations, which you may study at your leisure. They're mostly of Megan's likes and dislikes; her bath time, playtime, and so on. Mrs. Dugan cares for her personal grooming and the like. My housekeeper keeps to a rigid schedule herself. Should anything on the list conflict with your needs, please discuss it with her."

Jared rose from his seat, and Alissa did likewise, assuming their meeting had ended.

Picking up his brandy glass, he moved to the cabinet again. "We will see you at breakfast tomorrow." It was a statement, not a question.

"If you will allow me a few days to ease myself upon Megan, I think things will go much more smoothly for all concerned," Alissa stated, hoping Jared would agree. She needed time to read Agatha's journals.

The brandy eased into his glass, and he turned toward her, raising it in salute. "You are probably right." Then he swallowed a large portion of the amber liquid. "Should you need anything, let me know. Good day, Miss Pembroke."

Relieved she'd been granted a reprieve, Alissa hastily turned. Unfortunately, she'd forgotten her shoes were undone. On her first step, she walked fully out of one.

Noting her predicament, Jared headed in her direction, but luckily, Alissa grabbed the traitorous thing and stuffed her foot into it before he'd reached her side. Straightening, she nearly collided with her employer. And, for but a moment, blue eyes met green.

Jared's steadying hand fell from her arm. "On the morrow, Mr. Stanley will take you into Selkirk," he said as he moved back to the cabinet and his brandy. After another deep swallow of the fiery liquid, which seemed to cool the unexplainable blaze sweeping through his veins, he continued, "You are to purchase new shoes—a pair that fit your feet."

Embarrassed, Alissa whirled, fleeing the room, and Jared stared at the empty doorway, his glass held loosely in his hand, a perplexed frown marked deep into his brow.

CHAPTER
Six

Alissa sat to one side of the playroom, Agatha's small volume of Shakespeare's *Sonnets* in her hand, a letter hidden between its pages. Across the room, Megan played quietly.

It had been nearly two weeks since her arrival at Hawkstone, a miserable two weeks to be certain. If she wasn't engaged in an exchange of inhospitable words with Jared or in an earnest attempt to elude him, she was doing the same with Leona Dugan, the latter having become as great an irritation as the former.

Thankful Jared had allowed her the freedom to set her own pace with Megan, she'd utilized the interval to study Agatha's journals. According to the late Miss Pembroke, the first week or two, possibly longer, depending upon the child, should be the time of "acceptance." No attempts were to be made to work on the child's handicap until a semblance of trust and friendship was forged, Agatha's thoughts being the child could easily balk if a stranger were suddenly thrust upon him. Caution, kindness, and always keeping one's word seemed the orderly fashion in which Agatha had gained her "acceptance" with all her children. And that's what Alissa had planned to do with Megan.

Once she'd absorbed all the important information in the journals, Alissa was certain she could act as Agatha's surrogate. Preparing her own schedule, she'd approached Mrs. Dugan as Jared had suggested. Unfortunately, it did little good. In fact, she'd been shocked by the housekeeper's unwillingness to cooperate. It almost seemed that the woman didn't want Megan to speak, for Mrs. Dugan had denied each and every request, minor as they were.

"The child needs a long nap," the housekeeper had snapped when Alissa had innocently requested a change in the daily practice. "I lay her down at precisely two o'clock, and she'll not rise until half past three."

Alissa had wondered why a child of six needed such a lengthy rest, if one at all. And when she'd inquired such, she'd thought the ceiling had collapsed around her.

"If she doesn't have her rest, she's unable to stay awake through supper," Leona had informed her tersely.

"Then can't supper be moved to an earlier time? I'm certain Mr. Braxton wouldn't object."

"The evening meal has always been served at eight. It was his wife's wish."

"But his wife is no longer alive."

That had been the wrong thing for Alissa to say. Leona Dugan had glared her intense disapproval, then stalked from the room. Supper that night was at eight.

Several other issues had precipitated words between the two women, but Alissa had won on only one of those issues—supervising Megan's playtime. That concession came about when Jared had approached the pair on it himself. But, when she'd inquired about outside play, she'd been thwarted again. Megan had no suitable clothing for such an activity, and Leona wasn't about to dress the child like some street urchin. "A young lady of Megan's class should emulate those of her stature and no less," Leona had responded. And, again, Alissa had backed down.

As she remembered the small skirmishes, Alissa thought anew of going to Jared in hopes he'd act as peacemaker. Yet she feared another confrontation with the man. But in reality, there was only one reason why she maintained her silence: Hawkstone was her refuge, and inside its walls she was safe from discovery.

Shaking her head in defeat, Alissa decided it best to

remain the coward. At least for now. Yet, in order for her to continue her masquerade, she realized she'd have to keep a tight grip on her temper, especially since she was but a word short of letting it fly. Over the past week, she'd become very suspicious of the housekeeper. For any progress—a show of trust, a spark of friendship—she'd made with Megan during the light of day had been mysteriously stolen during the dark of night. And Alissa was certain Leona Dugan was the thief.

Enough! Alissa thought and refocused her eyes and watched as Megan played with three dolls: a father, a mother, and a small girl. She maneuvered them through the rooms of a large dollhouse, taller than Megan herself and very similar in structure to Hawkstone. Megan playacted mostly with the father doll who, through Megan's handling, showed a great deal of affection toward the smallest doll, the child. To Alissa, it seemed a bit odd that the mother doll, again through Megan's actions, virtually ignored her offspring, always brushing the child aside whenever approached.

Disturbed by this continuous play, which she'd observed almost daily, Alissa stood. "Come, Megan. Let's go into the gardens for some fresh air. The sunshine will do us good."

Megan glanced at Alissa, then back to the dolls. Finally, she laid them in their respective beds, each in a separate room, but not before the father doll had kissed the child good night.

With hopes the change of scenery would lighten both their moods, Alissa led Megan from the playroom, which was directly opposite Alissa's bedroom. As they headed toward the stairs, another door swung open. Leona Dugan stepped from inside.

"Megan, it's time for your nap," the housekeeper stated and reached for Megan's hand. "You'll need a quick wash."

"Her playtime isn't over," Alissa countered, weary of the woman's interference. "We are headed for the gardens and some fresh air."

An angry light speared Alissa. "Not in that dress," the woman hissed. "She'll soil it."

Alissa unconsciously hugged Megan to the folds of her skirt. "We'll take extreme care she doesn't."

"You'll not leave this house!" Leona said, her voice rising as she again reached for Megan's hand. "And that's my final word."

Her control snapping like a dried twig, Alissa blocked Leona's hand, then gripped her wrist. "Your final—I beg your pardon. She's still under my supervision, and we have twenty minutes of playtime left. And *play* we shall, dress or no dress!"

Suddenly, Leona's free hand poised, ready to strike; Alissa braced herself for the blow. If the woman wanted a cat fight, she thought, her eyes daring the housekeeper to follow through, she'd have one!

"Cease!"

Jared's thunderous outburst echoed down the hallway, and Leona's hand instantly dropped to her side. Alissa drew a steadying breath, but her eyes never faltered from Leona's. Not until she heard Jared's hard footsteps.

From the spot where he stood just outside his bedroom door, he bore down on the two women; a rolled newspaper swatted against his thigh, his eyes spewing green fire. To Alissa it seemed as though he were ready to reprimand a pair of errant pups. If she had any sense, she'd tuck tail and run! As she released Megan from the protective folds of her skirt, she felt her knees begin to quake, but she gathered what courage she could find and stood her ground.

"Ladies," Jared greeted them on a calmer note when he'd reached them, "that's if I may be so bold as to call you such." His gaze shifted from one woman to the other, making his displeasure known. As he squatted, he immediately noted Megan was visibly shaken by the sudden hostile display. "Sweet," he said gently, "there's a present for you in my room. If you're quick about it, I'll wager you can find it. But wait for my return to open it, okay?" Megan nodded with excitement. "Then I'll be but a moment."

Megan hugged her father's neck, then rushed down the hallway, eager to find her gift. When she was out of sight, Jared stretched to his full height. "Now," he said in a tone that could freeze a volcano's flow, "explain yourself."

Alissa noticed there was no plural to it and wondered if his fury was aimed only at her. Unable to hold his blistering gaze, her own dropped to his chest and the deep V created by the opening in his shirt, which dived almost to his waist. Blankly, she stared at the exposed chest while her mind raced, frantically searching for an answer.

Jared noticed the path her eyes had taken. He cared little if she was offended. His only concern was Megan's emotional state, and not this dim-witted woman's sensibilities. "Miss Pembroke," he commanded in a harsh whisper, "answer me!"

Alissa jumped. Amazingly, she found her voice. "Mrs. Dugan and I have had a difference of opinion on how Megan should spend her time." She fell silent.

"And?"

"That's all."

Through narrowed eyes, Jared studied her, then shifted his gaze. "And you, Mrs. Dugan? What's your side?"

Her hands clasped in their usual superior position at her waist, she looked her employer in the eye. "It was time for Megan's nap. I simply reminded Miss Pembroke of such."

"This display was precipitated by a *nap?*"

Before Alissa could respond, Leona defended herself. "This woman has disrupted Megan's schedule continuously. I cannot abide her interference a moment longer."

The dam burst. "My interference!" Alissa exploded in a low, controlled voice, so Megan would not overhear. "You're the one who's constantly interfered! You have no idea what the child needs—"

"Me!" Leona cut in. "You uppity old spinster, how—"

"Spinster? Uppity!" Alissa sliced back, forgetting whom she portrayed. "Why, you old stiff-necked—"

"Silence!" Jared commanded through his teeth. "I have little time for name-calling. I'm already late for an appointment in Selkirk." He glanced from one to the other. "And by my own admission, my temper is sorely pressed to contend with either of yours right now. So to prevent an out and out brawl among the three of us, I suggest we adjourn this little conference until I've returned from my meeting. Is that acceptable?"

Alissa looked to the carpet and nodded. However, Leona did not. "She's not helping Megan," the housekeeper argued. "The child is no better off than before she came. I doubt seriously—"

"Mrs. Dugan," Jared interrupted, his hard eyes upon her. "Is my suggestion acceptable?"

Leona's lips pressed together in a tight line; annoyance showed in her dark eyes, but she finally agreed with a quick nod. Alissa was astounded the woman hadn't been immediately discharged for her impertinence. Since Jared did not do so, it only reaffirmed her fear that he'd side with his housekeeper over her.

"Good," Jared said. "And to prevent any further disturbances, Mary will be in charge of Megan for the rest of the day. At seven, I want both of you in my study. We will settle this disagreement then. For now, I suggest you both keep to opposite sides of the house."

Leona turned cold eyes toward Alissa, then looked back to Jared. "As you wish. I will tell Mary she is to watch Megan." Then she turned and disappeared into the alcove.

"I hope, Miss Pembroke," Jared said when they were finally alone, "that in the future, you will not try to settle your differences with any of my staff by yourself, and especially in front of my daughter. Had you come to me first, it might have saved you the worry of this altercation and Megan the upset of witnessing it."

"I apologize, Mr. Braxton," Alissa whispered, hoping to smooth the waters, wondering whether she should try to explain why the incident had happened. If she botched it, he might very well decide to boot her out on her ear. As she thought about it, the scent of spicy cologne filled her senses; her eyes finally focused on his exposed chest. He's more perfect than Michelangelo's *David,* she thought, gazing at the finely honed muscle covered with sleek, tanned flesh, generously sprinkled with dark, springy hair. Embarrassed by her wild meanderings, she felt herself flush pink. "It will never happen again," she stated, but to her own ears, her voice sounded oddly hoarse. Was she speaking of her confrontation with Mrs. Dugan, or was it that she was enjoying the sight of his masculinity? Then in a rush, she breathed, "I promise."

Jared noted how her gaze skittered from his chest to the ceiling, then to the wall. He smiled to himself. He'd been none too pleased with her earlier display, just as she seemed none too happy with his present one. Wickedly, he felt tempted to punish her and considered what she would do if he were to press himself upon her and back her to the very wall she'd been surveying. No doubt, he concluded, his roguish eyes traveling the length of her, she'd faint!

Alissa remained on guard. She'd seen the glint in his eyes. She hadn't imagined it! It was the same cunning look that Charles Rhodes had bestowed upon her before he'd attacked! "I'm not a schoolgirl, Mr. Braxton, nor am I an imbecile. Henceforth, you should learn to mask your thoughts a bit better."

Not about to admit his dark intentions, especially when they were meant only in jest, he said falsely, "My apologies, Miss Pembroke, but I think you've misinterpreted what's in my mind. My only thoughts lay with the episode I've just witnessed. Until I'm assured which of you is in the right, I must assume both you and Mrs. Dugan are guilty. At seven, I'll hear your defense. Until then, Miss Pembroke." He nodded his dismissal.

Alissa turned in a flurry of skirt and rushed to her door several yards away. Had she misread him? she wondered, her hand shaking with a violent tic as she worked the latch. Stubbornly, it wouldn't open.

Jared chuckled beneath his breath. The dear woman was, no doubt, about to swoon, he thought, then noticed the small book at his foot. Retrieving it, he shoved the folded paper that had escaped it back between the pages. On silent feet, he came up behind her.

"Allow me," he said as he reached around her, his arm brushing Alissa's shoulder, and she felt herself on the verge of an hysterical scream. With a quick flick of his wrist, he turned the handle and pushed the door wide. He handed her the book of sonnets. "This, I believe, is yours."

Nervous fingers reached for it, but when her hand accidentally touched his, the volume fell to her feet, the letter spilling from between the book's leaves. Her stomach churned with fear as Jared stooped to retrieve the pair a second time, and she prayed, silently: *Please don't let him see the contents.*

"I see you're wearing your new shoes," Jared commented

when he rose from the vicinity of her hem. He handed her the book with the letter on top.

Relief surged through her as she took them, tightly gripping both as though her life depended on it.

"They look, uh . . . quite, uh"—should he speak the truth about the shoes?—"comfortable," he supplied. "Are they to your liking?"

"They squeak." Alissa shut the door in Jared's face, only to hear his deep chuckle filter through the wood.

"A suitable match, dear lady," he countered in a low voice to the locked panel. "You're both as stiff as the unfortunate animal that supplied the leather."

With a mock bow at the door, Jared turned on his heel and strode toward his own rooms. Although he was late for his appointment, he intended to speak with Megan. Through a series of hand signs, which the two had devised so Megan could communicate, he hoped to gain some insight on why the two women had been butting heads. He could not afford to dismiss either woman from his employ, but neither would he allow such a display of temper again.

As Jared entered his chambers, decorated in gold, white, and black, he placed the newspaper he still held on a side table. Again, the headline captured his eye: *Substantial Reward Offered for Capture of Covent Garden Actress.* Although he was eager to read it, he knew the brief article would have to wait. He had more important things to do at the moment. Placing a smile on his face, he strode from the small sitting room into his bedchamber. "Ah, sweet, I see you've found the present. Let's have a look at what's inside, shall we?"

Two doors down, Alissa weakly sank to the settee, the letter she'd feared Jared would see held tightly in her hand. Unfolding it, she read again the first line that was written in Eudora's expert hand: *Charles Rhodes is alive!*

Upon reading it the first time, Alissa had felt elation riot through her. In a quick series of thoughts, she'd packed her bags, said her farewells to all at Hawkstone, and was well on her way back to London and to those she cared for most. But, with the very next sentence, her hopes had plummeted into the depths of despair.

. . . I fear you cannot return, Alissa dearest, for you've been charged with attempted murder and theft. His father, the Earl of Creighton, has placed a large reward on your head. By reports, the rogue sports an ugly scar at his temple and is spreading the story you lured him to your dressing room with the promise of certain favors. Once alone, you bashed his skull and stole his purse, which was supposed to contain a tidy sum. He still lurks about Covent Garden, possibly lying in wait for another young actress. One would think that that alone would give him away for what he is, especially since the upper classes attend the opera these days. As you know, the Garden is not the most suitable of areas with the throng of pickpockets and prostitutes who gather inside and out. We can only pray Rhodes turns his hand with the next poor female he accosts. Then he will be exposed for what he really is. God keep you safe, dearest, and write.

Alissa refolded the letter and hid it in the book. Depression settled around her as she thought of Eudora's words. Surely, there had to be some way to free herself from this debacle. What she needed was a champion, a Lancelot, a knight of old, she decided, then scoffed at the thought. She knew not a soul who held such power, such status. Indeed, who'd be willing to wear her ribbon and slay the dragon which had entrapped her with his fiery lies?

Jared Braxton.

Alissa rolled her eyes and shook her head to clear it. She must be suffering from delusions. The man would never assist her, especially once she'd confessed all her deceptions. The truth discovered, he'd no doubt lock her in chains and deliver her to the dragon's lair as a sacrifice. It was hopeless.

A thought occurred to her. If she were to help Megan regain her voice, surely Jared would help clear her name in return. Although she'd willingly help the girl without any thought of monetary reward, she would not be opposed to an exchange of favors. Through a sense of gratitude, he might feel obligated to repay her. But she was certain, once he'd settled his debt, he'd wash his hands of her. He wasn't a man to condone lies, especially from a woman.

Knowing now, more than ever, the importance of remaining at Hawkstone, Alissa wished she'd held her temper in check earlier. Although she hated to admit it, Jared Braxton seemed to be her only hope. And to receive his help, she, in turn, had to help Megan.

Fretting over it did little good, she knew. Yet, somehow, she had to convince Jared to place Megan in her complete care, and she spent the rest of the afternoon constructing an argument that would sway him to that very end.

At five minutes to seven, Alissa headed toward Jared's study and their appointed meeting. Halting outside the library doors, she quickly rubbed her perspiring palms against the worn skirt of Agatha's gray gown. A bad case of nerves, she decided, then wished she were anywhere but here. Voices drifted from the small room inside, and she realized suddenly that Mrs. Dugan had already arrived. Perhaps the woman hoped to gain the upper hand by having a private discussion with Jared, Alissa thought, fearing the worst. But more to the point, Jared might have come to a decision before she'd even been given the chance to speak. Squaring her shoulders, she marched toward the door, praying for a reprieve.

"Miss Pembroke." Jared addressed her while he rose from his seat. "Please join us." He motioned to the chair next to Leona.

Despite her outward show of self-assurance, Alissa felt her courage falter. Don't fall apart now! she warned herself, then flopped into her seat as her wobbly legs gave way.

Noting her sudden descent, Jared raised a curious brow but held his tongue. As his gaze ran over her, he frowned at the ridiculous hairnet, which was perpetually worn to the middle of her forehead. Another inch and she'd snare her eyebrows, as well! Didn't the woman realize that that was not the way the thing was worn? he wondered, then whisked the annoying thought aside and took his own seat. "I was just telling Mrs. Dugan I've received a letter from my cousin, Robert Hamilton. He'll be arriving at Hawkstone in two days. Since he is my business agent and there is much to discuss, I'll be spending most of my time with him during his stay. Therefore, it is important we settle this matter, here and now."

Alissa relaxed. Apparently, there had been little, if any,

discussion about this afternoon's events. A brief glance at Leona confirmed her thoughts. The housekeeper's expression showed a surprising trace of anxiety. But as Alissa watched, her usual stern mask quickly slipped into place. There's still hope, Alissa decided.

Jared settled back in his leather chair. "Now, ladies, who would like to begin?"

Alissa opted to allow Leona to have the floor first. The housekeeper, wanting the last word, had decided the same with Alissa. Neither woman spoke.

"Come now." Jared looked from one to the other. "You both were quite vocal this afternoon. Has something transpired of which I'm not aware? Have you become fast friends, perhaps?"

Leona sniffed loudly. Hearing it, Alissa stared at the housekeeper, then looked to Jared. "Mrs. Dugan and I are not fast friends, which is unfortunate, especially since I believe we all have a common goal in mind—Megan's regaining her voice. Is that not so?"

His elbow propped on the chair's arm, Jared leaned his chin against his thumb, his forefinger stroked his lower lip. "Obviously, it is," he replied, wondering why she'd even broached the subject. Like an anxious barrister, she appeared ready to plead a case in which the outcome looked very dark. "That's why I hired you, Miss Pembroke."

Mesmerized, Alissa watched as Jared's finger played along his lower lip, caressing its angular smoothness, and once again, her imagination took flight. *Stop it!* she demanded of her senses, but she found she couldn't concentrate on anything but his handsome mouth. She blinked when she saw his lips move, then finally heard his words.

"Would you like to continue?"

"Y-yes, certainly," she stammered. "As you suggested, Mr. Braxton, I asked Mrs. Dugan for several changes in Megan's daily routine, one being her nap time." Her voice grew stronger. "Mrs. Dugan has denied all my requests, including shortening her rest period."

"I told you," Leona defended sharply, "Megan must have her rest to remain awake during the supper hour."

Alissa faced Leona. "Yes. So you've said. Yet when I have quietly looked in on her, I've found that she's not napping but sitting by the window, staring through the pane like a caged bird desiring its freedom. Although it may not be intentional, you've made Hawkstone her prison."

"You know nothing of the child," Leona scoffed. "It's a lie you tell."

Alissa turned her gaze back to Jared. "I do not lie."

His eyes steady on hers, he inclined his head an inch. "Continue."

"Why, then, Mrs. Dugan, is she forever in this house?"

"I explained that."

"You said she has no suitable clothing for play."

Leona's chin lifted. "That's precisely what I said."

"You also said she would soil the dresses she has."

"Yes."

"Then I suggest it is time you realize she is not an adult, nor is she a fashion plate. There is no need for her to be wrapped in frills, then made to sit in the corner because you're afraid she'll muss her finery." Alissa's gaze again met Jared's. "She's a small girl who needs her freedom so she can explore her surroundings and discover all there is to know. And that includes playing outside. Tell me what is wrong with Megan dirtying her hands with the rich earth as she fashions pies and cakes to serve at a pretend tea party with her dolls." Alissa implored. "Why can't she be allowed to frolic among the wildflowers that grow on the hillside or roll in the grass and smell its sweetness?"

"She's not some farm tenant's daughter!" Leona snapped, her forehead creased in anger, eyes shooting fire. "She's the daughter of the Ma—"

"Enough." Jared's low, menacing tone stopped his housekeeper short.

She's the daughter of the . . . what? Alissa wondered as she looked from one to the other, noting Jared's brief look of warning, and Leona's suddenly subdued manner. The master of Hawkstone, perhaps? All three knew he was that. Alissa's niggling suspicions began to rise anew.

Jared turned his attention to Alissa again. "You were saying, Miss Pembroke?"

Since Jared seemed willing to hear her out, Alissa was not opposed to taking advantage of the opportunity, and she shoved aside any thought of Leona's unfinished words. "I realize, Mr. Braxton, that you and Mrs. Dugan care deeply for Megan and that the two of you are highly concerned with her welfare. However, I feel, in the process, you've become overly protective. This isn't good, for you are robbing her of her childhood."

"You are certain of this?" he asked, his green gaze penetrating hers.

"As an outsider, I believe I can be more objective than those who are close to her."

"There!" Leona exclaimed. "She acknowledges she's an outsider. By her own admission, she cannot possibly know what Megan has suffered."

"I may not have been here to share Megan's initial grief over the loss of her mother. I can only imagine what a terrible shock it was to her—to you all. However, I am not a stranger to such a loss myself. My own mother's death was very traumatic." Alissa had to stop and clear her throat as the ever recurring tears stung her eyes like they always did when she thought of Rachel. Composing herself, she continued, "I can relate to Megan's fears and uncertainties. If she is ever to recover, you will have to allow her to face whatever it is that has caused her silence. Protecting her is not the answer. Continually keeping her inside the walls of Hawkstone only reminds her of her loss. Put her in my complete care, and I will do my best to free her mind of what's troubling her."

Not in the least convinced by Alissa's words, Leona pleaded with Jared. "Certainly, you don't believe—"

"Yes, Mrs. Dugan, I *do* believe what Miss Pembroke says is true. Although we've all meant well, we have most likely driven Megan further into her shell. Since I am probably more guilty than anyone of causing it, I will take full blame. However, I must change my ways. And so must you, Mrs. Dugan. You are a trusted and loyal employee, and I sincerely appreciate all your past efforts. But from this day forward, Miss Pembroke will be in full charge of Megan." Jared noted his housekeeper's startled look. "When Megan is well, she will be given over to your care again. For now, you will discharge your duties as my housekeeper. As always, I'm certain you will do an excellent job. I hope this meets with your approval."

Unable to hold her employer's gaze, Leona looked to the paneled wall behind his head. "As you wish, sir."

"Then, if you will excuse us, I'd like a private word with Miss Pembroke."

"Certainly." Leona rose and exited the room.

Alissa immediately felt her own flicker of guilt. She'd usurped Mrs. Dugan's authority over Megan. She'd even seen a shimmer of tears in Leona's eyes. Somehow, the sweetness of victory tasted very sour to Alissa. Very sour indeed.

Viewing the woman opposite him, Jared was amazed to see a touch of remorse bridge the features of her pale face. If anything, he'd expected her to gloat over having won the argument. He'd also noticed the look of pain in her eyes when she'd spoken of her mother earlier. By the quake in her voice, one would have thought she'd just lost her mother within the past year and not the fifteen years ago that had been stated in her letter. Perhaps the woman had a soft spot after all, he decided; then he said, "You seem quite distressed." He would have offered her a glass of sherry, but he didn't wish to hear a lecture on the evils of drink again. "May I have cook send up some tea for you?"

"No, I'm just saddened by this episode. I feel very badly about Mrs. Dugan—"

"Mrs. Dugan will get over it. Megan's needs come first."

"I realize that."

"Then, since you now have full care of my daughter, there should be no further excuses on any lack of progress because of interference from my staff."

Another ultimatum? Alissa wondered. "You must realize it will take time to gain her trust," she countered anxiously. "Even then, there are no guarantees."

"If you are as good as your former employers have professed you to be, there should be no worries—should there?"

"Mr. Braxton, you make it sound as though I'm some kind of god."

"Hardly. I simply have a positive outlook, which you seem to have lost. In fact, by the recent mellowing of your imperious manner, I'm inclined to believe you no longer hold any confidence in your own abilities."

"Imperious?" Alissa questioned, her eyes wide.

"If I may be so bold, Miss Pembroke, when we first met you were quite . . . uh, authoritative. Very self-assured." *Shrewish* would be the better term, but he opted not to voice his opinion. "But you seem rather depressed of late. Are you perhaps homesick for London?"

Yes, she thought, but answered, "No. There's nothing in London I miss."

"You are not ill, then?"

"Certainly not."

"Good." He hadn't thought so. For since her arrival at Hawkstone, her coloring had improved greatly, the shadows almost disappearing from beneath her eyes. Yet, to his eye, she was still a bit pallid-looking.

"Why all these questions, Mr. Braxton?"

"Because there is something troubling you."

"I'm afraid you are mistaken," Alissa denied, not quite meeting his gaze with her own.

"I am not, Miss Pembroke. You are hiding something from me. Of that, I'm certain."

Alissa's mind raced and she wondered if he'd somehow discovered the truth about her. "I—I am not hiding anything!" she lied.

"Too many falsehoods will condemn your soul, Miss Pembroke," Jared said, and noticed her startled glance. He thought he saw guilt there, too. "You need not protect Mrs. Dugan any longer."

Alissa frowned. "Protect Mrs. Dugan? I don't have the slightest idea what you mean."

"Then you are truly unaware Mrs. Dugan has been tainting Megan's thoughts and pitting her against you."

Her fear of discovery alleviated, Alissa felt dizzy with relief. Then she watched as Jared rose from his chair and circumvented his desk to angle a hip on the corner of its highly polished surface. "Were you or were you not aware of it?" he asked, his left hand bracing itself on his buckskin-clad thigh as he leaned toward her. "The truth, Miss Pembroke."

"I—I—" Why did he have to situate himself so closely? she wondered, her gaze traveling over his handsome face. Virile, powerful, masculine, and a *devil!* her mind calculated quickly, and she leaned back as far as her chair would allow, desperate to escape his magnetic force.

Jared smiled to himself. She looked like a frightened rabbit, ready to bound from a predator. Was she really that wary of him? Most women were overanxious to be in his presence. Why, whenever he'd make a grand entrance into a ballroom, he'd always been tempted to carry a cane with him, wielding it like a sword, to protect himself against the females who virtually attacked his person. For that very reason, he seldom attended such functions.

But prudish Agatha was the only one of her gender he could not win over—not with a smile, nor a compliment, nor with his considerable masculine charm. The only one, that is, except for *Celeste,* he thought cynically. His beautiful, shallow wife, Celeste. Angered that he'd even allowed himself to think of her, he scoured her image from his mind. Getting a firm grip on his emotions, he looked directly at the little frump not two feet from him. "Miss Pembroke," he coaxed gently, "the truth, please."

The sound of his rich voice vibrated through Alissa, and she felt her body react like a tuning fork. Every inch of her flesh quivered in response. Mesmerized, she found she couldn't answer, only stare at his long-lashed green eyes. Oddly, she felt as though she'd slipped into a trance, induced by an impelling trick of sorcery.

Noting the glazed look in her eyes, he wondered if the woman were subject to some sort of seizure, as well. He snapped his fingers in front of her face.

Alissa blinked. Answer him! she demanded of herself. "I had no proof, but I suspected Mrs. Dugan was somehow influencing Megan. May I ask how you discovered it so?"

Jared leaned back slightly, and Alissa breathed a bit easier. "Megan." He noted her confusion. "She's able to communicate through hand signs."

"She can!" Alissa exclaimed, sliding forward to the edge of her seat. In her eagerness to know more, she forgot she portrayed an expert, one who would not let something of such import slip by her. "Why didn't you tell me?"

Jared frowned. "I had assumed you'd noticed."

As she thought back on it, she realized she had noticed

some sort of signing from Megan. Being wrapped up in her own problems, though, she'd not placed much importance on it. Then she wondered if her outburst had roused his suspicions. Quickly she made reference to a passage in one of Agatha's journals. "You don't use the Abbé de l'Épée's method of signing, do you?"

"Who in blazes is the Abbé de l'Épée?"

"He founded the first school for the deaf in Paris between 1755 and 1760. He used sign language and finger spelling to teach his students. Quite successfully, I might add. But it matters not what form you use," she stated with an airy wave of her hand, hoping to impress him with her so-called knowledge. "Sign language has been in use since our ancestors crawled from their caves." She noticed his bland look. "Am I boring you with this information?"

"Exceedingly."

"I apologize, Mr. Braxton. And I apologize for not noticing Megan could communicate. My only excuse is I was becoming acclimated to my new surroundings, as well as still recovering from my illness. Please forgive my lack of perceptiveness."

"You are forgiven, Miss Pembroke. I don't expect you to know everything about my daughter in only a fortnight."

"Would you teach me the signs you've devised and their meanings?" Alissa asked. She was indeed eager to learn. Anything would be useful. Once his daughter was cured, she could then barter with Jared and have her name cleared. "It is important I understand what Megan is saying. It's very frustrating for someone when they cannot make themselves understood. I want to save Megan the stress."

"That's been one of my greatest fears, Miss Pembroke," Jared said, his own frustration evident. "Should she need my help during the night, or if she were to injure herself while playing outside, how could she call out so I might come to her aid? *That* is why, as you so aptly put it, she has been made a prisoner at Hawkstone. There's not a night that goes by that I do not check on her several times before she rises the next morn."

"I understand your fears. If you wish, henceforth, I will check on her while she sleeps. And I promise to stay by her side when we are away from the house. You will give me permission to take her outside, won't you?" she asked, her eyes locked with his.

"I will, Miss Pembroke."

Although he'd honored her request, Alissa knew by the look in Jared's eye, if anything were to happen to Megan, the responsibility would be placed squarely on her shoulders. Heaven only knew what he'd do to her. "Thank you, Mr. Braxton. I will care for her as if she were my own."

"I'll hold you to those words," Jared stated, his penetrating gaze promising her he would. "Your hand, please." Seeing the affronted expression that instantly covered her face, he almost chuckled aloud. "You do want to learn to sign, don't you?"

"Yes, certainly."

"Then give me your hand."

Her clenched fingers slowly uncurled, and the tips slid over Jared's calloused palm. He was an accomplished horseman, she knew, for she'd secretly watched from her windows as he fought for control over his thoroughbred stallion, Thor. Both beast and master had a temperament to match, but once Jared had gained the upper hand, the two would ride the hills and valleys. The thought of such freedom made her long more so for her own.

"Shall we begin?" Jared asked. Seeing her nod, he gently squeezed her hand in reassurance, knowing it was difficult for her to abide a man's touch. He marveled at its silky texture, certain the hand did not match the woman who owned it. Confusion marked his brow as his thumb lightly caressed her satiny smooth skin again.

Fire shot up Alissa's arm, and she jerked her hand free. Bewildered by the sensations he'd evoked, she stared at Jared, half-frightened by the man, half-longing for his gentle touch, again.

His gaze slowly climbed to Alissa's face, and Jared began to assess each feature, as though he were seeing them for the very first time. Ribbons of pink slashed her high cheekbones, and a straight, slender nose canopied a well-shaped mouth. Her full, lower lip trembled slightly as it separated itself from its mate to expose small, white teeth. With interest, Jared viewed the soft curves, and without thought, his own lips parted in response.

Then his eyes met hers. Clear, blue irises, framed by dark lashes that appeared dipped in pewter, stared back at him. What did he see in her sky-kissed gaze? Fear? Desire? No . . . *longing*. But why? he wondered, his eyes lifting to her winged brows, arching over enormous eyes, then to her smooth forehead and upward to . . . *that godawful hairnet!*

Jared blinked; his eyes quickly refocused. Pale-skinned, with deep hollows in her cheeks, dark smudges beneath her eyes, she once again became the same unappealing woman he'd first met.

What in blazes was wrong with him! his mind exploded as his brow folded itself into deep furrows. It seemed a continuous question of late. It kept rolling through his mind, over and over again, both day and night. The dreams . . . no, nightmares that perpetually plagued him . . .

Dash it all! He didn't want to think about them! Then he inwardly cursed himself, positive he was headed straight for bedlam, Agatha Pembroke the cause of his insanity!

Jared sprang from the desk and strode to the side table and the brandy. "I think it's best if Megan and I both teach you the signs we use," he stated in an agitated voice as he poured himself a healthy shot. "We'll begin our first lesson at supper."

Confused by his sudden anger, Alissa stared at his back. Undoubtedly she had done something to rouse his temper, but she couldn't fathom what it could be.

Having swallowed his drink, Jared dashed another large swig into the glass and gazed at the amber liquid. Should he keep to a steady diet of it, as he seemed prone to do of late, he was certain to find himself in the gutter. Again he found himself willing to blame Miss Pembroke for his lack of control. Deciding Megan didn't need a drunkard as a father, he set the glass aside and capped the decanter, the crystal top clinking roughly into place.

Jared turned and was surprised to see Megan's governess still in the room. All prim and proper-looking, the woman's eyes followed his every move. "If you intend to arrive in the dining room on time," he announced curtly, his eyes on the clock, "I suggest you find Megan and make your way downstairs. You have precisely five minutes."

"As you wish, sir," Alissa said, repeating Leona's words upon her dismissal, and rose. "We'll be most prompt."

Jared watched her graceful glide as she exited the room. Drawing a cleansing breath, he closed his eyes and expelled it from his lungs, wondering why he had attacked her with his words. The problem lay not with her, but with himself. The dreams . . . if they'd only stop! But with their growing frequency, he doubted they would.

Once Alissa hit the hallway, she ran down the corridor toward her room. The walls swayed and weaved, the carpet rose and receded. What was wrong with her vision? she wondered, then realized the distortions were caused by her tears.

CHAPTER

Seven

Bathed in silver moonbeams, draped in gossamer as translucent as a fairy's wing, the graceful figure of a woman danced alone in a forest's glade. A summer's breeze caressed her long, mahogany tresses, freeing and lifting them to cascade wildly around her slender body. Arms raised toward the luminous energy in the night's sky, she swayed sensuously as though she were beckoning to her lover.

His vision veiled in passion, Jared watched her inviting movements from afar, fire racing through his veins. Unable to keep from her a moment longer, he crossed the clearing without a sound. The night wind ruffled his hair, billowed his shirt, but it could not cool the hot flame burning in his loins.

Too many times she had escaped him, and he was always left wanting, tormented, his urgent desires unfulfilled. This time, he promised, he would discover her name; this time she would be his.

Behind her now, his arm encircled her small waist, and he pulled her hard against his chest. She did not struggle, but only moaned as though her own passion longed for fulfillment. Her head lolled against his shoulder, and Jared inhaled the sweet scent of lavender and wild rose as her silken hair brushed his cheek. His senses burst with the smell of her, his control shattered, and his lips urgently trailed the satin threads to her ear. Desperate to taste more of her, he turned her in his arms, and she arched, pressing her soft body fully to his. Her head thrown back, she offered her creamy throat, and Jared's lips traced its curve, upward to her jaw, her cheek; then with an agonized groan, his searching mouth captured hers.

Sweet and yielding, she responded, her lips parting, her small tongue seeking, teasing his. Lightning shot to his core, and his arms tightened around her. Needing her, wanting her, more than he could ever have imagined, he lowered her to the thick, fragrant carpet. The long grasses concealed them as he covered her lithe body with his own, his fingers threading through her hair to lift her face to his once more.

The fibrous strands suddenly coiled around his hands, binding them, and like a moth trapped in a spider's web, he found he could not break free.

"Spirits are the devil's henchmen," the shrewish voice echoed in his ears, and the gauze curtain dropped from his eyes to reveal the wan, hollow-eyed governess, lying beneath him. His hands still ensnared, he watched in horror as her pallid skin peeled from her face; black holes stared up at him from a mask of death.

Instantly, he rolled from the lifeless hag, yet his hands remained tangled, enmeshed. Wildly, his eyes focused to discover the cloying thing was a hairnet!

Then, like a living, breathing thing, it began to grow. It enveloped his face, his chest, his body—tightening, constricting, crushing the life from him. He couldn't breathe!

With a jerk, Jared awoke, his arms fighting down the bed covers that had wrapped themselves around his face, and cast them to the floor. Drawing a breath until his lungs burned, he exhaled slowly and shook his head to clear it.

Another nightmare! The damned things were coming more frequently, more vividly, until he was certain they were real and not some bugbear, chasing him through the night.

Still dazed, he leapt from his sweat-soaked bed, his naked body glistening in the moonlight that streamed through the windows. He moved to the washstand and bathed his face and arms, then worked downward to his feet. Once dried, he slipped into his quilted satin robe and lashed the belt tightly at his narrow waist.

He breathed steadily now, his head having cleared, and decided it was time to check on Megan. Knowing the way by heart, he left his quarters and traveled the darkened hallway. As his hand settled on the door handle, it was pulled from his grasp, and the panel swung inward.

Startled, he glimpsed the shadowy figure of a woman, the moonlight illuminating her silhouette from behind, and before he could move, she stepped headlong into his body. The force of it knocked her backward, and Jared's arm immediately encircled her waist, his hand clamping over her mouth to stop her scream. "Ssh, it's only me," he whispered, and felt her relax for an instant, then quickly stiffen against him.

Alissa's heart tripped wildly in her chest. With the length of her body pressed tightly to Jared's, she felt an odd sensation erupt somewhere deep inside, and it frightened her. "Let loose of me," she insisted in a harsh whisper, her hands pushing against his solid chest.

Jared honored her request. His arm slipped from her waist; the long strands of satiny hair brushed his hand. The feel of it surprised him, confused him.

"Why are you sneaking about in the dark?" she asked waspishly, incensed by the scare he'd given her, embarrassed by the reaction he'd caused.

"I could ask the same of you," he replied, leaning his shoulder against the door frame, his arms crossing over his wide chest.

"I was checking on Megan."

"So was I." Then he desperately searched the darkness, his eyes roving her moon-bathed outline, but she remained featureless as the night's luminescence reflected off her coarse cotton wrapper. A wealth of silky hair tumbled around her shoulders and down her back, a silvery halo crowning her head. Jared felt he was reliving his dream. Raw desire suddenly shot to his core. Stunned by its force, he pushed from the wood. "Go to your room," he ordered gruffly.

Surprised by his rough tone, Alissa stared through the

dark shadows, unable to see him. Then she sensed his movement, and fearing he was closing in on her, she fled Megan's doorway. Her shoulder brushed his chest, and his hand caught her arm. She tried to break free, but his fingers tightened, almost painfully.

"Henceforth," he said, in an oddly constricted voice, "keep to your rooms at night."

Then he released her, and Alissa rushed to her door, her silent feet sinking into the blood-red carpet. Once inside she settled against the locked panel, her body shaking from head to foot.

Her rapid breaths eased to a slower draw, and she tried to fathom what had suddenly made him become so threatening. She never completely understood the man, not from one moment to the next. Then she decided she never would. But one thing was certain. She planned to heed his warning. He could see to Megan at night, she would remain in her rooms.

Again making certain her door was secured, Alissa slipped from her robe, then climbed into her bed. Too weary to think, she settled under the covers and sank into a deep, soundless sleep, the incident forgotten.

Jared had lingered in the hallway, fighting for control. When the door handle jiggled, breaking the night's silence, he'd smiled derisively.

Had she tarried but a moment longer, she might have discovered herself pinned to the floor, he atop her, his carnal lusts responding to her writhing form, his desires raging out of control. At that moment, he'd cared not what she truly looked like, for in the darkness she could be whomever he'd wanted, whomever he'd desired. And he'd desired the woman in his dreams, the one who had beckoned to him, the one who had enchanted him, the one he'd held in his aching arms before she suddenly changed into a loathsome sight. As Megan's governess stood there, faceless, bathed in moonlight, she had suddenly become that woman, his *Hermia*.

Disgusted, Jared raked his long fingers through his hair. He was appalled by his thoughts, for he'd never force himself upon a woman. *Never!* he proclaimed silently.

He suddenly wondered . . . could it be possible there was

a dark side emerging from within him, one he never knew existed until now? Tormented by his dreams, his nightmares, he felt as though he were going insane!

After checking on his daughter to find her fast asleep, Jared strode to his rooms. Tossing the bed covers onto the mattress, he stripped from his robe, then lay naked atop the sheets. His arm propped beneath his head, he stared at the canopy. If only he could discover *Hermia's* real name, he thought. It was useless, though, for by the time he'd returned from Selkirk, his rooms had been cleaned and the newspaper discarded, the actress's true identity with it. Yet, if he *could* learn her name, perhaps he'd be able to find her and put an end to his nightly bedevilment. He scoffed at the thought. All of Britain searched for her without success. What made him think he'd be able to discover her whereabouts!

"Enough of this," he growled, weary of the whole thing. He needed to be up and about at sunrise. Yet, although he knew he needed sleep, he fought it, certain the agonizing fantasies would start anew.

CHAPTER

Eight

As Alissa slowly descended the grand staircase, in search of Megan's favorite doll, she carefully pondered the words she'd just overheard as two gossiping maids prepared Robert Hamilton's room, readying it for his arrival.

"I tell ye, he murdered his wife," the one had said, her voice filtering into the hallway through the open door, and Alissa had stopped short.

"If that be true, why ain't he hangin' from the gallows by now?" the other countered.

"'Cause they cain't prove he did it. He burnt up the evidence."

"Aw, yer daft."

"Ain't neither. The talk be, his wife had a lover here'bouts, and when he caught wind of it, bein' jealous and all, he killed her. Burnt her up, all crispy, he did."

Angered by their vicious prattle, especially since it could very well have been Megan who'd overheard their tripe, Alissa had stepped into the room. With her eyes condemning, her voice glacial, she'd said, "I suggest you both be about your business and leave the gossip to those who reside outside these walls, or I'll see to it you join them." Neither woman could face her, and with a last fluffing of the pillows, both had rushed from the room.

Although she knew their words had not an ounce of

credence, Alissa still found herself wondering about them. A seed of doubt, she thought, then wiped the entire episode from her mind.

Alissa's feet hit the landing between the second and first floors, and she descended another dozen steps, when she stopped to watch Mr. Stanley straighten his new livery, smooth the few hairs atop his head, and swing wide the front door to reveal a striking woman on the doorstep.

"Jared," she fairly gushed, "it's so good to see you again." Removing her light wrap and feather-bedecked hat to expose her fiery red hair, she shoved both into Mr. Stanley's arms. Then in a rustle of petticoats and green silk dress, she moved straight toward the handsome man, standing in the center of the entry hall. "Aren't you happy to see me?" she questioned with a pretty pout.

Alissa watched as the redhead raised her cheek for Jared's kiss, but he clasped her hands instead.

"Surprised is the better word, Patricia," Jared answered, holding her at a distance. "I wasn't aware Robert was bringing you along."

Not to be rebuffed, the woman brushed Jared's hands aside and raised on tiptoes, pressing her full lips against his. "Jared, dearest. You act as though we're strangers," Patricia admonished playfully. "It's only been a few months since we've seen each other. When Robert said he was coming, I decided at the last moment to join him. But it's Megan I want to see. However, brother-in-law, I somehow feel unwelcome."

"You're always welcome, Patricia," he lied, smoothly. "However, a little notice would have made Mrs. Dugan a bit happier. She hasn't prepared a room for you."

"Oh, tosh, the woman always wears a long face," she said with a small frown, then her lips broke into a teasing smile. "Just have my luggage sent to my usual room, the one across from Megan's playroom." Her hand lifted to straighten Jared's collar. "Mrs. Dugan can see to its preparation later."

Alissa realized the redhead referred to her own room and wondered if it would present a problem. As she viewed the beauty, she suddenly felt exceedingly plain. True, the original intent of her disguise was to appear somewhat dowdy, but once stripped of it, she doubted she'd ever be able to match Patricia's physical grace.

She watched the redhead's flirtatious advances, aimed openly at Jared. Alissa felt a twinge of anger, perhaps even jealousy. Certainly not! she told herself in haughty denial. But, oh, to wear fine dresses again, she thought, attributing the lingering emotion to mere envy.

Jared removed Patricia's hand from his chest, where it had lazily wandered and remained. Already, he was becoming annoyed with her feminine wiles. She reminded him too much of Celeste, not only in looks, but in her actions, as well. When he was young, he was easily aroused by such alluring displays, and his blood would stir, but now he was sickened by them. "The room, I'm afraid, is already occupied. You'll have to choose another."

"Occupied?" Patricia countered, a little more than surprised. "By whom?"

"By Megan's new governess."

Patricia's mind raced. She hadn't counted on this. "You never mentioned you were hiring a governess," she accused. "Why does the child even need one? I would think her family would be more understanding than some stranger. In fact, Jared, that's why I've come. I want to help—"

"Miss Pembroke," Jared called over his shoulder as Alissa turned, starting to retreat up the stairs. She'd listened long enough and didn't wish to become embroiled in a family discussion on what was, or was not, good for Megan. The one with Mrs. Dugan had been quite enough. "Would you please join us?" he finished.

Since his back was to her, she wondered how he could have possibly known she was there. Descending the remaining half-dozen or so steps, she felt Patricia's assessing gaze on her. Apparently satisfied that Alissa posed no threat, the woman smiled.

Just as she reached Jared's side, several footmen hustled through the doorway, followed by Mr. Stanley and two of Jared's servants. All were laden down with trunks, bags, and boxes of every size and shape. The ensuing commotion distracted everyone.

"It was your shoes," Jared said in a low aside to Alissa as he watched the men juggle Patricia's luggage.

"What are you talking about?" Alissa countered.

"The reason I knew you were on the stairs." His lips twitched and finally broke into a grin. "You're right, they do squeak. In the future, if you plan to sneak about, I'd suggest you oil them."

Alissa turned a stony eye toward him. If she had had a good-sized limb within reach, preferably the entire tree, she'd have crowned him with it. Nothing slipped past the man.

Suddenly a hatbox toppled from the towering stack in Mr. Stanley's arms, and Patricia shrieked in dismay. "Now look what you've done!" she cried, rushing to retrieve the spilled hats from beneath the man's feet.

Mr. Stanley—who Alissa had since learned was Jared's butler, manservant, and coachman, all rolled into one— shot his employer a pleading look. He then turned a disgruntled eye to the floor as he danced from one foot to the other, Patricia's hands nipping at his heels, while he tried to balance the remaining boxes, which shifted wildly in his arms.

"If this was a last-minute decision," Alissa spoke aloud, not realizing she did so, "I wonder what she'd have packed if her visit had been planned at length."

"I've been wondering the same," Jared replied in a dull tone, and headed toward Mr. Stanley.

When Jared had relieved him of the top three boxes, Mr. Stanley released a long breath. "Thought ye'd never get here."

"Jared, you really must hire yourself more competent help," Patricia complained as she rose from the waist with several hats in hand. The once beautiful chapeaus now resembled plucked pigeons, their plumes shattered, the down missing along their shafts. "Look! They're ruined!"

"I'll buy you a half-dozen others as replacements," Jared stated, "but I ask you to remember that you are the one who has elected to come to Hawkstone, uninvited. Therefore, you will not voice your displeasure with my staff."

Alissa was as much taken aback by his curt words as Patricia seemed to be. "I'm sorry, Jared," the redhead placated swiftly. "I've forgotten just how much Mr. Stanley means to you. How long has he been in your employ now?"

"A dozen years, miss," Mr. Stanley answered a bit tersely. "And they be right good ones, too."

"Enough, Mr. Stanley," Jared said as he shoved the boxes back into the man's arms. Taking the mangled hats from Patricia's hands, he stuffed them into the uppermost box, and smashed the lid on it. "Put these things in the corner and go find Mrs. Dugan. Tell her to open another room for our unexpected guest."

With a none too quiet snort, Mr. Stanley did as bade. Patricia quickly followed to orchestrate the placement of her luggage before another disaster occurred.

"Where the blazes is Robert?" Jared snapped, aggravated by the whole scene.

"Right here, cousin."

Alissa viewed the well-dressed man as he sauntered through the doorway, a foil-wrapped box, tied with blue ribbon, tucked under his arm. Tall and handsome, his hair a bit lighter than Jared's, he was not nearly as attractive as Jared, in her estimation.

"Do you always encounter this sort of chaos when receiving guests?" Robert Braxton Hamilton asked when he'd reached Jared's side. "Or is it only with Patricia?"

Jared arched a brow. "I suppose you were unable to convince her to stay in Edinburgh?"

"She wouldn't take no for an answer."

"Next time, don't mention you're coming. It'll save us all the aggravation."

"Ah, Robert," Patricia said, the words oozing out in relief as she moved toward the two men, "I see you've brought Megan's gift. I thought it lost in the melee." She took the box in hand and straightened the bright blue bow. "Where is my dearest niece, anyway?"

Jared turned to Alissa. "Miss Pembroke, please find Megan and bring her into the sitting room." He then motioned Robert and Patricia toward the mentioned room.

"Cousin, aren't you being remiss?" Robert asked, inclining his head toward Alissa, who had not yet moved. Noting Jared's confused frown, he prompted, "Introductions."

"Your pardon. Miss Patricia Southworth and Mr. Robert Hamilton, may I present Miss Agatha Pembroke, Megan's governess."

"Miss Pembroke," Robert greeted her, then bowed slightly. "Jared has extolled your excellent reputation from the moment he'd learned of your existence. I hope you can help Megan as much as you've helped the other children you've worked with over the years."

Alissa felt a bit nervous. The high praises belonged to another, yet she was the one to receive them. More expectations were being heaped upon her, and she began to feel the heaviness of her lies once more. "I shall do my best," she replied, wondering if it would be good enough.

"Miss Pembroke," Patricia said, virtually ignoring the amenities of their introduction, "I'm most anxious to see my niece. I have a gift for her, so please fetch her."

Alissa immediately bristled at the woman's condescending tone. "If I were a hound and Megan a bone, then, indeed, I would *fetch* her, Miss Southworth. However, neither one of us fits those qualifications. I will *inform* her of your arrival." With that, Alissa turned on her heel and marched up the stairs, wishing again she'd learn to control her temper.

"Close your mouth, Patricia," Jared said, and his sister-in-law snapped her jaw shut. "You will find Miss Pembroke to be an opinionated woman who speaks her mind quite freely. She has the propensity to try the patience of a saint. Even I have difficulty communicating with her."

"You are no saint, Jared," Patricia countered with a teasing smile.

"Hardly," he agreed. "But neither am I the spawn of the devil as Megan's governess believes me to be."

"Why, then, do you employ her?" Patricia asked, seeing her opening. "I'm certain, if you'd only let me try, I could have Megan talking in no time at all. How can a stranger possibly know what the child has suffered? I—"

Jared waved her off. "We've already been that route," he said, not bothering to explain Mrs. Dugan's similar concerns. "She needs an experienced teacher, one who's worked with children like Megan. As far as I know, Miss Pembroke is the only one of her kind."

Patricia instantly disagreed with Jared's statement, but she held her tongue. She'd learned long ago one didn't really win points with a man by being argumentative. Given a few days, she was certain she could change Jared's mind. After all, hadn't she come all this way to show him just how very nurturing and motherly she could be? It mattered not that she hadn't seen Megan for almost a year. Once she'd won over the child, the father was sure to follow.

How very foolish of Celeste, Patricia thought as she viewed Jared's handsome profile. Her sister never really knew what a catch she'd actually made. But Patricia was well aware of Jared's qualities, his money, his . . . no, he'd warned her never to speak or think of *that!* Very well, she wouldn't. But it made no difference. He was what he was, he couldn't deny it. Her sights were aimed. Just give her a few weeks, and she'd bag her quarry.

Upstairs, Alissa entered the playroom and Megan's expectant gaze turned toward her from across the room. Realizing the child was wondering over her misplaced doll, Alissa smiled and said, "I'm afraid I haven't found Mathilda yet. In fact, I had to discontinue my search because we have just received visitors. Your cousin Robert has arrived, and he has brought your Aunt Patricia with him."

Alissa noted that the spark of excitement that had entered Megan's eyes when she'd mentioned Robert's name had quickly died upon hearing Patricia's. But, then, she remembered Jared's rather cool response to the woman, and she wondered if both Braxtons regarded her in the same light.

"Your father has asked that we join them in the downstairs sitting room. So let's have a quick wash of your face and hands and run a brush through your hair. We want to look our very best."

Megan made a slow trek toward Alissa, her gaze downcast. Then she raised questioning eyes toward her governess. "Must I?" she signed with her small hand.

"Since your father has requested that you do, I think perhaps we should comply with his wishes," Alissa said, then noticed the child seemed overly anxious. "Are you nervous about seeing your aunt?" Megan nodded. "You don't have to be. Your father will be with you, and so will I."

Megan seemed to ponder Alissa's words. Over the past two days since Alissa was given complete charge of Megan, she hadn't been able to break through the barrier that the child had erected around herself, but she'd been able to whittle away at its edges, bit by bit, weakening its mortar, to form a tentative bond of trust with the girl. Yet, Alissa was well aware that the least little thing could cause the wall to reseal itself again.

"I promise you have nothing to fear," she said, knowing the child realized that in whatever Alissa promised, she always kept her word. "In fact, I believe your aunt has a wonderful surprise for you."

Megan's eyes brightened with anticipation. Finally nodding her assent, she took Alissa's hand. But as the two left the playroom for a quick grooming, Alissa wished she hadn't spoken so swiftly. Intuition told her that Patricia Southworth's concerns lay mainly with the father, not the daughter. And should the pretentious woman forget Megan's delicate emotional state and somehow hurt the child, then all that Alissa had accomplished would lie in ruin; Megan's growing trust in her would be destroyed.

When Robert and Patricia were seated in the small room, directly off the entrance hall, Jared asked, "May I offer you a glass of sherry, Patricia?"

"Thank you, yes," she answered as she perused the room and its soft blends of creams, blues, and violets, deciding she'd change the decor once Jared and she were married. "I might ask for a bit of nourishment, as well. We've been traveling since dawn."

"Here, here," Robert agreed. "And make mine a brandy, cousin."

Once cook had been notified and the drinks distributed, Jared sat opposite his guests. Raising his glass, he saluted both, then swallowed a small portion of his brandy. He'd been trying to cut back, but he had the feeling, with Patricia and Agatha in the same house, it was going to be doubly difficult to abstain.

Then, as he viewed his former sister-in-law, who chattered away about the latest gossip from Edinburgh, he again noted how much she resembled Celeste: the red hair, the gray-green eyes, the tilt of her head, the throatiness of her voice. Several years younger than Celeste, who would be twenty-six, if she'd lived, Patricia had always been the more stable of the two, which said little, if anything. Both sisters had been more concerned with the frivolities of life than the realities. Obviously, Patricia still was.

He couldn't figure why she was here. One would have thought she'd have taken the hint, as did the others, when he'd practically severed all contact with his late wife's family, shortly after her death. An occasional note or card exchanged hands through the mails, addressing the usual social amenities, inquiring about one's health. But other than that, no communication had been made, and certainly not in person. Yet, Patricia remained in touch more often than Jared would have liked, and usually it was with a surprise visit, like this one. Her unannounced visits normally occurred when he was in Edinburgh on business. In fact, she hadn't been to Hawkstone in ages, which in his estimation was a godsend for all concerned. "Patricia," he interrupted her regalement of the ball she'd attended last week, "May I ask why—"

"Megan, darling!" she exclaimed, cutting Jared off. Then she opened her arms, wide. "Come give Auntie Patricia a hug, dear."

Auntie? Alissa thought, fighting the urge to roll her eyes. The term belonged to a woman three times Miss Southworth's age. Looking at Jared, she noticed the slight twitch of his lips, the subtle arch of his brow, and the almost imperceptible nod of his head. He seemed to be agreeing with her. Quickly, she turned her attention to Megan.

Noting the child's hesitation, she leaned over and whispered, "Your aunt has come a great distance to see you. It would be nice if you were to greet her."

Megan viewed Alissa with wide, innocent eyes. They seemed to plead not to make her do it.

"Shall I come with you?" Alissa asked, for she saw no reason to force the child. "If you like, we can greet her together." She suddenly felt a vibrant presence and straightened to find Jared beside her.

"Come, sweet, we'll all greet your *Auntie* Patricia," he said, smiling. "You must forgive my former sister-in-law," he whispered to Alissa. "She's a bit theatrical at times."

"By chance, has she considered the stage?" she returned,

feeling an unexpected rapport, possibly because he seemed as put out with Patricia Southworth as she was.

"She's considered many things, but has never gone any further than the initial thought."

"Too bad. She might have great potential. London would love her."

"Are you an expert on the theater?" Jared asked, curious. Hoping she was, he wanted to discover the true name of his *Hermia*. "The London theater?"

Startled by the freeness with which she'd spoken, Alissa quickly answered, "No. I have no actual knowledge of the theater in London. I simply assumed, by her beauty and grace, all of London would have fallen at her feet." Another lie! And she wondered at what number she should mark this one, but she discovered she'd lost count. Then she heard Patricia clear her throat.

"Jared, if you and Megan's governess are finished with your tête-à-tête, I'd like to speak with my niece."

"As you wish, *Auntie,"* Jared said, and received a perturbed look from the redhead.

"You deserve to be teased, Patricia," Robert spoke up. "You've managed to present us all with the mental picture of a white-haired, raisin-faced dowager. I think 'aunt' would have sufficed."

"Oh, Robert, hush," she snipped at him.

"I have to agree with Robert," Jared said, defending his cousin. "Megan has not seen you in nearly a year. She does not remember you that well." He cast her a cautioning look as he released Megan's hand. *Move slowly,* it said.

Unwisely, Patricia ignored the warning and took Megan in a smothering embrace; her stifling kisses covered the child's face. Frightened, Megan pushed from her aunt's arms and hid in the folds of Alissa's dowdy gray gown. In an automatic response, she hugged the child close. Her intense gaze settled on Patricia, and Alissa directed a condemning look at the woman.

Patricia, however, disregarded the message and turned to Robert. She never dared look at Jared. "Hand me the box, please, Robert." He did, and Patricia held the foil-wrapped gift on her lap. "Megan, in my eagerness to show my affection, I managed to frighten you. I'm terribly sorry. Will you forgive me?" she asked, easing a smile onto her unlined face.

With a child's curiosity, Megan's wide eyes surveyed the beautifully decorated box, and she slowly nodded.

"Wonderful." Patricia patted the violet and cream striped silk cushion of the settee. "Sit here and let's see what's inside this box, shall we?"

Megan looked to her father, and seeing his reassuring nod, she moved from Alissa's side. Perching on the edge of her seat, then covering her small knees with her pink skirt, she folded her hands and waited.

"Wouldn't you like to open it?" Patricia asked.

Megan appraised her aunt for a moment, then accepted the gift and carefully began to unwrap the paper. Patricia, anxious for all to see the magnificent gift, became impatient and tore into the wrappings herself. After the ribbon and paper fell to the floor, the lid popped off. Inside was a doll, with red hair and an exquisite porcelain face.

Alissa thought it the most beautiful doll she'd ever seen, but Megan suddenly shoved the gift away. Surprised by her action, Alissa looked to Jared. His jaw locked, a nerve twitched along its edge. A definite look of murder flared in his eyes. And it was directed at Patricia.

Mrs. Dugan entered the room, then, carrying a heavily laden tray of assorted fruits, cheeses, and a plate of freshly baked croissants, cakes, and other pastries. "Might I help you?" Alissa asked.

With an effectual snub, Leona turned her eyes from Alissa's. "It's good to see you both again, Miss Patricia, Mr. Robert," she said, then she noticed the doll. "Oh, how lovely. It looks exactly like Miss Celeste, even down to the small mole at the corner of her mouth and the dimple in her chin."

"I'm afraid Megan doesn't like it," Patricia pouted.

"Doesn't like it? Megan," Leona said, "how can you not like it? It's a beautiful remembrance of your mother."

Megan's concentration dropped to her tightly clasped hands. Confused, Alissa didn't understand why she wouldn't accept the gift, or why Jared had seemed so livid over its presentation. Still, he remained stoically silent.

"I had so hoped she'd be pleased with it," Patricia said, sulking. "I had it specially made in France."

"Since your aunt went to so much trouble," Leona urged, "why don't you make a special place for it in your room?"

"Miss Pembroke," Jared commanded, his hard gaze still centered on his sister-in-law, "take Megan upstairs."

"But, Jared," Patricia objected, "I—"

"Say not a word. Miss Pembroke, please . . ."

"Should I take the doll, too?" Alissa asked, cautiously.

"*Yes,*" Jared hissed. When she and Megan reached the entry, he ordered over his shoulder, "Close the doors."

She pulled the panels shut and quickly led Megan across the foyer and up the stairs. She could only imagine what might be transpiring in the sitting room, but from the look in Jared's hard, green eyes, she knew it was not a pleasant scene. Not pleasant at all.

Once inside Megan's room, Alissa asked, "Do you want me to put the doll in the cradle with the others?"

Megan vehemently shook her head.

"No? Then where shall we put it?"

Megan grabbed the box and pointed.

"You wish for me to pack it away?" she asked, and saw her short nod. Not until today had Alissa known what Celeste looked like. All her portraits had been removed. In fact, there were no portraits on the walls whatsoever. It was as though the past had been stripped from the house, including all ancestral reminders. Again she wondered what secrets Hawkstone kept. Megan's, as well. "Your mother was very beautiful," she said, carefully placing the doll into the box. "We'll put this away, and perhaps someday you will want to display it."

With a violent shove, Megan almost knocked the box from Alissa's hands. Teary-eyed, she ran to her bed and bounded to the mattress, where she lay with her back to the room.

Finally switching her concerned gaze from Megan, Alissa stored the doll away in a drawer, then moved to the bed. Unable to tell if Megan actually slept, or if she simply pretended, Alissa pulled the cover up over the girl's shoulders and moved to a corner chair. Partially blaming herself for the child's woes, she kept a silent vigil.

Her troubled thoughts a jumble, for she couldn't understand Megan's tormented reaction to the gift, Alissa suddenly remembered the dollhouse. As she reviewed the girl's odd play with the dolls, especially the one representing the mother, she realized Megan hadn't been pretending at all! No wonder she'd refused the doll.

It seemed strange to Alissa that any child could feel such teeming anger, especially toward a parent. How sad, she thought, her heart twisting painfully, that the child's memories of her mother were so dark. Apparently, Megan was truly scarred by Celeste's rejection, if indeed that was the case, and Alissa couldn't imagine feeling so unloved. Thankfully, unlike Megan, Alissa had been spared the mental anguish of being openly spurned by her own parent. As she searched her memory for any hint of having known her father, Alissa felt the sudden sting of tears and quickly wiped all thoughts of the faceless man who had sired her away.

Again, she thought of Celeste and doubted the woman's selfish nature was the full reason behind Megan's silence. There had to be more to it, but she couldn't fathom what. Then she thought of the maids' gossip. Surely not! It was impossible. Jared Braxton couldn't possibly have murdered his wife.

Alissa refused to believe he could commit such a heinous act. Yet, by his own admission, he possessed a volatile temper. Once crossed, especially if he'd been cuckolded as the one maid had implied, then he might have been capable of anything!

As Alissa kept watch on the now sleeping child, she fought her growing doubts. And finally, she dozed, too, the truth still left undiscovered.

CHAPTER
Nine

"Jared," Patricia cooed, five days later, as they were gathered in the informal dining room for the afternoon meal, "you really must allow me to take Megan into Selkirk. Since the doll didn't suit her, perhaps she will find something in one of the local shops that would please her more."

"That's up to Megan," he replied as he raised his freshly refilled wine glass to his lips. Realizing it was his third in less than a quarter hour, he became annoyed with himself and set the thing aside. He'd been imbibing far too much, just as he'd predicted. But he'd been in need of a tranquilizing agent of late; his nerves were on the verge of splintering and his temper on the verge of exploding. As a result, his liquor supply was dwindling—fast. "And of course," he finished, "you must consult Miss Pembroke."

Wanting to protect the child, for Megan had withdrawn into her shell again, Alissa started to respond that it would be all right with her, *if* she were allowed to accompany them, but Patricia immediately leapt to a new topic. Annoyed, she transferred her gaze from the incessantly chattering woman to the reserved man sitting next to the redhead, opposite herself.

Robert, she decided, had been exceptionally quiet since his arrival. Although they'd all been chained to silence, because of the constantly clacking Patricia, Robert was probably the least talkative of all. Alissa noticed his eyes intent upon Jared, who, in turn, viewed Patricia with a somewhat dazed look.

There it was again, Alissa thought, noticing that certain something flash in Robert's eye. She'd caught the look on several occasions, mainly when they were gathered at meals, but she couldn't quite capture its meaning. The emotion had flickered so briefly, she wondered if she'd actually seen it at all. Whatever it was, it was always directed at Jared.

Perhaps he was trying to quietly signal his cousin, in hopes that Jared would somehow put a stop to Patricia's continuous babble. With luck, Jared would decipher the message, if that's what it truly meant, and bestow upon all who were within earshot the blessing of silence.

"Where's Megan?" Patricia asked, suddenly realizing her niece wasn't at the table. "She's not ill, is she?"

Alissa noted the false mask of motherly concern which had slipped over the woman's face, and again she decided Patricia should have been an actress.

The redhead set her napkin aside and placed her hand over Jared's where it rested along the tablecloth. "Perhaps I should see to her."

Having endured one episode too many of Patricia's theatrics, for she knew it was not the child who held the redhead's interest, but the father, Alissa tossed her own napkin onto the table. Her meal practically untouched, she rose from her seat. "Megan is resting, at the moment," she announced almost rudely. "She's already eaten and has gone to her room for some quiet time. Unfortunately, not all of us are so lucky."

Angrily, Alissa set a course for the doorway. Just as she passed through the panels, she heard Jared's full-throated laughter burst forth, and Patricia's incensed voice, "I find nothing funny in that impertinent woman's comment."

"You wouldn't, Patricia," Jared replied, his laughter subsiding to a deep chuckle. "But I, for one, am in complete agreement with her. Unfortunately, I was too much the coward to voice the words myself. Now, if you'll excuse us, Robert and I have some bookwork to finish."

Open-mouthed, Patricia stared after the two men as they disappeared through the doors. Then, forgetting Mr. Stanley stood in the corner, switching from one foot to the other, fighting to stay awake, she pounded the table with her fist, her gray-green eyes flashing in anger. The sudden thump jerked the butler to attention.

"That's the last time I'll let that plain-as-paste prude do that to me!" Patricia vowed aloud, determined to have the frumpish governess ejected from Hawkstone by nightfall. "She'll receive her just deserts, that I promise!"

Already in motion, his narrowed gaze aimed at the redhead's back, Mr. Stanley tripped himself up. *"Oops!"* It was the only warning Patricia received before the large bowl slid from the ornate silver tray.

"Eeeyow!"

Hearing the yell, Jared came sliding into the dining room, Robert at his heels, to see a glob of custard slide down the redhead's face and fall to the bodice of her gown.

Instantly, she leapt to her feet, turning on his manservant. "Why, you odious fool! Look at me! My hair! My dress! I'll have your head for this!"

Reaching her side, Jared had to forcefully bite the inside of his lip to contain his laughter. "What happened?"

"This fool, whom you call a butler, dumped the custard on me!" Patricia screeched anew. "He's ruined my dress!"

Still fighting for control, for Patricia looked like she'd taken a tumble into the slop bucket, Jared turned a curious eye to the man next to him. "Mr. Stanley?"

"Had an accident, I did. Heard her say somethin' 'bout just wantin' some *desserts,* so I served 'em up to her."

Jared had caught the stressed word. "I understand."

His man gave a quick nod. "Thought ye would." Then with a loud sniff at Patricia, he turned on his heel and headed for the door, his nose pointed at the ceiling.

Patricia glared after the man. If it weren't for the fact he'd heard her every word, she'd demand his punishment. But she could do nothing, not unless she wanted to confess her vindictiveness to Jared.

Jared's brow arched in question. "Just deserts? Would you care to explain, Patricia?"

"No . . . I mean . . . there's nothing to explain," she replied in a rush. "Mr. Stanley misunderstood . . . I mean, he's forgiven. Excuse me, I must change."

As he watched Patricia flee the room, he felt as though he were losing touch with all that went on in his home. The bookwork almost completed, his dealings with Robert were drawing to a rapid close. Most likely, it was more from his own swift doing, for he was anxious to see Patricia on her way. Once they were gone, he'd be left with Agatha Pembroke. That, alone, was enough to drive him insane!

Spinning on his heel, his cousin having retreated earlier, Jared strode back to his first-floor office, his study used for more formal meetings. If luck were with him, and he planned for it to be, he'd conclude his business by early afternoon on the morrow. Until then, he hoped he could keep his smoldering temper under control!

Alissa quickly ran along the garden path, her heart pounding in the same cadence as her feet. *Where can she be?* she wondered as she frantically skirted the exterior of the summerhouse, knowing it was one of Megan's favorite places.

When she'd gone upstairs, she'd glanced in to check on Megan and found her gone. A quick check of the entire floor had produced no results, not even her dared entrance into Jared's quarters. Again, she'd checked the girl's room. The drawer where she'd stored the doll had been opened, the empty box on the floor. Instantly, she'd feared the worst.

Now, as she stood in the gardens, not knowing where to search next, her fingers rubbed across her forehead, trying to stimulate her thoughts. *Think!* she told herself, but her massaging fingers became entangled in the hated hairnet, and in a fit of temper, as with the bonnet, she jerked the thing from her head to clench it in her fist. The light breeze caught a few loose tendrils of hair, caressing them, and it seemed as if once her head was free so were her thoughts.

"The east wing!" she exclaimed, and hiked her skirt. At a full run, she headed back toward the house.

"Do you have those figures for the net profits on last month's cargos from the Indies?" Jared asked after he'd reseated himself at his desk, the episode in the dining room set aside.

Robert turned from the window where he'd watched the suddenly agile Miss Pembroke flee the gardens. "Right here, cousin."

Jared stopped shuffling through the papers on his desk. "Well?"

"Your five ships brought in a profit of over £50,000." He handed the file to Jared, then silently reviewed the scene he'd just witnessed. Sealing his lips against sharing it with Jared, Robert stored the bit of information away for future reference.

Alissa made her way along the exterior of the desolate east wing, in search of an entry. Midway along the abandoned portion of Hawkstone, she found some narrow stone steps and descended them. A small door stood slightly ajar, wide enough for a child to squeeze through. Giving the weathered panel a good shove, she inched herself into the musty-smelling basement.

Her eyes finally adjusted to the bleak interior, and aided by the periodic streams of sunlight that shone weakly through the small windows, she quickly followed the dimly lit path, fighting the cobwebs knitted from wall to wall. At the end of the dank corridor, new wood blocked her way, and she decided, if the heavy boards were down, the course would lead her beneath the main house. As it was, she could go no farther.

Then, as she started to retrace her steps, intending to find the stairs leading up into the destroyed portion of the house, and hopefully to Megan, she noticed a recessed area. Her foot lifted, settling onto a stone step. Frowning, she debated whether to climb the passageway. Except for a murky shadow of light at the top, it was as dark as the grave.

"Megan," she called up the stairwell and waited, praying the child would appear. She tried again, but the house remained silent, no movement within.

Suddenly it occurred to her, if Megan had taken a misstep in the ruins, the child could be lying, helpless, unable to respond to her calls. A mental picture of a fallen beam, trapping Megan's small body, set Alissa into action, and although she realized the stairs could have given way from the blistering heat of the fire, she nonetheless shot up them. More webs swathed her face, and this time she was certain life scurried through the fine threads. Dashing safely to the main floor, she breathed a sigh of relief and pulled the silken strands from her face and shoulders, then knocked an uninvited traveler from her breast; the spider scrambled into a crack.

Not finding Megan on the first floor, Alissa hoped the east wing was constructed like the west and sought the alcove. Small arched windows lit the steps ascending from the basement, and Alissa decided the child had taken this path and not the narrower set of stairs she had followed. If she'd only thought to turn left instead of right when she'd entered, she'd have saved herself a scare.

Amazingly, as she followed the second-story corridor, cautiously stepping over fallen timbers, Alissa noted the scent of smoke still lingered. Its acrid bite sent a chill down her spine, and the words of the gossipy maids flashed into her mind. Again she considered whether Jared had truly plotted to murder his wife, having set their quarters ablaze while Celeste slept, then fled with Megan.

No! Jared Braxton was many things, but Alissa refused to believe he was a murderer.

Lifting her skirt, she stepped over yet another obstacle, her eyes intent upon her path. Then, she noticed them. Small footprints marked a trail in the soot and dust that covered the floor, and she quickly trailed them to the end of the hallway, into what she imagined was once a magnificent suite of rooms.

As she viewed her surroundings, she noted the interior was blackest here, the wall coverings fused into what was left of the interior walls. A four-poster bed lay blistered and broken, save for one spire, its surface charred. It stood like a hellish monument, a testament to the past.

Alissa wondered if this had been their bed. Then she briefly envisioned Jared's long, hard body covering the softness of his wife's, his passion taking hold. Quickly, she shook the thought from her mind and rounded the bed to stop in the doorway, leading into another room.

Near the corner, by the large, drapeless windows, sat

Megan, the porcelain replica of her mother hugged tightly in her arms. Her back to Alissa, she rocked to and fro; an odd chanting sound escaped her throat. To Alissa, Megan's movements seemed ritualistic.

Suddenly Megan shifted position to reveal a lighted candle. Before Alissa could react, she shoved the doll into the flame. Without hesitation, Alissa stretched the distance separating them, her hand knocking the doll into the corner, its china face shattering as it hit the wall.

The child jerked startled eyes to Alissa's face, then she sprang to her feet and ran. "Megan!" Alissa cried after her, but the child kept on running.

Quickly snuffing the candle and smothering the doll's dress, before Hawkstone burned anew, Alissa entered the hallway within seconds, but Megan was gone. Jumping the charred debris in her path, the doll still in hand, she ran to the alcove and descended the stairs to the basement Her feet flew along the passageway to the small door as she dodged a multitude of cobwebs again. Once outside, she headed toward the gardens, but Megan was not to be seen.

Her shoulders slumping in defeat, Alissa turned just in time to see a small form disappearing into a thick copse, heading toward the north fields. Casting the doll aside, she grabbed her skirts and ran after her. As she fought the thicket, she realized Megan knew these woods far better than she. Although the child was never allowed to wander the grounds by herself, Jared had taken her on outings whenever his time had permitted.

How far had she come? she wondered as she paused in her uphill trek to catch her breath, then glanced over her shoulder to barely see Hawkstone's chimneys.

Renewed by her short rest, Alissa topped the knoll to find a clearing. A small cottage stood in its center, patches of wildflowers bursting forth in the long grasses surrounding it. Quietly she made her way to the door, and as she stepped inside, she heard the strains of a throaty hum. As heartrending as its melody was, Alissa was relieved to hear it, and she followed its refrain of despair.

Huddled in a corner cluttered with broken furniture, Megan stared, eyes lifeless, as her body rocked in time to her intonation. Alissa surveyed her a moment, then whispered softly, "Megan." The child stopped her chant, but kept to her to-and-fro movement. "Megan," she said, the girl's name almost torn from her soul as she crouched next to her. "It's all right, darling. You've done nothing wrong."

The rocking stopped.

"Megan," Alissa said her name again gently, but the girl would not look at her. "What happened with the doll is my fault. Had I not promised you when your aunt arrived that you had nothing to fear, then your trust in me would not have been broken. If I had known her gift would upset you, I'd never have allowed her to give it to you. In fact, I'd never have taken you to greet her. But I didn't know. I made a promise that was based on assumption." It was true, for Alissa never thought an adult would purposely hurt a child. "And it was based on ignorance." Which was also true. Had Jared told her the truth about Celeste, none of this would have happened. She was angry with him for his stony silence and angry with herself for allowing it to continue. She only had her suspicions to go on, but she was certain that part of Megan's problem stemmed from being deprived of a mother's love. "Can you ever forgive me and be friends again?"

Still the child refused to respond, and Alissa's heart seemed to rend in two. "Sweet child," she breathed, her hand lifting to smooth Megan's tumbled hair from her brow, "there's so much sadness in you. If it were in my power, I'd take all your pain into myself, so you'd never have to suffer it again."

Megan blinked; her eyes searched Alissa's for a long, endless moment. Her own gaze never faltered as her heart beseeched the child to believe her, to believe she was her friend. Then, as she watched, tears formed in Megan's huge green eyes; they flooded and spilled over the rims.

Alissa pulled the sobbing child to her breast and soothed her with soft, gentle words. Her own heart ached with overwhelming sorrow as she began absorbing the small girl's pain. After a while, Megan quieted, and Alissa found the lace-trimmed handkerchief, tucked at her wrist, and dried Megan's eyes.

Taking the cloth, Megan blotted Alissa's face. Not until

then did Alissa realize she'd shared in the tears. But, when Megan pulled the handkerchief away, she frowned. Her small hand reached toward Alissa's face; her finger trailed lightly beneath Alissa's eye.

A grayish mark stained the once white handkerchief, and Alissa realized her makeup had smeared. Seeing the child's quizzical look, she said, "Just as you have secrets, so do I, Megan. One day we'll share them with each other."

Megan vigorously shook her head; fear etched her face.

"We'll share them when we're ready," Alissa said softly, "and not before."

Again, Megan studied Alissa's eyes, then nodded slowly. In that moment, both woman and child felt an instant bonding, and Alissa thought, if it had not been for the doll, she might never have been able to gain Megan's trust. Although tenuous, at least it now existed. Perhaps she should thank Patricia.

Never! she vowed in silent anger, knowing that if she hadn't found Megan in time, the child could have set herself afire, her silent screams gone unheeded. And all because of the redhead's interference—the presentation of the doll in particular. Patricia was a fool! Alissa raved silently. An empty-headed fool!

Feeling the touch of Megan's hand on her arm, she quickly masked her anger. "Let's say we return to Hawkstone before we're missed." Megan seemed hesitant, then Alissa noticed her concentration drop to the dusty floor, and she understood why. "What transpired in the ruins will be our secret. Your father and Aunt Patricia will never know about the doll. Agreed?"

Megan gazed up at Alissa, her eyes burdened with guilt.

"Are you afraid you'd be lying by not admitting what happened?" Seeing Megan's nod, she smiled gently. "If a person were to ask you a direct question and you were to answer no, with a shake of your head, when you should have said yes with a nod, that's a lie," she explained, having become an expert on the subject of late. "But if no one asks, you have not lied, because there is no answer until such time when they do."

Megan frowned and shook her head in disagreement.

"I see. Your father has taught you, if you've done something you shouldn't, then you are to confess it before you're found out, right?"

Megan nodded.

"Actually, your father is correct. An honest person always admits when he or she is wrong. But in this case, if we were to tell your father about the doll, I think he'd be very hurt. And he'd be very angry at your Aunt Patricia. She's the one who gave you the doll, and your father wasn't pleased she had." She noted Megan's questioning look. "Let's just say he knew the doll would bring you pain, not joy. And when you are unhappy, he is unhappy, as well. If he should ever ask about the doll, we'll tell him. But right now, I think it's best we wait until your Aunt Patricia leaves."

A small smile cracked Megan's face, the first Alissa had ever seen. Then the child jumped to her feet and swatted at her bottom.

Confused, Alissa gazed at her for a moment, then she laughed aloud. "No, Megan. If we were to tell him today, your father would not spank your Aunt Patricia. Although she deserves a good thrashing, she's a grown woman, and your father is too much the gentleman to do such a thing." Then Alissa doubted her words, for if Jared knew what had happened, he'd probably strangle the woman. "It simply wouldn't be proper," she finished.

Megan looked saddened by the news, and Alissa reassured her, "Someday your aunt will receive her due, but I don't think she really knew her gift would make you unhappy. She had hoped to give you a remembrance of your moth—" Suddenly the light drained from Megan's eyes. "I'm famished," Alissa said, quickly changing the subject. "Let's hurry back to Hawkstone and raid the kitchens."

Megan agreed, and they both stood. "You'll have to lead the way," Alissa said when they reached the door. "I must admit, I'm lost."

Megan took Alissa's hand, and the two started across the clearing, when the child suddenly broke into a skip. Laughing aloud, the musical sound of her voice rising into the air, Alissa joined in the romp. It was the first time since she'd left London that she truly felt happy!

* * *

A short distance from the cottage, at Hawkstone's northern boundary, a tall, muscular man sat astride his horse, his blue eyes surveying the woman and the small girl at play. A warm breeze ruffled his thick auburn hair, his white muslin shirt pasting itself to his broad chest; a frown etched his brow. When the pair disappeared into the thicket, he turned his horse and slowly headed up the hillside, pondering the graceful agility with which the woman moved.

"She's too damned young," Ian Sinclair mumbled aloud, then wondered if the local gossip had been correct. "Whoever she is, Woden," he remarked to his stallion, "she's *not* Agatha Pembroke."

The beast snorted in reply, its large head jerking against the bit, and Ian Sinclair gave him his head as the two raced homeward toward Falcon's Gate.

Having procured a snack for Megan, then repaired her makeup, Alissa headed down the hallway toward the alcove. Somewhere along the line, she'd lost her hairnet, but she was too angry to care. She hated the thing anyway.

As Alissa set her foot on the first-floor landing, Mr. Stanley had the sudden misfortune to meet up with her as he came up from the wine cellars. "Begs yer pardon, miss," he said, after he'd stopped short, avoiding a collision.

"Where's Mr. Braxton?" Alissa asked curtly.

Taken aback, he blinked twice. "Why, uh, he be in his office with Mr. Robert. I was just takin' 'em some brandy."

Alissa snatched the bottle from under Mr. Stanley's arm. "Don't bother. I'll take it to him myself." Then she turned on her heel and headed for Jared's office.

Wearing a perplexed frown, Mr. Stanley stared after her, the necks of the two wine bottles gripped tightly in his hands. Then he quickly marched into the kitchen and set the bottles on the table. "I'll be in cleanin' the silver," he announced, and cook dropped her jaw in surprise.

"Ye ain't never done it afore," the plump, white-haired woman said, "so why ye doin' it now?"

"Never ye mind," he retorted, as he snatched a glass from the oak sideboard. "And don't ye bother me none." Then he slipped into the small room, shut the door, and locked it.

A thump sounded on the wood. "Ye might do a better job of it, if ye'd take a lamp in there so ye could see."

"Hush yer lip," Mr. Stanley snapped, feeling his way along the cupboards. When he reached the corner, he squeezed into it and placed the glass, rim first, to the wall, his ear butting against its base.

Two raps sounded on the office door, and Alissa walked into the room without Jared's invitation.

Surprised, the master of Hawkstone leaned back in his chair and placed the top end of his steel-point pen between his teeth. He watched as she hefted the brandy bottle in one hand and immediately decided, if he were to speak too soon, she'd most likely lob it at his head.

He'd assumed correctly. As Alissa glared at him, the desire grew stronger to bounce the bottle off his skull, and she valiantly fought the urge to do so with every ounce of her might. Angry that he'd allowed his flighty sister-in-law to disrupt the serenity at Hawkstone, she was even more furious that he'd done nothing to stop her. Consequently Megan had been the one to suffer!

"Robert, Miss Pembroke and I have some business to discuss," Jared said, his eyes still appraising the woman. "If you'll excuse us, please."

"Certainly." Robert placed the file, which had hung in midair since her entry, back onto Jared's desk. "Some fresh air will do me good. I'll be in the gardens."

Jared waited until Robert had left, then said, "I take it you're upset about something."

"Upset?" she asked, sarcastically, the bottle rising and falling in her hand once more. "Why, Mr. Braxton, whatever gave you such an idea?"

"That particular brandy is worth more than a full month's salary for most. Take care you don't drop it." Then, amazed, he watched as she practically slammed the bottle onto his desk. "I suppose if I were to offer you a glass, you'd refuse?"

"Correct, as always," she replied uncivilly. When he tossed aside his pen and reached for the brandy to top off his own glass, she snapped, "You drink too much!"

Jared eyed her. Although she sounded like his Miss

Pembroke, spouting her words of abstinence, she certainly didn't act like the same woman. Something was amiss, for the fire in her eyes transcended any anger—no, fury!—he'd ever seen.

"Agreed," he stated, placing the bottle to the side. "Now, if you'd calm yourself, I'd be most happy to listen to whatever it is that has made you storm my office and disrupt my business." Jared pointed to the chair standing opposite his desk. "Sit, please."

"I'll stand."

"I said *sit!*"

Alissa suddenly lost her bravado; her anger subsided, for she knew Jared was the more volatile of the two.

When she was seated, he asked, "How may I be of help?"

"I want a place—a private place—where I might be alone with Megan."

"Is this house too small for your needs?"

"The size of this house has nothing to do with my needs," she countered. "I need privacy."

"There are locks on all the doors, Miss Pembroke. I would think—"

"Locks aren't good enough, Mr. Braxton," she interrupted. "I want a place away from the main house and all the interference within."

"If you are referring to Patricia, she and Robert will be gone on the morrow."

"I'm happy to hear it," Alissa responded, "but that's still not good enough."

"Do you want me to boot her out today?" Jared asked drolly, his brow arching.

"Would you?"

Jared chuckled. "In truth, I've been tempted to do so on more than one occasion these past few days. However, propriety does not allow such treatment of relatives, no matter how objectionable their presence might be."

"I understand your position, Mr. Braxton," she said, deciding against informing Jared of the chaos the woman had caused. "Yet, when Miss Southworth has gone, the problem will still remain."

"And what exactly is the problem, Miss Pembroke?" he questioned as he leaned back in his chair, steepling his fingers.

"Mr. Braxton, if Megan were given a change of scenery during the day, a private place where she and I could be completely alone, I'm certain her progress will move much more quickly."

"And, if I deny your request?"

"Then I will demand otherwise."

"Or what, Miss Pembroke?"

"Or I shall leave." She'd said the words before she'd realized their import. Cautiously, she watched for his reaction.

Shuttered eyes stared back at her. "Rarely do I allow such a threat to be made without acting upon it. And never do I allow a woman the opportunity to misuse her words in hopes I might rescind my position. Such feminine wiles are useless where I'm concerned. Experience has taught me long ago not to play the game. I will not play it now, Miss Pembroke. Now that you've been warned, are you still of the same mind?"

Her gaze locked with Jared's, Alissa wondered if Celeste had used such tactics to get her way. If so, perhaps as time went on, Jared had become deaf to them, not only closing his ears but his heart, as well. If Celeste were anything like Patricia, she could understand his ultimate distaste.

"Miss Pembroke," Jared said, interrupting her thoughts, "should I take you at your word?"

Alissa reflected a moment. "Mr. Braxton, I have become very fond of Megan and would hate to leave Hawkstone, but I fear I cannot help her unless I'm given a place where we will not be disturbed. I do not ask for myself, but for Megan."

"And if I don't, will you leave?"

"I will," she answered, knowing there was no point in staying. Still, she was utterly terrified of what might await her outside the walls of Hawkstone.

Jared eyed her. She'd made his decision easier. Suddenly he felt an odd twist somewhere deep inside. He'd come to admire this woman. In fact, he'd grown to like her. Probably because she'd placed no demands on him as a man. No demands whatsoever, except when it came to Megan. And, of course, when he drank too much, a difficulty acquired only of late.

Yes, he liked her, liked her wit, liked her ability to excite his mind. *And his body,* he admitted wryly, as his gaze ran over her face, then up to her uncovered hair, surprised he'd just noticed it. Was it a trick of light? Or were his eyes merely tired from his incessant viewing of the fine print in the ledgers? Whichever, at the moment, she appeared . . . attractive?

Jared closed his eyes and opened them slowly. The same. Attractive . . . almost pretty. Suddenly he decided it was time to visit Sara Longworthy, one of his former mistresses, to renew his acquaintance.

"Mr. Braxton," Alissa said softly, breaking his reverie. "Have you made your decision?"

"I have," Jared replied, and Alissa unconsciously edged forward in her seat, holding her breath, for she didn't want to leave Hawkstone. "Your request is granted."

Alissa sighed. "Thank you."

"Where do you—"

"I did some exploring today, while the house was quiet," she interrupted, "and I came upon a small cottage, north of here."

"It's the old gameskeeper's cottage. He's since passed away."

"May I also have a cart and pony?"

"If you do not wish to trek the mile plus each way, then yes you may. I'll have Mr. Stanley and some of my staff clean the place and make the necessary repairs. It should be ready within the week."

"Thank you, Mr. Braxton." She rose and went to the door.

"Miss Pembroke," he called, and she turned toward him. "Since I granted your request, I have one of my own." Seeing her raised brow, he finished, "Never do I want to see your head covered with that ridiculous hairnet again!"

"As you wish." She disappeared into the hallway.

Jared stared at the door. Suddenly, something else hit him. If the woman had such a weak heart, how in blazes did she find the cottage in the first place, much less return? Steepling his fingers again, he pondered the thought, then decided to keep a secret eye on Miss Pembroke. After all, appearances were, at times, deceiving.

CHAPTER

Ten

"It sure be a nice day fer a picnic," Mr. Stanley commented, hitching the sturdy pony to the cart.

"Indeed, sir," Alissa replied, a smile on her lips. "It's truly a glorious day." Standing by the stables, golden sunshine streaming down on her from a cloudless sky, she waited for Megan to join her with their picnic lunch. "Would you care to join us?" she asked as an afterthought. "I'm certain there will be enough food for one more."

"Why, thank ye fer the invite, miss," he replied with a wide grin and a bob of his balding head, "but I got work to be doin'. Might be acceptin' if ye asks me in the future, though." He straightened the harness. "If ye don't mind me sayin' so, yer and Megan's goin' to the cottage be a right smart idea. Thought ye handled the askin' 'bout it real good. Aye, real good."

"Oh?" Alissa turned a curious eye to the man. "And how is it, Mr. Stanley, you are able to form such an opinion? I thought Mr. Braxton and I were alone when we discussed it. Perchance, sir, do the walls have ears?"

Mr. Stanley twitched his nose, then sniffed. "Ain't seen none a-growin' on 'em," he said, eyes blinking rapidly. "O' course, that ain't to say otherwise, me eyes gettin' a bit blurred o' late. With a house as old as this one be"— he jerked his head toward the stone structure and shrugged

127

—"anythin's possible." Then he quickly rambled on. "Been seein' a change in the little lass, I has. Aye, she seems a might happier. 'Spects it be yer doin', miss."

"Why, thank you, Mr. Stanley. I do hope Megan is breaking free of what troubles her."

"Ye don't have to thanks me. All us here is the ones who should be a thankin' ye." He stopped his work for a moment. "Aye, smart man, his lo . . . uh, Mr. Braxton be, a-gettin' rid o' Miss Patricia and lettin' ye start to fix up the cottage, all in the same day."

"Smart man, indeed," Alissa agreed, remembering how Jared had pointedly denied Patricia's request to stay on at Hawkstone after Robert's work was finished. She'd wheedled and pouted and simpered prettily, but to no avail. And when Miss Southworth, with her volumes of luggage, and Robert, with his modest bag, had finally departed, the whole of Hawkstone seemed to breathe a unified sigh of relief. Once the visitors were gone, as promised, Jared had selected a half-dozen servants, and under Alissa's direction, the cottage was refurbished in less than a week, and during the past two, she and Megan had made daily use of it.

"Aye, he is at that," Mr. Stanley said. "Sometimes it takes a bit o' proddin', but 'ventually he sees—" A commotion rose inside the stables, drawing the man's attention. "That mulish crock, if he be mine, I'd have him gelded." He tossed the reins into the cart. "Be right back, miss," he stated, and stomped off to the stable door and down the long line of stalls.

Alissa blushed, for the man's anger was directed at Thor, Jared's stallion. A mare had just come into season, and the stallion, being confined against his will, had set to kicking the boards asunder. Deciding his mission might take some time, she wandered into the carriage house, several yards away.

Coming from the bright sunlight into the dim interior, she waited for her eyes to readjust, then tucked a stray hair into the bun at the nape of her neck. As she strolled past the fleet of carriages and coaches, she inhaled the scent of oils and waxes used to keep the lacquered woods from splitting and rotting. Again, she wondered at her employer's wealth. To purchase and maintain one coach was expensive, she knew, but the upkeep of so many . . . ? How could he possibly afford it?

Then, at the end of the line, she spied a canvas-draped vehicle, set apart from the others. Curious, she crossed the yardage and surveyed it. Certain it was a coach, she caught the edge of the cover, near what she thought was the door, and started lifting it.

Suddenly, a hand slammed against the coach; a startled cry escaped her lips as the canvas ripped from her fingers. Wide-eyed, she watched as Jared settled back against the vehicle. His arms crossing over his chest, an indolent smile split his face. "Have you taken to snooping as a pastime?" he questioned, his lazy green eyes surveying her.

Her mouth agape, Alissa didn't quite know how to answer. "N-no," she stammered finally.

"Then what do you call it?" Jared asked, still lounging against the coach.

"I—I was just admiring your fleet of carriages. This one caught my eye, and out of curiosity, I—"

"Snooping, as I said."

Alissa's lips pressed together in a tight line; she glared at him. Pompous, overbearing jackanapes! she berated him silently. Never mind that he was right! His high-handedness seemed a bit farfetched. In fact, he acted as though he were hiding something. Why else would he have made such an issue of her looking under the cover?

Then she remembered seeing something painted on the door. She'd only managed a glimpse, but she knew it was some sort of design. Considering Jared's odd behavior, it must be of great import, she concluded, her eyes still pitching daggers at him. Then she thought of sneaking back at a later time to discover what the insignia represented. If he believed her a snoop, then she'd honor that label.

"This area is forbidden territory," Jared said, reading her every thought. "Henceforth, you'll keep from the building, unless I give my permission. And, if need be, I'll put a man in here to keep you out."

"What a ridiculous statement," she said, airily. "Why would I want to spend my time in this place?"

"As you have so aptly put it, Miss Pembroke, 'out of curiosity.' But you know what happened to the cat, don't you?" Alissa's eyes widened, and Jared chuckled. "Megan is awaiting you." He straightened and his arms dropped to his sides, his loose-fitting shirt slit open down his chest. "I'd be most happy to escort you out."

His offer sounded more like a mandate, and Alissa dared not disagree. Lifting her skirts, she turned and marched from the carriage house, Jared close on her heels. Stupidly she felt like a stray goose being shooed back to the flock.

Once they reached the cart, Jared hoisted his daughter and the picnic basket inside, then offered Alissa his hand. She looked at it a long moment, remembering vividly the agonizingly sweet emotions that had claimed her the last time she'd placed her hand into his, and decided she couldn't withstand those feelings again. Ignoring him, she climbed into the cart herself.

"I admire a certain amount of independence in a woman," Jared said, handing her the reins, "but in your case, it leans more toward obstinance."

"You may call it what you wish," she replied, haughtily, "but, thus far, it has gotten me along without too much difficulty, and I expect it will continue to do so." Then with a flick of the leads, she set the pony and cart into motion, the large wheel almost rolling over Jared's feet.

Uncurling his toes inside his boots, Jared watched as she guided the pony up the lane toward the cottage. If he didn't have to oversee the mare's breeding, he'd follow and spy upon his daughter and her governess as he'd done several times these past two weeks.

Suddenly her musical laughter burst forth inside his head anew. Her wide smile flashed behind his eyes, and he could almost see the sparkle of merriment in her blue eyes as she danced among the wildflowers, her feet turning rapid circles, his daughter's keeping time. With the vivid scene etched in his mind, he wondered again how the sickly Miss Pembroke could suddenly have transformed herself into the sprightly creature he'd beheld. It was as though she were but a child herself, he thought, then frowned as the memory of her body, moving with gentle grace in the moonlight . . . no, sunlight. . . . Had he actually seen her at all?

An odd sensation stirred deep within him, and he realized he was mixing his dreams with reality—again! It was an agonizing pattern he could not break, always wanting, always desiring, never to be fulfilled. And what in God's name Agatha Pembroke had to do with it, he didn't know!

The sound of wood splintering snapped him from his reverie. "Here, ye dim-witted hack!" Mr. Stanley yelled, his words followed by a curse that fairly vibrated the stable walls. "If ye were a man, I'd turn ye into a eunuch!"

His man seemed in dire need of his assistance, so Jared strode toward the stables. In but a short time, he knew, Thor's torment would be put to an end. Once satiated, the stallion would prance the open pasture, his head held high, his tail arced like a flag. Unfortunately, Jared also knew his own agonies would persist—indefinitely.

"Let's have our picnic," Alissa suggested, removing the puppet from her hand. Megan did the same, then rose and placed the two toys on a shelf, each in its special place.

Having remembered the way Megan had played with the dollhouse, back at Hawkstone, she'd decided to use a set of hand puppets, hoping to draw the child out. Mostly, they played happy games, but upon occasion, Megan would sign to Alissa, "You be the child, and I'll be the mother." What transpired next always upset Alissa, for Megan would reenact the same scenario as she had in the playroom—the mother showing flagrant disregard for her offspring.

However, when Alissa would turn the tables, with herself portraying the mother and Megan the child, Megan would shake her head whenever Alissa showed affection while using the puppet, as if to say, "A mother doesn't act nice." Then Megan would proceed to show Alissa how she should move the figure to make their play more realistic.

Indeed, it was upsetting. But Alissa no longer *wondered* if Megan's play was a figment of her colorful imagination. No, it had become quite apparent that it was based on fact.

"Ready?" Alissa asked, Megan having retrieved the picnic basket from the table. Megan nodded, and they made their way to the small brook, several hundred yards beyond the cottage. After Alissa had spread the blanket, she opened the wicker basket to find fresh fruits, some cheeses, a crusty loaf of bread, and a nice raspberry tart. All that remained was the container of milk which they'd placed in the stream upon their arrival. "Go fetch the milk, will you please?" Alissa asked, taking the tin cups from the basket. "It should be good and cold by now."

Megan did not move, and Alissa looked up to see the child staring at a point beyond the flowing brook. Following the direction of the child's eyes, she noticed a man sitting astride a large, black stallion, just beyond the rock wall marking the boundary of Hawkstone. As he started to dismount, Alissa jumped to her feet and hugged Megan to the folds of her gown.

Broad of shoulder, narrow of hip, the stranger hurdled the wall and strode toward them through the stream, apparently not caring if he ruined his boots, his eyes trained upon both woman and child.

Oddly, Alissa did not feel threatened, but she took a protective stance, nonetheless. Should the man make an unfriendly move, she planned to instruct Megan to run, while she threw herself at him. What good it would do, she couldn't fathom, for he stood several inches over six feet and weighed, to her estimation, a good fifteen stone. He was hard muscle, not an ounce of fat to be seen, and she knew he could easily toss her aside with a simple flick of his wrist. Yet she hoped the fleet-footed Megan would have a sizeable lead, should the man decide to give chase.

Stepping from the trees that edged the brook, ducking the branches as he came, he stopped in the sunlit glade, not more than five yards from them. His blue eyes perused Alissa a long moment, then his gaze switched to the child at her side. "Don't you remember me, Megan?"

His deep voice, gentle as the wind, spanned the distance separating them, and Alissa felt Megan's head shake. Glancing at her, she noticed a quizzical frown on her brow.

"I thought not," the stranger said, and knelt to one knee, so he wouldn't seem so imposing. "If you have no recollection of me, by chance, do you remember a frisky pup named Merlin? I called him that because he'd disappear from my house and run off to visit a little girl who lived on the next lands. He'd be gone days at a time. As I remember it, the little girl would hide him in the stables and sneak food out to him whenever she thought no one was looking. But eventually, she was found out, and Mr. Stanley would leash the vagabond and put him in the cart, along with the little girl, and escort the two to my house, whereupon the little girl would tell me that if I'd been a good master in the first place, Merlin wouldn't have run away to seek attention elsewhere." Then the man whistled. "Merlin, come!"

A shaggy-haired dog bounded the rock wall, then on short legs, splashed through the stream, to rush through the stand of trees and halt at his master's side. With a shake that ran from his black dot of a nose to his stubby tail, he set a spray into the air, and received a curt command for his actions. Sitting on his haunches, his pink tongue lolling, his black eyes hiding under a disorderly thatch of gray and white hair, he whimpered, eager to be on the run again.

"It's been a good two years, but do you remember me now?" the stranger asked.

Before Alissa could stop her, Megan broke and ran into the man's embrace and hugged his neck. Merlin, wanting attention, as well, set up a loud yapping, but dared not break his master's command. Being ignored long enough, the excited bark finally changed pitch and escalated into a forlorn howl that pierced the ears.

Megan slipped from the man's arms and stooped to pet the little dog, then she hugged his neck. His wet tongue flicked over her face, and Megan quickly stood and wiped the kisses away. Then she looked askance at the man.

"You can play," he said, "but don't go beyond our sight. Understood?" Megan nodded, and the man came to his full height and watched as the two romped through the grass. "I apologize for the scare I gave you," he said, turning his attention to Alissa, moving toward her. "I'm Ian Sinclair, Megan's uncle." Noticing Alissa's frown, he corrected, "Actually, I'm her godfather, but she knows me as 'Uncle Ian.'" His eyes studied her again. "And who might you be?"

"Agatha Pembroke," Alissa stated a bit stiffly.

"Oh?" His blue eyes twinkled like sapphires in the bright light. "And who exactly is Agatha Pembroke?"

Alissa surveyed this Ian Sinclair. His auburn hair flashed red in the sunlight; matching eyebrows arched over mischievous long-lashed eyes. A slightly hawked nose sat above nicely shaped lips which were now split into a wide grin, exposing strong white teeth. His dress was as casual as

Jared's: white muslin shirt, topping buckskin breeches, tucked into highly polished, black leather boots. Perhaps all men dressed this way in Scotland, she thought, then caught the teasing light in his eye again. Straightening her shoulders, she said, "I'm Megan's gov . . . uh, Megan's friend," she stated finally.

Ian's gaze traveled the length of her, making Alissa feel highly uncomfortable. "Indeed," he said, his grin widening, "you might be at that." Then he strode off toward Megan and Merlin to join in their play.

Alissa stared after the tall man. What had he meant by his statement? she wondered, knowing he'd been amused by her. She couldn't imagine why—perhaps there was a spot on her nose, she thought self-consciously. All the better if there was, for it would reinforce her disguise. But, as she thought on it, she realized his manner leaned toward a complacent sort of ridicule, more teasing than taunting.

As she saw him give his full attention to Megan, Alissa felt her initial reserve dissolve. Indeed, he was no threat, she decided, watching as he stretched his finger to a blade of grass, allowing a woolly caterpillar to inch its tanned length. His deep laughter rang out as he insisted the multilegged creature's feet were tickling him. At first, Megan was hesitant about touching the crawly thing, but then, with Ian's encouragement, she took it on her finger. Her eyes brightened, and a wide smile slashed her face, then she turned and ran, Merlin quick at her heels, wanting to share her discovery with Alissa.

Ian followed at a slower pace, his eyes studying the woman, her finger lightly running along the soft bristles along the caterpillar's back, as she shared in his godchild's excitement. Agatha Pembroke she was not! He'd met the woman himself and had been instrumental in making certain that Jared was aware of her, relaying the knowledge through a mutual friend. At first he'd thought to expose the imposter, but the reports coming from Hawkstone, through Mary, who was betrothed to his trusted footman, Ned, were excellent. Megan was improving. For now, he'd keep his counsel and see how things progressed.

"Would you like to join us and share our fare?" Alissa

asked, breaking Ian's train of thought. "We have plenty, and you are most welcome."

"I beg your forgiveness, but I must be on my way," Ian replied graciously, then he saw Megan's disappointment. "Were it not for my having another commitment, I would stay. However, if you were to ask the same of me tomorrow, my answer would be a definite yes."

Megan tugged at Alissa's skirt, her eyes questioning, hopefully. "I see nothing wrong in repeating a picnic on the morrow," Alissa told the child. "And, yes, we may invite Mr. Sinclair to be our guest," she agreed, her motives not entirely unselfish. With luck, she hoped that future meetings with the man might supply the bits of information needed to fill in the missing pieces of the past, especially about Megan's mother. No one at Hawkstone was willing to speak of her; perhaps Ian Sinclair would. "I extend our welcome for tomorrow, Mr. Sinclair."

"I will be here at noon," Ian said cordially. "And, of course, Merlin, too," he added, noticing Megan's troubled frown. "Until then, I bid you a good day, Miss Pembroke." He bowed, his twinkling blue eyes again showing that certain mischievous light, then he hugged his godchild. "Come, Merlin," he said, then the two forded the small stream and hopped the wall. After Ian had mounted his horse, he threw a salute, then rode up the hillside, disappearing into the trees.

With their picnic lunch finished, the remains packed away, Alissa and Megan headed back to the cottage. The rest of the afternoon was filled with Megan learning her letters, a bit of simple mathematics, Alissa's reading an exciting fairy tale about a handsome prince who had to rescue his beautiful princess bride from the clutches of an evil sorcerer.

She also helped Megan practice making sounds. Upon finding the child that first time in the cottage and hearing her lamenting song, Alissa knew there was nothing wrong with the child's vocal cords. By placing Megan's hand against her throat, then making a humming sound so Megan could feel it, Alissa hoped the child could repeat the same vibration and strengthen her unused voice. More often than not, when Alissa would lightly place her fingers on Megan's throat, smiling her encouragement, no sound would come forth and tears of frustration would form in the girl's eyes, as they had today.

Not wanting to push it, Alissa suggested they do a stint of pantomime, which she'd taught Megan, and participated in herself, to show the child that her silence could be an art form in itself.

That night, as Alissa made her daily report to the ever imposing Jared, her nerves ajangle as always, she intentionally withheld the information about Ian Sinclair. Afterward, she decided that perhaps she should not have, but the choice had been made with Megan's welfare solely in mind.

"Ian," Alissa said as the two watched Megan and Merlin at play after one of their picnics, which had become a daily routine, "if you are Megan's godfather, why is it you never visit Hawkstone?"

Then she watched as Ian—a handsome man, but to her eye, not as exceptional as Jared—turned his head and stared off into the distance, his arm resting on his upraised knee. He seemed troubled, and she suddenly wished she hadn't asked the question, but it was something that had plagued her since they'd first met, two weeks ago.

"It's by mutual agreement, Jared's and mine, that I stay away," he finally answered.

"I—I don't understand."

Ian faced Alissa. "Our friendship is rather strained at the moment." He looked off into the distance again, falling silent.

"But surely, if you were such good friends—"

"Perhaps, in the future, I'll share our story with you," he said, then turned his mischievous eyes toward her. "Speaking of stories, is there one you'd like to share?"

"W-what do you mean?" Alissa asked in a rush, suddenly wary. She hoped he was teasing her again, as he always did. Yet, she feared she'd somehow awakened his suspicions. "W-why do you ask?"

"Let's just say, sometimes things are not what they appear to be. Are they, Miss Pembroke?" Alissa had no answer, and Ian hadn't really expected one. Stretching out, full-length, on the blanket, he linked his hands behind his head and stared up at the flotilla of white clouds sailing across a clear blue sky. "You are good for Megan," he stated. "She needs a special person like you."

"I'm not certain I can break her bonds of silence, Ian," Alissa stated truthfully as she viewed the little girl running through the field, Merlin by her side. "Sometimes, it seems an impossible task."

"It will take time. You must not give up."

"I'm not a quitter."

"No, you are not."

Alissa's gaze shifted to the man. "Sometimes, I feel there's more to her silence than simply the fire and her mother's death. Certainly that's part of it, but I have this feeling the crux of it goes much, much deeper."

"You may be right."

"Do you know something?" she asked in an anxious voice. "Please, Ian, if you do, share it with me."

"The man to answer your questions is Jared."

Alissa turned troubled eyes toward the ground. "He won't speak of that night . . . or of his wife."

"Then he is a fool to withhold the story, especially if it were to help his daughter."

"What should I do?"

"Ask him."

Alissa's eyes widened. Apparently, Ian was serious. She could just picture herself confronting Jared, yet another time. "Pardon me," she would say, "but I must know every detail of your life with your late wife—in particular, the night she died. And by the way, did you, perchance, murder her, like the gossips say?"

"Miss Pembroke . . . Agatha."

The sound of her assumed name broke through Alissa's thoughts, and she noticed Ian had come to lean on his elbow, facing her, his long legs shooting well off the blanket.

"That name does not suit you," he said, with a smile. "But it will have to do." For now, he thought.

Alissa frowned; a cautious look entered her eye. "What are you saying?"

Ian ignored her question, and with a sudden serious light in his eye, he said, "Jared is the only one who really knows the events of that night . . . at least, he's the only one who can *tell* you what happened." He rose to his feet, and Alissa gazed up at him. "Find the courage to ask him, and you may discover the key to unlock Megan's silence."

Her gaze fell from his. "I have no courage, Ian."

"You have much more than you know," he stated, then whistled for Merlin. "We must be on our way."

The shaggy pup came, full-speed, across the clearing and jumped into Alissa's lap. With a shriek, she fought to keep his licking tongue away from her face and neck. Thankfully, she succeeded.

"Heel," Ian commanded, and the pup, tail tucked, sidled up to his master's side. Megan joined the three, and Ian hunkered down. "I'll not be seeing you for a while," he told her. "I've business in Edinburgh, and then I'll be headed to London and the south of England. It will be a fortnight before I return to Falcon's Gate. I will think of you daily." Megan hugged his neck, and Ian placed a gentle kiss on her forehead. "Merlin and I will see you as soon as I return." He straightened and watched as Megan hugged her furry friend.

"We'll miss seeing you," Alissa said, coming to her feet. Indeed, she would, for he was the one true friend she'd made in Scotland. As she viewed Ian, she wondered why she compared all men to Jared. She didn't find Ian lacking, but neither did he have that special quality that made her heart skip in an odd beat, her breath catch in her chest. And she was angry with herself for allowing Jared to hold such power over her.

"I'll keep an eye out for you at the cottage," Ian said, bidding his farewell.

The two watched as man and dog crossed the stream. Ian mounted his horse and rode up the hill, out of sight. "He'll be back soon," Alissa said by way of reassurance to Megan. Then she realized the words had been meant for herself, as well.

CHAPTER
Eleven

While his hand rubbed the nape of his neck, Jared paced his office floor, his boots marring the polished oak surface. He stopped by the window to gaze in the direction of the cottage, but could not see it through the wall of shielding trees. Then, for the third time in less than five minutes, he glanced at the clock.

His daughter and her governess were nearly an hour overdue. True, their tardiness might have resulted from the late spring thunderstorm that had rolled through the valley earlier, the remnants of its passing still flashing in the distant sky. Perhaps they were on their way now, he conceded, but it gave him little peace of mind.

Since the cart traveled a dirt lane, a wheel might have easily mired itself in the mud. Or a rotten limb might have fallen, blocking their path. Lightning flashed on the horizon, and another scenario suddenly leapt into Jared's overactive mind to paint a horrifyingly vivid picture. If the governess had tried to return to the main house before the storm hit, then . . . Distant lightning flashed again, and he envisioned the bolt of fire crashing into a tree, splintering it, sending its top onto the cart.

He shook the ghastly thought from his head. Surely, she wouldn't have been foolish enough to leave the safety of the cottage. Yes, she would! For she was stubborn, obstinate—

mulish, to be precise! And if she thought she could make the mile-plus trek, beating the storm, she would have set off for the main house, Megan at her side.

Not able to withstand the suspense a moment longer, Jared strode to the door and jerked it open to reveal a startled Mr. Stanley, his fist raised, ready to pound the wood. "Have they returned?" Jared asked, anxiously.

"Sorry, ain't seen 'em."

"Send down to the stables. Have Thor saddled."

"The tar-headed knave be out front, awaitin' ye," he said with a scowl, rubbing his forearm where he'd taken a nasty nip from the stallion. The mark had healed in the two and a half weeks since its occurrence, but Mr. Stanley's temper over the episode had not. "He be muzzled, too!"

Jared smiled, patting the man's shoulder. "Thanks, my friend," he said, routing himself toward the front entry.

The burlap pulled from Thor's muzzle, the stallion tossed his head, and Jared sprang to his back and set the large horse into a full gallop toward the cottage.

Skirting the deserted lane, the pair traveled the woods, then topped the knoll to the clearing. The unhitched cart stood by the small lean-to, the pony sheltered inside. Seeing it, Jared felt the tension drain from his body and wondered why he had doubted the governess's intelligence. Any fool would have known she'd have waited out the storm, where she'd be safe and dry. No doubt, he decided, chuckling to himself, she was entertaining Megan with a dull read from one of his daughter's primers.

As he quietly guided Thor around the edge of the glade, following the line of trees, the wind caught the branches, sending a spray of water down upon them; Thor pranced nervously from the sudden shower. "Easy, boy," Jared crooned, patting the stallion's sinewy neck, then he dismounted and led Thor toward the cottage. Stopping thirty yards away, he draped the reins around a small bush, giving the stallion enough lead to graze, and set off alone.

With other matters claiming his attention, it had been nearly three weeks since he'd observed his daughter and her governess together. Knowing they were safe, lamps lit within the cottage to chase away the day's gloom, he decided to spy on the two. Under normal circumstances, he'd never have stooped to such skulduggery, but there was nothing one might consider the least bit normal about the perplexing Miss Pembroke.

In his presence, she would stiffen, her prudishness and cool reserve worn like a shield. But, when she believed herself away from his sight, she became an entirely different woman—lively, high-spirited—and her metamorphosis completely confused him.

On quiet feet, he crept toward an opened window, shadowed by an unpruned lilac. Suddenly, he stopped. A lilting voice, clear and true, drifted from the cottage, and an odd sensation of *déjà vu* spun through his head.

Impossible, he told himself, yet his ears said otherwise. And secretly he took in the sight.

An enthralled Megan sat upon a low stool, watching intently as Alissa reclined along the aged planks of the cottage floor. Pretending to rise from a night's sleep, she recited from memory: "'Help me, Lysander, help me! Do thy best to pluck this crawling serpent from my breast! Ay me, for pity! What a dream was here! Lysander, look how I do quake with fear. Methought a serpent eat my heart away, and you sat smiling at his cruel prey. . . .'"

Instantly Jared stumbled back, his eyes staring blankly. That long-ago April night, when he'd first seen his *Hermia* at Covent Garden, had somehow superimposed itself over this mid-June afternoon, the young actress and his daughter's governess becoming one and the same. Every graceful movement of her body, every word that escaped her lips was the same. The very same!

Confused, he silently turned and wandered toward Thor, his mind replaying the scene in the cottage, over and over again. Slowly he mounted the stallion and headed for home at a steady pace. Suddenly something clicked inside his head. His green eyes flashed in anger, and he pressed his knees into Thor's sides; the stallion tore into a gallop.

Crashing hooves hit the stone drive, and Jared jerked the reins, pulling Thor to a thundering stop. The front door swung open, and a concerned Mr. Stanley rushed down the stone steps. "Did ye find 'em?" he asked.

"Yes," Jared hissed, and Mr. Stanley instantly retreated a step to eye his employer warily. "Tend to Thor," he ordered

of the lathered stallion, then his boots crunched in the loose stones. Hard feet hit the steps with an angry tread, then the door banged shut.

"What's got him in such a stew?" Mr. Stanley frowned at the door, then felt a nip at his backside. "Here, ye pesky nag!" he yelled, swatting at Thor. "Ye behave, or I'll takes ye into town and have ye stuffed into a glue pot!" He led the horse off toward the stables, intermittently grumbling at the stallion, while scratching at his head, pondering his master's unexplained fit of temper.

Jared bounded up the last dozen steps, three at a time, and headed down the corridor to the west wing and *Miss Pembroke's* quarters. He found the door unlocked, which saved him the bother of kicking it down.

The door closed with a thump, and he turned the key. As he glanced around the room, he noted it was all neat and tidy, just like the woman herself. Then he headed toward the bureau, deciding, if he were right, and he was certain he was, her belongings would hold the truth.

Several tins of makeup sat in the vanity drawer, but it wasn't enough to prove his theory correct, so he moved to the armoire. Her drab dresses, two brown muslins and a gray wool, framed by threadbare petticoats, a high-necked nightgown, and a shabby cotton wrapper, plus her wool cloak, hung in the forefront of the wardrobe. He curled his lip at the lot, then shoved the articles aside to reveal a black velvet wrap and two fashionable dresses, hidden at the back of the closet. He fingered the blue silk material of one and smiled to himself, his thoughts growing darker and darker as the seconds passed. Quickly repositioning the clothing, he searched the shelves.

At the very bottom, pushed well out of sight, Jared found an old, worn petticoat, rolled into a bundle, a stack of journals beneath it. Scraping the shelf clean, he hunkered back on his haunches and untied the ends. Inside, he found his proof. "Whoever she is," he growled viciously, deciding at that moment her name was treachery, "she's played me for a fool! A goddamned fool!"

Again, his cold, furious gaze ran over the scattered articles, noting his letters to the real Miss Pembroke, a jewel case, Rede's *Road to the Stage*—a page tagged, explaining how an actor could assume the look of illness—a pair of kid slippers, a half-dozen letters from one Eudora Binnington, and a gossamer dress, Grecian in style, a costume . . . *her costume!*

Disgusted, he tossed the thing to the carpet and snatched up Mrs. Binnington's letters and began to read. A newspaper clipping fell from one, and he scanned it. *Alissa Ashford! Nineteen! Actress! Covent Garden! Attempted murder! Charles Rhodes, Viscount Rothhamford!*

That odious bastard? Jared thought, knowing the coward's reputation, well. An acquaintance, Matthew Etherton, of London, had challenged the man to a duel about five years ago. If he remembered correctly, Etherton's sister had been accosted by Rothhamford. In the end, Rothhamford never showed, having taken a sudden, extended trip to the Continent, and Etherton never had the satisfaction of drawing blood. Jared had heard, even to this very day, Rothhamford skirted any area Etherton frequented.

Examining the costume, he discovered the torn bodice. Instant anger raged through him. But why? Although he knew Rothhamford was a blackguard, it was Alissa Ashford who had duped him! He'd been harboring an imposter, a treacherous woman who could very well have injured his daughter's emotions. Megan might never recover! The fact was, he should be summoning the sheriff and see to it that this . . . this *actress* was taken from the premises in chains!

But, oddly, as Jared continued to read Eudora's letters, he began to feel a stirring of pity for the young actress; an empathy for her plight struck a chord somewhere deep inside him. Then, when he'd finished the last of the one-sided correspondence, he was able to piece together the sketchy information and understand how he'd become involved.

The plan, which he assumed had been devised entirely by Eudora Binnington, was an excellent bit of intrigue, quickly pulled together, assisted largely by fate, and of course, the real Miss Pembroke's timely, or untimely, demise, depending on how one looked at it. Fate, indeed! he thought, knowing if he were in a different frame of mind he might applaud the undertaking, for he could not have done as well himself.

But this Alissa Ashford, consummate actress that she was, had not seen fit to confess her deception once she'd escaped England. Instead, she'd continued her farce, knowing full well the import of her charade and the damaging effects it could have caused his daughter.

Megan, he thought, appraising what this might do to her. He pictured his daughter as she sat on the low stool, her eyes aglow with excitement and wonderment, while she watched "Miss Pembroke" act the part of *Hermia.* He could not deny that since her arrival Megan seemed far more communicative and considerably improved. Where once there was a blank stare, laughter now danced in her eyes. Where once she withdrew from a human touch, especially a woman's, now she was the first to reach out, showing no fear of rejection. And, should he decide to expose the young actress and have her arrested, he was certain it would completely destroy his daughter. With her newfound trust in women being irretrievably broken, she would be damaged for life, he knew. For that reason, and that alone, he was unwilling to allow his anger to be the source of his daughter's ruin. He would keep his discovery to himself.

His decision made, he sighed. Since he knew the viscount's reputation personally, he suspected Alissa Ashford had been accused unfairly, hence her deception. Yet, he still wanted his pound of flesh. The young actress wasn't about to get off so easily!

As he replaced the evidence, the jewel case caught his eye, and he peeked inside to find a smattering of worthless gems, mostly paste. Then he opened the white satin box with its embroidered *C;* his eyes widened. "Is she a thief, as well?" Jared wondered aloud, as he perused the sapphire brooch, knowing it was real. Plucking it from its satin bed, he inspected it closely. He found no discernible markings on its solid gold setting, nothing to tell of its ownership. Perhaps a gift from a lover, he thought, then felt an odd sort of rage fill him.

Considering the age of the satin box, he concluded it was a gift given long ago, a keepsake passed from one generation to another, possibly from mother to daughter. Yet, he wondered what the *C* represented. And its worth? He couldn't even fathom that.

There was no time to answer his silent queries, for he had other matters to settle. Tying the petticoat's ends together, he stuffed it back onto the shelf, the journals beneath, making certain nothing appeared to have been disturbed. The armoire closed, he paced the floor, devising a suitable punishment as reward for the little imposter.

After several false starts, the retribution either too severe or too light in nature, Jared paced all the harder, his brow furrowed in thought. Suddenly his shout of laughter filled the air. "Oh, my dear, prim and proper 'Miss Pembroke,'" he said, his tone smug, his green eyes sparkling with mischief. "I promise, you shall experience a night you'll never forget. Never!"

Then Jared quit the room.

Not more than fifteen minutes later, Alissa entered her bedroom and found a note tucked under the door. Opening the handsome piece of stationery, she read: *Miss Pembroke, I request we might forgo our usual seven o'clock meeting. Unfortunately, other matters will claim my attention at that time. However, I hope you will join me in the dining room at precisely eight-thirty. Your most obedient servant, J.*

Alissa's eyes beheld the boldly scrawled initial, her brow furrowing, and she wondered why he'd signed it as such and not Mr. Braxton. *J* seemed extremely intimate, more like something a husband or . . . a *lover* might use? Perhaps, his casual signature was simply part of his rebellious nature, his dislike of conformity. Then with a sigh she placed the note on her dressing table. At least she would have time for a short rest before their appointed meeting in the dining room. Kicking off her shoes, she settled upon the bed.

At half past eight, Alissa stood just outside the doors leading into the dining room and smoothed the skirt of Agatha's best gown, a bark-colored brown muslin. Weary of the plainness of her attire, she'd added a lace collar to the simple rounded neckline. It did little for the dress, but it made her feel a bit more feminine, which was exactly what she needed tonight, for her spirits were low.

Her hair pulled severely into its usual unstylish knot, the hollows of her cheeks and the delicate tissue beneath her large blue eyes darkened with makeup, her face and lashes powdered, she was ready for her nightly performance. Another stilted execution of a badly written play, she thought, tired of her impersonation. Yet, she knew there was little she could do, except continue the charade.

"You look quite lovely this evening," Jared said in a low, mellow voice, startling Alissa. Having purposely come up from behind her on silent feet, he reached around her, his arm brushing her shoulder as he turned the door handle. "May I have the pleasure of escorting you?"

Alissa gazed at him a long moment, noting his formal dress. His black silk jacket molded itself to his muscular shoulders, not an ounce of padding beneath. His white silk cravat, tied to perfection, was studded with a ruby. The silver waistcoat hugged his taut stomach; he did not wear a corset, as did many of his gender, she knew. Black trousers encased his long, sinewy legs to top a pair of polished half boots, made of the finest leather.

Her eyes traveled upward. His shiny hair lay in thick waves, the back caressing his collar; a lock curled over his forehead. His gaze held a lazy, seductive quality; a warm smile curved his lips. Suddenly his vital masculinity overpowered her, and as a woman, Alissa felt like a dowdy little frump.

"I await your hand, Miss Pembroke," Jared said, his arm poised, and Alissa nervously placed her fingers along his forearm. He led her to her chair, directly to the right of his own. "I've arranged for a buffet, so we might have more privacy," he said, his face close to her ear. "I hope it will meet with your approval."

As Jared's clean breath fanned her face, Alissa felt an odd sensation tickle down her spine, its warmth spreading to her limbs. "I—I have no objections," she said in a rush.

"Excellent," he drawled smoothly. "When it is time, it will be my pleasure to serve you."

"Where is Megan?" Alissa asked, just now remembering the child. She'd not found her in her room, and the girl was certainly not in the dining room. Suddenly Alissa felt highly uncomfortable being alone with Jared.

"She's already eaten and is with Mary," he said, moving to his own chair, his hand brushing Alissa's shoulder as it trailed along the back of her chair. She stiffened, visibly, but Jared paid it no heed. "First, we shall have some wine." Her mouth opened in protest, but he waved her off. "Mr. Stanley, if you will?"

The dubious butler carried the uncorked bottle to the table, his eyes shifting from his employer to the governess and back again. It had been a long time since he'd served a "private" supper in this room, the last one being to one of the master's mistresses. The wine poured, he turned a curious eye to his employer, waiting for the words that would confirm his suspicions.

"Thank you, Mr. Stanley," Jared said. "You may leave us now . . . and close the doors, please."

That's 'em, he thought. Then, with his eyes trained on Alissa, he said, "Be outside, miss, if ye needs me."

She gazed after the wiry little man as he stomped to the door. She wondered if he was trying to relay a message, then watched the panels shut with a decided thump.

"Miss Pembroke," Jared addressed her, and she turned to see him holding his wine glass. "If you would, please"—he motioned to her own glass—"I'd like to salute a lovely lady who's done so much for my daughter and myself."

"Mr. Braxton, I—"

"Please, Miss Pembroke. One sip won't harm you."

Alissa looked at the golden liquid. If she picked up the glass, as she was tempted to do, she'd be acting out of character. But it had been so long since she'd tasted a good wine, not that she'd imbibed frequently as herself, but an occasional glass had been a pleasure she'd enjoyed.

"I won't press you, if you feel it's against your nature," Jared said, softly, his gaze holding hers, "but I promise you'll feel no ill effects from one small sip."

Oh, tosh, she thought, knowing he was right. But it had been the soothing quality of his voice, plus the gentle light in his eyes that had actually convinced her. They had acted like a magnet, drawing her, tempting her. She lifted the glass and held it toward his.

Jared smiled lazily. "To an exceptional woman. May she remember this night always." Leaning toward her, he clinked his glass to hers and drank from the fluted vessel.

After she'd taken a small sip, Alissa couldn't decide if it

was the wine or if her chair had always been this close to Jared's. "I—I," she stammered, then she felt the brush of his leg against her skirt. "Mr. Braxton—"

"Jared."

Alissa stared at him, then blinked. "Mr. Braxton—"

"Jared," he insisted, smiling. "What is it?"

Alissa's mind raced. Not knowing what was wrong with the man, she thought he seemed . . . odd. Again she felt the caress of his leg against hers and jumped. Unthinkingly, she gulped from her glass.

"Tsk, tsk," Jared whispered teasingly. "A fine wine should be treated like a beautiful woman. One never takes it too quickly. No, it should be . . . *seduced."* Seeing Alissa's shocked expression, he fought for control, lest he laugh aloud. "One must inhale its fine bouquet . . . much like a woman's perfume. Did you know each woman has her own special scent? One that does not come from a bottle or a jar?" Her mouth agape, she shook her head; Jared's smile grew bolder. "You have your own," he said, in a smooth, almost husky whisper. "It's a mixture of lavender and wild rose, but beneath is the scent of woman, pure and sweet, untouched by worldly desires or the passions of men."

Caught up in Jared's silvery words, Alissa felt herself leaning toward him. Then she saw his hand raise, his finger nudged the base of her glass.

"Now, smell the bouquet," he said, and she did. It was heady, intoxicating, but she couldn't tell if it was the wine or if it was Jared that made her feel so giddy. "Take a sip and hold it in your mouth." Alissa complied. "Now let it flow over your tongue." She did. "Wine must be tasted to enjoy it, not just swallowed. The taste is a vibrant sensation," he murmured, softly, mesmerizing her the more. "From experience, I tell you, to taste your lover's skin is to inflame your desires. There's no emotion like it, sweet . . . Agatha."

The sound of the woman's name hit Alissa like a slap in the face; the wine rolled down her throat, choking her. Immediately, Jared jumped to his feet and thumped her back. His face split into a wide grin as he chuckled to himself. "Better now?" he asked, when her coughing fit had subsided.

"Much," she responded with a croak, then turned a

narrowed, watery eye upon him. "Sir, I hope the vein of your conversation will take a different slant, or I shall have to excuse myself, and you may dine alone."

Jared looked taken aback. "Why, Miss Pembroke, I had not realized I had offended you. I was simply trying to evoke the senses."

Angered with herself for allowing him the ability to evoke hers, Alissa was determined not to let it happen again and encased herself in haughtiness. "I found your subject matter rather indecent," she said, with a sniff. "It was certainly not polite conversation one normally shares at dinner."

"Your pardon," he said, smiling to himself. "I did not wish to offend. Perhaps some food will pacify you. Might I be entrusted to serve you?"

Alissa eyed him as he stood just to the side of her chair. "Your kind offer is accepted," she said regally. "I will leave the choice to you."

"My pleasure." Jared turned on his heel and strolled to the buffet. Lifting the tops on the chafing dishes, he began ladling up the fare, his shoulders shaking n silent laughter. "Here we are," he said, placing the china plate heaped with food before her.

Gazing at it, Alissa's eyes widened and she grabbed her fork to chase the sauce that threatened to overflow the plate. The man must think her a glutton! "Thank you," she said, frowning, then wondered how she could possibly capture a morsel without causing an avalanche onto the linen table-cloth.

Jared returned to the table with his own plate to see her puzzled look. "I'm afraid I've overdone it," he said, nodding toward her food. "Here." He took his fork and stabbed a piece of salmon from the conglomeration in front of her. "Open, please."

Alissa looked down her nose at the pink flesh, not an inch from her lips. He was treating her like a helpless child! Her mouth opened in protest, but the fork slipped inside before she could say a word.

"Cook prepares a most excellent fish, doesn't she?" he asked, as he broke a leaf from the artichoke, dipped it in a butter sauce, then held it for her.

"Really, Mr. Braxton—"

"Jared, remember?"

Alissa drew a long breath. "Jared . . . I believe I'm old enough to feed myself."

"Just one more bite."

She glared at him, but he refused to remove the leaf, so she opened her lips and sank her teeth into the tender end, while Jared slid it from her mouth. Some of the sauce trickled down her chin, and she reached for her napkin, but her host moved faster than she.

"All neat and tidy," he said, settling his napkin onto his lap. "More wine?"

"No!" she exclaimed, then noted Jared's raised brow. "I've had quite enough . . . thank you." Indeed she had! But it wasn't the wine she was thinking of. If he made one more false move, she'd take her plate and sit at the far end of the table!

"As you wish." Wisely, Jared left her alone. He didn't particularly want to wear her meal. "I was thinking perhaps you might enjoy a small shopping spree," he commented, and took a bite from his own plate.

"With Megan?"

"No, with me . . . for yourself, of course. My treat." He leaned back and gazed at her over his wine glass. "I'm tired of seeing you in the same boring dresses. I think silk would suit you better, perhaps blue to match your eyes." He referred to the dress he'd seen in the armoire. "They're a lovely color blue . . . soft, inviting," he said in a husky whisper, his smoldering gaze penetrating hers.

Dumbfounded, Alissa stared at him, and her fork clattered to her plate, splashing her bodice with sauce.

Jared hopped to his feet. "Here, allow me."

As if in a dream, she watched his deft hand slowly dab the napkin across her breasts, then her gaze slipped upward. With Jared hunched down, his face only inches from hers, a magnetic current passed from his eyes to hers, and she felt its forceful pull. An enticing smile crossed his lips; a dimple appeared in his cheek. Never having seen it before, she was tempted to touch it, and her hand lifted.

"There," Jared said, coming to his feet, breaking Alissa's trance. "The damage seems minimal."

The realization of what had just transpired hit home, and

she fitfully twisted the napkin on her lap. Unbelievably, she had allowed this man to intimately touch her! Embarrassed, she kept her eyes on her plate.

"Would you care for dessert?"

Jared's heated breath brushed her ear, and Alissa almost jumped from her skin. "N-no, thank you." Then she felt the gentle squeeze of his hands on her shoulders.

"Perhaps it's just as well," he said, sighing. "I've some bookwork to complete before I retire. It's been my pleasure to entertain you. I hope we might do it again in the near future . . . the very *near* future." Unable to find her voice, Alissa gaped at him incongruously, and Jared bit his lip to keep his chuckles inside. Then, taking her hand from her lap, he knelt on one knee. "'Good-night, good-night! parting is such sweet sorrow that I shall say good-night till it be morrow.' Shakespeare." He grinned. "But I'm certain *you* know his works far better than I." With a quick kiss on her hand, he rose and left the room.

Alissa stared at the closed door. He's a buffoon! Daft! An idiot! she cried silently. Waiting several minutes until she was certain the halls were cleared, she fled to her bedroom.

Locking the door behind her, she expelled her breath. Unable to fathom what had come over the man, she finally decided that the wine must have caused his strange behavior.

Although it was nearly half past nine, Alissa didn't bother to light the lamp, for daylight lingered seemingly forever in Scotland. She moved to the window and gazed at the patches of blue still lighting the late spring sky. Then with a sigh, she decided to retire for the night.

Fetching the cotton gown from the wardrobe, she threw it across the bed, her fingers working at her buttons.

"I've always wanted to see you in other than that frumpish sack."

Gasping, Alissa spun toward the sound of Jared's voice, nearly colliding with him. "What are you doing here?" she demanded, backing her knees to the bed, her hand gripping its post for support.

"Silk and satin would suit you better," he continued, his voice low, sensuous. "Undress for me."

Hopefully this was a continuation of the game he'd been

playing in the dining room, some sort of devilish prank. Certainly, he didn't expect her to comply! "Leave my room, at once, Mr. Braxton, or I—"

"Or what?" he asked, stepping closer, trapping her.

"I-I'll scream! You wouldn't want Megan to know what kind of man you really are!" she cried in desperation.

"Scream away," he stated with a cynical laugh. Her mouth opened, and he clamped his hand over it, jerking her against him, his arm tightening like a vise around her waist. Her body pressed to his, she struggled, but Jared's next words stopped her. "My sweet," he whispered sarcastically, "I'd think twice if I were you. Should you scream, I'll have little choice but to call the sheriff." He felt her stiffen against him. "It seems there's been an imposter in our midst, a fugitive from the Crown, who's gone undiscovered until today. There's a price on her head. A tidy sum, I hear. Is that not so—*Alissa Ashford?*"

Suddenly her knees gave way, and he pulled her tauter against him. His hand dropped from her mouth, and he settled her onto the bed. Lighting the candle, he turned to see her shoulders slumped in defeat.

"It was all for naught," she whispered weakly. "I can only beg your forgiveness."

Jared felt an odd twist of sympathy for her, but he immediately steeled himself against the emotion. She'd not get off so easily. His revenge wasn't complete. "Disrobe," he said, standing above her, and Alissa's gaze snapped to his face. "I want to see you as you really are." Her head shook in denial, but Jared pulled her from the bed. "Wash your face," he ordered, setting her in the direction of the small alcove and the basin.

On rubbery legs, Alissa slipped behind the screen. Tears stung the backs of her eyes, and she desperately fought to control them. He had not hurt her, physically, yet he was purposely trying to punish her. What had she expected? A mere tap on the wrists? Then she wondered how he'd discovered her true identity.

When she reappeared, his eyes drank in her healthy coloring. Her skin looked as soft as a babe's. "Take down your hair," he said, and watched as she slipped the pins from the tight knot. A wealth of shiny tresses fell around her shoulders and down her back, and he felt an odd tingle in his fingers, wanting to touch the silken threads. "Come here," he bade, his voice low, soft. "Put this on."

Alissa caught the wadded piece of material he'd thrust toward her. It was her costume. "You searched my things?"

"You gave me reason."

"What reason?"

Jared laughed, harshly. "My dear young woman, you act as though it is I who have committed the crime. Now put the dress on." When she turned to escape behind the screen, he stopped her. "Do it here!"

She cast him a mutinous look. "No!"

Jade eyes turned cold, hard. "You'll do as I say . . . or I'll do it for you."

Through tremulous fingers, the dress slipped to the floor. Tears pricked her eyes as she raised nervous hands to the back of her neck, slipping the buttons free. Her weak limbs quaked unsteadily, until she actually shivered, as if she were in the throes of a violent chill.

Viewing her lowered head, Jared saw her reaction. His eyes closed as he drew a deep breath. Although she no longer portrayed the prim Miss Pembroke, she retained a modesty of her own, and he couldn't allow her to go through with it. Expelling the air in his lungs, he spun her around, shoved her hands aside, and grabbed the material. Buttons shot everywhere, and Jared rammed the costume into Alissa's hands. "Get behind the screen and be quick about it!"

She ran to its security, several tears spilling down her cheeks, but with a swipe of her hand, she rubbed them away. The dress donned, she stepped into view, her hand holding the torn bodice in place.

Like a butterfly climbing from its cocoon, its jeweled wings unfurling to show its exquisite beauty, she, too, had changed into a vision of perfection, and Jared was astounded by her transformation.

"Come here," he ordered, and as she slowly walked toward him, he felt a hot stirring deep in his loins. Then she stopped before him, and his hand rose to thread through her silky hair, while his fascinated gaze traveled over her face.

Beautiful, he thought. And *real*. His thirsty eyes absorbed the look of her soft glowing skin. Like a babe's, he repeated in his mind, wanting to touch it. Huge sapphire eyes, topped by delicately winged brows and framed by long dark lashes, stared up at him, and he felt himself drowning in their alluring depths. His gaze slipped down over her straight, slender nose, to her soft lips, trembling with uncertainty, and he felt the need to gently caress them with his own. As he took in her entire length, he saw her as the wood nymph who had tormented him day and night, always leaving him wanting, never to be fulfilled.

"You've escaped me long enough," he said in a husky whisper. Then no longer certain she truly was real, he pulled her to him.

A raging fire scorched his veins as his fiery lips blazed over hers, his hot tongue probing their softness, urgently begging a response. His muscular arm slipped around her small waist, hauling her fully against him, while his long fingers splayed at the nape of her neck, pressing her face to his. Resisting the strange emotions clamoring through her tremulous body, his masterful mouth working its magic on hers, Alissa fought against his powerful hold. Her weak struggles inflamed him the more, as she writhed against his hardening body, and his hand slid down her spine, forcing her closer. Frightened by his masculine strength, his virility, her lips trembled; a whimper escaped her throat.

Hearing it, Jared suddenly realized this was not one of his dreams. Gently, he set her away and turned his back, fighting for control. "That was part of your punishment," he gritted out, knowing he'd punished himself, as well. Collecting himself, he walked to a chair. "Have a seat, Miss Ashford. We need to talk."

Warily, Alissa followed, her eyes surveying his every move. Then she lowered herself to the settee and watched as Jared folded his long frame into the chair, opposite her.

His emotionless eyes pinpointed her. "Explain why you have been impersonating Miss Pembroke."

Her concentration on her tightly clasped hands, Alissa told her story, relating how Charles Rhodes had accosted her, how she'd used the disguise to escape London, even how she'd studied the late Miss Pembroke's journals, hoping to help Megan.

"You expect me to believe you had my daughter's interests at heart?"

"I may not be as qualified as Miss Pembroke, but you cannot deny that Megan is far better now than when I first came here."

"No, I cannot," he conceded. "But when she learns of your deception, she may withdraw. In fact, because of it, she may very well be worse off than before."

"She's known for some time I wear a disguise. Likewise, she knows I am her friend, no matter what name I call myself. I have grown very fond of Megan. I would never hurt her . . . not intentionally. I told her once that I held a secret within me, and when I was ready, I would share it with her. She understood, and I'm certain she won't hold it against me, once she knows my reasons." She looked at Jared. He seemed unconvinced. "How did you discover my true identity?"

"That April night, when I was to retrieve Miss Pembroke, I, too, was at Covent Garden." He saw Alissa's eyes widen in disbelief. "A young actress caught my eye, but when act three had begun, she'd disappeared to be replaced by another. The portly little man in Stilton gave me a clue that she was in serious trouble, especially when the Crown had every man in England looking for her. But it wasn't until I went to the cottage today that I realized she'd been under my protection all along."

"Y-you were at the cottage?"

He smiled, knowingly. " 'Help me, Lysander, help me!' "

"You watched all of it?"

"Hardly. I take my Shakespeare seriously, Miss Ashford, and your portrayal of *Hermia* was exceptional. I remembered it well." He did not elaborate. Nor was he about to explain his dreams. "I'd heard enough to become suspicious. So I searched your rooms."

Alissa became suspicious in her own right. "You've been spying on us."

"Spying? Let's just say, I've been observing."

She wondered if he'd seen them with Ian and decided he

hadn't. For, if the rift between the two men was as serious as Ian had intimated, then Jared would have confronted her when he'd first discovered the fact.

"Mr. Braxton." Her teeth worried her lip. "D-do you think it might be possible for me to remain at Hawkstone?"

"What?"

"I—I was thinking of Megan. I've made some progress with her. She's able to make sounds. Given time, I'm certain she'll be talking."

"That's all fine and good, but deceit does not settle well with me," Jared snapped, coming to his feet. *"You* are a wanted woman. Although you claim to be innocent, I've no way of knowing what you say is true. If I continue to harbor you, and you're eventually found out, I'll pay the same price as you, Miss Ashford."

"I understand," she said, her gaze on her hands.

Jared looked at the top of her bowed head a long moment. Suddenly he became angry at all the emotion she stirred within him. He'd never wanted to feel anything for a woman again! In fact, he'd vowed long ago he wouldn't! Damnation! How did he get himself mixed up in all this? "I'll let you know my final decision in the morning." He strode to her door. "And I suggest you don't try to slip from this house under the cover of night. You'll regret it if you do."

As she watched the door slam shut, Alissa suddenly felt a spark of hope ignite within her. Since he had not said no, there still might be some small chance that he'd help her. She was willing to do anything he asked, just so long as he granted her a reprieve.

CHAPTER
Twelve

The next morning, a note was slipped under Alissa's door that read: *Agatha, meet me in my study in fifteen minutes.* The use of her assumed name stressed to her that she should be disguised. Again it was signed *J.*

Certain Jared had made his decision, Alissa entered the library, her stomach turning somersaults. Taking in a calming breath, she closed her eyes and prayed fervently it would be in her favor.

As she stood in the doorway to the study, she surveyed Jared as he leaned back in his chair, his head resting against the leather, the thumb and forefinger of his right hand massaging his eyelids. He still wore the same clothing from the night before, sans jacket, waistcoat, and cravat, his shirt studs missing down to his breastbone. Then his hand dropped, and he viewed her.

"Close the door and take a seat," he said, his face devoid of expression, and Alissa's hopes plummeted.

"I assume you've made your decision," she said, leaning against the closed door for support, should he say the words she most feared.

His tired eyes raked her face and body. He hadn't slept last night, having, intermittently, paced his quarters, then lain in his bed to stare at its canopy, then started the process anew. "I think it best you sit."

157

Alissa's legs teetered slightly, but she made it to the chair where she looked at him askance.

Jared drew a breath and cleared his throat. "I've made my decision, although I doubt you'll agree. The choice was extremely difficult. However, I saw no other way."

Her gaze dropped to her folded hands. "I understand."

"No, you don't," Jared said with a derisive laugh. "Alissa"—her name rolled through his lips like a summer's breeze—"look at me." He watched as her gaze climbed to his face. "My decision is based upon Megan's needs. Of course, there are conditions to it. After you've heard them, you will either accept my terms, or I'll have no choice but to notify the proper authorities."

Her heart sang in her breast. Her prayers had been answered! "Mr. Braxton, how can I thank you," she said in a rush, a smile lighting her eyes, then her face. "I promise I will—"

"Don't thank me," he said curtly, "and don't promise me anything. Not until you've heard my terms."

Alissa sobered. "I apologize. I thought you were going to allow me to remain at Hawkstone."

"You *will* remain at Hawkstone."

"Then what is the difficulty?"

"The terms, Alissa."

"Well, what are the terms?" she asked, anxiously.

Again, Jared viewed her a long moment. "We are to be married."

"Married!" she cried, springing from her chair. "You must be . . . daft!"

Overly tired from his long night of thought, first telling himself he'd marry her—for Megan's sake, of course—then telling himself he was insane for even considering the issue—a mistress was less bothersome—he had finally decided to make her his wife, and now, she had the audacity to look at him like he'd just crawled from beneath a rock! Instantly, his temper flared. "Agreed, I am daft!" he shouted, his eyes hard as moss-covered stone, "but the terms do not change. It's the sheriff or me. Now choose, woman!"

Stunned, Alissa fell into her chair. "I—I c-can't marry you."

"Why?"

"Because I don't love you."

The words hit Jared like a kick between the eyes. Never had it occurred to him that she'd reject him. Not for lack of love! True, he didn't love her either. But that was an entirely different matter! He'd made his decision, certain she'd leap at the chance. After all, he was a fine catch. Perhaps the best in all of Britain! And he decided to tell her so. "It may surprise you, Miss Pem—Miss Ashford, but if I were to snap my fingers, at least half the women in Scotland, and a good portion in England, as well, would come running to do my bidding. And if I posted one small sign in Selkirk today that read, 'Jared Braxton Seeks Wife,' there would be a line outside my gate on the morrow that would stretch from Edinburgh and back, thrice."

"It could stretch to London and back, thrice, Mr. Braxton," Alissa snapped, still suffering from the shock of his statement. "The fact remains, I do not love you."

"I said nothing about love," he countered, harshly. "Megan is the one who needs your love, not I. The decision was made solely with her in mind. She has come to trust you . . . in fact, she looks upon you as a mother figure, which in itself is a miracle. Even though Megan tried desperately to win her mother's love, Celeste never showed her the least bit of affection. For a small child, such neglect was hard to understand and very damaging. Not until you came along did she willingly open her heart again. You will not destroy her by leaving, and you cannot stay as Miss Pembroke!"

"But there are other women who can love her equally as much as I . . . perhaps someone whom you could love, as well."

"Patricia, perhaps?"

"No."

Alissa had said the word with such vehemence that Jared laughed, but it was not a kind laugh. "Precisely, Miss Ashford. Not only has Patricia attempted to use Megan to capture me, many others have tried the same ploy. Therein lies the problem—whom to trust. I learned long ago those of the feminine gender play a game—love's charade—when all they really want is what my money and station can afford them. In your case, however, I know you care nothing for me or my money, but you do care deeply for Megan and that is what is important."

Although she did not love Jared, as he had said, she had had hopes of using his money and station to her own ends. "My actions were not totally devoid of self-serving intentions," she said, hoping her confession would change his mind. "I, too, had wanted to use your power to help me."

"How so?"

"I had hoped, if I were to somehow cure Megan's muteness, I could ask your help in clearing my name."

"You were going to use Megan as a pawn?"

"No," she denied truthfully. "My thought was if I should give Megan back her voice, only *then* would I ask that you assist me. It would have been in lieu of monetary payment, that which you arranged with Miss Pembroke. Never would I have put my needs first."

"I believe you," Jared said, knowing deep down that despite her deception, she would never knowingly harm his child. "But there is a difference. Where you would ask one favor, the others would ask many upon many, until they had drained me of all I have. My choice has been made, and I will not change my mind. We shall marry."

Alissa shook her head in denial. "Y-you can't be serious! I won't do it!"

"It seems, Alissa, that you forget who holds the trump card here," he said, becoming irritated with the entire matter, especially her rebellion. "As I stated before, it's the sheriff or me."

"But—"

"If Megan agrees, then we will marry," he went on, ignoring her. "She is the one who holds the answer to your fate. In return, should she agree, I will do everything in my power to clear your name."

"B-but what about"—Alissa blushed—"about . . ."

Jared's lips twitched, his brow rising in amusement. "My husbandly rights?"

Alissa nodded.

"I'm not opposed to having more children," he stated, and watched as she went pale. "But there will be no pressure on you to perform."

He'd made it sound like a circus act, she thought in anger. This was not her idea of marriage at all. Certainly, she wanted children, but she also wanted a loving husband. Jared attracted her, made her feel things no other man ever had. Of course, her experience with men was practically nil. But love . . . ? She was certain that that was not what she felt for the man.

"Are you betrothed, Alissa?" he asked, interrupting her thoughts.

"No."

"Do you have a lover?"

"No!"

"Have you ever?"

"No!"

With her sharp denial, Jared felt an odd sense of relief rush through him. "Then I see no reason why we cannot marry," he stated as though the matter were settled. "Of course, first, you must convince Megan. You will explain everything in my presence. Should she agree, we'll be married as soon as things can be arranged." Then he stood, ready to shoo her out of his sight. "Oh, yes. During the day, you will continue to assume your disguise as Miss Pembroke. You will do so until your name has been cleared. In the evenings, however, you will become yourself." He rose, came around his desk, and lightly gripped her chin. "It's hard to believe," he said, turning her face from side to side, "that a few strokes of makeup, an old dress, and a spinster's hairdo could hide your beauty so well. When we are alone, I do not want it hidden from my eyes . . . ever. Now, are we to marry?" he asked, his eyes daring her to object.

Still stunned by Jared's proposal and the terms that went with it, Alissa stared at him and noted his stern look. All other options were closed to her. It was, as he'd stated, the sheriff or him. "You leave me no choice," she said, defeated. "We shall marry."

"Good. You've chosen wisely, Alissa."

Megan, excited over the prospect of having a new mother, one who would truly love her, had given her approval, and three days after Jared's ultimatum, Alissa, her beauty unveiled, stood beside him in a dimly lit church not far from

Selkirk, half-listening as the Reverend Mr. Jacobs recited the wedding vows from memory. His nasal tone vibrated through her, then she heard the deep timbre of Jared's voice as he repeated each word. Suddenly it was her turn, and in a weak, tremulous voice, she made her own pledge, stumbling several times as she did so. Jared's hand squeezed hers in reassurance when she forgot a complete passage and the minister had to restate it, then she watched as the gold band, studded with sapphires, was slipped onto her finger, and with a chaste peck from Jared on her forehead, the ceremony ended.

With the necessary documents signed, Jared stepped aside with the Reverend Mr. Jacobs. "Have you seen to everything?" he asked.

"There's no need to worry. Since Scotland is exempt from the Marriage Act, no banns needed to be posted, your bride did not need to prove residency, and no license was needed. An exchange of vows before witnesses is all that it took to make it legal. Your marriage certificate, sir." He handed the paper to Jared. "As always, your secrets are safe with me."

"Thank you, my friend," Jared said, squeezing Jacobs's shoulder, then he handed the man a purse. "For your orphans' fund."

"It is I who should thank you," the man said after he'd peeked inside, his eyes still round with surprise.

The men shook hands, then Jared walked to the arched doorway where his new bride awaited him, passing the time with Mrs. Jacobs, who had served as matron of honor. "Shall we, Mrs. Braxton?" he asked, extending his arm, and Alissa nervously placed her hand on his sleeve. "Mr. Stanley, I believe we are ready."

"Aye," the best man said, pulling at his stiff collar. "Be glads to get home, meself."

As the newlyweds traveled the road back to Hawkstone, Jared sitting opposite Alissa in the coach, he watched his wife in lazy assessment. She wore the blue silk, the one he'd found in the armoire, the gown's neckline curving low, the sapphire brooch pinned between her youthful breasts. Puffed sleeves capped her slim shoulders; seed pearls decorated the bodice in an intricate design. The silk molded her midriff and waist, to flare into a full skirt, covering her silk-slippered feet. "You're quite lovely, Alissa," he said, and she turned her gaze from the darkened roadway. "A man could not hope for a more beautiful bride."

Alissa's concentration dropped to the bouquet she held. "Are we really married?" she asked in a small whisper.

Jared chuckled. "Yes, Mrs. Braxton. In the eyes of God and man, we are married." She said nothing. "Having second thoughts?"

Her gaze snapped to his face. "I've said all along I did not wish to marry you."

"But my wish was that you did," he stated with superiority. "And, dear Alissa, I always get what I want."

"Through blackmail."

"This time, perhaps," he admitted. "But not so in the past. You will find our union will not be as distasteful as you might think. In the near future, you will have a babe to entertain you . . . perhaps two or three."

Her eyes grew round, and she finally found her voice. "You promised you would not press for your rights," she reminded in a rush. "I have a career—"

"Had," he stated. "Your days on the stage are finished. Should you feel the need to perform, it will be for my eyes alone."

Alissa could not find a suitable comeback. In her haste to escape the Crown's punishment, she'd given Jared Braxton the right to say what she could and could not do. She was no longer an individual who retained the right of choice for herself. No, she was owned by another—one who did not love her.

"I presume you now wish you'd chosen the sheriff over me?" he asked through the shadows. "If so, you are wrong in your assumption. I've done some investigating since I learned who you are. The Earl of Creighton, Rothhamford's father, has many friends in high places. If you had gone it alone, you would not have stood a chance. I, too, have friends. With my help, your risks of being convicted of the assault and robbery of one Charles Rhodes are far less likely. If you will be patient, I will prove it to you."

"And what shall I offer in return?" she asked in honest query.

"Yourself." Jared saw her stiffen. "Many couples marry

for other reasons than love, Alissa. And they parent a half-dozen or more children as a result."

"They also take lovers to compensate for their loneliness," she said, heatedly, knowing of several such marriages herself.

Jared's eyes narrowed. "In your case, you will not."

"And you?" she asked, detesting the thought of the double standard by which she'd be made to live, for she was certain he would take as many mistresses as there were days in the week. Yet, if she were of the disposition to search out a tender heart, then she'd, no doubt, be made to pay for her transgression. "I suppose you will be allowed as much freedom as you wish."

"Give me no reason to seek another," he said, thinking of his late wife and her frigidness, "and I shall search out your bed alone."

Certain she had spoken too soon, Alissa fell silent. Perhaps if she continued to refuse him, he'd find another for his masculine needs. Yes, that's what she'd do, she decided. She'd refuse him.

"This marriage will be consummated, Alissa," he said, reading her mind. "It is up to you how it is done."

"Y-you wouldn't use force, would you?" she cried, her eyes growing wide.

Jared chuckled knowingly. "Sweet Alissa, you are so naive. I'd never force you. I wouldn't have to, love. My experience is far greater than yours. I'm a master at seduction. No woman has ever refused me." Then he thought of Celeste—cold, selfish Celeste. Driven by his thoughts, he felt he had to prove his words. His new wife would not be like his first. "Come sit by me," he said, patting the empty space next to him.

"I'm quite comfortable here," Alissa said haughtily and without thought.

A cunning smile crossed his face. "Then I will come to you." He transferred his body next to hers, trapping her skirt under his thigh, then his hand hit the side of the coach, stopping her flight to the opposite seat. "Still comfy?" he asked with a grin as his free arm slipped around her shoulders, pulling her against him.

"Unhand me," she demanded, pushing against his solid chest. "If you touch me, I'll—"

"You'll what?" His hand released the coach wall and slipped around her waist, his grin growing wider. "Call the law down on me?"

Frightened, Alissa struggled the more. Visions of Charles Rhodes leapt into her mind. "Jared, please . . . don't."

Her attempts to free herself drove him onward. She would not be another Celeste. Never! When he wanted her, she would acquiesce, come to him willingly, her arms open, her body anxious for his entry. A moonlit glade suddenly filled the field of his mind; a free-spirited nymph beckoned to her lover, and Jared forgot all except the dream in his arms. "Don't deny me, Alissa," he whispered hoarsely, then he turned her face, and his mouth covered hers.

His lips probed softly, gently, Alissa fighting their tender persuasion, yet he refused to release her, his tongue tracing the fullness of her lower lip. Slowly, tenderly, he melted her, and of a sudden, she felt a spark ignite deep within her. At first, it frightened her the more, but the burning emotion kept increasing at a feverish pace, until fire leapt wildly through her veins, consuming her fears, and she leaned against him, her lips opening under his.

Her instant surrender rocked him, all thought of tender seduction fled, and he could no longer control the flame inside him. Raw desire erupted, an inferno blazed out of control, and his thirsty lips became demanding, forceful. In reckless abandon, his hand left her waist to glide up her silk-clad side, then cup her breast. His palm pressed the softness, then his fingers, eager to touch her flesh, moved to the swooping neckline of her gown and plunged into its depths.

Suddenly she stiffened; her balled fists struck at his chest, then she went limp. Jared pulled his mouth from hers to hear her whimpered plea, "Not again . . . dear God, not again!"

The piteous words hit him like spray from the North Sea on a winter's day, and he felt disgust replace his desire. He'd never lost control; he was always in command of himself— except with Alissa. Feeling the fearful quake of her body, he straightened her bodice, then gently held her against his shoulder.

Her tears soaked his coat, and a sinking feeling settled near his heart, and he tenderly smoothed the wisps of hair from her brow. Like a father comforting his injured child, he rocked her in his arms and crooned softly to her, "Ssh, sweet, don't cry. It will never happen again . . . I promise." As the miles passed, her sobs finally subsided into small sniffs, and she drew a long, shaky breath. "Alissa," he said, his tone low, regretful, "I apologize for my actions. I beg your forgiveness."

Her misty eyes looked up at him. "I—I realize you have the right to do with me as you wish . . . it's simply that you frightened me. You reminded me of . . . of . . ."

"Rothhamford," Jared stated, then saw her nod and decided he was no better than the lecherous bastard himself. "I admit I've behaved like a cad, an overanxious schoolboy who has not yet learned his manners. I will never again make unwanted advances toward you, no matter what my rights might be. This I promise you."

His words had sounded so genuinely sincere that Alissa could not help but believe him. "I—I know eventually we shall have to . . . to . . ."

"Make love?" Jared questioned, forcing back a smile. Her innocence intrigued him as she lowered her eyes and nodded. "I promise, Alissa, you will come to me willingly. I shall not force you. I also promise that when it happens, you will not be repulsed by the act. Know that it is a natural thing between a man and a woman. It gives much joy . . . a pleasure beyond words. When you are ready, I will teach you its ecstasies." She seemed embarrassed by his words, a bit skeptical, too, so he changed the subject. "The brooch you wear, was it a gift?"

"It was my mother's," she said, as she touched the precious remembrance.

"From your father?"

"I don't know. She never said."

"I don't understand."

"I never knew my father, Jared. He may have deserted us, he may have died . . . or he might not know I exist," she admitted in a weak voice. "Since I retain my mother's name, I can only assume that I am . . . illegitimate." She quickly turned her face away to stare out the window.

Jared squeezed her hand, then turned her face toward his with a gentle finger. "It is no crime to be such, Alissa. You are not accountable for your parents' actions. Don't think of yourself as any less important than those born from a union approved by the state and the church. It matters not where I'm concerned."

"You speak the truth?" she asked, surprised.

"Sweet Alissa," he said, his lips curving into a tender smile, "my first wife had a lineage as long as my arm and supposedly as pure as the first winter's snow, yet despite her birthright, her legitimacy, she had no redeeming qualities. She was selfish and uncaring. The only thing of beauty that came from her was Megan."

It was the first time Alissa had heard him speak freely of Celeste and his tone was contemptuous. Obviously, he had no feeling for the woman at all. But he had to have at one time. Why else would he have married her? She asked, "Why don't you ever speak of Celeste?"

"I have reason," he stated abruptly, saying no more. Then he shifted back to the opposite seat, and Alissa felt a sudden emptiness when he did so. "We'll arrive at Hawkstone shortly. Mr. Stanley will make certain no one sees us."

"Besides Mr. Stanley, does anyone else suspect our mission this evening?"

"Mission?" he asked, his lips twitching. "You make our marriage sound like some sordid bit of intrigue."

"When one slips from the house after midnight to say one's vows at a church hidden in the wood, I'd consider it a sneaky contrivance, wouldn't you?"

"I suppose you're right. I admit it took a modicum of maneuvering to make it all work. However, it was done to protect you. The only people aware of your true identity are Megan, the Jacobs, Mr. Stanley, and myself, of course. All can be trusted. You do realize we must continue this charade, until I've fulfilled my end of the bargain and have cleared your name."

"At which time I will be expected to fulfill mine," Alissa

finished with a sigh. To Jared, it had sounded like she was preparing herself to be recorded in the annals of martyrdom. "It matters not," she continued on the same toneless note. "A husband is a husband, any way one looks at it."

Jared's eyebrow rose. "I wouldn't know. I never had one."

Alissa smiled at his blasé tone. "If you had, Mr. Braxton, then I would not be in the position I'm presently in."

"No, Mrs. Braxton, you would not. But you have a husband, and I have a wife. Instead of bemoaning the fact, I think it best we play the hand fate has dealt us. In the end, if we are careful, we both might win. I can give you the basic comforts of life, plus the extra amenities of which most women only dream. In return, you will be a loving mother to Megan, something she has lacked all her life. Together, we might build an amicable relationship, one based on respect."

"But not love," she stated, feeling a twinge of sadness near her heart. She'd never known the love of a man, not even her father's, and Jared had said not to expect it from him. It hurt to think the emotion would always be lost to her.

Jared viewed her a long moment. "I've gone the route of love once, Alissa. It was a disastrous journey. Believe me when I say the emotion is not worth the pain."

Although she knew nothing of his first marriage or the reason behind Jared's cynical statement, she still disagreed, and she would have voiced her thoughts, but the coach pulled to a stop at the rear of the house, and Mr. Stanley climbed down from his seat and opened the door. "Follow me," he whispered. "I'll whistle if someone be lurkin' around."

Jared helped Alissa from the coach, then they followed Mr. Stanley into the darkened house. Like a cat, the wiry little man angled his way through the kitchens; the newlyweds followed, Alissa in the forefront. She tripped, her toe hitting a table leg; Jared bumped into her. Then his hands spanned her waist, his chest pressing to her back, and he began guiding her around the furnishings. He must be a creature of the night, she thought, wondering how he could possibly see in the blackened void, then he whispered, "The stairs are directly to your right."

Switching positions, Jared took her hand and led her up the steps and stopped inside the alcove, where he waited for Mr. Stanley's warning, Alissa again in front of him.

In the darkness, Alissa's remaining senses suddenly awakened. Jared's soft breath fanned the top of her head, and his spicy cologne filled her nostrils with its tantalizing scent. While his hands pressed gently against her waist, his chest molded itself to her back and shoulders. The sensations he evoked overwhelmed her; a thrill of excitement quivered through her.

Jared felt the tremor and, thinking she was chilled, covered her arms with his own, sharing his warmth. "Better?" he whispered, the gentle timbre of his voice sending another chill through her, and his arms tightened, pulling her closer.

Alissa did not object, for in the darkness, she could pretend her new husband had genuine affection for her, was showing her a measure of love, and she held the moment to her heart, knowing its tenderness would not last.

With her body curved to his, Jared felt desire spark deep within him again. She was soft, yielding . . . *his.* By right he could take her to his bed, and not a soul would object. No one, except Alissa, he thought, dejectedly. Their marriage was for Megan's sake . . . and his own, he feared. She'd been an intricate part of him, day and night. She was the woman in his dreams, and he desired her, wanted her . . . love had nothing to do with it. Yes, he wanted her now, but he also wanted her willingly.

He thought of their journey home from the church and of his heated response to her tentative kiss. Had he not been so eager, his fiery passion driving him onward, he would not have frightened her. She needed to be seduced, slowly, tenderly, but as long as the memory of Rothhamford's attack stood between them, he knew she would not desire his touch, his kiss.

Then, with the knowledge that he had to somehow free her of the memory and make the scoundrel release his hold on her, Jared decided that by week's end, he would face Rothhamford.

"'Tis clear," Mr. Stanley whispered through the shadows, startling the couple, who were lost in their separate thoughts.

"Thank you, Thom," Jared said, using the man's Christian name, finding his shoulder and squeezing it. "Your friendship is valued beyond words."

"'Twas me pleasure to help out. Sure were a surprise, though," he said of Alissa's true identity and the subsequent marriage, "but it be a nice one. Ye sure look right pretty tonight, mum. Right pretty. Well," he said with a small chuckle, "best be leavin' ye two alone."

"An excellent idea," Jared said in congenial agreement, and felt Alissa's indrawn breath, but before she could speak, his arm tightened around her waist. "Good night, Thom."

Mr. Stanley descended the stairs to see to the coach and horses, while Jared took Alissa's hand and pulled her down the corridor, stopping outside her door. "Should you become lonely during the night, Mrs. Braxton," he said in a teasing tone, "my rooms are but two doors away." Then he brushed her lips in a soft kiss.

Alissa stared after his shadowy form as he strode quietly to the end of the hallway. His door opened, then he whispered, "Good night, sweet," and the panel closed.

Inside her own quarters, her door secured should her husband decide to seek her out instead, Alissa gazed at her wedding band. Gold was for purity, the circlet for eternity . . . united forever, she thought, watching the moonlight reflect off the sapphires as she stood by the window. By legend, she knew, it was said a nerve ran from the ring finger of the left hand, directly to the heart. Was it true? she wondered, then decided it was only myth. Yet, when she slipped the band from her finger, she felt a painful twist near her heart.

Moving to the armoire, she pulled the petticoat from the shelf, and with one last glance, she placed her wedding band, along with the brooch, into the faded satin box. There it would stay until her name was cleared and her disguise dropped. The items hidden away again, her blue silk dress sheltered at the back of the wardrobe, she readied herself for bed. As she lay there staring at the moon as it crested outside her window, she suddenly realized the full import of the night's events.

Married, she thought. A wife, a mother . . . Mrs. Jared Braxton! A lone tear slipped down her cheek as she acknowledged that Alissa Ashford, actress by trade, was gone forever.

CHAPTER
Thirteen

"You seem preoccupied," Ian said, startling Alissa as she sat on the quilt, gazing out over the clearing to watch Megan frolic in the grass. "What momentous thoughts would make you deaf to my approach?" he asked, his smile teasing. "Has some disaster befallen the area while I was away?"

Yes, she cried inwardly, but held her tongue. "It's good to see you again," she said, quickly masking her thoughts, and held up her hands to him. Ian took them and squeezed lightly, then she slipped free. "We've missed you."

"You didn't answer my question," he said as he sat next to her, his own gaze beholding an excited Megan as a yapping Merlin ran round her feet. "What holds your thoughts?"

"Nothing of import," she lied, for she'd been thinking of her marriage, and Jared's absence.

"Braxton, I'd say," Ian stated, and Alissa's head snapped around. "I've been told I have an uncanny sense of knowing what others think."

"Obviously," Alissa said, a skeptical frown marring her brow. "But it would not be hard to determine the source of my thoughts. Lately it has been Megan's father."

"Has he been acting like an ogre? If so, I tell you his temperament is simply part of his personality, worrisome as it might be. Actually, it's a pretense. Under his ferocious lion's snarl is a tame little kitten who likes to be stroked."

Alissa laughed. "A pouting little boy, you say?"

"Something like that. Where is Braxton, anyway?"

"I've not a clue. He left four days past, on business." Was it? she wondered. Or was it pleasure?

"Well, he'll show up again . . . like a bad penny."

"Ian," Alissa scolded, "your trip made you rather surly. Did it not go well?"

"Fine, fine. It was actually most pleasant. London, as always, was exciting, depending upon what part one has the fortune or misfortune to live. I was able to take in a play at the Garden," he stated nonchalantly, then watched for her reaction. Not even a flinch, he thought, wondering if she was who he thought. While in London, he'd been able to trace Miss Pembroke to her last known address, a boardinghouse belonging to one Eudora Binnington. He'd also learned of an actress, Alissa Ashford, who had also resided at the same address and who was presently being sought by the Crown. "Have you ever been to the Garden?"

"Yes," Alissa admitted, plucking a piece of lint from her skirt.

"It's deteriorated somewhat since I'd last been there. The riffraff and all," he said, still watching her, "but the plays are still good. Well, enough of London. I've many more adventures to tell."

Relieved, Alissa listened as he regaled her with accounts of his journeys about Scotland and England; when Megan joined them, his stories became even more colorful. As she gazed at Ian, Alissa felt a comforting warmth. The man was a friend, a true friend. Eventually, she would confess her identity. But at the moment, she was under direct orders from her husband to keep her secret quiet.

Guilt suddenly crept upward, making her feel a bit strange. Knowing of his hostilities toward Ian, she considered whether she was disobeying Jared's wishes in another way. Although he'd never verbally forbidden her to see Ian, simply because she'd never mentioned their encounter and subsequent friendship, she feared she might be creating a more volatile situation by allowing their secret meetings to continue.

As she thought about it, she knew Ian's shared moments with Megan were not in the least detrimental. In fact, he, too, had been able to draw her out. Should the time come that Jared discovered their rendezvous, as innocent as they were, then she'd deal with it accordingly. For now, she would enjoy Ian's company. After all, she needed a special friend, one who did not make demands.

"Has the master returned to Hawkstone?" Ian asked, two days later.

"No. It's been almost a week since he left."

"Well, as I said—"

"Like a bad penny . . . I know," Alissa said, then laughed. Although her laughter's light melody filled the glade, deep down, she wondered if Jared's continued absence actually meant he'd already sought another to warm his bed.

Jared entered the room at the private gentlemen's club as if he owned the place, poured himself a glass of brandy, then sat in a vacant chair, opposite Rothhamford. It had taken him this long to find the whoreson, but it had not been time wasted, for he'd discovered a lot about the man's character, all of it bad.

"Good to see you again, Rothhamford," Jared said as he leaned back in the cordovan leather chair, raising his glass in salute. "You're looking well."

Hearing his titled name, Charles Rhodes stopped his dissertation on a particularly fine horse he'd come upon and pivoted his head to look down his nose at the stranger. "You say something?" he inquired in his usual nasal tone.

Jared studied the flatulent man. Thinning hair, combed to cover a bald spot, crowned his egg-shaped head. Spiked, bushy brows topped heavy-lidded eyes that drooped along the lower rims; a bulbous nose, tipped upward at the end, resembled that of a pig, while sagging jowls hung down onto a stunted neck.

Then his gaze traveled to Rothhamford's flabby mouth and watched as it pinched itself into the position of annoyed superiority. As he thought of those lips traveling over Alissa's soft skin, Jared felt hot anger shoot through him, but with great effort, he kept his temper in check. "I said you are looking well, considering the bad round you took." Jared frowned. "I say, nasty scar, there." He watched as the man's hand touched his temple. "Hope it doesn't give you much bother."

"Uh, I don't believe we've met."

"Braxton, Jared Braxton," he said, extending his hand and receiving a limp shake in return. "And we did meet, several years past . . . the Derby, remember?"

"Right, right," Rothhamford agreed, not remembering this Braxton fellow at all. "Good to see you again."

"I thought you'd remember," Jared said, tonelessly. "Have they caught the rapscallion who accosted you?"

"She's still at large."

"She? I thought you were attacked by some street urchin."

"Not quite. Good lord, man, don't you read the papers?"

"My estate is in Scotland. I've just come to London on business. I'd heard you were in some sort of fracas, but didn't hear the details."

Rothhamford perked up. This was his chance to relay the story, yet another time, with all its embellishments. "I say, we were just about to adjourn to the game room for a hand of whist. We seem to be out a man. Would you like to join us?"

"Certainly. I must warn you, though, I haven't played for some time, so I might be a bit out of practice. You'll have to bear with me . . . oh, and I assume we will carry a wager?" Jared took a large quantity of folded bills from his inside coat pocket and saw Rothhamford's eyes widen.

"Why, certainly," Charles said, pounding Jared's back, reaching up to do so. "You can team up with my father, Sidney Rhodes, the Earl of Creighton. He's a dastardly good player. Rather a sore loser, though. So you'd better bone up fast. By the by, what title do you hold?"

"Nothing as impressive as yours, my lord," Jared said, then watched as Rothhamford puffed himself up.

After the introductions were made—the earl and Jared paired against Charles and one Jonathan Grimes, Esq.—the four settled at the table. "Would you give a refresher course?" Jared asked, and the earl's gaze snapped to his face.

"I thought you played, Braxton," he said, then the short, thin man looked pointedly at his son, but Charles pretended to be settling his feet under the table with great interest. "In whist, all fifty-two cards are dealt, the dealer turning up the last card, which is trump, and placing it on the table. When the first trick goes round, counterclockwise, the dealer then retrieves the card and either plays it or places it in his hand. When a suit is played it must be followed. If one does not have a particular suit, he must play a trump card. If he has no trump, another card can be played. When a team takes six tricks, the team gets a point. If a team takes all thirteen tricks in one hand, it's called a slam."

"Oh, yes, now I remember," Jared said, frowning. "Shall we begin?" He played the first two rounds, purposely losing for his partner and himself. The earl seemed to be on the verge of apoplexy when Jared played a large trump, the ace of spades to be exact, on a harmless set of cards, the five of hearts the largest shown so far.

"Don't you have a smaller trump, man?" the earl asked.

"I have the deuce."

"Damnation! Why didn't you play it?"

"I told you I was a bit rusty."

"Rusty! I'd say you've gone to seed!"

Rothhamford chuckled. "About time you lost, Father. You usually slam us every time."

As the game continued, several interested gentlemen from the peerage gathered around the table, mostly to chuckle at Jared's inept plays, which further inflamed the earl. Red to the roots of his white hair, Sidney Rhodes's blue eyes were practically popping from their sockets, and his acquaintances were enjoying the sight immensely.

Then as things got considerably worse, the earl and Jared being soundly trounced, a new wager was made, Rothhamford betting his month's allowance on the round. The earl had balked at first, then glanced at Jared; a cunning look entered his eye. "Agreed," the earl said, smiling. "Deal the cards, Braxton."

Spades were trump again, Jared turning up the deuce, placing it on the table. Then, waiting his turn, he leaned back, dividing his cards according to suit. "You never did tell me about your experience, Rothhamford."

"Right, right," he said, laying down the five of diamonds. "I did promise, didn't I?"

"When and where did you say it happened?"

"April . . . Covent Garden."

Jared plucked the deuce from the table and tossed it onto the trick, pulling it. "Bad area, of late . . . pickpockets and all, bandying about outside. Why were you there? The gentry usually attend the opera, nowadays."

"Playing trump already?" Charles asked, then seeing Jared's nod, he settled back with a frown. "I was there because I wanted to see some Shakespeare."

"Excellent choice," Jared said, then placed the three of spades on the table. "Who did it?"

"A young actress, Alissa Ashford."

Again Jared pulled the trick, then played the four of spades. "Oh? How did it happen?"

"The little trollop lured me to her dressing room, bashed my head, and robbed me."

Jared bristled at the slur, but he kept his cool and played the five of spades. "After the play?"

"I say, don't you have anything besides trump?" Rothamford asked, losing yet another card.

Jared smiled. "I'm not at liberty to say. But perhaps we could make a wager on it . . . a friendly one between the two of us?"

Charles considered it. When the first trick had been played, only one trump had appeared and Braxton had thrown it. That meant Braxton held all trump. Seeing an easy profit, he said, "Certainly, but I'll wager you have all spades."

Jared frowned. "Are you sure?"

"Do you take me for a fool?" the viscount asked with a chuckle.

"As you wish," Jared said, placing his wager on the table, between the viscount and himself. Then the six of spades hit the surface. "Was it after the play?" Jared repeated. "Or was it between acts when you were attacked?"

"After act two, I believe," the viscount said, anxious over yet another lost card. His allowance was quickly deteriorating, but excitement leapt inside him, for Jared's spade had taken the trick.

The seven turned face up. "Why were you backstage?"

"I was visiting in the green room. Get on with it, man," Rothhamford said, wanting to see the next card.

Jared threw the eight of spades. "Odd, Madame Vestris doesn't allow visitors backstage during the play."

"Well, I was, and that Ashford woman lured me into her dressing room."

Jared swept the trick. "How?" The nine of spades fell onto the table.

"She saw me and offered to make it worthwhile if I came with her."

Ten of spades. "Madame Vestris told me Alissa was onstage, and there were too many players backstage," Jared commented, after he pulled another trick. "If they'd seen you, you would have been asked to leave."

"Well, then, I was already in her dressing room," Charles said, as he watched the jack of spades hit, more interested in the cards than his words.

Collecting the last trick, Jared threw the queen of spades. "Why?"

"Because," the viscount spouted, seeing his pleasures for the next month passing before his eyes. Without funds, what would he do? Yet, his side wager would hold him for a while. "By God, man," he said, excitedly, "you do have all the trump!"

The cards raked in, the king of spades hit the table, and Jared demanded, *"Why?"*

Charles threw his useless card in with the others. "Show me the last one," he ordered, eager to see what it was.

"Not until you've answered my question," Jared said, waving the unseen card like a scrap of meat before a ravenous dog. Rothhamford grabbed for it, but Jared jerked it to his chest. "Tell me why you were in Alissa Ashford's dressing room."

"Because, she was nothing but a lowly actress . . . a little tease. She'd denied me twice . . . wouldn't have anything to do with me, so I waited for her. When she came in, I tried to persuade her to let me . . . let me . . ." He snapped his mouth shut, and watched as Jared turned his card, flicking the back with his finger. *"Deuce of hearts!"* the viscount exclaimed, in disbelief, and the crowd that had gathered began to mumble among themselves. Then as an added shock, he saw his father's hand slam onto the table, revealing the ace of spades. "Something's not right here!" Charles cried.

"By God, you're right," the earl bellowed, "and it smells worse than the Thames!"

"B-but you played out of order. You have to follow suit!"

"And follow suit I shall, you sniveling idiot!"

"I—I don't understand," Rothhamford said, his eyes wide with confusion. "Why didn't you play the ace the first trick?"

"Charles, listen closely," his father stated, punctuating each word as though he were speaking to an imbecile. Indeed he was, for his son had just confessed to a roomful of his peers that he'd made false accusations against another. "When the hand began, I thought it would be a bit of a lark to play as stupidly as Braxton had. If he'd lost his money to you and Grimes, there, then all the better, especially when my loss would still be kept in the family. But the more spades Braxton turned over, the more interested I became in your babble. Do you have any idea what you were saying while Braxton was flipping up his trump?"

"Saying? Why, he asked me about being accosted by that actress."

"You stupid fool!" the earl shouted, pointing a rigid finger at his son. "You were the scoundrel in this supposed assault, weren't you? *You* attacked the actress, not the other way around!"

Suddenly the viscount remembered every word that had slipped from his mouth. Hearing the distasteful grumblings coming from his peers, Rothhamford defended, "Yes . . . but—"

"You bastard! Why?" Jared demanded, his voice as sharp and as cold as honed steel. "Why the hell would you put someone through such agony! Do you have any idea what she's suffered because of your treachery?"

"What's she to you?" Rothhamford snapped back, angered that Braxton had trapped him into a confession. "She's a simple commoner . . . an actress."

"Alissa Ashford is my *wife!*"

179

The words rolled over him like a tidal wave, and seeing the green fire in Braxton's eyes, the viscount paled to the color of his starched white shirt. With a quick turn of his head, he looked to his father, seeking help.

"You'll not get any assistance from me," the earl told him. "I've gotten you out of your last scrape. I'm washing my hands of you. Braxton can feed you to wolves, for all I care." Knowing his family's reputation had been ruined beyond repair, the Earl of Creighton stalked from the room.

"B-but . . ." Rothhamford stammered, then realized he'd get no sympathy from anyone around him and shot from his chair, intent on fleeing.

On him in two strides, Jared grabbed the viscount's collar, pulling him up short. Balancing on tiptoes, Rothhamford was marched toward the table and slammed back into his seat, where in a cowardly slump, he gasped for air.

"There is a matter of signing a few documents before you take your leave," Jared said, withdrawing several papers from his inside breast pocket. "Now write."

"I—I don't have a pen."

"Here's one," a spectator announced, carrying quill and ink to the table.

"Thank you," Jared said, angling his head in a slight bow. "Now, shall we begin?"

"What should I say?" the viscount asked.

"I could think of a few words," another spectator shouted from the corner, and laughter erupted, then settled quickly.

"Thank you, gentlemen," Jared announced, "but I think it best if I dictate. Although I'm in complete accord with your thoughts, my wife will read these papers, and I do not wish for her to blush at the wording."

"Might it be possible for us to get our own statement?" another man asked.

"When I'm through with the viscount, you may do with him as you wish."

"Here, here!" all the men shouted in unison, and Rothhamford paled anew.

"Do you, perchance, have a notary on the premises?" Jared asked, then heard an "aye" from the group. "Now, Rothhamford, I believe we can begin."

As Jared began to dictate, Charles carefully wrote each

word and signed each paper. When he was finished, the notary asked if this was done by his own free will. The viscount started to protest, but one look at Jared's hard eyes silenced him immediately. The documents signed and sealed, Jared slipped all but one into his pocket. "This goes to whomever has the power to drop the charges brought against my wife." He handed it to the notary. "I trust you will deliver it."

"Indeed I will," the man said. "In fact, you may want to inform your wife that she might wish to bring charges against Rothhamford."

"I'll inform her of her rights." Then he turned to the viscount and leaned close to the man's ear. "I must thank you, Rothhamford, because if you weren't such a whore-son, then I'd never have met Alissa. But, if I ever hear of you accosting another female, you will see me again, and I won't be as kind as I have been tonight." Then Jared picked up his winnings, rotated on his heel, and strode from the room.

"Who was that man?" Rothhamford asked when Jared had vanished into the night. "How did he get in here?"

One of the lingering spectators bent to the viscount's ear, and while the rest watched, a few with knowing smiles on their faces, he whispered something of import.

Rothhamford jerked upright. "You must be joking!" Then he saw the slow shake of his informer's head. "But, but—"

And, as the men watched, Rothhamford's eyes rolled to the back of his head; his face hit the table. "By jove, I think he's fainted!" someone shouted.

Outside, Jared strode to his coach, his feet ringing with a confident step against the cobblestones, his walking stick twirling in his fingers. "Well? Did ye gets the bloke's confession?" Mr. Stanley called from his seat.

Jared smiled, while patting his coat pocket. "Did you doubt I would?"

"Did ye have to trounce him? Or was it done all peaceful like?"

"Let's say a little of both."

"Ye talk in riddles," Mr. Stanley grumbled.

"Rothhamford's pockets are considerably lighter . . . but his face is still intact, although his integrity is not."

"Well, ye gots a strange way of makin' the bloke pay fer his transgressions."

"He's paid his due," Jared said, certain Rothhamford would be disowned by his father, the Earl of Creighton. "Now, let's be on our way."

"Where to, gov'nor?"

Jared opened the coach door and announced, "Mrs. Eudora Binnington's." Then he settled inside, a wide grin splitting his face.

"Ian," Alissa said, several days later, as she tossed another stone into the stream and watched the circles ripple wider and wider until they disappeared, then she sighed. "Do you think he murdered her?"

Ian gazed off into the distance to see Megan and Merlin at play. "The servants have been talking again, I see," he said, straightening from the tree trunk where he leaned, sucking on a tender blade of grass. "True?"

"Yes," Alissa admitted, her eyes downcast. "Some time ago, I overheard two maids gossiping. It made me angry. It could have easily been Megan who'd walked down the hall to hear them viciously attacking her father. I told them to be on with their work. Yet . . ."

"Yet they managed to plant a seed of doubt in your mind," Ian finished for her.

"I suppose." She turned to him. "Do you think he did?"

"I've told you before, Jared is the only one who knows what happened that night. Only he holds the answer."

"Yes, I know. But do *you* think he did it?"

"I suppose all of us are capable of doing things we normally wouldn't when pushed to the end of our endurance."

"Ian, answer me," Alissa demanded.

"No, I don't believe he killed Celeste."

"Will you tell me about her?"

Ian gave a short, abrupt laugh. "What is there to say about her?"

"I wouldn't ask, if it weren't important."

"All right," he agreed, tossing the green stem aside. "Celeste was a beautiful woman, and she knew it. High-strung would describe her, and never happy. Jared couldn't satisfy her needs. She always insisted on a new gown or a new piece of jewelry. 'I want' was her motto, and Jared tried in every way possible to please her, but it was never enough. She was very spoiled, shallow, flighty, self-centered, selfish . . . I could go on and on, but what's the point?"

"How did they meet?" she asked, not believing Jared would choose someone like Celeste for his wife.

"At a ball about eight years past. Her beauty was what caught his eye. At four and twenty, Jared was not as wise as he is now. Experience has opened his eyes to the true meaning of what love should be, or at least I hope it has."

"I doubt it," she mumbled, but Ian caught her words.

"Don't tell me you have a schoolgirl's crush on the dark master of Hawkstone?"

"No, certainly not," she denied in haste. "How preposterous of you to ask."

Ian chuckled. "Dear Aggie, Jared could charm the fangs from a serpent, if he so desired. Don't think for one moment that you're immune to his masculine influence. If you do, you're in for a shocking surprise. Not many women can break his spell once they've fallen under it."

True, she thought, for as the days had passed, Jared's absence had begun to worry her, and she'd found herself thinking of him more and more, until he had consumed her entire mind, leaving room for little else. Her days were full of him, her nights the worst of all, for he came to her in her dreams, and Alissa had felt stirrings deep within her that she thought to be improper for a virgin.

Yet, what confused her most was she carried those feelings into the daylight hours, and they would erupt at the oddest times. All she had to do was close her eyes and picture Jared's face, and a strange longing would burst forth, without warning. An odd warmth would spread deep into the pit of her stomach, leaving her breathless as it suddenly radiated through her entire body. Yes, she decided, she was under his spell, and she was certain it was too late to break its bonds.

"He'll be back soon," Ian said near her ear. "Then you'll probably wish he was gone again."

Alissa turned and smiled. "You are probably right." But, instantly, she doubted her words. For each day without him seemed like an endless space in time, lacking worth, lacking substance, lacking meaning. Indeed, she was trapped in a masque of enchantment, Jared her fascination.

CHAPTER
Fourteen

In the library, Alissa stood on tiptoe reaching for a volume of poetry, her finger picking at its binding. With the shelf too high, she became irritated and jumped, but missed. An arm stretched from behind her, startling her, and a masculine hand covered the volume, slipping it free. Alissa whirled. "Jared," she breathed, happy to see him. "You scared the wits out of me!"

"Were you engaging in some form of new exercise?" he asked, a teasing smile curving his handsome lips. His right forearm rested itself on the shelf, the book dangling from his thumb and forefinger. "Or were you after this?"

"Thank you," she said, accepting the book. "I wanted something to read."

"What? Bored with Shakespeare?"

"No. Just wanted a change."

"Did you miss me?" he asked, his emerald eyes smiling into hers.

"Yes . . . uh, that is, Megan did."

"And you didn't?"

"That, sir, will remain my secret," she said, with a haughty tilt of her head.

Jared's hand rose to capture her chin. "I have no fear in admitting my loneliness," he said, then his face lowered toward hers. "I missed you, sweet."

Realizing his intent, Alissa swiveled her entire body, hoping to escape, but Jared trapped her, his hands hitting the edge of the shelf behind her head. "W-what do you want?" she asked, her eyes wide.

"Just one small wifely peck to say welcome home."

"I-if I give you one, will you let me pass?"

Mischief danced in his eyes. "Of course."

She viewed him through narrowed eyes, wondering if she could trust him. Probably not, but she knew he would, undoubtedly, keep her here until she honored his request. Jared was just stubborn enough to wait hours, days, perhaps weeks. "All right, but remember it's one kiss, then I can be on my way."

"Agreed."

Closing her eyes, she tilted her face to his and pursed her lips, waiting. Her lids popped open at the sound of his chuckle. "Why are you laughing?"

"You look . . . uh, never mind."

"I look what?"

"I refuse to say, madam, lest you be offended."

"I know how I look; but remember, it is you, not I, who wish me to stay in this disguise, Mr. Braxton."

"I have reason, Alissa."

"To protect me, of course."

He didn't answer. As his gaze traveled her face, he knew he could not tell her of Rothhamford's confession. If he did, he was certain she would press for an annulment. She would be free to leave . . . leave Megan . . . leave him. And he did not want that. To keep her, he knew he must court her, woo her, seduce her with tenderness. "Shall we try again?" he asked, a lazy smile breaking his lips. "But this time, relax, sweet. Before you looked too much the martyr. All I want is a kiss from my wife." Then his hand slipped around the nape of her neck. "Now, kiss me, Alissa."

The tender caress of her name drew her deeper under his spell, and she raised her mouth to his. The gentle meeting of their lips lulled her, soothed her, and before she was ready, his head raised, and she felt herself leaning toward him, seeking more of him.

"Thank you," he said, his heavy-lidded eyes searching hers. "'A thing of beauty is a joy forever,'" he whispered, then drew away completely, his finger tapping the book in her hand. "Keats."

Alissa blinked. As he stood there, smiling at her, she decided he was the most handsome man she'd ever seen. The smart cut of his gray coat, the neatness of his perfectly tied cravat, the smooth lie of his waistcoat against his taut stomach, the long line of his gray striped trousers, topping his polished leather boots, all combined to create the flawlessly stylish gentleman whom every woman longed to have at her side. But as she mentally viewed herself, she knew no man would want to be seen with her. "When can I be myself?" she asked, not knowing she did so.

"Tonight," Jared whispered, taking her hand, "when we are alone." Then he clicked his heels, bowed, and placed a soft kiss on her fingers. "Until then, love."

As she watched him stride from the room, a self-confident air about him, Alissa leaned against the bookcase, and as a soft smile curved her lips, she sighed. Then Ian's words suddenly flashed through her mind—"Don't tell me you have a schoolgirl's crush on the dark master of Hawkstone?" —and she sobered from her childish reverie. She was acting like an enamored adolescent, barely out of pigtails!

Tonight! her mind screamed, and she jerked erect. *When we are alone.* What did he intend? Surely, he didn't . . . ? No! He'd promised her he would wait! Was he about to renege? Well, she'd just see about this!

With a determined step, Alissa left the library, going in search of Jared. Stopping Mr. Stanley in the hallway, she demanded, "Where is your master?"

At her waspish tone, Mr. Stanley's eyes popped wide. "W-why, he be headin' fer the stables the last time I seen him, mum."

"Thank you," she said, curtly, and headed toward the alcove, her steps firm, purposeful.

"Storm's a brewin'," Mr. Stanley mumbled to himself, then grinned, realizing his master had finally met his match. "Gots himself a fiery one, he has." Then with a merry whistle, he toted the trunk to Jared's quarters.

When Alissa reached the stables, she was informed that Jared had taken Megan for a ride astride Thor. She'd just missed him. In fact, she found that that was to become the standard saying of the day—"You just missed him, Miss Pembroke"—and she began to wonder if everyone at Hawkstone was protecting him. The insidious rogue! Disgusted with the whole lot, she finally gave up and went to her rooms.

As she sat on the settee, reading the volume of Keats, she saw a movement near the bottom of her door. A note had slipped under, and Alissa hopped to her feet. Jerking the panel open, she found the hall empty. The door banged closed, and she stooped and retrieved the note, recognizing the stationery as Jared's.

Sweet,—Since you cannot traipse the halls without your disguise, I asked Mr. Stanley to set a light supper for us in your room. I wish to spend time alone with you, so that we might become better acquainted. As promised, I ask no more, other than you wear the blue silk as on the night we wed. Until eight.—J.

Alissa reread the passage, "As promised, I ask no more . . ." He'd not forgotten his vow after all, she decided, realizing she'd worked herself into a dither for naught. Yet, the thought that the two of them would be locked behind closed doors—in her bedroom, no less!—still frightened her and she wondered if she would succumb to his charms as Ian had predicted. According to her friend, no woman was capable of denying Jared anything . . . ever!

Yet, why should she? He was her husband; she, his wife. Eventually, she knew, she must allow him into her bed. From the sound of his note, he was simply trying to build a rapport between them. There was no urgency on his part, no demands. Perhaps he wanted to court her. Alissa smiled at the thought. Marriage first, courtship second. Rather like the cart before the horse, she decided, but realized that at least he was willing to make those amends, knowing some men would not. It might be pleasant, she concluded, then felt a thrill of warmth spread through her. Perhaps, in his own way, he would eventually learn to love her, and she him. Or was she starting to love him already? No . . . yes . . . oh, tosh! It was an impossible situation, she decided, then headed toward the bell cord, ringing for Mary and hot water for a bath.

At eight, Mr. Stanley having already set their supper for

them, a light tap sounded on Alissa's door. Smoothing the skirt of her blue silk gown, she walked toward the panel, her knees vibrating in tune with her heart.

"Beautiful," Jared breathed as he stepped inside and closed the door. His heated gaze assessed her at length; Alissa blushed. "Don't be embarrassed, love, when your husband says you are beautiful. Nor by the look in his eye, when it says he is pleased with what he sees."

Alissa did not know what to say. She could quote impassioned words of love as she glided across a stage, but she felt it impossible to recite her own, and she wondered if he expected her to reciprocate.

Jared laughed; its low, sensuous quality drew Alissa's attention. "You seem to be at a loss for words, love." His finger tilted her chin up. "Let me help. Tell me I am . . . handsome."

"Y-you're handsome."

"Virile."

"Virile," she repeated, and blushed anew.

Jared smiled. "And a conceited bore."

"And a con—" She laughed. "Indeed, you are."

"Conceited, yes . . . boring, never." He winked, then grinned, the dimple showing in his cheek again, and again Alissa suddenly wanted to touch it. "Shall we make our way to our table?"

Her gaze slipped upward from the indentation. "Yes. I'm famished." She felt his hands settle at her waist.

"So am I, Alissa," he whispered. "So am I."

The husky tone of his voice rocked her to the core. For food? she wondered. Or did he hunger for her?

Jared moved around her and pulled out her chair. "Madam." He waved her to her seat. "Since our repast consists only of one course and dessert, might I offer you some wine now? Or will you tell me it's the devil's brew?"

Alissa looked up at him. "If I were still in disguise, I'd have to spout the need for temperance. But I'd never do so as myself."

"A lush, you say?" he teased, pouring the wine, then sat across from her. "I hadn't counted on this."

"I drink only on occasion, usually special ones."

"And is this one special?" he asked, raising his glass.

"Yes, it is," she answered, her glass rising, too.

"Then I salute you, Mrs. Braxton. May our life together be long and happy." Jared clinked his glass to Alissa's, then drank; she did the same. "Did I ever tell you how wine shouldn't be swallowed, but *seduced?*"

Thankfully, the fluid had already cleared her throat before his words hit her ears. "You did, sir," she countered, curtly, then noticed Jared's grin. "You're most fortunate, Mr. Braxton." She noticed his quizzical look. "Wine is far better consumed than worn."

"Agreed," he said, chuckling. "Now, let's see what fare we have." He snatched the covers from their plates and placed them on the tray beside the table. "Roast lamb with mint sauce, boiled asparagus, baked potatoes, and lobster cutlets, and . . . hmmm, strawberries and cream for dessert."

Their meal was enjoyed with good conversation, Jared ever attentive to Alissa's needs. His words were teasing, then tender, then teasing; his gaze was always upon her. His deep laughter reverberated through her when she'd say a particularly witty thing. Never was he argumentative, not even when their views clashed on politics, religion, or women's rights. "I've married a hoyden," he announced, when she told him women should not be considered chattel. Then he chuckled. "Of course, you're used to being independent. Perhaps, when you realize how wonderful it is to have a husband, you might change your rompish views."

"I do not consider myself a mannish female nor a bold woman. I do, however, believe women should have more rights than they do, at present. That way they won't have to be so dependent on their husbands or families."

"Your pardon," Jared said, a teasing light entering his emerald eyes. "I did not mean to offend. In fact, as a peace offering, I extend to you my word that you shall be my equal."

"In all things?"

Jared frowned. "In all things," he said finally.

"Then I shall take Thor for a canter tomorrow."

"Over my dead body, madam!"

"Then your agreement is worthless; we are not equal."

"Equal does not mean I will allow you to kill yourself!

The stallion will tolerate no one on him, except me. Even I have trouble controlling him. His temperament is like—"

"Yours?" she finished, smiling.

Jared laughed, its deep rumble filling the room. "Exactly. Thor and I are a perfect match in that respect. You cannot ride Thor," he stated with finality. "However, there is a gentle little mare that would suit you and your temperament perfectly. Her name is Sweet Honesty. If you'd like, we can go out tomorrow."

"I'd love to," Alissa said, her eyes aglow with excitement.

The sight of her lovely face filled with innocent, childlike expectation momentarily took Jared's breath away. Such a simple gift, he thought. And she seemed overjoyed by it. Then he thought of Celeste and the mounds and mounds of jewels she'd demanded, never satisfied with a one, always wanting more. Suddenly he remembered his own gift to Alissa. "While I was away," he said, pulling the velvet box from his coat pocket, "I got you a little something . . . a wedding gift."

Alissa accepted the box with nervous fingers. "I—I have nothing for you," she said, embarrassed by the fact.

"Alissa, this is my gift to you. I want you to enjoy it without thought of reciprocation," he said, a sincere light entering his eyes. "Now open it."

The lid crested to reveal a set of pendant earrings. The blue sapphires, surrounded with diamonds, winked up at her and tears of joy filled her eyes as she gasped with pleasure. "They match my brooch," she said, lightly fingering the stones, gazing at them in awe. "I—I never expected such a beautiful gift. How can I thank you?"

Jared quaffed the golden wine and set down his glass. "A kiss will do nicely," he teased.

Alissa viewed him a long moment; then she rose and walked the few steps to his chair. He remained seated, his face unreadable, and she bent over to lightly brush her lips against his. Then she felt the pressure of his hand at her waist, urging her to him again. "Once more, Alissa," he whispered, huskily, "please?"

As she looked deeply into his hooded green eyes, she saw there were no demands, just tenderness and . . .

expectation? Without thought, she moistened her lips, the tip of her tongue gliding along their softness.

At the sight, Jared drew in his breath; lightning shot to his loins. Did she believe him made of stone? he wondered, then realized the action had not been meant to incite, her innocence being too pure to know what it had done to him. Then her face lowered a second time, and his parted lips received hers, soft and caressing. He felt the pressure of her breasts against his shoulder and chest, and the temptation to touch their fullness, fondle their perfection, rose inside him anew. Fighting his urge, forcefully keeping his desires in check, his fingertips tightened at her waist, like those of a man who hung at the edge of a cliff, ready to slip into a roiling surf below.

As her kiss deepened, Alissa tasted the wine on his lips. *Intoxicating,* she thought, but it was not the wine that brought the word to mind. It was Jared. Knowing it, she opened her lips more fully against his, searching for that heady feeling only he could bring forth. At her waist, his hand gripped tighter and tighter, yet it felt painfully sweet, and wanting to sample more of him, her tongue tentatively touched his lower lip, then it slipped inside, savoring his own.

With an agonized groan, Jared suddenly set her away and viewed her through heavy-lidded eyes. She seemed lost for a moment, not knowing what had happened. With a quick move, he shifted in his chair, to hide his arousal, then let out a low laugh, but to his own ears it sounded a bit stilted. "Thank you, my sweet," he said, his voice strangely tight. "Your gift was much more impressive than mine."

A flush crept up Alissa's face, for she'd just realized how very wantonly she'd acted. Trying to hide her embarrassment, she turned and walked toward the settee, where she stood, her eyes lowered to the carpet.

Gentle hands squeezed her shoulders, a light kiss settled on the crown of her head. "I shall take my leave now," Jared whispered, wanting to stay, knowing he must go. "I've enjoyed our time together, Alissa. We shall do this again tomorrow night. Until then, sweet." With one last gentle pressure, his hands dropped from her shoulders.

Feeling an emptiness overcome her, she turned to see him

at the door. "Jared." He turned to her. "Do I not get a good-night kiss?"

"Not tonight, love," he said, his hand on the handle. "You need time . . . and so do I." He threw her a kiss. "Good night, sweet. Dream of me." Then he was gone.

Dream of me. That's all she did of late. But dreams offered her no fulfillment . . . only the real Jared could do that. But he did not love her. Would he ever? she wondered, her fingers reverently touching the sapphire earrings. Perhaps someday, she would escape her dreams, her masque of enchantment, Jared becoming her reality.

"Megan seems quite content," Jared said as he watched his daughter pick a bouquet of wildflowers; then he reclined on his elbow and looked up at his wife. "I never realized how very peaceful this glade is, until today. No wonder you and Megan picnic here so often."

"Y-yes, peaceful," Alissa agreed, placing the last scraps of their meal back into the wicker basket.

He perused her. "Why are you so nervous, love?"

Alissa continued with her task, her eyes never leaving her hands. "Nervous? You must be mistaken."

"We have a chaperone, if that is what worries you. I shan't take any liberties with my daughter so near."

"I never thought you would," she said matter-of-factly, brushing a crumb from the skirt of Agatha's brown dress.

"Not even a slight hope that I might?" he asked in an expectant tone.

She turned her face and smiled. "No, dear husband. I fear, sir, the anticipation of such an occurrence has been all yours. I hadn't even thought on those terms until you just made mention of it."

Jared settled a playfully peevish look on her. "Rather dispassionate of you to say your husband sparks no secret yearnings within his new bride. My ego is crushed."

"Your ego, should you decide to lay it before the entire British army, would feel little ill effect, even after a six-month march."

"Ho!" he exclaimed, trying to fight back a grin. "You think my arrogance that audacious? Or is it the Queen's own men you call weaklings?"

The light of mischief danced in her eyes. "I say your cockiness becomes you . . . most of the time."

"And when does it not?"

"When we have a disagreement."

"And have we had a disagreement since we wed?"

"No, nothing of import."

"Then, that in itself should tell you I wish to make our marriage work," he said, his tone serious. "You know I'm an impatient man, more often than not. My temper is worse than most—"

"True," she interjected, and he smiled.

"Yet, Alissa," he continued, gently, "I have not pressed you for other than a kiss in the three weeks since we've wed. Nor have I lost my temper." He saw her dubious look. "Well, almost never. But when you do something foolish, like stepping behind Thor, I'm bound to explode. One thrust of his hoof, and you'd be permanently injured, if not dead!" he exclaimed, heatedly, thinking of this morning in the stables when she'd passed directly behind the skittish beast, gently patting his buttock. Thor's hock had risen, and if he, Jared, hadn't seen the roll of the beast's eyes, heard the angry snort, and thrown his own weight into the stallion's flank to knock him off balance, the hoof that had kicked upward would have hit Alissa squarely in the chest. Even now, as he envisioned the scene, he felt drained; a sick feeling settled inside.

"I've learned my lesson," Alissa said, quietly, remembering how her short life had passed before her eyes when she realized the stallion was about to kick. At that moment, her only regret centered on not having known Jared's love. She'd have died with her husband's name on her lips had he not rammed himself into Thor's side. When she'd realized she still lived, she'd thrown herself at Jared, intending to shout her need of him. But he'd grabbed her arms and shaken her, bellowing his rage to all of Hawkstone. His tirade done, he'd swept her up, set her on Sweet Honesty, then mounted Thor, Megan before him. Not a word was said until they'd reached the glade. As she remembered his temper, she whispered, "I know never to disregard your warnings again."

"My warnings are given for a reason, Alissa. In Thor's

case, I do not want to see you harmed. I apologize if I hurt your feelings when I shouted at you in the stables, but I thought I'd lost you, and my only remembrance would have been the touch of your lips."

She felt the heat rise to her face; her gaze dropped to her hands. A gentle finger tipped her chin upward.

"Look at me," Jared said, and she did. "As I was about to tell you, my patience is growing weaker and weaker by the hour. I want you," he said, huskily. "All of you. Tell me I can have you. Tonight."

The desirous look in his eyes melted any reserve that remained. Why didn't she allow him his rights? Did she not want to discover what mysteries a man and woman shared? Wouldn't they, then, be bonded more closely, to actually become one? Not only in body, but in spirit, as well?

When she did not answer immediately, Jared urged her toward him, hoping to persuade her with a kiss. But a sudden racket in the woods beyond the stream jerked her away; her head spun toward the noise. "What's wrong?" he asked.

"N-nothing . . . I—I . . ."

"It was a hare," he said, pointing to the rabbit as it bounded up the hillside.

Relief coursed through her veins when she realized it wasn't Ian and Merlin. Since the moment that Jared had insisted they picnic in the glade, she'd been fearful they'd come upon his estranged friend. And her intuition told her it would not have been a pleasant scene, if they had. Each rustle of the wind through the trees, each scant sound of the forest's inhabitants had stretched her taut nerves to the point of snapping, for something told her that if Jared ever discovered she knew Ian, she'd pay a heavy price as a result.

Concerned eyes surveyed her. She'd suddenly gone pale. "Alissa, what is it, sweet?"

"I'm just a bit jumpy. I suppose my near accident has made me a little anxious," she lied, not knowing what else to say. "Every time I think of it, I grow weak." Which was the truth.

"Then perhaps we should head back to the house. A shot of brandy and a short rest will help soothe your nerves. Tonight, I want you relaxed."

"What are you proposing?"

"I'm proposing we become husband and wife as God intended and as I desire."

Alissa's mouth opened to make comment, but Megan ran up on quiet feet, three braided wreaths in hand. Placing crowns of wildflowers on Jared's and Alissa's heads, she curtsied. The last she placed on her own head and motioned for Jared and Alissa to rise.

"I believe we have a princess who wishes to be honored with a bow," Jared said, rising to his feet. Alissa did the same. After they had made the proper show of courtesy, Megan clapped her hands.

"If you are of such noble blood, then who are we?" Alissa asked of the child and watched as Megan placed both hands at the sides of her head, her fingers stretching upward to the sky.

"She says we are the king and queen, of course. And as all good royal persons do, it is time we seek out our palace. Our subjects must wonder where we are."

Seeing Megan's disappointment on having to leave the glade, Alissa said, "When we get back to the house, we can have a round of charades in the downstairs sitting room, if your father agrees. But, afterward, we shall have our naps," she stated, seeing his raised eyebrow.

With everyone in agreement, they packed up their things and headed toward Thor and Sweet Honesty, tethered not far from the cottage.

From the hillside, Ian watched the threesome, his forearm leaning on the pommel of the saddle. "Well, Woden," he commented to his horse, while surveying the tender ministrations being paid by his estranged friend to the young woman he knew as *Aggie,* "it seems love has come to Hawkstone, but methinks King Jared is only vaguely aware it has." Quietly, he turned his horse toward Falcon's Gate.

As Jared, Alissa, and Megan made their way to the sitting room from the rear of the house, the three in high spirits, Jared leaned close to Alissa's ear. "I'm rather weary of charades. Do we have to play yet more?"

"Yes, and as you've stated, we will continue to do so, until you've cleared my name. You have only yourself to blame, sir. I am willing to unveil myself upon request," she said, without thinking, and heard Jared's groan of anticipation.

"Tonight, love," he whispered fervently, causing Alissa to blush as they entered the sitting room. "Tonight."

"Well, darling," a woman's voice cooed, prettily, stopping all three Braxtons in their tracks. "It's so nice to see you've found your way home."

CHAPTER

Fifteen

"Patricia!" Her name erupted from Jared's lips as though he'd been beset by the plague. "What in blazes are you doing here?"

"The word *no* is not in her vocabulary," Robert said from the corner, a brandy glass in hand. "But, then," he offered with a shrug, "perhaps, I do not pronounce it correctly."

The redhead sent a condemning look in Robert's direction, then strolled toward Jared, her green silk dress swaying in time with her hips, a teasing smile lighting her eyes. "Robert is such a bear. He forgets that he had no transportation and would not be here himself had I not offered my coach." Then she raised on tiptoes and placed a kiss full on Jared's mouth.

Astounded, Alissa watched the woman's wanton show of affection. A sisterly peck it was not! Worse yet, Jared did not see fit to end the brazen caress! "I've missed you," Patricia whispered when her mouth finally pulled away.

Missed him? Alissa thought. Was she referring to the length of time since she'd last left Hawkstone? Or had her loneliness been precipitated by a more recent parting? Since Jared hadn't shown even an inkling of affection toward the redhead during her last visit, at least not in Alissa's presence, she suddenly wondered if her husband's hasty "business" trip, only days after their marriage, had in truth been a fraudulent pretext—the redhead's arms his actual destination.

Jared glanced at Alissa, noting her mutinous glare. She resembled a lioness ready to pounce. Still dazed by Patricia's arduous kiss, he took the woman's arm and led her to the settee. Had he not been suffering from the shock of seeing her, he would have pushed her away. But she'd come upon him so unexpectedly, he'd not been able to react. There had been no response to her kiss on his part, but he knew Alissa thought otherwise. "Have you been offered some refreshment?" he asked, finally finding his voice as he sat next to Patricia in hopes of keeping the two women apart. One misplaced word, and they'd be at each other's throats, he knew.

"Mrs. Dugan is bringing tea and cakes. But, of course, I know you prefer brandy. Robert," she called over her shoulder, "fix Jared a drink."

"What? Orders already?" Robert asked, in mock amazement. "Let's not be so hasty, Patricia. You've not snared my cousin, yet."

Patricia's head swiveled toward the man with such force that everyone thought it would topple from her shoulders. Jared's lips twitched, trying to hide a grin. His eyes sparkling with amusement, he looked directly at Alissa and winked; she could not help but smile in return. Perhaps she'd assumed incorrectly. Mistress, indeed! But . . . as a lark, perhaps he intended to pit one against the other: wife versus mistress; winner takes all.

"Miss Pembroke, please come join us," Jared said, motioning to the chair closest to the settee and to him.

Patricia viewed Alissa with a caustic eye; then the redhead's gaze settled on Jared in irritation. "Can't we have a family visit without Megan's governess continuously at our side?"

"Would you prefer I dismiss her?"

"Yes."

"Well, then, I suppose I've no other option," he said, and noticed Patricia's shoulders square, anticipating her victory; Alissa's slumping in defeat. "Miss Pembroke, *I* ask that you stay. The choice, of course, is yours."

Surprised, Alissa noticed her husband's gentle regard and

realized he'd given her a choice for a reason. She could either stay at his side, should she want to be near him, or she could leave the room and escape Patricia's hateful slams. Gratitude sparked in her eyes. "Thank you, Mr. Braxton," she said, almost reverently, "but I believe I shall retire to my rooms for a rest. I hope you'll understand."

"I do, Miss Pembroke," he said with a slight nod, acknowledging her wishes were acceptable. "Oh, Miss Pembroke," he called in afterthought, stressing her assumed name to relay the importance of her disguise, "we shall be dining at eight. Please bring Megan with you when you come. In fact, I believe it's time for her nap, also. Perhaps you can see her safely upstairs."

"I shall be most happy to do so, sir." With one last glance at her husband, Alissa took Megan's hand and escaped the room. Poor Jared, she thought, uncertain whether or not he had the strength to withstand the woman's gibberish and still maintain his sanity.

She wondered if he was strong enough to fight off Patricia's advances, as well. A warm and willing body, here and now, might be far more appealing than awaiting a skittish wife, not knowing when or if she'd ever give herself willingly. But would he choose just any woman to fulfill his needs? Although she suspected Jared's carnal appetites were more powerful than most, she was certain he was far more discerning in his selection of a partner than the majority of his gender. Patricia Southworth did not fit his requirements. Of that, she was positive. Yet, she found herself questioning whether she met those discriminating requirements herself.

That evening at supper, Jared purposely sat Alissa to his right; Patricia took the chair to his left, Robert settling beside the redhead.

"Where is Megan?" Patricia asked Jared, shaking open her napkin with an annoyed flick of her wrist, upset because he'd seen fit to seat the governess and not herself. "I thought *she* was supposed to bring her along."

"Megan complained of illness," Alissa answered, her eyes making contact with Jared's, and he received the message there was nothing amiss, except the child wished desperately to be excused. "She's in her bed, asleep."

"If she's ill, why aren't you with her? She might need your

care." Patricia pulled her gaze from Alissa and turned to Jared. "Really, you should find a competent individual who shows more concern for the child."

"And I suppose you have such an individual in mind?" Jared asked, his elbow leaning on the chair's arm, his jaw resting against his thumb.

"No. But I'd be happy to find someone. Miss Pembroke *obviously* is not acceptable. Not by my standards. And I would hope not by yours, either."

"She's more than acceptable to me," Jared countered, his cool gaze pinning the redhead to her seat. Weary of the woman's prattle, of her interference, of her superior attitude, and especially of her attacks on Alissa, his tolerance snapped. "Since you've no say over my child—nor, might I add, Patricia, will you ever—I'll make the decisions I believe best for her. *Your* wishes do not matter!"

Surprised by his curt statement, Patricia's eyes widened. Then, she watched Jared's warm regard settle on the governess. Realization hit her with the force of an exploding volcano. Surely not . . . impossible! He wasn't in love with this vile little creature, was he?

Through narrowed lids, she studied the pair. Daggers dipped in hatred flew from her eyes, aimed directly at Alissa. She was a witch! She had to be! Otherwise, no man could possibly find the unsightly female the least bit attractive. Yes, that's it! She's blinded him with some sort of potion that she's sprinkled on his food or slipped into his drink. Why else would Jared ignore her own beauty to gravitate to one so plain? Convinced this was the case, Patricia decided she'd find the evil concoction, present it to Jared, and expose the ugly thing for what she actually was. Once freed from his curse, he'd turn his affections to her. Patricia was certain of it.

To Alissa's relief, the meal progressed without further disruption; Patricia remained in a silent huff throughout. Robert, quiet as always, drank more than usual; and, as Alissa had noticed on his first visit, he still directed odd looks at Jared. Finally, they all went their separate ways, Jared whispering he'd meet her in the garden, by the summerhouse, in an hour.

Moonlight shone through the latticework, framing the

columns of the summerhouse, creating diamond patterns along the floor. The scent of roses filled the air as it traveled on the light summer's breeze. A night for lovers, Alissa thought as she waited for Jared, still entrapped in her disguise. Looking out over the rail at the garden, her anticipation grew with each passing moment. With her thoughts on her husband, she'd come to a decision. They would truly become man and wife, as he had promised . . . and as she wanted . . . *tonight*.

A gentle arm slipped around her waist, pulling her back against a warm, solid chest, and Alissa suddenly felt exhilarated by his familiar touch. "Jared," she whispered longingly.

"I missed you, sweet." His breath fanned her hair, then he turned her in his arms. "Kiss me, Alissa. Kiss me." And his head lowered, his mouth capturing hers, and she dissolved against him, her lips opening in complete surrender to his demands.

Her wild abandonment surprised Jared—hot desire shot to his core, and he pulled her more fully to his hard length. Willingly, her body melted to his and her slender arms encircled his neck. A violent need surged through him, rocking his masculine form to the foundation of his soul.

Somewhere in the back of his mind, he wondered why she'd come to him so easily. He prayed he was the sole cause of her surrender. But he suspected that Patricia had somehow spurred her on, making her give herself before she was truly ready. If that were the case, he did not want her. Her regrets would come on the morrow, he knew. She must come to him freely. Yet, with her lithe body so close to his, beckoning him on, her soft lips and velvet tongue teasing, tasting his own as it darted tentatively, naively, he found he could not stop himself. Her reasons be damned!

The fiery possession of his smoldering lips, slanting fiercely across hers, sent wave upon wave of heated emotion coursing through Alissa's quivering body. Frightened, yet spellbound, she could not decide whether to flee or to stay. Then his splayed hand slid from her waist, down over her hip, to press urgently against the base of her spine, molding her, fitting her to his hardened body. His masterful lips left hers, grazing across her cheek, leaving an urgent trail of kisses in their wake. "I want you," he whispered at her ear. His swirling tongue invaded and teased its delicate folds, and a shiver of ecstasy quaked through her as he nibbled the lobe. "But only if you give yourself freely, Alissa." Then his flaming lips blazed over hers once more.

His urgent plea spiraled through her head and penetrated her drugged senses to fix itself in her brain. *Freely, Alissa,* she heard again inside her mind, and her responsive lips hesitated. Jared instantly felt her slight withdrawal, and with a strength he did not know he possessed, he dragged his aching lips from hers and set her away, then smoothed the wisps of hair from her face. "You must not come to me because you fear I will seek another. You'll be mine because you want it for yourself, as well."

"B-but . . ." *Yes!* She wanted him, wanted his love, wanted his child. She knew he would offer his body, give her his child, but would he ever award her his love? Then she decided naively that the bond of a child, one created from their union, would surely make him love her. "Jared, I—"

"Hush, sweet," he said, fighting down his raging desires, not giving her the chance to deny her need of him. "Our time together must wait. When our guests have gone, and we're alone, I'll teach you all the pleasures that await you. Until then, we must be patient." His last words were more for himself than Alissa, he knew. Taking a deep breath to cool his ardor, he drew her close, settling a gentle kiss on her forehead.

Several yards away, spiteful gray-green eyes surveyed the couple as they tenderly embraced in the summerhouse. "How touching," Patricia hissed beneath her breath, then turned on her heel and stormed back up the path. Now, more than ever, she was determined to find the potion that had bewitched Jared. Tomorrow, she thought. She'd find it tomorrow. If not then, then the next day, or the next. But she'd find it! No matter how long it took! "Witch!" Patricia gritted between her teeth as she reentered the house. "I'll see you burned at the stake!"

The next morning, Jared and Robert headed off to Melrose to settle some labor problems at a tweed mill Jared had recently invested in. They would not be back until late.

Once her husband had left, Alissa quickly gathered Megan and their lunch, escaping to the cottage, away from Patricia.

In the afternoon, the two picnicked near the stream, disappointed that Ian and Merlin did not show. But Alissa decided that perhaps it was best he hadn't, for her conscience would have bothered her the more.

Instead, they practiced making sounds, Megan's voice seemingly growing stronger. But still the child would not speak, and Alissa decided that Megan's words were imprisoned within a dark cell, deep inside the child's mind, and not simply locked in her throat. If she could only find the key to free her stepdaughter, whom she'd come to love as her own, and unshackle her words, but Alissa suspected that the chains that bound the child were much stronger and far heavier than anyone realized.

Finally, the time came to return to the house. As she and Megan headed down the lane, Alissa wished Jared were there to foil Patricia's sharp tongue.

Mrs. Dugan stood just inside the door as the pair entered the kitchen. "You're wanted in the foyer," she said to Alissa, her eyes cold. "I'll see Megan upstairs."

Confused by the housekeeper's abruptness, Alissa frowned, then glanced at cook, noting she seemed awfully fidgety. "Who is it?" she asked, not knowing who'd want to see her. No one knew she existed outside the walls of Hawkstone. Except Ian. Surely, he wouldn't . . . no! Perhaps it was Mrs. Jacobs, for the woman had promised, on the night that she and Jared had wed, to pay her a visit in the near future. Receiving no answer from the stiff Leona, Alissa bent to Megan. "Go upstairs and wash up. I'll be along shortly." Megan nodded and followed the housekeeper to the stairs, and Alissa headed toward the front entry.

As soon as the governess passed through the doorway, cook headed toward the other one. On quickened feet, she waddled as fast as her stout legs could carry her to the stables.

"Seize her!" Patricia shouted, her rigid finger pointing directly at Alissa the moment she appeared. "She's wanted by the Crown!"

Suddenly two burly men were upon her, grabbing her arms, and Alissa felt as though she were trapped in the throes of a bad dream. "Let go of me!" she cried as she was dragged the rest of the way into the foyer.

"Are you Alissa Ashford?" a portly man asked authoritatively, a heavy frown marking his brow.

"W-who are you?" Alissa asked, struggling against the meaty hands shackling her arms. "Let loose of me!" she demanded, but the men's hands only tightened, painfully.

"Are you Alissa Ashford?" the man repeated.

Glaring up at the man, she refused to answer.

"Of course, she's the actress whore!" Patricia shrieked. "Look at the makeup, the costume! I've already shown you the evidence!" She stabbed a finger toward the collection of Alissa's personal articles, scattered on the floor near the redhead's feet, dumped there in a fit of anger. "Not only did she try to murder a viscount, but she's a thief, as well!"

Dazed, Alissa watched the woman's hand come from behind her back to reveal the sapphire brooch and earrings, plus Alissa's wedding band. "They're mine!" she cried, again struggling against the men, and again she felt the enforcement of their grips.

Noting the feral look in Alissa's eyes, Patricia shrank momentarily. "Arrest her!" she cried, fearing Alissa might break her bonds. "Get that imposter from this house!"

"Miss, I ask again, are you Alissa Ashford?"

She met the man's eyes. "I shall not answer until you tell me by what authority you have invaded this house!"

"My authority lies within the law. I am John Graham, sheriff in these parts. Now, answer my question."

Alissa's eyes widened and a sinking feeling settled inside her as she watched the sheriff withdraw Eudora's letters from his pocket, the newspaper clipping on top.

"Are these yours?" he asked.

Suddenly the blood drained from her head, and her legs gave way, but the insistent bonds kept her upright. Doomed, she thought. *Oh, Jared, where are you?* her heart cried silently. *Why did you have to leave me?* But any hopes that he might somehow save her were instantly erased. Even if he were here, she knew he'd be powerless to help. She was a wanted woman. It was useless to deny it. "Yes," she said tonelessly, certain her fate had been sealed. "The letters are mine. I'm Alissa Ashford."

"I'm sorry, miss," the sheriff said, his tone sympathetic. "I've no choice but to arrest you for the attempted murder of Charles Rhodes, Viscount Rothhamford, and the theft of money from his person."

"What about these?" Patricia harped smugly, thrusting the sapphire jewelry at the sheriff. "If you inquire further, you might find their actual owner."

John Graham took the jewels and slipped them into his pocket. "Will you go peacefully?" he asked, and Alissa nodded.

"You're not going to chain her?" Patricia cried in a strident tone. "You're fools, if you don't!"

The two deputies seemed to take her at her word and one quickly produced a set of manacles. "Put those away," the sheriff commanded. Then he turned. "I suggest, Miss Southworth, henceforth, you keep your nose about your own business. Or I shall arrest you for obstructing the law."

Patricia's eyes widened. "Y-you can't mean that!"

"Indeed, I do," the sheriff lied, his eyes hard upon the redhead. Then he took his prisoner's arm in a gentle grip and began escorting her toward the door.

Her eyes suddenly growing misty, Alissa's step faltered, and she glanced one last time at the beauty of Hawkstone. Setting it to memory, she hoped it would see her through as she withered away in some damp cell, deep inside a faraway prison reeking of human excrement and rotting flesh. The thought sent a nauseating chill through her, and she stumbled again. Then a picture of her husband filled her mind; tears brimmed her eyes. *Farewell, my love,* she bade silently, certain she'd never see his handsome face again.

"We have to go, miss," the sheriff said in a gentle tone, and Alissa nodded, taking her last dozen steps toward her final destiny.

Abruptly, with a force beyond that of a violent wind, the door flew wide, crashing into the wall beside it; a towering, masculine form stood on the threshold, framed by blazing sunlight, his hands knuckled against his lean hips. "What the hell's going on in my home?" he thundered, then stepped inside, his green eyes flashing with acute anger. "The explanations had best be good."

"Jared," Alissa whispered, breaking free of the sheriff's grip, running toward her husband.

The two hefty deputies set off after her, and as Jared's arm settled around Alissa's trembling shoulders, drawing her close to his side, he commanded, "Halt! Or you shall both rue the day you've placed your filthy hands on my wife!"

Her husband's words reminded Alissa of the man from the coach in Stilton when his wife had been set upon by the constables, having mistaken the woman for herself. Did Jared love her as much?

"Wife!" Patricia shrieked, having just digested the word. Her mouth snapped shut as Jared turned a cold eye in her direction.

"Yes, Patricia," he said, his voice like arctic air. "My wife . . . Alissa Ashford Braxton."

"Y-you knew?" the redhead stammered. "But, Jared, she tried to murder someone . . . a viscount. She's a thief, too. Look," she ordered, filching the sapphires and ring from the sheriff's pocket, displaying them to Jared. "Where could that lowly little beggar possibly get these? She's stolen them, I say!"

Jared scooped the lot from Patricia's outstretched hand. "This," he said, holding up the brooch, "is a keepsake from Alissa's mother. This is her wedding band." He slipped it onto Alissa's finger. "And these"—he dangled the earrings on high—"are my wedding gift to her. I had them made to match the brooch, as you can see. If you don't believe me, Patricia, I'll be happy to give you the name of the jeweler in London."

"London?" Alissa questioned, confused.

"Yes, sweet . . . London." A gentle smile curved his lips. "There's much I need to tell you, but first I'd like an explanation from all present as to why my house was invaded and my wife manhandled."

The sheriff cleared his throat. "I received a message, sir, that you were unknowingly harboring a fugitive—Alissa Ashford. She's been wanted by the Crown for some time now, and I had to confirm or deny the report. I hope you understand."

"I do, sir," Jared said. "However, I'd like to know who sent this information to you."

"Why, it was Miss Southworth."

Jared cast his gaze on her. "And exactly how did you discover Alissa's true identity?"

Realizing her chances of ever capturing Jared and his wealth were now trashed, Patricia vindictively thought to repay him. His trollop of a wife, too! "I—I searched her things," she admitted, a mutinous glare entering her eye. "But that's neither here nor there. The fact remains she's wanted! She must be arrested!" Again, her rigid finger stabbed toward Alissa. "Now take her!"

"I suggest everyone remain calm," Jared stated when he saw the deputies move again. "Miss Southworth's incendiary accusations are false, and I'd hate for you gentlemen to suffer because of her lies."

"Sir!" the sheriff interjected. "Miss Southworth is correct. I've a warrant for your wife's arrest."

"Since the time that warrant was issued, other information has come to light. If you'll follow me, I'll prove the charges against my wife have been dropped." The last word rolling from his lips, Jared heard Alissa's gasp. "Gentlemen . . . if you will?" He took his wife's hand and led her down the hallway to his office, the sheriff and his men following close behind. After retrieving the notarized papers from a locked drawer, he handed them to the sheriff. "These documents are proof of my statement."

"I see your meaning," the sheriff said once he'd read the signed statements of Viscount Rothhamford. "My apologies to you and Mrs. Braxton."

"You are not to be held accountable, sir. Bad news always travels far swifter than good. I'm certain the information would have reached you, eventually."

"Yes, well, uh . . . ." the man said, hesitating. "If you know the laxness of our officials in such matters, then why didn't you come to me with this information yourself?"

"That, sir, I shall first have to explain to my wife," he said, looking at Alissa, noting the frown marring her smooth brow. Was there resentment in her blue eyes, as well? he wondered, and knew he couldn't fault her should she feel such an emotion. "I'll see you out."

Tucking the papers into the breast pocket of his coat, he

gripped Alissa's arm and led her back to the foyer. Her heels seemed to dig into the floor as they went. There would be hell to pay once the house was clear of the unwelcome group, he was certain. Then he glanced up the staircase to see Patricia's feet hitting the treads as fast as they could go. "Miss Southworth, descend this instant!" he ordered, and she stiffened. "Lest you'd like for me to come after you, I'd suggest you do as told."

The sheriff debated if he should stay to prevent a possible murder, but his men were of a different mind and their feet were already scrambling toward the door. As the deputies reached the open portal, Robert and Mr. Stanley appeared and elbowed their way inside, the two burly men scurrying out between them. Deciding no physical harm would come to the redhead, the sheriff nodded his good-bye as he passed the two newcomers, closing the door behind him.

"Seems we got here just in time," Mr. Stanley said as he watched a scowling Jared stride past him, his master's hand squeezing the redhead's arm. Then Jared ushered the woman into the sitting room; the door slammed shut. "Are ye all right, mum?" he asked Alissa above the shouts, both male and female, coming from behind the closed door. "I feared he wouldn't gets here in time."

"How did he know I was in trouble?" Alissa asked, then jumped when a vase crashed against the sitting room wall.

"Cook sent a lad from the stables. Told him to go all the way to Melrose, if he had to. He caught up with us 'bout a half mile out, a-shoutin' the sheriff were a-takin' ye away."

"But I thought you were to be late."

"We completed our business, early," Robert said, from across the huge entry where he lounged in a chair, his arms crossed over his chest. "As soon as the boy started shouting, my cousin was out of the coach. The poor lad was nearly knocked from the horse. Most inconsiderate of Jared. Then he was on the nag's back and headed to Hawkstone. The question is, why?"

He sent her a probing look, and Alissa felt a chill run down her spine. Pulling her eyes away, she thought to question Mr. Stanley further, but another vase crashed, and a violent curse erupted from Jared. Fearing he was on the verge of strangling his former sister-in-law, she said, "Mr. Stanley, perhaps you should intervene."

"Don't thinks I'd better, mum. When he gets himself worked up like he is, it's best we all stay out'a his way."

Her anxious gaze darted to Robert. He seemed content to stay where he was. "Patricia can fend for herself," he said, not moving.

"It's not Patricia that I'm worried about!" she retorted, then marched toward the door herself. But just as she reached for the handle, the panel swung open and the redhead stormed out, brushing Alissa aside.

Jared followed, rubbing his shoulder. Seeing Alissa's questioning glance, he said with chagrin, "I neglected to sidestep one of her missiles." Then he called to his manservant. "Inform Miss Southworth's footman to ready her coach. She'll be leaving within the quarter hour. Send some maids to help with her packing. They are not to worry about neatness. And make certain she leaves without further damage to my home."

"Right, gov'nor," Mr. Stanley replied. "Hopes this'll be the last we sees of her." With a distasteful sniff, he set off on his errand.

"Might I now receive an explanation?" Robert asked, rising from his chair to saunter across the marble floor and stop by the couple. "If you'll excuse my ignorance, why the haste to save Miss Pembroke?"

Jared chuckled. "The real Miss Pembroke is no longer among the living, Robert. The woman you see before you is a young actress who was falsely charged with attempted murder and theft. She came to us in disguise, as she stands before you now. Her real name is Alissa Ashford—"

"Braxton," she finished, to see Robert's startled look.

"You're *married?*" he asked uncomprehendingly.

"Yes," Jared said, his arm surrounding Alissa's shoulders. "So, if you'll excuse us, we have some matters to discuss, privately. I doubt we shall see you until the morrow." With a nod at Robert, he urged Alissa toward the stairs, his arm settling around her waist as they ascended.

From below, Robert stared up at the couple, his eyes

narrowed ever so slightly. *Married,* he thought, pondering this unexpected revelation. After Celeste, he'd never thought his cousin would take that step again. "Enjoy your lives together," Robert said, barely above a whisper, then turned on his heel, going in search of a brandy and a quiet place to ponder Jared's startling admission.

CHAPTER
Sixteen

A bewildered silence had cloaked Alissa, almost since Jared's timely arrival, but as she rose up the grand staircase, she pondered all that had happened, and the truth climaxed sharply in her mind. Her husband had deceived her, and without reason! Animosity burst forth inside her, and as soon as her feet hit the second-story landing, she broke from his encircling arm, picked up her skirts, and marched down the hallway toward the west wing with an angry step.

Jared stared after her a moment, confusion knitting his brow. Then, in several long strides, he overtook her, caught her arm, and stopped her progression. "What has set you off?"

"Guess," she retorted, then slipped free of his grasp and started toward her room again, but Jared blocked her path. "Out of my way, sir."

"Alissa, if you'd calm yourself and let me explain—"

"Explain what? That I've been cleared of the charges brought against me, but had no knowledge of it, because my husband, for reasons only he knows, decided to keep the information from me? In the meantime, I've been subjected to wearing this ridiculous disguise, which I hate with a passion. I'm set upon by some dim-witted woman who throws herself at my husband as though she were a cat in heat and decried by that same woman as being incompetent and told I should be booted from my own home to satisfy her pretentiousness. Then, while I'm away, she searches my personal possessions and summons the sheriff, whose thugs have bruised my flesh, as well as—"

"Your pride?" Jared asked softly, fighting back a smile of admiration. *By the gods, she's beautiful!*

Her eyes narrowed at him. "And my pride!" she admitted, angrily. "All because you didn't have the decency to tell me that the viscount had rescinded his lies! What else is there to say!"

"Thank you, perhaps?"

"Thank you! You must be daft!"

"Actually, it took some bit of doing to trick him into a confession. My idea, admittedly, was a bit cracked at first, but through my cunning and superior intellect, I managed quite nicely to dupe him."

Alissa glared the harder at him, her lips pressing into a mutinous line. "I speak not of your intellect, sir, but of your deception. Why did you not tell me of my exoneration the instant you'd come home?"

"What?" Patricia chirped sarcastically from behind Jared and Alissa as she walked over the carpet toward them. "A lover's quarrel already?" She drew on her gloves. "Poor Jared. Your haste in choosing a mate may very well haunt you to your grave. What a pity."

Her control snapping, Alissa turned blistering blue eyes on the woman. "Miss Southworth," she addressed, her smile saccharine, "if you value each silken strand upon your head, I suggest you pick up your feet and follow the stairs to the front entry. Or you may find a sudden urgency to seek out a wig maker."

Jared chuckled. "If I were you, Patricia, I wouldn't tarry. My wife has an extremely excitable disposition. One can never be certain what she might do when her temper's roused."

"I hope you have an *extremely* long and *exceedingly* dull life together," the redhead bit out hatefully. With a toss of her head, she turned on her heel; her half-dozen trunks, carried by as many footmen, followed her down the steps.

The front door slammed into place, and Mr. Stanley's

snide shout rang through the house. "And a good riddance to ye!"

"I second that," Jared commented, smiling, as he tipped Alissa's chin upward. "Long? I certainly hope so. Dull? I sincerely doubt it."

Alissa felt herself melting under his warm gaze. Instantly she remembered their discussion. "You've not answered my question," she said, breaking free of his hold, trying to regain her former anger.

Her husband's smile grew lazy. "I will, love . . . tonight."

Tonight! her mind exclaimed, thinking of how he'd caressed the word. If he thought she would now be a willing wife, especially after his deliberate subterfuge, he was sadly mistaken!

We'll see, he countered silently, reading her every thought. "For now, love, you may seek your room and shed your disguise."

Rebelliously, she thought of wearing the ugly thing forever.

"I'd better never see you in this garb again," he ordered, his hand motioning to the shabby gray dress. "If I do, I'll remove it from you myself." He inclined his head. "Until tonight, sweet."

Alissa stared after him as he made his way toward his study, then she fled to her room. Hurt, confused, and angry, she stripped from the horrid disguise, then rang for a bath. As she waited for Mary, she creamed the makeup from her face, then scrubbed her skin with a vengeance. Afterward, she pulled the pins from her hair and brushed it until her scalp tingled from the harsh pull of the bristles.

Immersed in the hot water, her long hair cascading over the edge of the tub, Alissa rested her head against the polished copper. Her fury started to subside as the warmth relaxed her, and a sleepy lethargy overcame her. As she closed her eyes, she slipped into a dreamlike state. For a long time she lay in the water, her mind reminiscing, wandering backward in time.

Gentle hands stroked the length of her hair, and she thought of her mother, brushing and taming Alissa's wild mane, the two talking of their hopes and dreams, like mothers and daughters do. But Rachel could no longer share her wisdom, gained from her experiences, which was exactly what Alissa needed. Even Eudora was too far away to help decide which path she should now take: Should she stay at Hawkstone . . . or should she return to London?

Splayed fingers tenderly massaged her scalp, and Alissa moaned with pleasure. "You are more beautiful than I had ever imagined, love," a husky masculine voice whispered near her ear, and her eyes slowly opened to see Jared's handsome face only inches from her own.

Her hands flew from the sides of the tub to cover her nakedness, but he caught them in one of his own; his heated gaze caressed her. "No, don't hide from my eyes. There should be no shame in allowing your husband full view of your exquisite body."

As he beheld her, her firm breasts crested higher in the water, their pink summits drawing into taut peaks, and Jared felt a flame ignite in his loins. Down her creamy skin, his gaze traveled to her slender waist and hips, then stopped at the dark triangle above her sleek thighs. Hot desire shot through him as he imagined his fingers tangled there, discovering the magic hidden in her delicate, satiny folds, slipping deeper to touch her silken moistness.

His breath shuddered through him as he fought the urge to lift her from the tub, take her to the bed, and lie with her. He'd come here to explain why he'd kept the truth from her, but he had not thought to find her thus. As if in a trance, she'd lain before him, a sea nymph, inviting his touch. He should have left then, he knew, but she'd not condemned his hands in her hair, so he believed she'd wanted him to stay. Too late, he'd realized she'd been between wakefulness and sleep. Now, aroused by his thoughts, his fantasies, he couldn't make himself leave, and his hand tightened in her long tresses; his face lowered toward hers.

Frightened by his lustful gaze, Alissa attempted to break free, but his hand bound tighter, taming her struggles. "Open to me, love," he urged, unknowingly hurting her, tugging again. She gasped, and his foraging lips took hers in a soul-rending kiss, his searching tongue slid across the softness of her lips, then it thrust deep into her mouth. A wild surge of heat shot through Alissa, settling at her core, to throb and pulsate; a warmth flowed from within, leaving her breathless. She couldn't allow this . . . not until their differences were settled. And she fought to free her lips to tell him so.

With the sound of her whimper, Jared's lips grazed across her cheek. "Don't fight me, love. You're mine." Alissa's mouth opened in protest, but his plundering lips drowned out her cries. His shackling hand loosed her wrists and plunged into the water, capturing an alluring breast, his thumb teasing its studded nipple.

A vibrant chill shuddered her entire length, settling at the juncture of her smooth thighs as his tantalizing fingers taunted her flesh, gently cupping, molding, shaping it to his masculine hand; she groaned with pleasure. "Good?" he asked, his lips leaving hers, again.

Hearing his husky voice, Alissa's brain slowly absorbed its meaning, then she realized she had to stop this madness. Her arm scooped through the bath; water splashed like a wave. Doused in the face, Jared jerked away, and Alissa scrambled from the tub. The large bath sheet covering her from shoulder to ankle, she backed into the corner, quivering from head to foot.

Jared shook his head like a dog, flinging water everywhere. Rising to his feet, he turned his back to her. "We need to talk," he said, in a low, shaky voice, then strode from the small chamber. Alissa followed, her toweling wrapped securely around her, and stopped by the screen. He glanced at her as he dried his face and hair with a cloth he'd grabbed on his way out. "You don't have to dress. What I have to say will take only a moment." Seeing her cautious look, he added, "I'll not touch you again."

Her gaze followed as he strode to the settee to flop down on it in disgust. But she suspected the emotion was aimed at himself, not her. A long sigh escaped him as he looked up at her. "Alissa, I apologize for what just happened. I should have left when I'd found you."

"Why did you enter without knocking?"

"I did knock. You didn't answer. The door was unlocked . . . when I found you, I . . . ." Still feeling the effects of their encounter, the heat continuing to pulsate through his body, his words died in his throat. How could he explain his needs to her? "The reason I came to your room was I couldn't wait till tonight to explain why I had kept Rothhamford's confession a secret. You were already angry, and if I had allowed you to stew, by tonight, I knew you wouldn't listen at all."

She came forward a bit and sat on a low stool, near her dressing table. "You're probably right," she said softly. "Why did you hide the information from me?"

"We've both played our own deceptions, Alissa, each for his own reason. Yours being to protect yourself from an unfair accusation that could have sent you to prison for life. Mine, because I feared once you'd learned that your name had been cleared you'd press for an annulment."

He continued to gaze at her a long moment, and Alissa wondered if she would indeed have done so. He rose, and she watched him pace the room, his hand raking through his thick, damp hair.

"I forced you into a marriage you did not want. Again, I had my reasons for doing so. Megan would have been shattered if you had left her, and I thought if we married, it would help her. You know I have no objections to having more children," he said, and watched her blush slightly. "But in order for us to have come together as man and wife, I had to dispense with Rothhamford's hold over you. Each time I touched you, I knew you thought of him. Hence, I went to London. But on my way back, holding the papers that said you were free, I feared you'd leave Hawkstone. We had not yet consummated our marriage, and considering the conditions under which we wed, no court would deny your request for a dissolution of our vows. So I held the truth from you, hoping I could persuade you to come to my bed willingly. Once you did, you could not leave."

"You would have tricked me into your bed in order to hold me?" she asked softly.

"Yes."

"Why?"

"Megan could not withstand your loss."

"And you?"

"I, too, would miss you." Not hearing a response, Jared headed toward the door. "You are free to leave Hawkstone, Alissa. I will not stop you."

Leave? her heart questioned. Was that what she wanted? No! This was her home, with Megan . . . with Jared. She had nothing else. He was her husband; she, his wife. And whether he truly loved her or not, he was kind, giving, protective, and caring. "Jared," she called almost anxiously as he turned the handle on the door. "Don't leave."

Hearing her plea, he drew a long breath, releasing it slowly. "If I stay, you realize what it means," he said, in a low timbre, still facing the door.

"Yes," she whispered, her eyes suddenly growing misty. One part of her shouted with fear, the other with anticipation, but through the discordant emotions, she knew Jared was her destiny. "I wish to be your wife," she said finally.

Jared turned and leaned back against the locked panel. "Then come to me, love," he said, and prayed she would. In a slow, faltering progression, she moved toward him, until she stopped a half-dozen steps away. "Closer." Three more steps, and she hesitated again, her eyes downcast. He lifted her chin. "Are you certain?"

Her searching gaze met his. "Yes."

"Show me your beauty," he commanded gently, and watched as the towel slowly slipped from her shoulders, down over her breasts, exposing their youthful perfection, then dropped the length of her body, to lie in folds at her feet. The sight of her naked form, blushing in virginal modesty, rekindled the banked fires in him, and he sucked in his breath. "I offer you one last chance to renounce me," he said, in controlled agony.

"I am yours."

"Then so be it," he groaned, and swept her up into his arms. His stride firm, he carried her to the bed, where she slid his length to her feet.

The covers flew to the end of the bed, and Alissa felt herself floating onto the cool sheets. Suddenly thirsty for the sight of his male form, she watched as Jared stripped off his clothes. When she saw the evidence of his desire, her gaze skittered to the opposite side of the room.

Jared chuckled as he eased himself beside her, pulling the cover over his hips, hiding his arousal. "You've done this to me, sweet," he said, smiling, his splayed hand gliding over her taut stomach, and her blush deepened. "Alissa," he said softly. "I want to make love to you. Don't be afraid, sweet." His hand swept upward over her satiny skin toward her breast. As his fingers captured the silken globe, he felt her jerk. *Rothhamford, the bastard!* he thought with such vehemence it reflected in his eyes.

"Have I displeased you," she asked, in a small, quivering voice, wondering if he was angered by something she'd done. Or, perhaps, it was something she had not done.

"No, love," he whispered achingly, wanting desperately to erase Rothhamford from her memory, forever. "Never will you displease me." Then his gently persuasive mouth took possession of hers, tenderly coaxing a response, and her petal-soft lips opened like a flower under his. His eager tongue invaded the honeyed recesses in a teasing, tantalizing foray. Her response, timid at first, grew bolder, and she drew his tongue deeper into her mouth, and Jared could not suppress his groan of pleasure. Desperation shuddered through him, and he suddenly lost all sense of Alissa's needs, his own raw desires erupting forcefully.

His hand hungered to explore the mysteries of her body and sought its repletion. As the satiny texture of her skin enticed his fingers, the heat of his magical touch sent tantalizing shivers down Alissa's spine to radiate outward to every nerve she possessed. His intoxicating kisses, his masterful tongue darting wildly, drugged her senses, and she felt herself melt against the sheets. She wanted something. But she didn't know what. She knew only Jared could supply the remedy to cool the fever building inside her.

Fiery lips blazed the curve of her neck, his hot tongue seeking its pulse, then swirling toward her breast, capturing the taut nipple to suckle gently. His strong hand slipped low over her stomach, his searching fingers dipping between her thighs. She jerked again and closed her legs, embarrassed by his sudden intimacy.

"Don't seal yourself to my touch, love," he whispered huskily, his heavy-lidded gaze seconding his plea. "It's part of making love . . . to prepare you for the ecstasy we'll share."

Her anxious eyes searched his. He did not lie, she knew,

and she slowly relaxed beneath his touch. Shackling his own desires, Jared's gaze never left hers as his gentle fingers glided along the satiny folds, seducing a moist warmth from within her. Then he tenderly probed and heard a gasp of enjoyment as he penetrated her silken bonds, his thumb gently caressing her bud of ecstasy.

She was ready, he knew, but he wanted her more so, and again his lips captured hers, his tongue thrusting intimately, matching his rhythmic fingers. She writhed wildly, her soft cries of rapture filling his ears. He parted her thighs and settled between them. "Put your arms around me, love," he instructed, as he positioned himself, and she encircled his neck. "Now look at me." His desirous gaze penetrated hers as he slowly channeled into her.

The hot, satiny feel of her almost undid him, and he stopped momentarily, fighting for control. Reaching the thin barrier, he urged softly, "Give me your lips, sweet." And his mouth lowered over hers. When she was dizzy with his kiss, his hand slid under her hips, and he thrust forward, swallowing her cry of pain. Instantly, he stilled, waiting. "The worst is over, love. Now the pleasure begins."

Alissa felt a rigid fullness glide upward inside her as Jared eased deeper and deeper. Completely sheathed, he began to move. Each thrust of his hips created a new excitement, until Alissa was wild with want. "Jared, please . . ." And she heard his deep, masculine laughter.

"Move, sweet." And his hand directed her hips to pace with his own. She twisted beneath him, and he felt his restraint snap. All his energies throbbing at his center, his mouth took hers in a fierce, slanting kiss. Then, as her hips arched wildly, her fingers threading through his hair, her tongue mating frantically with his, her ecstatic moan filled his head, and he felt her caressing spasms. Its rhythm rocked him, and with a shout of ecstasy, Alissa's name rising above it, Jared climaxed deep inside her.

Satiated, his breathing settling to a normal pace, Jared feared his superior weight might crush her and rolled to his side, bringing her with him, their legs entwined, their bodies still linked. With gentle fingers, he swept her luxurious hair from her face, gazing at her in awe. Never had a woman given herself so freely to him. Her naivety set aside, she had come alive under his tutelage, willingly offering herself, begging for the unknown pleasures only he could give her.

As his new wife shyly hid her face against his chest, he thought of his first. Celeste and her stiff movements, or her lack of them, always complaining he'd muss her hair, or bruise her ivory skin with his lips, leaving his disgusting love marks on her—it was like bedding a corpse! When he'd finally turned to other women to fulfill his masculine needs, they all had performed in accordance with his wishes, but that was exactly what it had been—a performance.

But Alissa, sweet and yielding, had given him the gift of herself. He'd been the first, the only, and he would teach her how to love him by loving her. He envisioned the endless nights of ardor they would share, her virginal modesty eventually being replaced by a woman's knowledge, her own lips and hands worshipping his body. Yes, he would teach her *all* the ways to love him, by loving her in every way possible. Except with his heart, he admitted cynically, knowing that such emotions were reserved for fools and poets. The soft whisper of his name broke his thoughts. "What is it, sweet?"

"Shouldn't we dress, now?" she asked timidly. "The sun has not yet set and—"

He chuckled. "We shall lie abed and watch its light fade from the sky through your window."

Her eyes widened as she turned scarlet. "But the servants . . . and Megan . . . and Robert!"

"Mr. Stanley has been instructed to keep the household running without me. Megan is with Mary, and my cousin can fend for himself."

"You thought to seduce me all along?" she asked accusingly.

"I had thought to seduce you even before I knew your true identity." He chuckled at the surprised look in her eye. "I thought I suffered from dementia, but there was something about Miss Agatha Pembroke that caught my interest. It certainly wasn't her looks. But she kept slipping in and out of my dreams," he confessed, smiling. "As did a certain young actress whom I'd seen at Covent Garden. The two would intermingle, sometimes becoming one. I think my subconscious had been trying to tell me something, don't you?"

"I can't imagine why," she said facetiously.

"Nor could I, at the time." He cleared the frown from his brow. "It was not your physical beauty that attracted me, for you hid it well. What made me take notice was something else. But to discover your fairness, especially as you are now, makes you all the more desirable." His hand curved over her smooth breast, his thumb teasing the nipple anew, and Alissa felt a tingling sensation shoot to the juncture of her thighs. Noticing the rekindled fire in his eyes, she fought to flee the bed. "You will not escape me," he said, his smile growing wicked, as he clamped his arm over her waist. Then she felt the surge of his arousal against her leg, and her eyes widened.

"Y-you don't expect to—"

"Yes, sweet. Until the sun rises tomorrow."

In a quick move, she slipped from his grasp and pulled the sheet high upon her neck. "You have not yet answered my question."

"What question?" he asked, reaching for her.

"Had you planned to seduce me?"

"I thought I'd answered that."

"Hardly. When you came in here . . . before all this happened . . . tonight. . . ."

Jared chuckled as he slid along the sheet, edging closer to her. "I'd hoped it would end like this, but my intent was to explain why I kept the information about Rothhamford secret. After you heard me out, I'd planned to offer you your freedom, which I did. You made the choice to stay, Alissa. Now I choose to love you again." He reached for her and pulled her close to his body, and she gasped at his strength. "Just look me in the eye, sweet," he said, as his head rested high on his hand, the other traveling low on her stomach, then his fingers slipped into her curls. "This is my home," he told her, his gentle fingers entering her. "No other shall ever seek refuge here, promise me."

Her huge eyes stared up at him and she nodded, wondering if he thought she would cuckold him. Had Celeste?

Surely not! Jared was all a woman could ever want. His masterful hands and tantalizing lips could satisfy any female. They had her! And she blushed anew.

"Tell me," he said, his fingers lightly teasing her until she felt herself relax in wanton surrender.

"I promise," she said breathlessly, then moaned in wild delight, feeling that special warmth surge through her again.

His heated gaze still held hers. "What do you promise?"

"That no one shall have me but you."

His magnetic gaze seduced her, and she slowly placed her hand on his chest. Solid, virile, masculine, she decided, as she threaded her fingers through the crisp fur growing there. Feeling the rougher texture of his flesh, she marveled at the difference between man and woman. Then more boldly, her hand edged downward, and she heard the rasp of Jared's indrawn breath as his desire-laden gaze beseeched her to search lower. Knowing she held power over him, the same as he held it over her, she sought and found his erect member. His eyes closed, a look of pain crossed his face, and she instantly released him.

"I hurt you?" she questioned innocently, and heard his ragged laugh.

"No, sweet," he groaned. "When we have been together longer, you'll understand. Now hold me, love." Her gentle touch almost undid him again, but he fought for control. Then he moved in her hand, showing her what he desired. Shyly, she tried to please him, then with more understanding, she did, and with his own hand actively ministering to her, his lips captured hers in an achingly endless kiss. Their tongues entwined, mating in furious delight; then Jared's mounting desires ready to erupt, Alissa's hips twisting wildly, he tore his mouth from hers and hoarsely demanded, "Lead me home, Alissa . . . lead me home."

And she did.

At breakfast, Alissa lowered her fork and glanced up to see her husband's warm gaze upon her; a lazy smile curved his lips, and she blushed. Her own gaze fell to her plate.

Their night of lovemaking had not ended until dawn, their passions finally satiated. But, now, as she pondered her wantonness, she felt embarrassed. The hardest thing she'd ever done in her life was to walk from behind their closed door to face, again, all those residing at Hawkstone. Every last one of them knew what had kept the master's attention through the past evening, as well as the entire night!

"You'll get used to it, sweet," Jared whispered as he leaned close to her ear and squeezed her hand, resting along the table. "None of us would be here now, if it were not for the private times a man and woman share together. Just hold your head high and look them in the eye; the house will soon quiet of its gossip."

"I doubt it."

Jared chuckled. "You fear they heard your cries of ecstasy?"

"Jared!" she admonished, then looked around the room.

"We're alone, sweet. In fact, we might be for quite some time. I have a feeling that everyone here is afraid to walk into a room where we've closed the door."

"In the dining room! You can't mean—"

Jared laughed at her innocence. "Passion, my love, does not know the name of a place, nor does it care if it has a feather mattress. It simply needs a man and a woman to find its fulfillment."

"But—"

"Shall I show you?"

"Again?"

"Always." And he watched as she blushed anew when she realized his meaning.

The door suddenly opened, and Robert strode through, but stopped short when he saw the magnificent beauty seated at the table. Recovering, he sat to Jared's left. "Well, I thought never to see you *this* early," he commented, snatching a muffin from the plate. "I can't say that I'd blame you, though, if you were to disappear for months." He turned to Alissa. "This surely is not Miss Pembroke?"

"No," Alissa said, looking him directly in the eye as Jared had suggested; she found it helped. "Miss Pembroke unfortunately passed on some time ago."

"Unfortunately?" he asked. "Or fortunately?"

Taken aback by the hard look in his eye, Alissa stared at

him, then she heard Jared say, "Both, Robert. Unfortunate for the dear woman herself. But most fortunate for me. I wouldn't have met Alissa, unless dear Agatha had taken the opportune time to transcend these earthly bounds. Heaven has her now, and I have an angel from on high."

"I believe she's turned you into a poet, cousin," Robert gibed. "Of course," he said, rising, stuffing another muffin into his pocket, "a beauty like hers has encouraged many a man to pick up the pen and pour his heart and soul onto the parchment. Why should you be any different?" Theatrically, his hands covered his heart. "I must confess I can think of a rhyme or two myself."

All bawdy, Alissa thought, her eyes narrowing.

"Well, I'm off for a ride through the countryside," he informed them, striding to the door. "Lovers should definitely be left alone." Then the door thumped closed behind him.

"I should box his ears," Jared commented in a growl.

Alissa smiled brightly. "You'll get used to it, sweet."

"Madam, I'm beginning to find it easier said than done. But, of course, the reason behind the teasing is worth every annoying bit of banter that touches my ears." He smiled. "Now, I believe we were discussing dining rooms . . . or was it passion? I'd be more than happy to show you—" The door opened again, and when Jared saw it was Megan, his mouth clamped shut. "Good morning, darling," he said when she reached his side, and placed a fatherly peck on her forehead.

"You should have joined us earlier, dearest," Alissa said, smiling over Megan's head at her husband, and received a disconcerted look in return. "Let's fetch a hot plate, shall we?" She rose and guided Megan to the buffet.

As Jared watched the sway of her hips, last night's memories came flooding through him, and he quickly adjusted the napkin on his lap. Some rules would need to be laid down to his daughter about entering his rooms at will. It mattered not if it was in broad daylight, either. A lazy smile crossed his face. The new mistress of Hawkstone would be kept quite busy, but not with household matters. Unmaking the bed would be the most she'd be allowed to do in the way of labor; the rest he would attend to himself. Quite happily so, he decided.

After the threesome finished their breakfast, Jared suggested they go upstairs. When they reached Alissa's door she was surprised to see her personal items were being moved two doors down.

"Close your mouth," he said, nudging her chin upward. "My room is the farthest from anyone's ears." He nodded toward Megan, who had signed she wanted to carry Alissa's blue silk dress and now was helping Mary. Then he noticed his wife's shocked look. "Have no fear, love. I swallowed most of your ecstatic cries with my kisses. However, I'm not certain of my own." She reddened further, and he laughed. "Don't be embarrassed, sweet. You should be proud you can evoke such passion in your husband."

Stepping from her father's room, Megan ran up to them and took Alissa's hand, urging her to her new quarters. Once inside, Megan skipped off toward the armoire to again help Mary. Alissa felt a bit awkward as she gazed at the gold, white, and black decor. She'd been in here only once, when she'd frantically searched for Megan, to eventually find her in the east wing. Jared still did not know of the doll's destruction. And possibly never would. As she glanced at the huge bed, draped in gold and black satin, she noted it was twice the size of her own, and she imagined Jared's long body lying in its center, she cuddled close to his side.

"We only need a small portion of it, sweet," he whispered, his hot breath fanning her ear. "As soon as the room clears, we shall discover which area provides the most comfort."

Startled by his boldness, she turned to make a retort. What could she say? Especially with Mary and Megan within earshot! Apparently, Jared realized her predicament, for he grinned lazily, challenging her with his eyes to make a comeback. She flashed him a superior look, telling him with her own eyes he'd better behave or she'd slap his hands. But Jared mistook her meaning.

"Don't ever think to settle our differences in bed, love," he said, a subtle threat laced through his tone. "I'll not have a cold body next to me again." Then he strode toward the chair near the armoire and fell into it, waiting for the room to empty.

Alissa's confused gaze followed him, but her attention turned to Megan, who had moved to her side, then she glanced at the dress Mary held on high. "My clothes!" she cried, realizing the ones she'd left in London were now here at Hawkstone. "Where did you get them?"

"While in London, I stopped to visit with Mrs. Binnington. She sent them along with her love."

"She knows about us?"

"Yes. In fact, the poor woman almost fainted from relief when I told her." He chuckled, his temper having subsided. "I'm certain she'd thought I had come to accuse her . . . to exact some sort of punishment. But once all had been said and done, she seemed quite happy to know you were now my wife."

"You charmed the stockings off her, I suppose?"

"Certainly," he admitted conceitedly. "By the way, she is coming for a visit about month's end." He watched a surprised delight spread over his wife's face and smiled to himself. "In the meantime, I've planned a trip for us."

"Where?" she asked, her hands settling on Megan's shoulders, and both gazed at him in expectation.

"The three of us are off to Edinburgh on the morrow."

Megan broke from Alissa's gentle hold to run and hug her father's neck, overjoyed at the news. His brow rose. "Don't I get a hug from my wife, as well?"

Alissa slowly walked toward him. "Only if you promise to take us to the Royal Theatre. Megan has so wanted to see a real play."

"Influenced by an actress, I suppose."

"Possibly." She leaned down and kissed his upturned cheek. "It'll be a wonderful holiday. Thank you."

"With my two leading ladies by my side, how could it not be?" he asked, smiling a bit wickedly as his hand slid low over her hip, making Alissa straighten with a jerk. "Mary," he called over his shoulder, still chuckling, "have Mr. Stanley bring up my surprise."

Several minutes later, Mr. Stanley, followed by two other servants, carried box after box, marked by the finest fashion houses in London, into the room. Watching his excited wife and daughter tear through the wrappings, strewing lids and tissue paper all over his room, Jared began to wonder if *love* might not be such a bad thing after all.

CHAPTER

Seventeen

A low hum of voices chorused through the Royal Theatre in Edinburgh as the throng settled into their seats. In their private box, Alissa fanned herself as the excitement grew around her. Next to her, Megan gaped in awe. Not every day did a child of six attend a play, and Alissa smiled, noting the girl's expectant look.

"You're beautiful, love," Jared whispered in his wife's ear as he leaned intimately close to her.

Alissa turned a teasing smile on him. "So are you."

Jared's throaty laughter drew several curious glances from the boxes sweeping the circle beyond theirs. Smiling, he inclined his head toward the onlookers; each bowed in return. Then behind their fans and cupped hands, he noticed the speculations passed one to the other. "I believe the word is *handsome,* sweet," he said, while wondering if he'd be approached during the break. "Women are beautiful; men are handsome."

"In my eyes, you are beautiful," she countered, her captivating smile melting his heart. "Tell us how we match up," she said of Megan and herself. "Shall we pass for those of the peerage?"

Jared quickly masked his surprise over her words and surveyed her lithe form swathed in a white satin gown, the bodice beaded with tiny pearls; her intricately styled hair, woven with white rosebuds; the silk lace shawl, draped over her gloved arms; and the ivory fan in her hand. "You look like a marchioness. And Megan looks like a princess."

His daughter smiled up at him, then straightened the satin skirt of her dress, which matched Alissa's, except for its decolletage and length, and turned her eyes back to the activities below. "Thank you again for our beautiful gowns," Alissa said, her gaze warm. "They fit perfectly."

"Indeed, they do. Mrs. Binnington assured me the dress we'd taken on our shopping trip had been an exact fit. Megan's size I already knew. But beware, my love, should you start gaining weight, you'll be left without a stitch."

Alissa blinked. Did he think she ate too much? Then noting his gaze rested upon her stomach, she caught his meaning and cast her eyes about to see if anyone noticed the flush rising on her cheeks. "Your talk is inappropriate."

"It is fact, love. If it hasn't happened already, it will soon. It can't be helped, especially when we're not apart for more than a few hours at a time." His words turned her a flaming scarlet, and she snapped her fan open, hiding her face behind it. He chuckled, his smile growing wicked. "I would have it no other way. Nor, might I add, would you, love. In fact, I recall, approximately two hours past, we—" Jared's breath whooshed from his lungs as a pointed elbow jabbed his side. "I'll tell you later," he rasped, the houselights dimming slowly.

The curtain rose, and Alissa noticed Megan sit taller in her seat. As the lines flowed from the actors' lips, she turned her attention to the stage. Ten minutes along, the actress playing the lead marched across the front of the stage, her lamenting verse recited from memory. The woman turned, the train of her gown swinging wide behind her. Alissa gasped; her hands gripped the chair's arms. My God! She's too close! her mind shouted, realizing the woman's flowing dress was about to brush one of the lamps lighting the stage. Halfway rising from her seat, she started to cry out, but her throat refused to shout its warning.

"What's wrong?" Jared asked, leaning toward her, touching her arm. Anxious cries erupted from the audience, and he turned to see the flames licking up the back of the actress's gown. A shrill scream sliced the air, only inches from him, yet he couldn't fathom its source. Then he glanced at his daughter.

Alissa squatted before the child, shaking her slender shoulders. "Megan!" she called, yet the girl's screams still pierced the air. "She's all right. Look!"

Onstage, the lead actor had swept off his cape to smother the fire; the audience breathed a relieved sigh as they saw there was no actual injury, but Jared paid it no heed. In one swoop, he lifted his screaming daughter into his arms and strode from their box, Alissa running behind them.

By the time they'd reached the entrance, brushing past those who'd fled the unnerving scene, Megan had quieted. Her jaw clamped rigidly, her wide green eyes stared unseeingly, and her small body quivered as though she'd been taken with a chill.

Out on the street, Jared glanced up and down the long line of carriages, frantically searching for their own, but Mr. Stanley had already spotted them. The team of horses drew to a bone-crushing stop, and he jumped from his seat. "What be the matter with her?"

"Get us to the hotel, then find a physician," he ordered, and strode to their open carriage, Alissa still following close behind. "Help me with this sleeve," he commanded her when they were seated inside, Mr. Stanley whipping the horses into a full gallop, and she pulled his arm free of his coat. His daughter cradled close to him, he wrapped his coat around her to warm her shivering body. "Megan, sweet, it's all right. Papa has you, love," he crooned, rocking her in his arms. "He won't let anything happen to you."

Alissa heard Jared's ragged, indrawn breath, his face turning heavenward. Eyes closed, his features twisted in emotional pain. "What do you think it is?" she asked, placing a gentle hand on his. His anguished gaze held hers a long moment. No answer came forth. Then his attention switched back to Megan as he spoke softly to her again.

Confused, Alissa surveyed him. Did he blame her for insisting they take in a play? All was right, until . . . My God! The fire! Did any of this have to do with Celeste?

The carriage suddenly came to a stop outside the hotel,

and Alissa followed Jared up to their suite. With Megan swathed in blankets, they awaited the physician's arrival.

"She's suffering from extreme shock," the white-haired man said, placing his stethoscope into his bag. "Her mind has closed itself off. I'm sorry, but there's nothing I can do." He squeezed Jared's shoulder, consoling him. "If she should have the terrors again, give her a few drops of this. It should settle her nerves. But only a few drops, mind you. Laudanum is a powerful drug. It can be habit-forming, and quite dangerous to one so young. Tomorrow, if she's not better, I suggest you return home. Familiar surroundings might help, and her own physician knows her needs better than I."

"There is nothing we can do?" Alissa asked, anxiously.

"Talk to her. Tell her of your love. She's able to hear you. One's hearing never shuts down, not until we've met our end. If you need me, send your man around."

"Thank you, sir. My husband and I appreciate your concern and advice."

"See to him, too," he said, nodding in Jared's direction where he stood by the bed. "He's on the verge of coming unglued. Are you sure you can handle this alone?"

"Yes," she said with certainty.

"Then you're stouter of heart than most ladies. Here are some smelling salts, just in case."

Alissa gently pushed his hand away. "I'm not a swooning woman who takes to her bed whenever a crisis arises. Thank you, anyway."

He smiled. "No, I can see you are a woman with strength. Much more than even your husband might realize. Good night, Mrs. Braxton. I hope all goes well for your daughter."

After the doctor left, Alissa turned to see Jared slumped over in a chair, his head held in his hands. She hurried to his side. "Jared?" she questioned, dropping to her knees beside him. "What's wrong, my love?"

He jerked his fingers through his hair, his breath pulled between his teeth in a rush, and when he finally turned toward her, Alissa almost fell away. She'd never seen such volatile anger in anyone's eyes.

"Do you blame me?" she asked hesitantly.

He stared at her, then shoved from his chair and paced the

room. His hand scoured the back of his neck, and he shook his head. "No. I blame myself."

"Why?" she asked, not understanding.

"Because it is my fault that she's like this."

Alissa studied his agitated movements. Finding the courage, she stated, "It has to do with the fire at Hawkstone."

"Yes," he hissed vehemently.

"Tell me about that night."

Hard green eyes turned on her; he laughed cynically. "This was to be sort of a honeymoon for us, Alissa. Not a discussion of my first wife's death."

"Circumstances have changed things, Jared," she said, her voice growing stronger as she came to her feet. "If we are to help Megan, I must know about her mother. From the first, whenever I asked about Celeste, you managed to dodge my questions. Other than assuming she was much like Patricia, I know nothing of her. Except you allow her to stand between us! This time I'll not let you shun the issue!"

Amazed by her righteous anger, Jared viewed her at length. "You're very perceptive, Alissa. I have let her stand between us and for that I am sorry."

"The fire, Jared. Tell me of that night."

He released a long breath, then strode toward his vacated chair and pulled its mate over to face it. "Have a seat." He sat heavily in his own chair, his forearms bracing themselves on his thighs as he leaned forward. His hands were clasped, thumbs pressed to one another. "I must explain, Alissa, my first marriage went from one of love—a mistaken emotion on my part—to one of tolerance," he said, the dark memories flooding through him. "When I married, I thought I loved Celeste, but as time went on, I realized I'd simply been infatuated with her physical beauty. After Megan's birth, Celeste refused to allow me into her bed. At least, not without payment."

"What do you mean?"

He laughed cynically. "She was willing to sell herself to me for a new gown, a piece of jewelry, or whatever met her fancy at the time. At first, I subscribed to her little game by buying her favors. But her cold responses soon cooled my desires. Any feelings I had for her finally died. I allowed her to remain at Hawkstone only because she was Megan's mother. Celeste stayed only because of my station and wealth."

"And the night she died . . . what happened?" Alissa asked, reaching out to him.

Jared looked at the soft hand covering his, then took it in his own. "The night of the fire, we argued," he said in a low, controlled voice, fighting down his emotions. "I had come home to find her in her room, pacing the floor like an anxious cat. I don't remember what I said to her, but it set her off. She accused me of being with my mistress—"

"Were you?"

Jared looked at Alissa. "Yes," he said finally, then waited for her condemning words. They never came. "She knew I entertained other women, but it had come about only in the last year of our marriage. Although she refused my advances, she still wanted no one else in my bed. She was demented . . . I'm certain of it."

"You cannot be blamed for seeking someone to show you kindness," Alissa said, with understanding. "She pushed you into another's arms."

"Most women would not admit that, Alissa," he said, a weak smile on his face. "I soon discovered why she'd brought up the subject that particular night. Cloaked in false indignation, she informed me she could no longer abide my 'adulterous affairs.' She was leaving me. Weary of her threats, her tantrums, her coldness, I toasted her decision with the brandy I held, offering her my blessings. She seemed startled that I would allow her to leave so easily. Perhaps my uncaring attitude damaged her pride, because it loosened her tongue."

"And?"

"I was told she'd found a new love . . . a man who would care for her better than I. 'My sincere sympathies to the poor fool,' I said, and was told he wasn't *poor*. She informed me they'd loved each other for years and it was only now that she'd decided to go to him. I told her to be off as quickly as possible. But, as she started gathering her jewels, I informed her she'd take nothing but the clothes on her back . . . she went wild. She started throwing things— cursing the day she'd met me. I merely laughed at her and started to leave the room, intent on washing my hands of the whole episode. But then she hit a chord in me that I could not—would not—abide. . . ."

His voice trailed off, and Alissa tenderly squeezed his hands, knowing there was only one thing the hateful woman could have used against him to hurt him. "Megan?"

"Yes, Megan. Celeste cursed our daughter . . . said she hated her . . . wished Megan had been born dead. She kept at it . . . wouldn't shut up. Something snapped inside me. I remember throwing my glass across the room and going after her. I suppose she recognized the anger in my eyes for what it was. I could have killed her. Sometimes I think I actually would have, except . . . ." The force of his memory hit him so hard a shudder racked his entire body and his eyes closed in pain.

"Jared," Alissa whispered, gently, "tell me." If he could only voice it, she thought, then perhaps Celeste's ghost would be exorcised, gone forever. Now, more than ever, she knew the events of that night still haunted him. And he carried the emotional scars, from that day to this. "Except what?"

"In defense," he whispered, "or anger, I don't know which, she grabbed a book from the table to hurl at me. In the process she knocked over the lamp . . . the oil spread over the cloth, the flames after it. She was too close . . . her gown caught. I tried to help her, but she fought me . . . ran from me. Her screams were unbearable. It was too late . . . she threw herself through the window, her lover's name on her lips. The drapes caught as she did so. They went up like a torch. I couldn't extinguish them, so I found Megan and alerted the house. We saved all but the east wing."

A picture of the actress leapt into Alissa's mind, flames licking up her skirts, then it suddenly transposed itself into a vision of the faceless Celeste. Was it possible . . . ? "Jared, that night, where did you find Megan?"

"She was in the hallway, outside our rooms."

"And where would you have expected to find her?"

"Four doors down, asleep in her bed," he answered with a frown. "Why do you ask?"

"Is it possible . . . I mean, seeing the actress tonight, do you think—"

"My God!" he cried, finally understanding Alissa's meaning. "I never realized . . . I only thought she'd suffered a paralyzing shock because of the fire itself and the fact her mother had died in it. But she'd heard Celeste's hateful words. She'd actually witnessed her mother—Damn it all! Why hadn't I recognized it before!"

"It doesn't matter. We know what has happened to cause her reaction tonight, and we'll be able to help her."

Jared enfolded Alissa in his arms. "Why does a child so young have to suffer so much?"

He had not expected an answer, and Alissa did not offer one. As they continued their vigil, she kept thinking about her husband's words.

Cold and heartless, Celeste had nearly destroyed two lives, as she had her own. No wonder Jared viewed love so cynically. On the night they'd wed, he told her the emotion was not worth the pain. Now, she understood why. Yet it angered Alissa that he believed all women were like his first wife. Especially her. His words, warning her he'd not allow a cold body in bed with him again, forcing her to promise him, while he'd made love to her, that she was his home and no other would be allowed to seek refuge in her except him, came to full fruition in her mind. He *had* been cuckolded! And apparently he knew the man's name. Unknowingly, she voiced her disbelief aloud, "Ian?"

Jared's head snapped around. *"What?"*

Alissa blinked. "I'm sorry, I didn't hear you."

"Perhaps not, but I heard you, madam. How do you know Ian Sinclair?" Her startled look confirmed she did. "Don't lie to me, either. It won't wash, Alissa."

"We met at the cottage. He came upon Megan and me while we were picnicking one day."

"The bastard trespassed?" he hissed, then wondered if it was only his land which had been invaded. But, immediately, he realized he'd allowed his distrust of Ian Sinclair to dictate his thoughts. His wife had come to him pure, virginal, and she'd not been out of his sight since the day he'd first bedded her. "You'll not have any further communication with the man," he ordered, coldly, grasping her chin. "Understand?"

Rebelling against the insinuation written in his gaze,

Alissa pulled free. "Ian Sinclair did not cuckold you in the past. Nor would he do so now, sir. I believe him when he says he's still your friend. Unfortunately, you're not wise enough to recognize the fact."

She started to rise, but he caught her arm. His grip bit painfully into her flesh. "If I ever learn you've gone against my orders, there'll be hell to pay, madam. So heed my warning. Stay clear of Sinclair."

Jared let loose her arm, and Alissa walked on stiff legs to Megan's bed. His threats had made her bristle. If there were only some way to convince him . . . but she knew her words would settle on closed ears. Tamping down her anger, she spoke to Megan, instead, as the doctor had suggested.

Little communication fell between Alissa and Jared the remainder of the night, Ian Sinclair standing between them like a stone wall. By dawn's light, Megan hadn't improved, and they headed back to Hawkstone.

As Jared carried his daughter into the house, his silent wife behind him, he glanced at the figure framed in the sitting room doorway. Without missing a step, he recovered from the shock of seeing the all too familiar face.

Damnation! Had the whole world gone mad? he wondered. Or was it only his doorstep that seemed beset by fools and interfering relatives of late?

Turning to Mr. Stanley, he shifted his daughter into the man's arms and ordered him to take her to her rooms. As Alissa moved around him, he caught her arm. "I'll be detained a few moments. Please see to Megan for me."

"What's wrong with the child?" Edward Braxton asked, moving into the foyer. "And who's this woman?"

Not knowing the man's identity, Alissa resented his authoritative tone. "And who, sir, are you?"

"*I*, young lady, am—"

"An interloper," Jared finished for his father, his tone frigid. "I don't remember issuing you an invitation to my home. However, since you've taken it upon yourself to come at will, I suggest you find a comfortable spot and stay put. I have more urgent matters to attend to right now."

When the man finally stepped from the shadows, Alissa gasped. Save for the color of his eyes, and his silver hair, he was an older version of Jared. "He's your *father?*"

"He sired me," Jared said, his cold eyes on the man.

"I'd better go," she said, deciding it best to leave the men alone. The way the two had sized each other up, she was certain they were ready to stretch the entry ten paces and fire! "If there's any change, I'll send Mary for you." Then, without thinking, she stood on tiptoe and kissed Jared's cheek.

As she lifted her skirts to climb the stairs, she heard the elder Mr. Braxton say, "So, you've taken to keeping your mistress on the premises, now."

"You, sir, are a fool!" Jared countered, angrily. "The young lady you have just maligned is not *my* mistress, but *the* mistress of Hawkstone. Alissa is my wife."

"Wife!" his father shouted, but Alissa did not linger to hear the rest. By no means did she wish to become embroiled in another family row. Patricia's maliciousness had been enough for her tastes. She could only imagine the malevolence that would come from her father-in-law's lips.

Over the next three days, Alissa stayed at Megan's side, Jared coming in every hour. Each time he did so, his temperament had worsened, and she felt certain his father was the cause. Only once did the man himself come into the room.

Upon entering, he had refused to address Alissa, choosing to remain aloofly silent. Then, to her dismay, he'd sat in a corner chair for a good half hour. The man's stony presence unnerved her, his narrowed gaze inspecting her every move, and when she felt certain she was on the verge of delivering a well-deserved rebuke to the arrogant man, he rose from his seat and left. She'd not seen him since.

Fortunately, Megan had begun to regain a sense of reality. Apparently, the familiar surroundings and the gentle words of encouragement from Alissa and her father were acting as the needed medicine the doctor had prescribed.

On the afternoon of the fourth day, while Megan slept, Mary at her side, Alissa descended the stairs, heading toward the kitchens for a cup of tea. As her feet hit the diamond-patterned marble flooring, she stopped short. Shouts came from the direction of Jared's office, rebounding through the halls. Slowly traveling toward the back of the house, a frown settled upon her brow. Several servants, who milled around the area, dusting nonexistent cobwebs, suddenly scurried off to attend to other chores. Eyes narrowing, her arms crossing over her breasts, she stood directly outside the closed door, listening to the heated discussion.

". . . a common actress! You young whelp! Haven't you the sense to marry into your own class?" Edward Braxton barked. "I should disown you!"

"You forget, *Father,*" Jared shot back, "when you practically accused me of murdering my first wife, I renounced all claim to your estates, your monies, and your titles! I don't give a fig for any of it!"

"You cannot simply renounce a title, you dim-witted fool! Despite what you say, you're the Marquis of Ebonwyck! And when I die—which, by God, will be another fifty-six years hence, if I have anything to say about it—you'll be the Duke of Claremore!"

Outside the room, Alissa lifted her chin from the vicinity of her chest and snapped her jaw shut. *Marquis of Ebonwyck? Duke of Claremore?* Was this some sort of absurd joke? Then Jared's words boomed through the door.

"I can do whatever I damned well please! All who reside within a fifty-mile radius of Hawkstone know they had better not address me by anything other than *mister.* I have not been called by my title for two years now, and I'll not be called by it again. As soon as my son is born, I'll gladly make a formal surrender of my title, which others have done in the past, whereupon it can be conferred on him, making him the heir apparent. And *that,* Your Grace, I shall do!"

"So, she's with child already!" the duke accused, hotly. "Your reckless behavior in pursuing a willing piece of flesh has trapped you. Fool! Didn't you think to pay her off instead of marrying her!"

"Alissa was a virgin when I took her to my bed. Our marriage came first, sir!"

"You don't mean to insinuate that you love this commoner, this—this actress?"

"Love has nothing to do with it!" Jared shouted, his sardonic words slicing through the wood straight into Alissa's heart. "She pleases me. At least she willingly shares my bed! That's all I want from her. But since you are so worried about your damned title, I tell you this: When I impregnate her and she bears me a son, then your worries are over. If she does not bear me a son, then you know as well as I that Megan, being a Peeress in Her Own Right, can carry the title through her to her own son. Praise be you're of the old Scottish line! Save that Megan's child will not carry the name Braxton, at least, there will be yet another Duke of Claremore! And furthermore, you—" The door suddenly flew inward, and Jared swallowed his heated words as he viewed Alissa standing just inside its frame.

"You, sir, are an ass!" she hissed at her husband, her blue eyes flashing in anger . . . and hurt. "Deceptions abound within you, my lord." She spat the form of address as though she'd just ingested poison. "Is it an affliction that is common among all the nobility?" she asked, sarcastically, and Jared realized she referred to Rothhamford, as well as himself.

"Is it your custom to eavesdrop on a private conversation at will?" the duke asked, condescendingly.

"Your Grace." Alissa inclined her head in mockery. "Eavesdropping is reserved for those who press their ears to the walls and doors. Since the entire household has been alerted that I am considered to be, in your eyes, a trollop, a lowly commoner, who's trapped the Marquis of Ebonwyck into marriage, I do not call it eavesdropping!" Her eyes shifted from the duke to Jared. "Likewise, they also know my husband is pleased with my performances in bed and I'm to be considered, by him, nothing more than a brood mare! Of course, it's expected I shall produce a male heir so his father will have a descendent on whom to place his esteemed title." She noticed Jared's gaze fall from hers. Guilty as charged! she thought. "Since the two of you have been so forthright in expressing your feelings, I shall be equally as honest. As for any desire to be called a marchioness, I disavow it! As for producing an heir to satisfy the childish desires of a pompous old man, I shall not do it! And, finally, Lord Ebonwyck," she said, walking up to her husband, poking a finger into his solid chest, "you'll find the pleasures I gave you are now but a memory. I'll not be used by any man, whatever his purpose. You're no longer welcome in my bed, sir!"

Sufficiently cowed, Jared watched his wife whirl in a flurry of skirt. "Alissa," he called, but the door slammed behind her. He should go after her, he knew, but he was certain she'd throw his explanations and apologies back in his face. Feeling he'd been kicked in the gut, he sank into a chair.

"The girl has spunk," Edward Braxton stated with admiration. "Haven't had a woman dress me down like that in a good thirty-five years. Deserved it then, too."

"What happened?" Jared asked uninterestedly.

"Why, I married the young lady, of course."

"Mother gave you a tongue-lashing?" he asked, remembering her gentle, soft-spoken nature.

"Only once. It was before the announcement of our engagement. She'd caught me in the gardens with a rather striking blonde. The young woman had complained a lash had fallen into her eye, and still being a bit wet behind the ears, I'd fallen for her story. Your mother came upon us just as the young lady threw herself into my arms. I shan't ever forget your mother's fury . . . beautiful, passionate, she was, her green eyes flashing in anger. That's when I knew I loved her." Jared's father patted his son's shoulder. "Buck up, lad. She'll cool off. Turn on that Braxton charm of yours, and she'll fall into your arms again."

"I suppose you used your 'Braxton charm' on Mother?"

"Naturally."

"And how long did it take you to convince her the blonde meant nothing to you?"

"A year."

"A year!"

Edward chuckled. "In your case, it might take two. Your wife's temperament is far more volatile than your mother's was. You'd best prepare yourself for a long siege. A few diamonds might help appease her."

"Not Alissa," Jared grumbled.

"Then I suggest you discover what it is she really wants from you."

"If I knew that, I'd offer it to her now." He jerked to his feet. "Damnation! Nothing goes right of late!" Wanting to be alone to think, he strode to the door, where he turned a caustic eye on his father. "I've some things to attend to. You'll have to entertain yourself for a while."

The Duke of Claremore watched the door close on his

son's back and shook his head, partially blaming himself for the split between his son and new daughter-in-law. Edward Braxton's opinion of Alissa Ashford Braxton had changed the instant she'd burst into the room. He'd seen the hurt in her eyes, masked by anger, and he knew it had been caused by his son's words, more than his own biting remarks.

Apparently, she'd known nothing of his son's link to the peerage. The contempt in which she held their class had been made quite clear. She'd spoken of deception being an affliction of all nobility. What that was about, he'd have to discover. But she'd not married his son because of rank or title, that he knew. And when he'd suggested appeasing her with jewels, Jared had inferred nothing of a material nature could buy her. That left only one thing, and Edward knew its name.

"You foolish pup," the duke said to his absent son. "If you'd drop the scales of cynicism from your eyes, you'd see what it is she needs to bring her back to your arms. I could tell you, but you would not believe me. So, until you shed your blinders, you'll be made to suffer."

Deciding that talking to the walls did him little good, he thought to visit with his granddaughter, the only heir he might very well have, thanks to his interference. And with a firm stride, the Duke of Claremore quit the room.

CHAPTER
Eighteen

Sweet Honesty crested the hill, Alissa atop her back. *"You look like a marchioness."* Jared's words rang through her head, infuriating her the more. *"Have you taken to snooping as a pastime?"* The coach! The design had been a crest! *"She's the daughter of the Ma—"* The master of Hawkstone? No! Leona had been about to say the *Marquis of Ebonwyck! Fool!* she berated herself silently. All the signs had been there! How could she have missed them?

Seeing horse and rider bearing down on him across the glade, Ian Sinclair hopped to his feet, then grabbed the winded mare's reins. "Aha! I see the butterfly has emerged from her cocoon!"

Blue fire crackled in her eyes. "You knew, didn't you!"

"That you weren't Agatha Pembroke? Certainly. It was I who'd made certain Jared knew of her. A friend helped—"

"Not that!" She slid from the saddle, Ian catching her waist. "You knew he was a marquis! Why didn't you tell me?"

Ian chuckled. "You didn't ask."

"Ask! Was it necessary?"

"Why should his title bother you?"

"Because," she said peevishly.

"All is not wedded bliss, then?"

"You know we're married?"

243

"Certainly. There's little I don't know that goes on at Hawkstone."

"You've placed a spy in our midst," she accused.

Ian chuckled anew. "Hardly. A member of Jared's staff is betrothed to a member of mine. I had nothing to do with placing Mary at Hawkstone, but through her, I'm kept abreast of the important happenings."

"Tell me something," Alissa said, eyeing him carefully. "Why didn't you tell Jared I was a fraud when you'd first discovered the fact?"

"Because I knew you would be good for Megan."

She tilted her head. "And I suppose you hold a title, as well?"

"Actually, I'm an earl . . . the Earl of Huntsford, at your service, Lady Ebonwyck," he said, bowing. "Any other questions, my lady?"

As Ian lashed the reins to a tree limb, Alissa viewed him. Yes, there were several, but how to approach them was the problem. Sighing, she finally blurted, "Jared believes you cuckolded him. Is it true . . . was Celeste your lover?"

"*No,* Alissa. She was not," he answered, firmly, truthfully, and Alissa believed him. "When did Jared say this?"

Alissa told him of their disastrous trip to Edinburgh, of Megan's frightful shock, and of their subsequent suspicions that the child had actually witnessed her mother's death. But she did not speak of Jared's command that she not see Ian again. Ian Sinclair was the only one she could confide in at the moment and receive sound advice from in return.

"Is Megan all right?"

"She is improving daily."

Ian suddenly erupted. "Damn Celeste! She's caused more problems than she was worth."

"She died with your name on her lips," Alissa whispered, watching for his reaction. It was one of complete surprise.

"I have no idea why," he said, holding her gaze. "Celeste made several advances toward me the last two years of her life. Physically, she was a very tempting woman, but I swear I never encouraged her. Jared was my best friend. I'd never cuckold him." Then, as he gazed at Alissa, Ian wondered if his statement were completely true. Never with Celeste, he knew. But Alissa? Yes, he admitted, for he no longer viewed her only as a friend. His heart seemed to do odd things, of late, whenever she was near. Great care had to be taken, he knew. "You appear to be in need of a friend. Can I help?"

"No," she said, deciding it best that Ian not involve himself. "I must face my problems alone."

"Should you change your mind, the door to Falcon's Gate is always open."

"Thank you, Ian. I appreciate your kindness." She raised on tiptoes and kissed his cheek.

Hidden in the copse, across the clearing, Robert Braxton Hamilton watched the intimate display. "Well, Jared, old boy," he said, chuckling, his horse's ears the only ones to hear, "you seem to have the damnedest bit of luck with your wives." Then he turned the gelding and quietly headed back to Hawkstone, planning to have a friendly visit with his uncle.

Jared left Megan's room and strode down the hallway in search of his wife. When she'd returned to the house after her outing, she'd gone straight upstairs. At supper, she'd sent word she'd be dining with Megan and attending to the child's needs. He had not pressed seeing her, believing the more time she'd had to herself, the more receptive she'd be to hearing his explanations. Then he wondered if the delay had only helped fuel her fiery temper the more.

Entering his chambers, he found them empty. He searched the bath area. Still no Alissa. Where the blazes was she! Then he noticed her brushes were missing from the dressing table. A frown marked his brow and he quickly searched the drawers and the wardrobe. Gone! All her things were gone!

In a firm stride, he hit the hallway again. By God, she'd better not . . . He stopped in his tracks. Light flowed from under the door to her old room, and Jared released his breath and smiled. Since she hadn't left Hawkstone, perhaps her anger was only superficial. A few tender words, a gentle touch, and a persuasive kiss might be all that was needed to collect her forgiveness.

His hand on the latch, he found it locked, then back-tracked to his room, fetching the ring of keys from his bureau drawer. Silently, he opened the door to see his wife standing by the wardrobe, wearing a sheer nightdress, hanging up the last of her gowns.

"Have you lost your sense of direction?" he asked, closing the door.

Alissa spun toward him. "No," she snapped. "I know exactly where I am."

"And where is that, love?"

"In *my* room. And don't call me that!"

"Love? Why not?"

"I resent your use of the word," she said coldly, pulling on her wrapper, the belt left untied. "Now if you'd please leave, I'd like to retire for the night."

"It makes no difference which bed we sleep in," he said, starting to unbutton his shirt. "This one is as comfortable as mine." He bounced upon the mattress, then lay back, his hands linked beneath his head. "Come join me, sweet."

Rebellion flashed in her eyes. "If you think you're sleeping here, you're sadly mistaken, sir. Now get out!"

"I sleep where my wife sleeps," he answered smoothly, smiling. "And she sleeps where I do."

"I no longer consider myself your wife," she said frostily. "So leave."

Jared swung his legs over the side of the bed, and Alissa breathed a sigh of relief, certain he was about to honor her request. But to her surprise, he stalked toward her, a cunning look in his eye. Hastily, she turned, intending to flee behind the dressing screen. But Jared blocked her path and pulled her against him.

His heated gaze traveling her face, he whispered, "You're beautiful when you're angry, love." And his mouth began its descent toward hers.

Alissa struggled against him, then whipped her head to the side. "I told you not to call me that!" she gritted out between her teeth. "You know nothing of the word."

"Don't I?" he asked, his lips traveling near her ear. "I know it is a wasted emotion. It's the feeling of the flesh that counts, Alissa. My body loves yours each time we are near." His hand slid down her spine to cup her bottom, pulling her fully against him. "It desires you now, love. Feel it?"

Through the sheerness of her gown, his rigid need made itself evident, and she felt her traitorous body coming to life under his masterful touch. "Stop it!" she demanded, trying to break free. "You care nothing for me! You only want me to bear your children and satisfy your lusts! Let me loose!"

Jared's lips continued their onslaught, moving across her cheek to her ear, his massaging hand molding her hips to his. "Don't fight me, love. I can make you forget the things you heard. They were said in the heat of the moment. I—"

"They were said because you believe them. You think of me as a prized mare to stud with, a paid paramour to give you pleasure. I am neither!"

His tongue swirled the delicate folds of her ear; Alissa shivered. Fire leapt in her veins, and she tried desperately to extinguish the desires only he could evoke. Feeling her sudden response, Jared was certain he could break down her barriers. A few more kisses, a few more words, and he'd have her melting in his arms, begging him to take her, love her. During their blissful nights, their bodies eagerly entwined, he'd learned each secret place that, when touched, would heighten her desires. Turn on that Braxton charm, his inner voice told him as he swept her into his arms and carried her to the bed.

The instant Alissa hit the mattress, she scrambled to its side, but Jared caught her, dragging her back, his leg and arm clamping over her. "Don't try to run, love. I want to ask your forgiveness," he whispered, his lips close to her ear again, his hand moving over her silk-covered breast. Then his mouth traveled to her throat, a vulnerable point, he knew, and his tongue slid over its satiny smoothness, lingering at its throbbing pulse.

His alluring mouth caused the familiar vibrations to erupt deep in the pit of Alissa's stomach. *He knows you too well,* she thought, a pleasurable moan escaping her lips, and she heard Jared's chuckle. Struggling against his mastery, fighting his deliberate seduction, she heard the cautioning words, *Jared can charm the fangs from a serpent,* and blurted without thinking, "Ian warned me. . . ." She swallowed the rest as Jared's face suddenly rose above hers.

"Ian?" His cold emerald eyes stared down at her as his rough hand edged slowly upward from her breast to her throat, pausing a second, then framed her face. "Never mention his name again. Not in my arms, not in my bed, not

in my house!" Then his mouth crashed down on hers, hard and angry, his fingers biting into the tender flesh along her jaw. With a growl he released her and sprang from the bed, then strode to the door. "On the morrow, you'll move your belongings back to my room. And don't ever lock a door against me again," he said, removing the keys from the lock, where they still dangled. "When I want you, nothing will keep me from having you . . . you know that. By our very vows and the laws of Britain, I own you. Take it as truth, *love.*"

"Don't call me that!" she cried, but the door slammed before her words were out.

Staring at the wood, she felt a tightening in her chest, like a hand gripping her heart, squeezing it until it would burst. *Jared's hand.* He didn't love her; he never would. He *owned* her. She was no different than a stick of furniture—chattel. Most likely disposable, as well. On that thought, she rolled to her side, the pillow smothering her tears of pain.

On the far side of the house, in his study, Jared sank into a chair, a brandy glass in his hand, the decanter on his desk. Downing the amber liquid, he poured himself another, then another. He felt sick, but not from the liquor. He had thought he could charm her, woo her into his bed and make her forgive and forget. What conceit, he thought, knowing even if he had made passionate love to her, it would not have settled their differences.

Alissa was exceptional. Bright, intelligent, forthright . . . not a woman who could be duped so easily. Beautiful, passionate, giving . . . the woman he wanted. Each time he'd called her *love,* he'd felt himself beginning to believe in the emotion again—until she'd mentioned *Ian Sinclair.*

Was the bastard trying to cuckold him again? he wondered, slamming his empty glass onto the desk, pouring himself yet another. He'd cared not that Celeste had had a lover. His anger had resulted when he'd discovered the rake's identity. The dark memory of her cry as she'd crashed through the window, Sinclair's name ringing like a death knell from her lips, filled his head. Then his mind's eye saw the book she'd thrown, lying open at his foot. Flames licked at the note hidden within, curling around the words, devouring the sickeningly sweet platitudes and the boldly scrawled signature—*Ian*. The sight of it had confirmed Celeste's dying proclamation—his best friend had maliciously trespassed, breaking the bonds of trust. He would not encroach again! Jared decided in anger.

Then, his wits dimmed by the drink, Jared thought of Alissa lying in her bed alone. If he kept her there, day and night, she'd have no time for another. Swallowing the last dregs in his glass, he quit his study and weaved toward his wife's bedroom, the buttons on his shirt freeing themselves. Inside the darkened room, he stripped from his clothing, then plunged beneath the covers to hear Alissa's startled cry. Before she could move, his muscular arm clamped over her waist. "I'll make you forget him." And his mouth lowered, searching for her lips.

His brandy-laden breath repulsed her, and she turned her face away, shoving at his shoulders. "Get off me!" she ordered, sickened by his clumsy attempts to seduce her. "You're drunk!"

"Only with your beauty," he whispered, his words slurring, his heavy hand capturing her breast; she pushed it away. "Ah, sweet, I just want to pleasure your body. Don't be so unsociable."

"Unsociable!" she screeched, struggling against the slackened weight of his body. "Why, you arrogant buffoon! Nothing you'd do could please me!"

"Not even this?" His hand slipped between her silk-covered thighs, his lax mouth traveling the curve of her neck. He felt her sudden jerk as his fingers began their awkward search. Misinterpreting its meaning, he whispered, "Are you sure, love?"

Love! The word hit her with the force of a violent wave. Angered by his assumption that she'd succumb to his "charms," whether he be drunk or sober, she pushed his face from her throat, then squirmed from his hold, sliding to the edge of the bed. "Get away from me, Lord Ebonwyck. I warn you now. Leave or pay the consequences."

The brandy clouding his judgment, Jared chuckled thickly and levered himself onto an unsteady elbow. "Ah, sweet," he said, his lopsided grin flashing in the moonlight streaming through the window, "you know I have the power to take you anytime I wish. Make it easy on yourself. Don't fight me. Come here," he urged, patting the sheets near his waist. "Come here, sweet."

"No."

"Do you wish me to force you?" he asked, proudly knowing he held the key to unlock her desires.

While Jared thought to ravish her senses by kissing her with his masterful lips, teasing her with his expert hands, until she was wild with want, surrendering herself to him willingly, Alissa thought the term *force* meant defilement. Her eyes widened and she froze.

When she did not answer, he reached for her. "Then so be it, love."

"No!" she cried, her arms flailing outward as his powerful hand drew her toward him. Her fingers groping frantically, they caught the edge of the night table, and she twisted, trying to escape him. In desperation, she grabbed the first object she touched, the brass candlestick, and swung it in a weak arc; Jared's firm hold suddenly went limp. Immediately a picture of Charles Rhodes's blood-splattered face flashed through her mind. Dropping her weapon, she sat upright, fear surging through her. My God! Was he . . . ?

His moan lifted to her ears, and Alissa breathed a sigh of relief. Then her fingers gently searched through his thick hair along his scalp to find the rising lump. He moaned again, but this time it strangely sounded like the purr of a cat. Then she realized he was snoring.

"Oooh! You drunken sot!" she cried as she bounded from the bed. She snatched the coverlet from his limber body, grabbed her pillow, and turned on her heel. Certain she would not be bothered the rest of the night, for Jared was out like a snuffed candle, she nonetheless marched across the hall and entered Megan's room. Checking on the child, she found her asleep and settled onto the chaise. "Let's see you try something now," she whispered angrily, knowing full well that Megan would be the perfect deterrent should he awaken before dawn, his amorous flights of fancy still twirling through his muddled brain. "Pleasant dreams, *my lord,"* she said, punching her pillow, taking her wrath out on it. With a last angry swat, she pulled the cover over herself and closed her eyes.

Sunlight spotted itself fully on Jared's face, and he

swatted at the obnoxiously bright beam. But the movement caused a violent pounding in his head, and he winced. Rolling to his side, away from the morning sun, he eased open a crimped eyelid. After a moment, its twin loosed itself and widened; he blinked. Noting his whereabouts, he jerked upright.

"Damnation!" he cried in agony, his hands clamping tightly to his head, trying to hold the intense pain at bay.

At first he thought the brandy had caused his godawful headache. But, now, as his fingers gently probed the mysterious lump he'd found rising along his scalp, he doubted that the drink alone was the culprit. Slowly, the past night's events began trickling through his fog-laden brain, and with a groan he sank back onto the mattress. *Alissa.*

Suddenly the door flew open, and Jared grabbed the sheet, flinging it over his nakedness; his head suffered severely for the quick movement.

"Oops," Mary said, blushing. "I—I thought the room empty, sir. I didn't mean to disturb ye. I—I—"

"What do you want?"

"The mistress said I was to move her clothes, like ye ordered."

"Can't it wait?"

"No," Alissa said, coming into the room. "If it's to be done, then it will be done now."

Jared groaned and rolled to his side. "Then be on with it." But, immediately, he regretted his words. The wardrobe door squeaked on its hinges to pierce his eardrums and scrape down his spine. His stomach turned a somersault, and he swallowed hard, willing it to behave. The screech continued as she purposely swung the door back and forth, grabbing her dresses from within, until he was certain his jittery nerves would climb straight through his skin. "Stop that racket!" he growled.

"But you ordered it done," Alissa said, holding back a smile as she moved the door again.

His stomach lurched again. "Forget what I said!"

The hinge squeaked anew. "You are certain, my lord?"

"God, yes," he moaned. "Now leave me in peace."

"As you wish, my lord." Her eyes on her husband, Alissa closed the wardrobe door with a thump; his whole body twitched. Dismissing Mary, she walked to the side of the bed. "Might I get you something?"

His bloodshot eyes viewed her at length, then he slowly levered himself up and leaned back against the headboard, the pillow behind him. "Some powders for my head."

"I'll ask Mrs. Dugan to prepare you some." She turned to leave.

"You wouldn't know how I came by this bump on my head, would you?"

Innocent eyes turned toward him. "Bump?"

"Yes, madam . . . a bump."

She shrugged. "Perhaps you fell."

"Perhaps . . . but I doubt it."

"Well, my lord, if you have no recollection of how you received your injury, I suppose it shall remain a mystery to us all."

His eyes narrowed. "I have my suspicions, madam." He noticed her raised brow. "Correct me if I'm wrong, but I believe this is a battle injury. Perchance, has war been declared upon me?"

"That is a possibility, sir."

"And shall I be forewarned of any further aggression?"

"A good general never sends advance word of his battle plan to his enemy. However, you might consider that your wound may have resulted, not from a premeditated attack by your opponent, but from a sudden need for defensive action. If one is threatened, then one must act."

Although they spoke in riddles, Jared understood Alissa's meaning, all too clearly. In the light of day, he regretted his heated words, informing her that nothing would stop him from having her, that he *owned* her. His hot temper and angry words, he knew, had only served to drive the wedge deeper between them. He'd never use force on her. She was far too precious to him to ever hurt her like that. Yet, she had to understand that any contact with Ian Sinclair was strictly forbidden.

"Being last night's aggressor, I offer my apologies and an immediate truce. However, let it also be known, if I find a marauder has encroached on my territory, especially when I've given fair warning against such an intrusion, I will defend what is mine . . . to the death, if necessary. Is that clear?"

Immediately Alissa realized the term "marauder" referred to the Earl of Huntsford. "Yes, it is clear." Then knowing his mind was closed to all discussion of his estranged friend, she turned and started for the door. "I'll have Mrs. Dugan prepare a draught of powders for you."

"Alissa," he called softly, and she faced him. "Don't break our truce by defying me. Peace is far better than war."

"Peace, my lord, comes only through understanding. Unfortunately, that is something you apparently lack."

As he watched the door close, Jared knew the battle lines had been drawn. No doubt, he predicted, a long siege would ensue before he'd finally break down her defenses.

An uneasy tension settled upon Hawkstone over the next several days, everyone noticing the way the new mistress treated the master with polite coolness. "They've gone back to separate rooms," the servants reported to each other, whispering their thoughts behind feather dusters and stacks of linen being carted to the isolated beds. Not knowing the details, they assumed it had to do with the Duke of Claremore's verbal altercation with his son, the Marquis of Ebonwyck, over the younger man taking a "commoner" for his wife. Even among the staff, there had been an invisible line drawn, half being for the "actress," half being against her. "She shouldn't have married above her station," some said with a sniff. "She knew nothin' about his title, so it ain't her fault!" others defended. But their bickering was kept quiet, Lord and Lady Ebonwyck unaware of the turmoil they'd caused.

At first, Jared watched his wife, searching for a vulnerable point where he might sneak behind her armaments. Subtle teasing did no good, nor did his rakish attempts at seduction. Polite reserve had no effect on her, either. He went from perfect gentleman to devilish rogue and back again, but, to his surprise, he found her immune to any ploy he used. So much for the Braxton charm, he thought, peevishly, wondering what in blazes it would take to persuade her to come back to his bed! At wit's end, he found he was quickly losing his patience.

"Give her time," his father said one afternoon, while the two were cloistered in Jared's study.

"I'm not about to wait a year!"

"I estimated two," the duke said, chuckling.

"Blast it all! Why did you ever come here?"

"To see my granddaughter, of course, and to try to mend the fences between us. It's been over two years since Celeste's death and our subsequent row. Since you had elected not to come to me, I came to you." He eyed his son carefully. "You never did tell me what happened the night she died. I know I had accused you—"

"Of murdering my wife . . . I'd hoped you knew me better."

"I said those words because you refused to share what had happened that night. You'd skirted the issue to the point of rousing suspicion. I'd known that your marriage had gone sour. What was I to think? In my state of anger, I accused you, wrongly. I know that now. I apologize."

Jared studied his father a long moment. "Accepted."

After the two had shaken hands, drawing each other into an embrace, the duke asked, "Will you share that night with me?"

"Don't ask, Father. Celeste is gone, and it is best the memories of her death be left buried alongside her."

"You shouldn't keep it inside you, son. It's not healthy. You should share the happenings with someone so you might purge yourself of any guilt you still carry."

"I carry no guilt," Jared snapped, angrily, knowing he lied. Had Megan not heard them arguing, she'd not be in her present state. Had they not fought, Celeste would still be alive . . . and he'd still be trapped in a loveless marriage. But, being well connected and having the wherewithal to do it, he could have petitioned for a divorce. Stupidly, he had not done it sooner, believing Megan would have somehow suffered because of it. In the end, she'd borne a greater burden, more so than if he'd cast her heartless mother out—alive. "I won't discuss it, so let it drop."

"As you wish," the duke said, not wanting to disturb the shaky foundations of their renewed relationship, certain that, in time, he'd discover the truth. "As for Alissa," he said, changing the subject, "I suggest you indulge her. Be patient with her. Treat her with reverence. By all means, no matter how many times she shuns you, keep your Braxton temper in check. I tell you from experience, you'll regret it if you let it loose."

"I suppose Mother taught you prudence in that area."

"Damned right she did. I hated sleeping alone."

"I understand your meaning. We're of the same cut."

"Perk up! By winter, hopefully, she'll be warming your bed, instead of a heated brick."

Jared scowled. "An encouraging word, if I've ever heard one." Then he poured himself a light brandy and raised his glass. "I'll not share my bed with a brick. And that, sir, is a promise." With a salute, he downed it.

In a secluded spot in the garden, Alissa sat on a low stone bench, her favorite spot, thinking about her plight. Should she stay in a loveless marriage—loveless on her husband's part, that is? Or should she leave him, return to London, and resume her career on the stage? It was a difficult decision. Especially when there was a child involved—possibly two. At present, she couldn't bring herself to leave Megan, not when the girl needed her. But should she decide to take the coward's way out and run, there remained the possibility that she'd be raising a child, hers and Jared's, alone. Remembering her own experience, a child deprived of a father's love, she couldn't decide what course to take. Although her mother had tried to fill the void, Alissa still felt a certain emptiness. Silently, she'd grieved for her unknown parent, even to this day.

The wind picked up, and an odd creaking sound met her ears. With a sudden leap, she bounded from the bench; the Grecian statue that stood directly behind it crashed into its center. Her hand pressed against her wildly pounding heart as she gazed in disbelief at the broken stone seat, the heavy sculpture, shattered in three large pieces, lying across it.

Her rapid pulse slowing, Alissa released her breath. Three near misses in as many days, she thought, her shaky hand rubbing her brow. First, a loose piece of carpet had snagged her foot on the stairs, almost tumbling her down their entire length. Thankfully, she'd grabbed the rail, stopping her sudden descent. Next, while she was riding Sweet Honesty, the saddle girth had broken, sending Alissa to the ground. Fortunately, she'd only been bruised, but if they'd still been at a full gallop, as they were moments before . . . she shuddered to think what might have happened. Now, the statue. Before, she'd thought the accidents to be just that— accidents! But now, she doubted they were. Was someone deliberately trying to . . . *kill her?*

Jared?

No, she denied, again erasing the memory of the gossipy maids' words. Again, she refused to believe him capable of murder. He had not killed Celeste. Nor was he trying to kill her. Then who? Robert? Edward? Mrs. Dugan? Alissa wondered if she was simply misreading the incidents; then she decided they were probably nothing more than odd happenings.

Erosive crumblings caused by the weather met her eye as she examined the pedestal. Then she noticed the lip of the supporting platform showed new breakage, but decided it could have occurred when the sculpture fell. Shrugging off the episode, she made her way back to the house, intending to report it to Mr. Stanley. She refused to speak to Jared.

As she entered through the glass doors into the downstairs sitting room, a familiar voice filtered to her ears from the foyer. Could it be? she wondered, scurrying toward the sound.

"Dearest child, it's so good to see you again."

"Eudora!" she cried, and ran into the woman's waiting arms.

CHAPTER
Nineteen

After depositing Eudora's luggage in her bedroom, Mr. Stanley excused himself and left the two women alone. "Dearest, come sit by me," Eudora said, turning concerned eyes upon Alissa, who sat in the empty space on the settee. "Something seems to be troubling you."

"I don't know what you—"

"Alissa, you cannot fool me. What's wrong?"

She dropped her eyes to her hands and sighed. "Everything's wrong, Eudora."

"You mean Jared Braxton, don't you?"

"Yes." Her eyes met Eudora's. "And he's not simply Jared Braxton. He's the Marquis of Ebonwyck . . . his father is a duke!"

"Marquis?" Eudora asked, surprised, then laughed. "I'd think your troubles were over. A marquis . . . what more could you want?"

"A man who loves me."

Eudora frowned. "Are you sure he doesn't?"

"Yes! He's told me it's a wasted emotion."

"But you're in love with him."

"No!" Alissa disavowed in haste. Then, seeing Eudora's skeptical look, she whispered, "Yes, I love him. But it angers me to admit it."

"Why?"

"Because . . ." Alissa fell silent.

"You'd like to see the shoe slipped onto the other's foot. Namely, the Marquis of Ebonwyck's . . . correct?"

"For once, I'd like to know what it means to be loved by a man. My husband considers me chattel. He needs me only to satiate his lusts and bear his offspring. Otherwise I'm a whiffet . . . a nobody."

Eudora remembered the marquis's unannounced visit in London. Once she'd recovered from the initial shock of seeing him, as well as the discovery that the two were married, she'd paid close attention to Jared Braxton. While on their shopping excursion, contrary to most men, he had behaved as though he'd enjoyed the outing. And she had noted that he'd spared no expense, purchasing the finest and most costly of gowns, rejecting design after design, until he'd found the ones that were "distinctively Alissa." But, most important, when he'd spoken of his new bride, a certain light had entered his eye. Having seen it many times before, mainly in her own husband's eye, Eudora was certain she'd not mistaken its actual meaning. "Tell me why you think this," she said at last, believing the younger woman had somehow misconstrued her husband's true feelings.

For the next half hour, Alissa explained the events leading up to her marriage and what followed. She even told of her friendship with Ian Sinclair. "Jared doesn't believe me when I tell him Ian did not cuckold him. If he ever had the capacity to love a woman, Celeste managed to destroy that part of him. Megan is the only one to whom he willingly gives his heart." She paused. "Eudora . . . I fear I'm with child."

"Oh, dearest, how wonderful!"

"No, it isn't," she said, rising to pace the room. "I plan to leave Jared. But I—"

"Have you thought this through?"

Alissa looked at her friend. "Yes."

"And do you realize, if you should desert him, it may bode ill for you? I've little doubt he'd make every effort to find you. He'll take your child from you . . . it is his right, you know."

"He's unaware of my condition."

"Then keep it that way . . . for now, at least." Eudora smiled. "From what you've told me, dear, I think your marquis is not immune to love. He's simply afraid to admit to it."

"You think he loves me?" she asked incredulously.

"I do. The problem is . . . how to make him confess it to you, as well as himself."

"If you're planning some sort of deception again, I'll not have any part of it. Jared and I have duped each other too many times already. There's no trust left between us. Besides, he once informed me that engaging in feminine trickeries, like coquettishness or attempts to make him jealous—"

"He's already that," Eudora cut in, then noticed Alissa's questioning gaze. "Ian Sinclair," she said knowingly. "Although you might believe differently, especially when your husband is so candid with his words, deep down, he knows you've been faithful to him. If he thought otherwise, he'd have gone after Sinclair by now. I suggest you break off any contact with the earl, at least until the marquis is made to see reason. If you don't, you might find one or the other lying in a pool of blood. You wouldn't want that on your conscience."

Alissa shivered at the thought. "I could never forgive myself should anything happen to either of them."

"I know that, dearest." Eudora rose, walked to Alissa's side, and embraced the younger woman's shoulders. "Don't worry about it. If you have no contact with the earl, then nothing will happen. As for your husband, I think that if you'd simply be your charming self, he'd soon discover he cannot resist you. It's sort of like dangling a carrot before a donkey. The tempting morsel, which stays just beyond its reach, eventually leads the stubborn creature wherever you wish it to go."

Alissa laughed, lightly. "Eudora, you are truly *wicked.*"

"Me?" she questioned, her laughter blending with Alissa's. "Whatever makes you think that?"

Supper that night was to be a formal affair to celebrate Eudora's arrival and Megan's recovery. With the older woman's help, Alissa composed three notes, requesting that the men join the ladies in the downstairs sitting room at seven sharp. Unknown to the men, however, the women planned to delay their entrance.

Her luxurious hair intricately styled, Alissa wore her blue silk gown, Jared's favorite, with her sapphire brooch and matching earrings as the only embellishments. "How do I look?" she whispered as the three paused in the foyer at ten past seven.

"You'll knock the stockings off him," Eudora replied, then smoothed the gold silk skirt of her gown and straightened her shoulders, her head angling, regally. "I believe you said there was a duke on the premises. Shall we see if we can find him and finagle an introduction?"

Alissa's musical laughter erupted. "I'm certain when he sees you, he'll be most anxious to acquaint himself. In other words, Eudora, you'll knock the stockings off him."

"I never doubted I would," she said, smiling, a knowing twinkle in her eyes. Then she bent to the little girl who'd stolen her heart the moment they'd met. "Megan, dearest, it's time for our grand entry. Shall we allow Alissa to go first?"

Megan gave a quick nod of consent, and Alissa smoothed her own skirt, then walked the few paces to the door. As the panel swung wide, Jared paused in mid-sentence, then shoved himself to attention, his arm dropping from the mantel where it had leaned casually. His breath caught in his chest.

Beautiful, he thought as his heart made an odd trip over itself several times. Strangely, he felt as though he were suffering the pangs of a schoolboy's crush. "Ladies," he greeted them with a nod, never taking his eyes from his wife. "It is our pleasure to have you join us."

"Thank you, my lord," Alissa said, a captivating smile crossing her soft lips.

His gaze latching on to it, Jared sucked in his breath; fire scorched his veins, yet he managed to swallow his groan of longing. Dragging his eyes from his wife, he looked to Eudora as she passed through the doorway. "Mrs. Binnington, it's a pleasure to see you again."

Just having noticed the statuesque beauty, the Duke of Claremore suddenly propelled himself to his feet, and Jared wondered if a spring had popped through the cushion where the man sat. Then, noting the interested sparkle in his father's eye, Jared swallowed a chuckle. "Father, I'd like to introduce Mrs. Eudora Binnington of London." He observed his father's disappointment on hearing the conventional title, proclaiming her married. Taking pity on him, Jared added, "Mrs. Binnington is a widow." The duke's smile brightened. "And this is my father, Edward Braxton, the Duke of Claremore."

Eudora inclined her head slightly as she slipped into a small curtsy. "Your Grace."

"Mrs. Binnington, it is my pleasure."

"You may call me Eudora, Your Grace."

"And I am Edward," he said, quickly cutting through all the formalities that went with his title, raising a startled brow from his son. "May I offer you a sherry, or some wine?" the duke asked, leading Eudora to the settee, seating her next to his former position.

"Thank you, Edward. I would enjoy a sip of something, but I shall allow you to choose."

As Alissa watched her friend at work, she bit her lower lip to keep from laughing aloud. She wondered what the duke might say when he discovered Eudora had been an actress, as well. Then she felt her husband's hand at her arm. Glancing up, she smiled. Again, Jared's breath caught. "I'd prefer a glass of wine, my lord, if it's not too much trouble."

"I'd gladly give you whatever your heart desires," he whispered as he led her to a chair, his appreciative gaze upon her.

Seeing the heat in his eyes, Alissa nearly missed a step, and as she glanced at him through her lowered lashes, she wondered if his profession was true. Everything, she decided, except his heart.

With Alissa seated, Jared walked back to Megan and squatted. "It's good to see my princess all bright and well again." He folded her into his arms for a hug, then rising, led her to another chair. "What would you like in way of refreshment, sweet?"

Robert hopped to his feet. "A lemonade, I'll wager."

As Robert made his way to the sideboard for Megan's

lemonade, Alissa watched him, carefully. From the moment she'd entered the room, she'd felt his gaze upon her. Yet, viewing him, she found nothing in his demeanor to indicate the ill will she'd felt coming from him. Realizing she was still jumpy from her earlier mishap in the garden, she decided that perhaps she'd been mistaken and brushed aside her uneasy feelings.

"I'd like to propose a toast," Robert said, when all the drinks were handed out, his eyes settling on Alissa. "A healthy and prosperous life to us all."

It was not an unusual toast, she acknowledged, after sipping her wine. But, just the same, when he'd made it, she'd felt a strange chill race along her spine. Again she dismissed her anxiety, attributing it to a bad case of nerves.

"That brooch?" Edward asked with odd curiosity, drawing Alissa's attention. "Where did you get it?"

"It was my mother's, Your Grace. I inherited it when she died."

Edward frowned. "And who was your mother?"

"Rachel Ashford. She, too, was an actress."

He made no further comment and turned his attention back to Eudora.

As the night progressed, Alissa paid close attention to being her "charming self" as her friend had suggested. Each time her laughter rang out, sounding like a crystal bell to Jared's ears, an untamed longing shot through his famished body. Her engaging smile mesmerized him. Her soft voice bewitched him. Her graceful movements lured him, until he felt certain he'd go insane with desire.

Having turned on the sum total of his own charm, he couldn't quite fathom why it had no effect on her. She listened attentively to his conversation, laughed at his witticisms, and returned his devastating smile with one of her own. But whenever he'd thought himself to be making progress, she'd retreat ever so slightly. No one else seemed to have noticed her withdrawal. No one, except him.

After retiring to the sitting room again, Jared leaned his elbow against the mantel and sipped his after-dinner brandy, his eyes intent on his wife. At his wits' end, he found himself tempted to slam the glass down, scoop her up in his arms, and quit the room for his own. Propriety disallowed such action, however, so he remained impassive and suffered in silence.

"It's growing late," Alissa said finally. "Although it's hard to leave good company, I think Megan and I should retire."

"I'll see you both upstairs," Jared said, her words barely having left her mouth. His unfinished brandy settled on the mantel. "Mrs. Binnington . . . gentlemen . . . please feel free to visit as long as you wish. I'll see you on the morrow."

Alissa looked to Eudora and saw her reassuring nod. Jared's hand at her elbow, he guided her from the room. With his bedtime story finished and Megan asleep, they stepped into the hallway, the door closing quietly. "You look beautiful tonight, Alissa," he said, leaning a hand against the frame of her own door, again turning on his charm. "More beautiful than I ever remember."

She smiled. "Thank you, my lord." Then as his head lowered toward hers, she slipped inside her room.

Jared's head snapped back as the panel shut in his face. Frowning, he stared at the wood a moment, then pushed from the jamb, turned on his heel, and strode to his own room. Stripped of his clothing, he lay upon his bed, making a thorough mental search, cataloging the night's happenings. What would it take to bring her back into his arms? he wondered, knowing he'd already used every irresistible influence he possessed. Nothing worked!

Completely baffled, he rubbed his hand over his face, punched his pillow, and settled deeper under the sheet for another night in his lonely bed. What in damnation did she want from him! he grumbled silently, rolling to his side. Gowns? Jewels?

But he'd already tried that route by presenting her with a satin ball gown, direct from Paris; a velvet, mink-lined cape; and a diamond bracelet, all in the past week, only to find she still wore the dresses she'd purchased before their marriage, plus her own jewelry, his wedding gift being the one exception. The false charges had already been rescinded against her, so he couldn't tempt her with that promise. And he'd accorded her a leg up in society by sharing his name and title with her. Obviously, she was unimpressed with either. So, what in blazes could he possibly give her that he hadn't already!

His love, Alissa thought as she stared at the star-studded sky through darkened windowpanes. That's all she wanted from him. True, he seemed willing to give her everything . . . except his heart. She wondered if she should accept his protection, his name and title, his generous gifts, and settle for those alone. But she couldn't. She wanted none of it without his love. On a sigh, she turned and slipped into her lonely bed, praying that Jared would let loose the strictures that bound his heart.

Jared sat reclining in his office. After more than a week of Alissa's remaining just beyond of his grasp, he felt himself on the verge of complete madness. Unknowingly, she'd teased him, taunted him, until he'd felt certain the primitive side of him would erupt, and he'd drag her, yelling and screaming, possibly clawing at him like an angry cat, up to his room, where he'd dump her on his bed and make wild, passionate love. . . .

Love. The magic word rebounded through his head and jerked him upright. Suddenly it all came crashing down around him. That's all she'd ever wanted from him! But was he capable of sharing such an emotion? Did he even know its true meaning?

His usual cynical thoughts on the subject worked themselves to the forefront of his mind. He'd thought himself in love once, but Celeste had managed to destroy all his feelings and, in the process, had left him jaded. Then, as he compared the two women—his first wife against the second —he discovered there was no similarity at all.

Never had one woman evoked so much emotion in a man as did Alissa in him. She had the power to bring his temper to a roiling boil, yet he would rapidly cool it, fearing to let it loose should he hurt her tender heart. His jealousy had raged when she'd innocently mentioned another man's name, but he'd tamped it down, somehow knowing she'd never debase their vows. In her guileless way, she made him laugh, genuinely so. Her captivating smile melted his soul, while her artless touch inflamed his body, his untamed desires nearly consuming him. Indeed, she was like no other woman he'd ever known. If it were not so, then why had he been at his wits' end all these agonizing days since their estrangement, trying to discover the secret to bring her back into his arms?

In truth, he'd forced her to marry him, using Megan's welfare as an excuse. He'd deceived her about Rothhamford's confession, fearing she'd ask for an annulment. Had tried desperately to persuade her to come to him again after she'd overheard the heated exchange between his father and himself, only to botch it all. Why . . . ?

Because, you idiot, you love her!

Jared felt a swelling in his chest; the heavy weight he'd carried all these years had been lifted. A shout of laughter rang though the room, joy filled his heart, and he leapt from his chair. He actually loved her. *Alissa, heart of my heart, I love you.*

Determined to find her and tell her so, he strode toward the door, a wondrous smile lighting his face.

Alissa rounded the foot of the staircase, clutching a sealed note in her hand, and quickly made her way toward the kitchens in search of Mary. When she reached Jared's office door, her heart skipped several times, a nervous reaction. Swiftly she scurried past on silent feet, then curved around the corner and breathed a bit easier.

Jared flung the door wide to see the tail of his wife's lavender skirt disappear toward the kitchens. With a wide grin on his face, he stalked her, in hopes of catching her in a darkened corner, where he'd profess his undying love, take her into his arms, and kiss her until she went limp.

When he hit the back hallway, he found not a trace of her. Yet, the element of surprise was all-important to him, so on quiet feet, he rushed to the kitchen doorway and stopped short. He pressed himself back into the shadows when he heard his wife's voice; his lighthearted smile vanished, instantly.

"When you reach Falcon's Gate, Mary, please give this to the Earl of Huntsford. No one else must see it . . . understand?"

"Yes, mum. I'm to give it only to the earl."

"That's correct. Now go."

Tucking the note into her apron pocket, Mary bobbed a curtsy and headed toward the back entry. Alissa waited but a moment, then turned and dashed to the back staircase.

Jared's angry strides carried him across the tiled floor only a second after Alissa had disappeared. Catching the closing door with his hand, he jerked it from Mary's grasp. "You have something in your pocket I want. Hand it over."

Wide-eyed, the quaking servant girl stared up at the master of Hawkstone. "B-but—"

His hard gaze bored into her. "Now, Mary." Nervously, she slipped the note from its hiding place and, with shaky fingers, placed it onto his outstretched palm. "You may go now. But if you breathe a word of this to anyone here or at Falcon's Gate, you'll immediately be dismissed from my employ, and you'll not find work in this district again. Is that understood?"

"Y-yes, s-sir," she stammered, her knees vibrating in time with her words. "I-it's me d-day off, s-sir—"

"Then go about your business." The door slammed after the frightened girl as she scurried down the path.

Jared weighed the note in his hand, then angled himself through the room, heading for his office. Inside, he slammed the door and ripped through the seal. Anger filled him as he read the words.

Ian—I send this to tell you it is not wise for us to meet as we have. Should Jared discover us, I fear the consequences. I will keep in touch through Mary. Ever, Alissa.

After he'd read it twice, the note curled slowly in his tightening fist. *"Fool!"* he berated himself harshly, his recently opened heart snapping shut like a trap. *"Damned fool!"*

"You seem upset." Robert's voice came from the corner; Jared's gaze jerked toward him. "Is something amiss?" his cousin asked.

His ire masked, Jared strode toward his desk. "What are you doing here?"

"We had an appointment to review the cargo on your ships at nine . . . it's ten past, now."

Jared settled into his chair, resting his elbow on its arm, and rubbed his fingers across his forehead. "I forgot."

"A lover's spat?" Robert asked after eyeing Jared at length. "If you need a sounding board, perhaps—"

"Fool!" Jared denounced himself again, only half-listening to Robert's words.

Furiously, he tossed the note onto his desk. It skittered across the surface to land on the carpet, and Robert stooped to retrieve it. As he glanced at the crimped paper, two words met his eye. Ian. Alissa. Seeing them, he placed the note on the center of Jared's desk and said, "I'd hoped you wouldn't discover the truth about them."

Cold eyes slowly climbed to Robert's face. "You knew they were meeting and didn't report it to me?"

"Yes, I saw them in the glade by the cottage while out riding, several weeks past," he confessed, carefully choosing his words. "I was surprised, then embarrassed by what I saw. I'd hoped—"

"Hoped what!" Jared's hand slammed onto the desk. "I want the truth—all of it! Now!"

"Your wife and Sinclair—they kissed."

Jared rose, slowly stretching to his full height. The vehement look in his eyes caused Robert to pace back a step. "You're sure of this?"

"I do not lie. I saw them, I swear."

Through shuttered eyes, Jared studied his cousin, then he quit the room.

Upstairs, Alissa tidied up the last scraps of stationery, placing the lot in the drawer. Relieved she'd caught Mary before the girl had left for Falcon's Gate, she hoped Ian would understand her hastily scratched message. It was best they didn't see each other, as Eudora had suggested. Yet she feared, if she didn't show up at the glade, Ian might come searching for her, hence her note to him. Besides, there seemed little sense in the man wasting his time by making a daily trek to the stream when she could just as easily inform him not to come.

Without warning the door crashed to the wall; a sudden cry escaped her lips as she spun toward the noise. Then, Jared was upon her in four long strides. Harsh hands grabbed her arms, jerking her against him. "I've one question," he said, his voice cold, ominous. "Have you met with Sinclair since I forbade you to do so?"

Alissa blinked, then began to struggle against him. "You're hurting me."

He shook her. "Answer me!"

Recognizing the volatile anger in his eyes for what it was, she nodded, then hurriedly said, "Only once."

"Has he ever, madam, felt the press of your lips?"

Her eyes grew round; she blanched. It had been only a small peck, she thought, wondering how he could have possibly known of it. "No!" she cried, hoping to ward off a confrontation between Jared and Ian. "I never—"

He shoved her away. "Madam, your eyes say otherwise."

As he strode toward the door, Alissa ran after him. "Jared"—she caught his arm—"where are you going?"

"To search out your lover and dispense with him, once and for all."

"Please . . . don't. I swear, nothing happened between us." He seemed not to hear. "Jared," she pleaded as she threw herself against him, her fingers twisting in his shirt. "I kissed him on the cheek . . . that's all. He's my friend. I tell you nothing happend . . . *I love you!*"

The last three words tore straight to his core; his contemptuous gaze raked her face, and he jerked her against him, his mouth crashing down on hers in a fierce, angry kiss.

Alissa tried desperately to respond, but his deliberate cruelty frightened her; a whimper trembled in her throat. Hearing it, Jared tore his mouth aside and shoved her away. "It won't work, Alissa. You say the words, hoping I'll believe you. But I know you're only trying to protect him. Your guile sickens me."

In disbelief, she watched as he slipped the key from the lock; the door swung on its hinges and slammed shut. Hearing metal scrape into the lock, she threw herself against the wood. "Jared, please!" she cried, her fists pounding furiously. "You're wrong! Please don't do this! Please . . . please . . . !" No response came, and she sank to the floor, her cheek pressed to the door. "It's you I love," she sobbed brokenly. "It's you."

His mind already set, Jared strode the hall, closing out her anxious cries, and headed for the stables. With Thor saddled, he bounded to the stallion's back and spurred him into a full gallop, heading to Falcon's Gate.

Ian Sinclair's startled butler fell back as the door was shoved inward, Jared striding into the large mansion without preamble. "Find your master," he demanded, his eyes hard as stone. "Tell him Jared Braxton is here."

"C-certainly, my lord." And the man scurried off.

"Jared. What brings you here?" Ian asked, coming into the huge entry, but he stopped in his tracks as his estranged friend turned toward him.

"You common bastard," Jared hissed, eyes narrowed. "Twice you've cuckolded me. Now I'll put an end to your chicanery."

"What the hell are you inferring?"

Jared laughed, raucously. "Sinclair, you truly believe I'm stupid, don't you? She's already confessed to your little rendezvous in the glade. You've trespassed for the final time."

"Nothing's happened between Alissa and me. I swear."

"The same as nothing happened between Celeste and you?"

"You know it didn't."

"Still denying it, Sinclair?"

"I never touched Celeste. I didn't love her."

"But you love Alissa, right?" Jared asked, his madness driving him a step closer to Ian. In disillusioned anger, he added, "Since she doesn't sleep in my bed, then she must be in yours. Conveniently, she's made herself your whore."

"Hold your tongue, man," Ian said, his voice threatening, eyes cold. "You'll not call her that."

"I'll call her what she is," Jared answered, purposely baiting his opponent to ensure the proper outcome. "Paramour. Trollop. Harlot. Bit—" The flat of Ian's hand connected with Jared's cheek, turning his head sideways. Slowly swinging it back, he smiled, coldly. "I accept your challenge. Since you've been kind enough to make it, I'll set the rules. We'll dispense with the proper etiquette. No seconds are needed. Ready your pistols, *sir*. Be at the glade within the half hour." He turned and strode toward the door. "I'd say it's a fair place to die, wouldn't you? And, remember, if you don't show, Alissa will suffer for your cowardice."

"Braxton—" The door banged shut, and Ian swallowed his words. Releasing a long breath, he made his way to his study and retrieved his dueling pistols from the locked cabinet. The man was insane . . . completely insane. Or was he? he questioned, realizing he'd been duped into making the challenge. Yet, he dared not back away from it, certain Alissa would suffer Jared's reprisal.

After saddling his horse, Ian told a servant to summon the physician in Selkirk and lead him to the glade. An ominous feeling overtook him. Blood would be spilled.

"Where's the damned key?" the duke shouted, then snatched the ring from Mrs. Dugan as she rushed up beside him.

"Hurry, Edward!" Eudora implored. "She's hysterical."

The duke quickly unlocked the door and turned the handle; Alissa burst into the hallway. "We must stop him!"

"Stop who?" Edward Braxton asked, not knowing what had caused the fuss, only that Eudora had anxiously called for him to find Mrs. Dugan and the keys. "And why were you locked inside your room?"

"I don't have time to explain. Eudora can tell you."

As the group rushed down the hallway toward the alcove, Eudora hastily apprised the duke of his son's intentions. "He's bent on killing Ian Sinclair," she finished as they reached the kitchens.

Edward caught Alissa's arm. "Does he have reason to, young woman?"

Alissa shook his hand free. "No, Your Grace. His imagination has run wild. There's nothing between the Earl of Huntsford and myself, except friendship." Then she turned and rushed off to the stables, the duke and Eudora following her.

"Eudora, order my son's room prepared, just in case the worst comes about," Edward said, impatiently waiting for Mr. Stanley to saddle their horses. "Plenty of clean linen and hot water. Ho! You there," he called to one of the stable boys. "Head into Selkirk and alert the physician there's trouble at Falcon's Gate. Hurry, lad!"

The boy quickly slipped a rope bridle onto the nose of an old gelding, hopped onto its bare back, and rode off at a steady lumbering pace toward town.

"Give me a leg up," Alissa ordered the moment Sweet Honesty came into view; Mr. Stanley's cupped hands boosted her astride the mare. "We'll cut across country. It's faster."

Then she turned Sweet Honesty and headed toward the cottage. Don't let it be too late, she prayed, edging the mare into a full gallop, the Duke of Claremore and Mr. Stanley close behind. *Please, Jared, my love, don't do anything foolish!*

In the glade, Jared and Ian stood back to back, pistols loaded and cocked, barrels pointed heavenward, resting at their shoulders. "Start the count, Sinclair," Jared commanded.

"You hotheaded catch colt," Ian returned, angrily. "If you're so intent upon dying, then you start the count."

"If I die, it's a certainty you will, too. My *faithful* wife will be left with nothing."

"Then it's to the death, Braxton. I'll not leave her to suffer at your hands. You've gone insane! You'll be damned for it!"

Jared laughed, roughly. "Then I'll meet you in hell, *friend.*" And he began the count.

Sweet Honesty crested the hill in time for Alissa to see the men step the last few paces. An eerie slowness seemed to orchestrate their movements, and her mouth opened to emit a cry, but her voice suspended itself in silence.

"Ten," Jared shouted and started to pivot and level his pistol, Ian's moves duplicating his own. A shot rang through the glade, exploding like cannon fire; Jared stumbled back, a jolt of pain racking his body. In disbelief, he stared at the red stain spreading across his white shirt. *Blood?*

"Jared!"

The terrorized scream of his name drew his fading

attention and he turned on unsteady legs. His vision blurring, he tried to focus his eyes. A horse and rider bore down on him. "Alissa?" he questioned, somehow certain it was his wife. "W-why . . . *why?*"

Then, strangely, Jared found himself staring into a dark abyss. His knees buckling, he slipped into oblivion.

CHAPTER

Twenty

"Jared?" Alissa cried as she slid from the saddle and dropped to her knees beside his fallen body. Shaky fingers touched his blood-splattered shirt, covering his upper left chest. "Oh, Jared . . . why did you do this?" A shadow fell across her, and she gazed up.

Ian read the frightened question in her eyes. He bent to one knee, braced his pistol across the other, and felt along Jared's neck, searching for a pulse. "He's alive," he said, laying his weapon aside. "We need to stem the flow of blood."

A length of her petticoat ripped free, Alissa folded it and gently placed it over the wound.

"By God, man, you fired too soon!" the Duke of Claremore accused, having leapt from his horse, his hand clamping onto Ian's shoulder. "I should throttle you! Coward!"

Ian rose. "My weapon is still loaded."

Edward Braxton's eyes narrowed. "Prove it!"

Retrieving his pistol, Ian walked several yards away, the duke on his heels, and aimed it at the ground. The sudden explosion startled Alissa, and she screamed, "Stop this madness! It matters not who shot him! We must get him back to Hawkstone!"

No sooner had the words left her mouth, than a buggy careened up the lane and across the glade, two lads on horseback behind it. Mr. Stanley caught the reins, steadying the lathered horse, as the elderly Dr. Drummond sprang from his seat. Without preamble, he knelt and examined Jared's wound. "Let's get him back to the house."

Carefully lifting Jared, the duke, Ian, and Mr. Stanley gently set him inside the buggy, then mounted their own steeds. His head resting against her shoulder, Alissa continued to apply pressure to his wound.

"Hold tight," the doctor said as the vehicle began moving again. "Should he start bleeding more, tell me." Then he snapped the whip, sending the horse into a fast trot toward Hawkstone.

Her lavender day dress stained with Jared's blood, Alissa stood next to the doctor, sterile cloths ready upon request. A moan erupted from her drugged husband's lips as the man probed his flesh, searching for the shot, while Ian held him down. Feeling suddenly light-headed, she fought for control. Usually strong of stomach, she decided it was her condition that caused the nausea. Her arrested fear that she might lose her husband suddenly welled up inside her and she prayed with all her might that Jared would live to see his new son or daughter.

"There . . . I've got it." Dr. Drummond turned and dropped the lead ball into the basin. Next came a bloody swatch of cloth, a remnant of Jared's shirt, which he pitched alongside the lead shot. "Now hand me the antiseptic."

The bottle and a clean cloth were passed to him. "Will he be all right?" Alissa asked.

"If his body can ward off any infection . . . we must be cautious, however. Should he start showing signs of a fever, notify me at once." After taking several stitches, he bandaged the wound, instructing Alissa on how to change the dressing. "Keep him sedated with the laudanum. From what little I've been told, I take it his hotheadedness got him into this." Drummond looked pointedly at Ian. "I don't want him trying to leave his sickbed to take after you again." He headed toward the door. "I'll be back on the morrow. If you should need me sooner, send round for me."

From the moment the silver-haired man stepped from the room, Alissa kept a continuous vigil, Megan at her side.

Eudora, Edward, Mr. Stanley, and Ian all took turns staying with the pair, Mrs. Dugan bringing hot tea and food to the room, periodically. Robert made his appearance at will.

"If Sinclair didn't down him, who did?" Robert questioned his uncle on one such visit.

"We haven't the slightest . . . a hunter . . . a poacher."

After a moment or two of pacing around, Robert quit the room.

Despite everyone's urgings, Alissa refused to leave Jared's side. She ate little, if anything at all. Then, late into the night, several hours before dawn, her greatest fear came to fruition. Jared's brow flamed with fever as a violent chill overtook him. Rousing Mr. Stanley from the corner chair, where he slept, she sent him after the doctor, then heaped cover upon cover over Jared.

"There's probably some cloth fragments still in the wound," Dr. Drummond stated, sighing. "I had hoped I'd gotten it all." He placed a fresh bandage over the festering wound, covering the angry red marks branching outward from it. "There's not much I can do."

"He's not going to die, is he?" Alissa asked, wildly. Ian quickly stepped from behind her, his hands settling on her shoulders. She gazed at him and pleaded, "There must be something we can do."

"I'm sorry," the doctor said, gently. "We'll have to wait it out." His gaze firmed on Ian's. "Use any resource you have."

As soon as Drummond left, Ian turned to Mr. Stanley. "Go fetch Nanna. Tell her your master has a poisoning in his blood."

"Right, yer lordship." Mr. Stanley headed for the doorway. "I'll get her here in a flash."

Alissa fixed questioning eyes on Ian. "Who's Nanna?"

"She's an old woman who lives on my estate. She's probably a century old, if she's a day. Some say she's a witch. I say she's a healer. If anyone can help him, Nanna can."

Staring down at her husband, Alissa felt the sting of tears behind her eyes. "What would I do without him?"

"It is not a question you need to ask," Ian said, comfortingly. "He'll survive to see and to hold his new son."

Her head snapped around. "Who—?"

"Eudora has told us. She's worried about you. Especially when you refuse to eat. It's not good, Alissa, that you spend so much time here. One of us can tend to him."

"I'll not leave him." She then wrung out another cool cloth, placing it on Jared's fevered brow. "Don't leave me," she whispered in his ear. "Please, don't leave me."

Within the half hour, the door flew back on its hinges, and an old crone, stooped and aided by a cane, limped into the room. Her skin looked like aged parchment; gray hair sprang from her head, wild and untamed. Her sharp eyes pierced the occupants of the room; then she ambled toward the bed. "Out'a me way, lass," she ordered, prodding Alissa with her cane.

Alissa's gaze latched onto Ian. He nodded reassuringly, and she slowly stepped aside to watch as gnarled fingers slipped the bandage from her husband's chest.

"Eeh, 'tis bad," Nanna said, and turned to Alissa. "The croaker, did he put anythin' on the wound?"

"Antiseptic."

"Bring me sack and kettle," the crone called to Mr. Stanley, and he quickly did as told. Then all three eyed Nanna as she took the lid from the black iron pot and skimmed a moldy substance from the broth inside, slapping it onto a clean linen bandage.

When she realized the woman intended to place it on Jared's wound, Alissa opened her mouth in protest, but Ian bent to her ear. "Let her do what she knows best."

"But—"

"She has the power to heal. Her cures go beyond those of most folk medicine. Drummond knows it. Because of his oath, he won't say her name aloud, but she's the 'resource' he spoke of."

"If anything happens to him—"

"I'll take full responsibility."

An agonized moan tore from Jared's lips as the old woman's fingers probed his injured flesh. Alissa's fists balled, and she bit her lip to keep from ordering the woman from the room.

"Hot water," Nanna demanded, sharply. "Needs to draw some of this poison from him 'fore I dress it."

Ian slipped the kettle from the coals in the fireplace, carrying it to her, and in disbelief, Alissa watched as the crone plunged a clean cloth into the steaming liquid up to her wrist. Was she human? she wondered, noticing not even a flinch from the woman.

"I need ye to hold him down. He might be drugged, but he'll feel this for certain."

Once Jared was restrained, Alissa holding one wrist, Mr. Stanley the other, and Ian pressing his bulk over the Marquis of Ebonwyck's middle, his hands bearing down on Jared's upper arms, Nanna dropped the hot cloth onto the wound.

Jared writhed; a tortured cry broke through his lips, and all three fought to constrain him. Even though he was virtually unconscious from the laudanum, Alissa was astounded by his strength. Then she remembered that night when she'd thought he'd intended to ravish her. Not so, she decided, realizing if that had truly been his purpose, he'd have succeeded, easily.

The cloth was dipped again. "We have to repeat it thrice."

"Are you up to it?" Ian asked, noting Alissa's pallor.

"Yes," she said firmly.

"Hold him," the hag ordered; the cloth was dropped again.

After it was all done, Alissa felt a sob rise to her throat, but somehow, she contained it. Gentle fingers brushed the hair from Jared's hot brow, and she bent to kiss his cheek. "The worst is over, my love. Soon you will be well."

Ian helped her from the side of the bed, and they watched as Nanna placed the prepared bandage over the wound. Then she mixed a concoction of herbs in water and spooned it between Jared's lips, allowing it to slowly trickle down his throat. "He ain't to have laudanum. Vile stuff, it be. These herbs will make him sleep and help heal him. Mix a pinch in this much water"—she crooked her fingers an inch apart—"and don't touch that patch on him. I'll be back next sunup."

Mr. Stanley kept back a pace as he followed Nanna out of the room, her sack and kettle in hand. "You'd best get some sleep," Ian said, after the door closed. "I'll take watch over him."

"No, I'll not leave him."

"Alissa—"

"Ian, I am mistress of this house. Do not try to tell me what I can or cannot do."

"Then we shall keep watch together."

"I'd prefer to be alone with him for a while."

He gazed at her a long moment. "As you wish. If you need me, I'll be outside in the hall."

Alone with her husband for the first time since he'd locked her in her room, Alissa sat on the bed, taking care not to jostle him. Her hand slid over his as she spoke softly, "It's important, my love, that you fight this infection. You have a strong will, a strong body . . . don't let it defeat you. Megan needs you. I need you. Our child needs you. Please, don't leave us."

Another day and night passed, Alissa close to her husband's side. Despite everyone's efforts, she refused to leave him. Eating little, she dozed occasionally in the chair beside his bed, only to awaken the instant she heard his moan. When his fever raged, she cooled his brow and body with wet cloths, struggling against his flailing arms and delirious curses.

"Alissa? Sweet? I . . . I . . ." His fists balled. *"Alissa! Deceptive witch! I almost believed . . . Damn you!"*

The venom in his voice hit her like a physical blow. Fighting back her tears, she attended him, gentle hands working to make him comfortable, feeding him his medicine to ease his pain.

Then, just as quickly, the fiery heat would leave him, and a violent chill racked his body. "C-cold . . . s-so c-cold," he bit the words between chattering teeth, and she'd heap the covers on him, sometimes lying next to him to share her own warmth.

In those moments he clung to her, and she to him. Tears formed in her eyes as she feared she'd lose him, their last words said in anger. But seldom did she let them flow.

The old crone came again, and upon examining the wound, a doubtful look entered her eye. But she reapplied her treatment, this time Edward, Ian, and Robert restraining him, while Eudora comforted an anxious Alissa.

Immediately afterward, a pale Robert left the room, the

duke cursed, and Ian sank into a chair, his hands raking through his hair. "Why the hell didn't he believe me?" Ian asked of no one in particular.

Nanna mixed a new concoction of herbs for Jared to ingest, then left, Mr. Stanley carrying her sack of medicines; the process to be repeated at dawn on the next day.

Only once did Alissa dare leave him. Having sent Eudora for more water, she'd forgotten to ask for fresh linen and towels. When she returned, she found Robert hovering over him, his fists clenched tightly. Instantly, she feared something had happened to Jared and rushed to the bed. "Robert, is he all right?"

The sound of her voice startled the man, and as he spun toward her, hard eyes met hers. "Yes . . . I was just checking on him." Then he strode from the room.

Alissa could not fathom why Jared's cousin acted in such an abrupt manner. But, then, she realized everyone reacted differently to a crisis. Perhaps, he's simply distraught, she thought, shrugging away the incident.

About midnight on the third day, Alissa sat alone in her ever-present vigil. By her own declaration, this time of day was her private time with Jared. Strangely she felt a presence behind her and turned to see Megan. The child's wide eyes were teary and sorrowful.

"Come, darling," she entreated, folding the girl into her arms, drawing her onto her lap. "He'll be all right. Believe it, and it shall be so."

Through her hand signs, Megan asked question upon question, and Alissa answered as best she could. "Yes, Megan, he knows we are here. I talk to him, constantly, the same as I did with you when you were so ill. Your father spoke to you, too. Do you remember?"

Megan's brow furrowed, then a light sparkled in her eyes, and she nodded.

Alissa smiled. "The doctor in Edinburgh told me that a person's hearing never shuts off, no matter what the body does. . . ." Except in death, she thought, but held her knowledge. "That's why we told you how much we loved you . . . that you would be fine, and you are. I do the same with your father. Even if he doesn't respond, I know he hears me." Jared groaned; his head twisted on his pillow.

"His fever is rising again," she said, setting Megan on her feet. "I need to bathe him." Moving to the night table, she discovered the pitcher almost empty. "I'll have to fetch some more water. Will you be all right alone with him?"

Megan placed her small hand on her father's brow. New tears formed in her eyes, but she quickly wiped them away as she nodded.

Alissa viewed her carefully. The poor child had recovered from one emotional shock, only to be thrust into another. Twice Megan had been in the room when Jared had gone into his fever; she'd fled in tears. Now, Alissa wondered, if she should leave her, in case Jared should start his wild thrashings. Yet, if Megan were chased from the room, she thought it would only upset her more. Explaining what she might see and hear, Alissa said, "Don't be frightened. You must understand, it is the fever that makes him act so strangely."

Megan nodded she understood; a confident look entered her eyes.

"Then, I shall be right back." On swift feet, Alissa rushed down to the kitchens for some cool water. But the return trip took her longer than expected, a light-headedness overtaking her as she climbed the stairs. She fought it off, however, then traversed the hall to her husband's room. As she quietly stepped inside, she immediately stopped and drew back into the shadows to watch the scene unfolding before her.

Megan leaned close to her father's ear, her mouth working open then closing; as always, when they'd practiced, an odd garble escaped her throat. Tears of frustration gathered in her wide green eyes, then rolled down her cheeks, but this time she refused to give up. Her small hand rose and nudged his burning face closer to hers. And with one last effort, Megan finally pushed the sounds through her lips: "P-Papa . . . p-please d-don't die."

Tears of joy and sorrow filled Alissa's eyes and heart; she knew, if anyone could rouse him to fight harder, his daughter could. Yet, if he fought and lost, would he have known the ecstasy of hearing Megan's sweet voice, once more? No, not consciously. "Say the words again," she said, surprising the child, then walked on shaky legs to Megan's side, the pitcher wobbling in her hand. "Tell him, darling. Talk to him. He'll hear you. Tell him of your love."

"Papa . . . papa, I l-love y-you," she said with more self-assurance. "Don't die . . . please don't leave me."

Heartened by Alissa's gentle smile and tender words, Megan continued to speak, her voice growing stronger and stronger. And, as the night progressed, both wife and daughter whispered their encouragement, their hopes, their fears, sometimes in anger, sometimes tearfully. But they never let up.

Unable to sleep from his worry over his son—his daughter-in-law, as well—the duke entered Jared's room to halt in his tracks. "Papa," he heard his granddaughter say, "do you remember . . ." As she went on with her words, Edward's watery gaze connected with Alissa's, his praises of thanksgiving written there. One more miracle, he prayed. Just one more.

Then, as the pink of dawn glowed on the horizon, Jared started perspiring, soaking his sheets. "The fever has broken," Nanna announced, proudly, her crooked fingers pulling the bandage free. "The infection is gone." She seemed surprised. "There be a stronger medicine that made the miracle besides mine." She patted Alissa's shoulder. "You gave him life again, lass."

His body washed, dry sheets placed beneath him, and another herbal drink ingested, Jared lay in a restful slumber, Alissa still hovering at his side.

"Now, dearest," Eudora said authoritatively, drawing Alissa's attention, "you shall have a warm bath and slip beneath the covers of your own bed for a much needed sleep."

"Indeed she will," the duke piped. "I'll not have my new grandson's health jeopardized because his mother is intent on staying with her husband. Now, daughter," he said, surprising her. "Take yourself off to bed."

"But—"

"I think you're outnumbered," Ian interrupted, and smiled. "Jared's in fine shape. You're not."

Suddenly, Alissa realized she was indeed tired and offered

a weak smile. "I suppose you're right. But I go only with the promise that as soon as he awakens, one of you will wake me. Do I have it?"

"You do," the three said in unison.

Her hand lightly brushing a lock from Jared's brow, Alissa gazed at him a moment, then bent to his ear. "Welcome back, my love." And she pressed a light kiss on his lips.

Eudora came to her side. "Come, dearest. I'll help you to bed."

"We'll call you the moment he wakes," Ian promised again. "From what Nanna said, he'll be out for several hours. Now off with you."

After she'd eaten a light breakfast and bathed, changing into a silk nightdress, Alissa slipped into her bed and fell into an exhausted, yet restless sleep.

In Jared's room, while the duke and Ian kept watch, Edward finally said after a long silence, "From listening to my son's ramblings, plus through what little Eudora has been able to tell me, this so-called duel was precipitated because he believed you'd cuckolded him—not once, but twice. Is this true, Sinclair?"

Ian looked at the man. "You've known me since I was in short pants. Do you think it's true?"

Edward's lips tightened. "I didn't accuse you of doing it . . . I asked if that's what caused this unseemly incident to come about! An answer, please."

"Unfortunately, Your Grace, yes. Jared, for some ungodly reason, not only thinks I've imposed myself physically on Alissa, but he'd accused me of it with Celeste, as well. I am innocent in both cases."

Edward Braxton eyed the Earl of Huntsford at length. "I believe you." Then he said, "Jared has never opened up to me about Celeste. I'd consider it a favor if you were to tell me what you know of their marriage . . . and her death, if possible."

Ian almost refused. But upon reconsidering, he decided it best to clear the air. As he quietly spoke of Celeste's shallow nature, a trait she'd hidden well from the duke, and of her refusal to share Jared's bed after Megan's birth without a bribe, Edward seemed taken aback.

"Several times, she threw herself at me," Ian stated, angrily, "but I refused. Jared was my best friend. I know nothing of the night she died, except that Jared severed all relations with me immediately afterward. When I came round to discover why, he accused me of cuckolding him. I denied it, of course, because it wasn't true. But he wouldn't listen. Somehow, I doubt that he cared if Celeste had friendships with other men. But something must have given him the idea I was involved with her. Alissa told me that Jared had relayed to her that Celeste had died with my name on her lips. I've no idea why. I never encouraged her. I hardly spoke to her. It all remains a mystery to me."

"And Alissa?" the duke asked. "What of her?"

Ian looked to his hands. "I'll admit, my feelings for Alissa are far different than they were for Celeste. But as you've seen for yourself, she loves your son, not me. Alissa and I are simply friends. Besides, I still consider Jared my best friend. I'd never encroach. Never."

"You are an honorable man, Sinclair. My son could not have a better friend than you. It's a shame he's too thick-headed to realize it."

"Since Jared is on the road to recovery, do you think we should set ourselves to finding who shot him?"

The duke's brow furrowed. "Do you believe it was done on purpose?" He saw Ian's shrug. "My thoughts had lain along the line of poachers . . . a stray shot from afar. Perhaps—" The door opened, and upon seeing Eudora, Edward fell silent.

"She's sleeping," the woman said, seeing their questioning eyes. "The poor child's head barely hit the pillow and—"

A groan rose upward from the area of the bed; all three moved toward it. "He's coming out of it," Ian said, glancing at Eudora. "I hate to do it, but we promised her."

"I'll get her."

Jared's ponderous hand ran over his face; he grimaced when it dropped to his chest, pain shooting through him. A heavy eye opened to fall shut. He tried to open the other, but it seemed an impossible feat.

Jared couldn't quite grasp what his problem was. He felt

as if he were struggling, hand over hand, upward from the depths of a black cavern. Attempting to take a deep breath, he lurched and groaned. His chest hurt like hell. Why?

The haze clouding his brain suddenly cleared, and his eyes opened to find Ian Sinclair standing over him. "The bastard is in my own house," Jared rasped, then coughed; his face twisted in pain. "Unfortunately, Sinclair, I survived."

"I never intended to kill you, Jared," Ian said, stepping closer. "In fact, it wasn't my shot that injured you."

His short, cynical laugh erupted, and Jared paid for it, but he wouldn't allow it to show on his face. "Whose, then? Did you pay one of your servants to accomplish what you knew you couldn't?"

"You're still suffering from the fever."

His memory sharpened with every word that passed Ian's lips; his mind saw Alissa riding toward him across the glade. "I have it! It was my beloved wife. She feared she'd lose her lover! I had no idea she was a marksman. Another point in her favor, eh, Sinclair?"

Ian was fast losing patience; his eyes narrowed. "Again, I'll excuse you. The fever has obviously numbed your brain."

Jared pulled his bored gaze away. "Where is my *faithful* bride, anyway?"

Edward stepped forward, stating curtly: "At the moment, she's resting. She's been at your side constantly these past four days."

"Obviously, you had the sense to keep someone with her."

The duke felt his anger rise. With sheer willpower, he kept it in check. "You dolt! You wouldn't be here at all if it weren't for her! She helped save your life!" A snort of disbelief erupted from his son; Edward ignored it. "When your fever broke, Eudora insisted she lie down. She did so under protest. She had to think of the child she carries."

Child! Jared's gaze widened, then it narrowed as it hit Ian. "Yours or mine, Sinclair?"

The insult was too great. "You unfeeling bastard!" The indignant words escaped between Ian's teeth as his fist balled and rose. "I should beat the truth into—"

"Don't!" Alissa commanded, having heard the exchange from the doorway. A driving pang had pierced her heart with each insensitive word Jared had uttered. Especially his last. Then as she stepped from the shadows, her emotionless gaze met her husband's.

Her luxurious hair cascading around her petite form, falling to her slender waist, she looked so very frail. Streaks of purple slashed beneath her tired eyes, and Jared realized the marks were real, not some trick of makeup. Unable to hold her vacant stare any longer, he faced away.

"Since he refuses to open his heart, the truth will always elude him. Don't waste your anger on him, Ian. He's not worth the effort."

Her words pricked Jared like a sharp knife. His gaze bounced off his father, to see his disgust, and ricocheted back to his wife. Megan stood at her side, looking at her askance. Alissa nodded, and his daughter came to his bedside.

Huge eyes, so much like his own, gazed at him; then she opened her lips. "Papa, I love you."

Not absorbing what he'd heard, his gaze lingered, searchingly. His brow furrowed. "Sweet?"

"I love you, Papa," she repeated, smiling. "You've come back, just as Alissa said you would."

His good arm surrounded his daughter as joyous tears glazed his eyes and cramped his throat. Over Megan's silky head, he viewed his wife. *Alissa,* he thought, wistfully. Through her love and understanding, she'd allowed him to regain his daughter, unbroken, renewed. How could he repay her? Blank eyes held his only a moment; then he watched as she turned and left the room.

Suddenly an unbearable ache compressed his chest. It had nothing to do with his wound, he knew. *Alissa,* he cried, silently. With his bitter mistrust and heartlessly cynical words, he'd driven her away. And he was certain her love was now lost to him—forever.

CHAPTER

Twenty-one

Jared withdrew another article of clothing from the wardrobe and packed it in his portmanteau.

"Yer lordship, sir, do ye still needs me help?" Mary asked, in a frightened little voice. "If not, Mrs. Dugan has some work for me."

He glanced in her direction, noting the nervous twist of her hands, and immediately took pity on her. "You may leave in a moment, Mary. First, I wish to apologize for the way I behaved the day I intercepted Lady Ebonwyck's note. It was extremely high-handed of me."

Since a member of the peerage never apologized to a mere servant girl, Mary blinked in surprise.

"When I return from Edinburgh, I'll have a fine gift for you to make up for my abominable behavior."

She blinked again. "Oh, yer lordship, ye don't have to do that!"

"It's my way of saying I'm sorry."

She smiled. "Thank ye, sir . . . I mean, yer lordship, sir." She turned to leave.

"Oh, Mary," he called, and she pivoted. "What time is your mistress to return from Selkirk?"

"Megan and her ladyship should be home soon. If ye remember, Mr. Stanley promised he'd be back by noon to take ye on to Edinburgh."

Jared sighed. "Yes . . . I remember, now. That's all." He watched the door close, then jerked another article of clothing from the wardrobe.

Each minute seemed like an hour when Alissa was away. Why it would make any difference, he had no idea, for he'd not seen her since the night he'd awakened from his fever, three weeks past. And he wanted to, desperately. But it seemed the entire household conspired against him. And rightfully so.

From the moment he'd uttered his unconscionable accusation that she carried another man's child, Hawkstone had become a house divided, its master ostracized. The congenial Eudora had instantly turned frosty. Mr. Stanley, his trusted servant and longtime friend, had taken to grumbling and scowling at him. His father had called him an "incorrigible idiot!" and a "blasted fool!" Even Mrs. Dugan had sniffed her distaste while managing to *accidentally* spill hot broth on him, not once but twice, while he remained in his sickbed. As he dressed today, he'd noticed his inner thighs still retained a red mark where the searing liquid had branded him. Fortunately, the woman had not aimed her sights higher.

Only Robert had remained an ally, but he was now in Edinburgh, sent on ahead to conclude some business. Using that same ploy himself, hoping that while away he could discover the solution to regaining Alissa's heart, Jared planned to join his cousin later tonight. He needed time to think.

Then he thought of Megan. Of course, being sweet and innocent, she had no knowledge of the undercurrents flowing through Hawkstone. "Why did you make Alissa cry?" she'd asked one day while visiting him when he was still abed. Embarrassed, he'd not been able to admit the truth, and she'd quickly admonished, "You're not very nice, Papa, to hurt her so."

'Innocence dwells with wisdom . . . ,' he quoted Blake silently, thinking of his daughter. "'. . . but never with ignorance,'" he chastised himself aloud, ending the quote. "Guilty as charged!"

With a sigh, Jared wadded up another shirt and threw it into the portmanteau. *Alissa,* his mind whispered plaintively, wishing forlornly for her return, not just to Hawkstone but to his arms, as well. Surely, there had to be a way to win her love anew. Too late, he'd recognized that she'd truly loved him, unselfishly, completely. For, as he'd lain abed in a surly mood, bits and pieces of the happenings during his fevered state had come filtering back to him. Soft hands had gently cooled his brow and body. Whispered words had filled his ears and heart. *I love you, Jared. Please, my love, return to me. Megan and I need you. Our child needs you.*

Her remembered words ate deeper into his soul, and Jared struck his hand against the armoire. Damn his hide! How could he have been so stupid! After all that she had given him, he'd repaid her with heartless disdain. Indeed, as his father had stated, he was a *blasted fool!*

A sudden shout sounded in the hallway, and he strode from his room; Ian's feet ran across the blood-red carpet toward him. "Come, man, Mr. Stanley's been shot! The coach is overturned."

"Where's Alissa? Megan?" Jared asked anxiously as the men struck a course toward the back stairs. "Are they—"

"They're nowhere to be found."

Jared felt an ominous dread jolt through his chest. "And Thom? Is he . . . ?"

"He's alive, but dazed. The shot grazed his temple. He keeps mumbling something about Alissa and Megan being spirited away by three men wearing masks. Other than that, I couldn't make heads or tails out of his ramblings."

Jared stopped just long enough to gather his pistols, shot, and powder, then headed toward the stables. With Thor saddled, the two men rode across country toward Falcon's Gate.

"Thom . . . what's happened?" Jared asked as soon as he saw his friend, noting the man's head bandaged with a blood-soaked piece of linen. "Where are Alissa and Megan."

Thom Stanley's head rolled on the pillow toward his employer. "Gone . . . they's gone. Nabbed by three men wearin' masks. I tried to stop 'em, but . . . but . . ." His eyes rolled dizzily, and he blinked, fighting for consciousness. "They came out of the copse by the road. Was upon us 'fore I knew what was happenin'. I—"

Just then Dr. Drummond bustled into the room. "Step aside," he said to Jared and Ian. Peeling the bandage away, he examined the wound, cleaned it, and stitched it up, a round of curses received for his efforts. "Lucky for you, sir, you have a thick skull."

"Lucky fer ye, these gents was a-holdin' me down," Mr. Stanley snarled in return.

Dr. Drummond ignored him. "Keep him abed for a few days. He's suffered a mild concussion, but he'll recover. I'll return on the morrow to look him over again."

"Ye better brings an army with ye," Mr. Stanley called after him. "These gents won't be here to help ye."

Jared nodded, confirming his manservant's words, and Dr. Drummond rolled his eyes, then left the room.

"Thom, can you tell us which way the men went?" Jared asked, urgently wanting to be on his way.

"Cain't say . . . sorry." His suddenly watery eyes looked away from Jared's. "It happened so quick-like . . . I reached fer me pistol . . . and everythin' went black. When I woke, the carriage was in the ditch, the horses gone . . . so was the mistress and little Megan."

"I found him stumbling along the road," Ian supplied, "and brought him here."

"Will you be all right?" Jared asked, squeezing his man's arm, and saw Mr. Stanley's nod. "Then you stay put. Ian and I will find these brigands. And ease off on Drummond. He's only trying to help you."

"Huh, the man's a quack." He saw Jared's stern look. "Fine, I'll be as docile as a babe."

"I'll take that as your solemn word." Jared straightened from the bed. "We must be on our way."

"When ye catch 'em, give 'em a good thrashin' fer me 'fore ye kills 'em all."

"I'll do that," Jared said, anger roiling inside him. "I promise."

Searching the area near the overturned carriage, Jared and Ian found not a trace of his wife and daughter or of the men who'd taken them. Alissa's purse lay by the wreckage, several large bills inside, and Jared decided that robbery was not the motive. "What was the purpose of all this?" he inquired, not expecting an answer, yet hoping he'd receive one. "There's no note for ransom. Nothing."

"I cannot answer," Ian said, his hand clasping Jared's shoulder. "But I think we'd best alert the sheriff, then gather some provisions. I doubt they traveled the main road. Three men with a woman and child would be too conspicuous. If we're lucky, we might find a trail through the woods."

Both men agreed to meet at the site within the hour, then went their separate ways. Having apprised his father of the situation, Jared hurriedly collected several blankets and enough food for a week, should his search take him longer and farther than hoped. Two leather pouches of gold were slipped in with the rest to use as an incentive to free his wife and daughter.

"Are you certain you're well enough to traipse the countryside, looking for them?" Edward asked, concerned. "What if there's a confrontation? Your wound is barely healed. You can't go it alone."

"Ian will be with me," Jared answered, making the last tie in a leather thong, securing the blankets. "I have no choice, Father. My wife and daughter are in danger." And new babe, he thought, knowing in his heart it was his. He brushed past the duke, heading for the door. "Keep tight to the house, just in case a message comes with their demands. If it's money, then pay them what they want. Give them the whole damned estate if that's what it takes . . . all of it. Just so long as Alissa and Megan are returned to us."

"Good luck, son," Edward called after Jared's retreating form. "Godspeed." But the door closed before his last word was out. Releasing his breath, Edward went in search of Eudora to break the news to her and to offer his comfort. Together they anxiously awaited any news of Alissa's and Megan's plight.

After an hour's search in the wood, Jared finally found a scrap of silk pinned to an overgrown thistle. Certain it came from Alissa's dress, they fanned out, discovering hoofprints, which led in a northwesterly direction. On a continuous ride, following the tracks in the soft earth until it became too black to see, the two men camped for the night; at dawn they were on their way again.

Four hours later, they came upon an old woman with a pushcart, and she pointed them toward the central highlands. Jared tossed her several gold sovereigns, which she promptly bit with her sparse collection of teeth, then smiled and placed them in her purse next to the coin the other gentleman had given her earlier.

But in short order their progress halted as a sudden, violent rainstorm sent them in search of shelter. "Damn this delay!" Jared ranted in the confines of the leaky stable, water pouring through the shoddy roof. Frustrated, he raked his hand through his damp hair. "We should be out after them."

"You can't see a blasted thing through those sheets of rain. The wind alone will unseat you from Thor's back," Ian said as a gust hit the rotting boards, their rusting nails emitting an eerie creak. "We'll be lucky if we leave this place alive!"

"In the meantime, their tracks are being washed away!"

"I'm afraid, my friend, they've been that long ago."

Jared settled into the dank pile of straw, his forearms resting across his upraised knees. "What purpose did they have in taking them?"

Ian gazed at Jared. "A conspiracy, perhaps?"

Jared's head snapped around; a harsh laugh erupted. "Toward what end?"

"Perhaps it's a ploy to draw you out."

"Me? I have no enemies!"

"You bear a scar that may indicate otherwise. I did not put it there. Nor did Alissa."

Jared turned away. "I know that."

"I'm happy to hear your admission," Ian said, chuckling. Then he grew serious. "Since we are guiltless, then obviously someone else wants you dead."

"Who, pray tell?"

Ian eyed Jared a long moment. "Where's your cousin?"

"Robert? He's in Edinburgh."

"Are you certain?"

"I sent him in that direction. I was headed that way myself, until Alissa and Megan . . ." Jared's eyes narrowed. "You must be daft! He hasn't the nerve to shoot a pigeon, much less a man. Besides, what would he gain from it?"

"You tell me, *Your Grace*. As the heir apparent, you'll be addressed as such one day. Has a nice ring to it, don't you think?"

Jared snorted, then just as quickly sobered. "What makes you think Robert is involved?"

"His actions while you were on death's doorstep."

"Which were?"

"Odd . . . very odd," Ian stated, with frankness. "He seemed distressed, but not that you might die. Quite the opposite. He seemed more upset that you might live. You know his background. His father hated the Braxtons. When orphaned at thirteen, he certainly was old enough to carry that resentment with him when your father took him in. Perhaps his being the 'poor cousin' has festered in him all these years. With you dead, he has the chance to become the Duke of Claremore."

"Ridiculous . . . we're from the old Scots peerage; Megan inherits it all. She'll hold the titles for her own son."

"But what happens, Jared, if you, Megan, and your unborn child all cease to be? Who benefits then?"

The knowledge hit him between the eyes like the potent kick of a mule. His words grating viciously, he acknowledged at last, "The benefactor is . . ."

"Robert!" Alissa cried, her excited voice echoing through the cavernous interior of the old burnt-out kirk where they'd been held these past two days. Saved! her heart sang, joyously. Then, certain she'd see Jared step over the threshold, the remainder of their rescue party at his heels, she rushed forward, Megan directly behind.

"Stay back," he ordered coldly, and she stopped short.

Hazel eyes emitted a feral gleam as Robert's lip curled maliciously. Instantly, her heart sank like a lead weight. *"You!"* she accused, angrily. "You're the leader of this vile group!" Protectively, she drew Megan close to her skirts. "Why, Robert? What madness has inspired you to have us carried here?"

"Not madness, *Lady* Ebonwyck. Cunning. You're to be used as bait."

A feeling of dread shuddered through her. Then her eyes

widened as he withdrew a knife from his belt; his thumb scraped over its finely honed tip. "B-bait?"

He stopped his movement and sucked a drop of blood from his thumb. "There's no other way I could find to get Jared here, except through the two . . . uh, three of you." He looked to Alissa's still-flat stomach. "Can't forget the last Braxton bastard, can we now?"

He's insane! Alissa thought, trying to remain calm. "What do you intend, Robert?"

"Intend? Why, I'll await the arrival of your devoted husband. He's surely that. You should have seen him these past few weeks, pining away for his lost love, his dear sweet Alissa. Sickening, to say the least. Too bad my original plan hadn't worked. Quite brilliant of me to orchestrate the duel between my lovesick cousin and Ian Sinclair. A few seeds of jealousy planted—"

"You insidious bastard! *You* shot Jared!"

"Name-calling will get you nowhere. But you're right. After he'd intercepted your note to Sinclair, I informed him, in a distraught manner, of course, that I'd seen you kissing the earl. I didn't lie, exactly, for I did see you kiss the man's cheek. I simply expounded a bit, played on his jealous nature, hoping he'd go off half-cocked. But after he'd left, I was afraid Sinclair might not follow through . . . possibly only a grazing of his flesh. So I followed Jared from Hawkstone to Falcon's Gate, then to the glade, and hid in the trees. Unfortunately my horse bumped my arm . . . my aim was off a few inches. Needless to say, if the nag had behaved, I wouldn't have had to stage this little abduction to lure him here!"

Alissa's mind suddenly raced. The carpet on the stairs, the broken saddle girth, the statue in the garden, they weren't accidents! "You were behind my mishaps, too!"

Robert laughed. "Knowing my cousin's manly appetites to be overly strong, especially with a wife as pleasing as you, I knew he'd plant his seed, swiftly. Hence the 'mishaps.' It seems, however, that fate was with you, Alissa, all three times." He edged a leg onto the scarred oak table, then jabbed the knife into its wood. "But this time, I'll control the outcome."

As the firelight reflected off the shiny blade, protruding from the center of the table, Alissa's eyes widened again. *Remain calm,* she ordered herself. But the bile rose to her throat, and she suddenly became light-headed—a recurring effect of her pregnancy, she knew—yet she fought off the dizziness.

"Had my original plan worked," Robert continued, "you and Megan would have met with a carriage accident . . . oh, let's say, a month or so after my cousin's funeral. But now, with Jared on his way, I'll kill three . . . uh, four birds with one stone." He sighed. "Such a pity. Of course, Jared will be the last to go. I must allow him the pleasure of seeing your deaths first."

Alissa felt Megan edge closer to her, and she held the child tight. He truly was insane. "Why are you doing this?" she cried, praying Jared wouldn't find them. At least, then, he'd be safe. "What motive could you—"

"The money, the lands . . . Hawkstone. And, of course, I plan to be the next Duke of Claremore. But, in order to ascend to such distinction, I, first, must be rid of the Marquis of Ebonwyck. With all of my uncle's heirs tragically deceased—killed by some unknown brigands—I plan to console him on his loss. In time he will decide the line must continue . . . he's too conceited for it not to. He'll simply need to petition the Queen, along with the Lord Lyon, and the title can be passed to me without a hitch. Then, when the time is prudent, poor Uncle Edward shall meet with an accident of his own. Naturally, I'd like to enjoy the bounty while I'm still young."

"You're insane, Robert," Alissa said, finally voicing her thoughts. "You won't get away with it."

"Won't I? I almost succeeded once, through Celeste."

Alissa pressed Megan's head close to her and covered her ear. "Celeste?" Then the entire picture came into bright relief. "You made Jared believe he'd been cuckolded by Ian."

"It only took a few love letters, signed supposedly by Ian's hand, offering a few promises of finer jewels and more fashionable gowns, trips to Paris . . . all of which Jared was, toward the end of their marriage, unwilling to give. The woman was a shallow, frivolous bitch, just like Patricia. But

I should have known Jared couldn't be provoked to challenge Sinclair. He didn't love her enough. You, on the other hand, are quite a different matter. He truly does love you. A shame that such a flatulent emotion will lead him to his death." He rose from his perch. "Now, into the corner. We have a short wait ahead of us. A few hours . . . more or less."

"With luck, he won't find us!" she cried angrily.

"That won't happen, I assure you."

"What makes you so certain?"

"I've spent a small fortune to ensure he does. A few coins, and a willing finger will point him this way. He's being led like a lamb to the slaughter. Now get over there."

Alissa led the frightened Megan to the far corner as Robert had instructed, then whispered, reassuringly, "We'll be all right. Don't let him distress you, dearest. He is deranged. And because of it, he thinks he holds a great deal of power. He underestimates your father's strength and intelligence, however. It will be his downfall, I promise."

If her words were only true, instead of wishes, she thought as she huddled close to Megan. *Oh, Jared,* she prayed. *Stay away, my love. Stay far, far away.*

Under the cover of darkness, the Marquis of Ebonwyck pressed himself to the rough stones and edged silently closer to the man standing guard at the far side of the kirk. Barely inches from him, Jared's hand snaked out and tapped the man's shoulder. Startled, the brigand turned; a fist met him square in the jaw, sending him to his knees. A well-aimed boot followed, and he fell to his face, unconscious.

Two down, and one to go, Jared thought as he quickly wrapped a length of leather thong around the man's hands and feet, then stuffed a gag into his mouth, leaving him like the first. Again, he edged along the stone to the corner. A quick glance and he espied the man guarding the entry. Damn! Where's Ian! he wondered, anxious to make a clean sweep of it.

Having found the kirk with suspiciously little trouble, the two had hidden on a nearby hillside in a stand of trees, lying in wait until darkness had settled. Together, they'd planned to take down the first of the brigands, then Jared would take the second, himself. Once done, he'd wait for Ian's signal and create a diversion, while Ian attacked the third from the rear, leaving Jared to storm the interior and face the final and most treacherous of all.

If he'd had any doubts that Robert might have been involved, they had disintegrated the instant he'd seen his cousin riding down the lane toward the kirk. Anger directing him, Jared had almost given himself away as he lurched to his feet. Thankfully, Ian had tripped him up, then sat atop him. "Cool your head," he'd ordered, in a harsh whisper. "Before you reach him, Alissa and Megan will be dead!" The moment the words had left Ian's mouth, Jared's hot anger had turned to cold cunning. Robert would rue the day he was born! This he'd promised.

Another glance around the stones, and Jared caught the flash of white cloth from the opposite corner of the building, Ian's signal that he was in position. With a scuff of his boot, Jared began kicking loose stones across the ground. The sound turned the third brigand's head, then his body. He moved toward the noise, his pistol drawn, ready.

On quiet feet, a solid tree limb in hand, Ian came up behind the man. A dried twig snapped under his foot, and the man swung in his direction. Powder flashed as the pistol exploded. Wood met skull at the same instant, and the man was felled like a giant oak.

Already on the move, his own pistol braced, Jared cursed the unexpected eruption. His element of surprise was gone. Still he burst through the doorway to stop short.

"Set aside your weapon," Robert ordered coldly, his arm wrapped tightly around Alissa's torso while Megan's long tresses were bound around his hand, keeping her in place. "Or your wife's throat will suffer."

His heart pounding erratically, Jared viewed the knife tip as it indented the fair skin of her throat. Then his gaze met Alissa's. Wide, sky-kissed eyes stared back at him, but he saw no fear. A message passed between them, and he groaned silently. *I love you, too, sweet Alissa.* Then he slowly lowered his pistol.

"Don't do it, Jared!" Alissa cried out. "He means to kill us all!" She winced as the point dug deeper into her skin.

Cold anger filled Jared as he watched the trickle of red

flow down her ivory skin. "You'd best give it up, Robert. You won't win."

"But you will lose," his cousin countered. "All three of them."

Hearing Ian come up behind him, Jared set his pistol on the table. "Let them go and we'll let you pass."

"You really believe I'm a fool, don't you, cousin?" Then his eyes snapped to Ian. "Ready three horses, now!"

"Do as he says," Jared ordered, feeling Ian's hesitation, his eyes never leaving Robert's. Then he noticed the movement of Alissa's hand, Megan watching it. If it would only work, he thought, reading the signs. "You can have it all, Robert," he said, trying to distract him. "My rights to my father's title . . . everything." He caught Alissa's eye, then nodded imperceptibly, telling her he understood. "Just let them go."

"How can I have it all when you're still alive? An impossibility, cousin."

"It is not, if I sign it over to you."

"Won't work. I want more than the lands and the money. I wish to be the *next* Duke of Claremore."

"Nothing is impossible, Robert," he said, watching the count of Alissa's fingers. "If Alissa, Megan, and I left Scotland, without a trace, then it might be assumed we are dead. My last will and testament can name you as benefactor. Only the Crown can grant you the rest."

"And what promise do I have you'll hold to your word?"

"That's all I can give . . . my word. You have it now, Robert, if you let them go. Otherwise, you will lose all. There's no other choice."

As he considered Jared's words, Robert's hold slackened and Alissa felt it. Instantly, her third finger popped out. Seeing it, Megan hiked her foot, ramming it into Robert's shin; Alissa went limp, sliding down his body, then her elbow hit his groin. Sickening pain racked Robert's entire body; his arms dropped, and Alissa and Megan scampered to freedom. Before he could recover, he was hit by the full force of Jared's lunging body.

The knife flew from Robert's hand, skittering into the corner as hard, angry fists pummeled his face and body. Twice he managed to strike back, hitting Jared directly in his tender wound. Pain shot the length of his body, but Jared ignored it, his fist crashing again into Robert's jaw. Again. And again.

Blood combined with sweat, its odor filling Alissa's nostrils; the sound of knuckle crushing bone vibrated in her ears. She suddenly felt nauseated. "Stop, Jared! You're killing him!"

Her cry filtered into his brain, then a hand jerked him back. "Enough, friend," Ian said. "He's already unconscious."

The red haze cleared from Jared's eyes and he saw his cousin lying upon the stone floor, his face broken, bloody. Shaking his head, the last remnants of his fury left him, and he turned to face his wife. Their gazes held for a long moment, and their thoughts seemed to transcend the space between them.

His arms opened, and without hesitation, she flew into his loving embrace. Then his lips sank, meeting hers in an achingly poignant kiss. Tearing his mouth free, he whispered, huskily, "Alissa, love, I feared I'd never see you again."

The words seemed torn from the very depths of his soul, and she was filled with resounding joy. "Nor I you, my love."

Then she pulled away slightly, and he turned to catch his daughter up in his arms to hold her tight. "Soon we'll be on our way home," he said, setting Megan on her feet; then he moved off to help Ian.

Home, Alissa thought, smiling softly. Never had a word sounded so wonderful to her. *Home,* she repeated again, knowing, as she gazed at her husband, she was already there.

CHAPTER

Twenty-two

Once Robert and his hired thugs were deposited with the local authorities, the foursome headed homeward. Stopping at the lane leading to Falcon's Gate, Jared's hand stretched toward Ian's. "I could never have done it without you. Thank you."

Ian smiled, his hand clasping Jared's. "That's what friends are for. Remember it."

Jared returned his smile. "I'll not forget it, Ian. Foolishly, I had allowed myself to be blinded to the truth," he said, remembering how once Robert had regained his senses, his tongue had loosened, and he'd voluntarily recounted his treacherous acts, including his involvement in writing the love letters to Celeste, signing Ian's name. Realizing that their estrangement had been caused by his cousin's maliciousness, plus his own foolishness, the Marquis of Ebonwyck had made amends with the Earl of Huntsford. "Never again. You're a true friend." He let loose Ian's hand. "Remember, you're always welcome at Hawkstone . . . but wait a week or two before you call." His warm gaze settled on Alissa. "I'll be busy."

A fiery flush instantly brightened her face; affronted, her eyes widened. "S-sir," she sputtered, "I believe—"

Ian laughed, then cleared his throat. "I'll leave the three of you, before I become embroiled in a family dispute. See you in a fortnight," he called as he turned Woden and headed down the lane.

"I simply spoke the truth, madam," Jared said, a teasing smile lighting his eyes. "As a matter of fact, we'll both be busy . . . urgently so."

Alissa turned dancing eyes upon him. Unable to stop the laughter bubbling to her throat, she let it fly. Its musical quality vibrated through Jared, and he reached for her, but she quickly turned her horse and set it into a gallop toward Hawkstone.

With Megan bouncing along on another horse, Jared kept Thor to a walk. A wicked grin crossed his face. "Love," he said, watching his wife's retreating form, "whether you know it or not, you're headed exactly where I want you."

"What, Papa?" Megan asked, her curious eyes upon him. He smiled and winked. "Nothing, sweet."

Hearing his son's voice in the hallway, the Duke of Claremore bounded from his chair in the sitting room and trotted to the door.

"Eudora!" his voice boomed through the house. "They're back!" A delighted smile lit his face and eyes as he lifted his granddaughter high. "Welcome home."

Appearing at the top of the stairs, Eudora swept downward in a flash. "Oh, my dears, thank God you're safe." She threw her arms around Alissa, hugging her close. "I'd feared the worst, but I should have known the marquis would rescue you." She turned smiling eyes to Jared. "I was told you were willing to give all you owned, so long as they were both returned safely. I assume all is settled between you?"

"Indeed, madam . . . save for a few minor details," he answered, drawing Alissa closer to his side. "When we are in private—" He gasped as Alissa's elbow hit his ribs. "I believe my wife wishes for me to remain silent on the subject." He rubbed the tender area, his lips twitching as he viewed her indignant scowl. "I shall defer to her better judgment."

As the two women and Megan walked toward the sitting room door, the men following, Edward chuckled. "Your mother had a similar way of silencing me. My instep still suffers from the blows of her heel. For safety's sake, you might wish to invest in a suit of armor."

"Since it will be too cumbersome to discard when the mood strikes, I believe I'll take my chances and bear her bruises."

"I catch your meaning," the duke said, slapping his son's back, then they both guffawed, drawing Alissa's petulant eye. Catching the look, Edward harrumphed and whispered, "I think we should curb our discussion, lest she attack both of us."

"A coward, Father?"

"Never. But one woman's wrath is enough."

Jared looked at him askance, then smiled. "I take it Eudora was not content with your waiting."

"Not in the least." His father grinned. "But there were benefits, as well."

"Used the Braxton charm, did you?"

"Naturally."

As the group settled in the sitting room, Jared began to tell of their adventure. His father was noticeably taken aback when he learned his nephew had been the leader of the group. "I suppose we failed him," Edward said, shaking his head. "Perhaps his father's hatred of the Braxtons had been instilled too deep for us to turn it aside."

"What made the man hate you so?" Alissa asked, not knowing Robert's background.

"It began over thirty years ago, when Robert's mother, my sister, had been betrothed to a young man of good standing, an earl's son. The marriage had been hailed by both families and was to take place in the spring of the coming year. Unfortunately, Sybil met Miles Hamilton, a lesser son of a baron." Edward noted Alissa's impeaching look. "It had nothing to do with his standing in the peerage, my dear. It was his boorish manner and arrogant presumptuousness. Seeing his chance to attain power and money, he seduced my sister, got her in a family way, then challenged her fiancé to a duel, killing the young man outright. Hamilton promptly married her, thinking he'd won. But my father, livid over the scars the family had suffered because of Sybil's scandalous behavior, quickly disinherited her and cast her from the fold. Afterward my father suffered greatly, for she died in childbirth. Raising a son by himself, Miles Hamilton took to the bottle, drowning his sorrow . . . but it had nothing to do with the loss of my sister. He became a social outcast, without a farthing of his own. Naturally, he placed the blame on the Braxtons."

"And Robert?" Alissa asked.

"Robert was thirteen when his father took a drunken spill from his horse, breaking his neck. I immediately took the boy in, hoping to give him a good home. He was a sullen, peevish lad, at first spouting his hatred for the Braxtons, like his father had before him. As time passed, I thought he had overcome his anger. I suppose he never did."

"Don't blame yourself, Father," Jared said, patting the man's shoulder. "You did everything you could to help him. He remained his father's seed." He moved to his wife's chair and edged a leg onto the arm. "Not everyone is as lucky as I to have a sire such as you." He glanced at Alissa, instantly noting her troubled look. "What is it, love?"

Tear-glazed eyes stared up at him. "I—I was just thinking that perhaps it's best I know nothing of my own father. Especially if he was anything like Robert's."

Just then Leona Dugan marched into the room, carrying a hefty tray of refreshments, a bandage-crowned Mr. Stanley following her. "I found the best bottle of wine ye had," he offered, holding the dusty bottle high in his hand. "I'd say this be a time fer celebration."

"Agreed," Edward said, his eyes meeting Eudora's with a knowing look. "I'll get the glasses."

Alissa sprang from her chair. "Oh, Thom, it's good to see you're on the mend. Jared said you'd not been seriously hurt, but I couldn't wait till I saw for myself."

"Wish I coulda been more help to ye," he said, scuffing his toe in the carpet, shrugging.

"You did the best you could," she offered, hoping to raise his spirits. "I couldn't ask for a better friend and coachman." Then she placed a kiss on his cheek.

Blushing, he grinned. "Thank ye much."

"Don't get any ideas, Mr. Stanley," Jared said from where he sat, looking at his man with mock sternness. "Or you might be sporting a scar to match the other."

"Could say the same about ye, as well," he countered, a brow raised. "She be too good fer either of us anyway."

"True," Jared said, grinning. "But I hope to persuade her to stay . . . with me, of course."

Feeling Mrs. Dugan's presence at her side, Alissa turned. "Yes?"

"I-I just wanted to say how glad I am you're back, Lady Ebonwyck. Welcome home."

Close friends they might never be, but a look of understanding passed between the two women. Respect for each other held their regard. "Thank you, Leona."

"When we've had our toast," Jared said, "I'd like to order up baths for my wife, Megan, and myself. We're rather weary from our journey."

After all their glasses were raised, the wine swallowed, Mr. Stanley and Mrs. Dugan left the room with Megan at their sides. As soon as the door closed, Edward waved Alissa toward her chair and waited until she had reseated herself next to Jared. He cleared his throat. "To go back to the subject we were on before we were interrupted, Eudora and I have a story to tell that might heal some old wounds," he said, again seating himself beside Eudora.

Jared settled more comfortably on the arm of his wife's chair and rested his hand along its back, close to Alissa's head. "You sound as though the two of you have unearthed some great mystery, Father."

"Actually, we have. But, considering the way my new daughter reacted when she discovered you were of the peerage, I'm not quite certain I should broach the subject now."

"Stop talking in riddles, Edward," Eudora admonished, frowning at him, "and get on with it."

"Of course, madam. But I believe you have the evidence."

As Alissa looked to her husband, she saw his shrug. Then she noticed Eudora slip her hand into her pocket to withdraw something. Her hand opened. "My brooch!" Alissa cried, uncomprehendingly. "What's this all about?"

"It's about a young woman who has no knowledge of her father, but should have had a long time ago," Eudora explained, "and I'm afraid it is partially my fault that she did not."

ou know who my father is?"

"Was," Edward said gently, and noted her crestfallen face. "His name was Geoffrey Chapman."

"Chapman!" Jared exclaimed, coming to his feet. What the hell else could happen to cause them problems! "If you are about to tell me she is my first cousin—"

"Sit," Edward commanded, waving him down. "There were other Chapmans running about besides your late mother."

"Cousin?" Alissa inquired, just grasping Jared's mother was a Chapman, as well. "Please explain."

"Certainly, dear," Eudora said, then looked at the duke. "Edward, please."

"Yes, well, you and Jared are cousins, but a half-dozen or so times removed. Your children will suffer no abnormalities," he stated, "if that's what's upset you, son."

Jared relaxed. "Thank God for that!"

"Perhaps I should tell Alissa's mother's side first," Eudora said, softly. "Rachel Ashford, as you all know, was an accomplished actress. She'd met a young man by the name of Geoffrey Chapman, who immediately fell in love with her. Since he was of the peerage"—she noted Alissa's startled look—"he was the Earl of Benton, my dear. Fearing a match between them might lead to little else but trouble, Rachel balked at his attentions. But Geoffrey refused to give up. Eventually he was able to convince her to marry him, secretly. It was not long afterward that his family found out about it, and they pressed for an annulment. It was a bitter confrontation, Geoffrey's father threatening to disown him because he'd married a common actress."

Edward cleared his throat. "Sometimes we of the peerage display exceedingly bad manners. I apologize for mine."

"Anyway," Eudora continued, "one day your father simply disappeared without saying good-bye. Believing he'd buckled under to his family's pressure, she assumed he'd deserted her. By then she was with child and tried several times to find him. But the Chapmans refused her even the simplest of courtesies. She was turned away at every juncture. Never hearing from your father again, she vowed never to speak of him, and she never did. Her heart had been broken." Eudora sighed. "Your mother swore me to secrecy. Hence I was silent, even after her death. I'm sorry, dearest."

"You are forgiven, Eudora," Alissa said, the tenderness she felt for the woman displaying itself in her eyes. "A promise is a promise. But what does the brooch . . . was it a gift from my father?"

"Indeed it was," Edward said, going on with the story. "When your father married your mother, he gave her a gift . . . this brooch. Remember when I asked you about it?" He saw Alissa's nod. "Well, I thought I'd recognized it. It wasn't until we were waiting for your return that Eudora and I began to piece this story together."

"How so?" his daughter-in-law asked.

"The Chapmans had a vested interest in the East India Company. The sapphire in this brooch came from Kashmir, in northern India, and was placed into this setting. It was passed to Geoffrey when his mother died. I'd only seen it a few times, but I remembered it well."

"What happened to my father?" she asked, then felt Jared's hand slip over hers, squeezing it tenderly.

"Your father did not desert your mother. Quite the contrary. Since he was to be disowned, for he loved your mother too much to leave her, he decided to make his own fortune. After a heated row with his father, during which all ties between father and son were broken, your father discovered a ship was leaving for India, and he quickly booked passage on it. As the family gossip would have it, he entrusted a servant with a note addressed to your mother, explaining what he was about and asking her to wait for him. Unfortunately, fate, it seems, played a beggarly trick on the two lovers. First, the note was intercepted, hence your mother's believing she'd been deserted. Next, your father's ship was caught in a terrible storm off the coast of India . . . all souls were lost."

Alissa's eyes widened. "She was never told?"

"Eventually, she discovered his loss," Eudora said. "But she never knew the circumstances behind his leaving . . . or his death."

Alissa's heart suddenly ached for her mother . . . and her father. How could anyone be so cruel as to keep two people apart when they truly loved one another? "I'm not certain that I'd want to be known as a Chapman," she stated, sudden anger in her voice. "Damn the lot for their subterfuge!"

"Geoffrey's father paid his own price for his deception," Edward stated. "Besides losing his eldest son, he also lost his two younger. One was killed in a duel after he'd been caught cheating at cards; the other drowned in the Thames after being robbed by a band of thugs. Milton Chapman, too, has since died, a broken and lonely man for his treachery."

"There's something I want you to see," Eudora said, rising, taking the brooch to Alissa. "Press this stone," she said, handing her the brooch and pointing to a small diamond. Alissa did as told; the sapphire suddenly sprang away from the setting on its secret hinges. "This was your father."

A handsome man with hair and eyes the color of her own stared back at her. She gazed at Geoffrey Chapman, the Earl of Benton. Tears formed in her eyes, and she tried to blink them away. Then she felt the nudge of Jared's forefinger under her chin.

"It's all right, love. He did not leave you willingly. No man ever would."

She smiled weakly. "You are right . . . about my father."

"I am correct about the other, too," he said, speaking of himself.

"That is a promise?"

"It is."

As the tears cleared from her eyes, she and Jared read the inscription written opposite the miniature of her father, a hidden promise of his love: *Forever one heart with thee.*

"It is a promise I make to you, as well," Jared whispered close to her ear, and Alissa felt the warmth of his words surround her heart.

"And I to you," she whispered.

A knock sounded on the door, and Mary peeked in. "Excuse me, but yer baths are ready."

Jared rose to his feet. "Thank you, Mary." He pulled Alissa from the chair. "Madam, we are wanted upstairs." A cry escaped her lips as he suddenly swung her up into his arms. "We shall see you on the morrow," he announced to his father and Eudora, then strode toward the door.

"Put me down," Alissa demanded, kicking her feet as she heard the duke's knowing chuckle. "You're making fools of us."

His feet touched the stairs. "What's foolish about a husband wanting to be alone with his wife?"

"But it's still daylight!"

"All the better. It'll save the expense on the candles left unburned. I want to see you, love. All of you."

As they reached the top of the stairs, Alissa's eyes met Mr. Stanley's. "I see she's a-stayin'," he said, grinning. "I'll brings ye some supper, later."

"I'll ring when we need sustenance. Till then you may guard the hall. We're not to be disturbed."

"Right, gov'nor."

"You insufferable buffoon!" she cried just above a whisper when they'd turned the corner. "How dare you intimate to the servants that we . . . we . . ."

He chuckled. "We what? Are about to make love?" Alissa's mouth drew into a tight line, and seeing it, Jared said, "I simply issued an order. Thom's assumption is his own . . . correct, but his own."

"Ooooh! If I were a man—"

"If you were a man, madam," he said, with a grunt, "I wouldn't be carrying you down this hallway."

"Your wound!" she said, anxiously. "Put me down before you hurt yourself."

He nodded toward his door. "Turn the handle."

"This isn't my room!"

"Turn the handle." She did, and after they had entered, Jared kicked the door closed with his foot. "This, madam, is *our* room." He carried her to the bathing chamber. "And this is *our* bath."

Alissa slid along his body to her feet. "Surely, you don't expect . . . ?"

He began unbuttoning her clothing. "I do." Becoming frustrated, he finally rent the gown in two, surprising his wife. "I'll buy you another . . . a dozen if you'd like."

Their clothes fell away, and Jared lifted Alissa in his arms, then plunged into the steamy water, settling her down in the large tub across his lap. She moved against him, and he sucked in his breath. Hearing it, she turned to face him, sliding her body over his length.

"Do you know what you're about?" he asked in a husky whisper, feeling the rise and fall of her slender form as it floated above his, teasing him, unmercifully.

"I do," she replied, her eyes locked with his.

"And do you know the outcome?"

"Yes."

"Is it what you want?"

"Yes," she replied throatily.

With an urgent groan, he swung his arms from the sides of the tub, surrounding her. His searching lips captured hers in a hungry, wildly poignant kiss. His tongue probed gently, and as she allowed it entry, his hand slid over the curve of her spine to caress her hips and knead the softness of her bottom.

Then, his mouth suddenly tore aside. "I can't wait, love," he growled, his hands shifting her thighs across his hips, opening her to his rigid desire. Positioning himself, his hands gripped the moons of her hips and eased her down.

Filled with him, Alissa felt the burning need to move. And she did. A violent shudder racked Jared's entire body, his breath caught raggedly, and she gazed deeply into his passion-glazed eyes. Knowing she held power over him, possessed the ability to drive him half mad, she moved in the same provocative motion. Then, suddenly, her eyes widened as his powerful hand pressed her closer, his own hips meeting her rhythm. A chuckle rumbled from his solid chest. "It works both ways, sweet," he whispered against her throat, sending delightful shivers through her.

As Jared's lips tasted and teased her honey-flavored skin, white-hot desire shot through Alissa's veins. His tongue traced the sensitive curve of her throat, gently soothing the small nick made by the vicious blade, and her head arched backward, giving his mouth full rein. An aching torment sparked deep in the pit of her stomach, building into a fiery inferno, and a moan of pleasure erupted from her throat.

The seductive vibration filled his ears, teased his lips. Then her entire body arched as it pulled upright, straddling him; her arms lifted her luxurious mane, her hands clasping behind her head. Like the pagan goddess in his dreams, she swayed in a dance of passion. Full ivory globes tempted him, and his impoverished hands were suddenly filled with them, gently molding them, cupping them, urging them to his starving lips. Then, as his tongue tormented and teased the responsive nipples, her moan of pleasure erupted anew, and his steadying hands slid to her waist, guiding her undulating form, rocking it against his hardened contours. "That's right, sweet. Coax me, caress me! Share your fire!" he cried, huskily.

Inflamed by her untamed ardor, her nymphlike grace, he felt her body surge against him, seeking the ultimate pleasure only he could give. His fervent gaze memorized her ardent look as she succumbed to her desires, drowning in sweet surrender. Her pulsing spasms enticed him, and his passion blazed uncontrollably. Wildly, he thrust upward, his own desire bursting forth, filling her, her name torn from his lips in an agonizingly sweet melody.

Spent, Alissa fell against him, and Jared held her close. "I love you," he whispered, with aching poignancy, his lips traveling her cheek; a tear fell from his eye to slip unseen into the bath. *Oh, how I love you. And, through my own stupidity, I almost lost you.* His arms tightened around her.

As the water cooled, his passions momentarily sated, he rose with his wife in his arms, afraid to let her go, lest she disappear. Setting her on her feet, he ministered to her, drying her from head to foot. The towel quickly rubbed over his own body, he swung her high in his arms, carrying her to their bed.

Tearing the covers aside, he placed her reverently upon the sheets, then lay beside her. "I love you, Alissa," he said, his throat aching with joy, and fear, his gentle hand traveling the plains of her smooth stomach. "Forgive me . . . please . . . for all the unkind things I said. I was wildly jealous . . . afraid you didn't love me . . . I wanted to hurt you, as much as I was hurting."

"Ssh," she whispered, her finger covering his lips, then her hand rose to brush away a lock of hair from his brow. "I know why it happened, and I forgive the words, for I know they were not said by the real you."

"I've been such a fool, Alissa. I'm not certain I can forgive myself. My babe grows inside you . . ."

"My love, why do you chastise yourself so?"

"Because . . ." How could he explain what he needed to hear from her lips . . . the reassurances that would heal his jaded soul? "I . . ." He fell silent.

Reading the display of emotions in his emerald eyes and on his handsome face, Alissa realized what he wanted, needed most of all. "Jared . . . I love you. I love you from the depths of my soul. I love you with every inch of my heart. And I always will."

"Alissa," he whispered, his eyes glowing with joyous tears, his heart expanding tenfold. His splayed fingers wound through her hair. Then his mouth lowered over hers, embracing her lips in a tenderly sweet, achingly wonderful kiss. "My precious love, I had vowed never to give my heart to a woman again. But I was wrong, sweet. I never really knew what love was until I found you. You are my love, my life, my soul . . ."

And as Alissa pulled her husband into her arms, her heart swelled with the greatest pleasure imaginable. At last, she knew totally, completely, the love of one man. And just before Jared's lips took hers, she whispered the hidden pledge of love, "Forever one heart with thee."

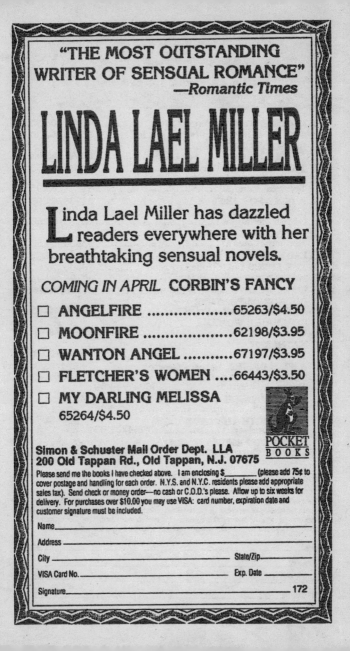